STOLEN *Words*

HIGH TOWER, 1

INDIA CAEDMON

STOLEN WORDS

India Caedmon, Publisher

This book is a work of fiction. Names, characters, places, and incidents either are products of the author's imagination or are used fictitiously. Any resemblance to actual persons, living or dead, events, or locales is entirely coincidental.

Cover by: Rupa Limbu

Edited by: Ariana Bloodgood

ISBN-13: 978-0-692-99945-5

First Edition: December 11, 2018

10 9 8 7 6 5 4 3 2 1

www.indiacaedmon.com

This is for you.

"True love begins when nothing is looked for in return."

— ANTOINE DE SAINT-EXUPÉRY

CHAPTER ONE

They called it the Mighty Ike. Grayson called it a floating, seasick-inducing hell. He leaned over the edge of the aircraft carrier and gasped for air.

Familiar footsteps approached from behind, and a hand gripped his shoulder with a firm squeeze. "Lovely day, huh?"

Grayson's lungs clenched. "It's cloudy. You *do* realize this?" He wasn't in the mood for Lance's positivity.

"I knew you didn't like water, but this is a side of you I've never seen. It's only been one day at sea." Lance released him and stretched his arms wide. "How are you going to train the Reactor Division? And don't call in sick, because there's no way I can handle that."

A moan escaped from the pit of Grayson's chest, and his stomach rolled. All the oxygen was stripped from the air.

Day one, eighty-nine more to go.

The mental pep talk didn't work. They never seemed to work.

He finally managed to stand semi-straight and adjusted the lapels of his charcoal suit.

Lance ran his hands over his chest and down the forest-green cashmere of his sweater. "We aren't at the High Tower Lab; you don't have to wear your suit here."

Grayson's ears rang from the pressure building behind his eyes. Just watching Lance's subtle movements made his face squinch.

"Lighten up for once." Lance slapped Grayson on the back. "It's March—the first day of spring!"

Grimacing, Grayson nodded toward the tower at the center of the ship for Lance to lead the way back into the main office. He might have been sick, but he wasn't about to let them be late. Lance still hadn't met the entire team, and this was the morning Grayson was going to introduce him to the staff.

Everything blurred together as Grayson slithered past the airmen settling on board. His hearing was the only sense not failing him, as his TLD badge clinked with the top button of his suit jacket. He adjusted it with clammy hands. The last thing he wanted was to damage the small light on the rectangular card that measured radiation exposure.

Radiation poisoning. He scoffed. Wouldn't that be just his luck?

Silence met Grayson, as he strolled through the door that was propped open and walked to the head of the table. Everything was so cramped, he couldn't help but stub his toes on every chair and cabinet corner. He held back his grunts. Lance followed swiftly and effortlessly behind. He really needed to tone down his smile. It was pissing Grayson off.

After the younger officers were introduced, Lance talked about himself like usual. People gravitated toward his obnoxiousness. Grayson was no charmer. He knew his talent. He was a closer. He preferred to be blunt and cut to the chase—there was nothing wrong with that. The two made a good team, as long as a woman wasn't around to distract Lance. His eyes followed any giggling, wiggling, or protruding body part owned by a busty blonde.

Luckily, they were surrounded with uniformed men.

"...Grayson is the brains here. I'm just the sidekick making sure he doesn't fall overboard." The room erupted in laughter, except for Grayson. "Thank you for letting us join you, while your pilots complete their carrier qualifications. We'll be out of your hair before your deployment this summer. I'll *definitely* stay out of the way, as Grayson works with Captain O'Hare in the reactor spaces...unless you want an explosion."

Why was everyone laughing? An explosion on Ike would be catastrophic.

"We're here, at your disposal, for the next three months."

Thank God, Lance was done. Four minutes seemed to drag on for an hour. The mention of three months made Grayson's head spin. New York was even more far away.

Grayson shook hands with the officers in the small space that continued to blur under his tunnel vision.

3

"Lance, I'm going to retreat now. I need to…find my stomach."

Lance chuckled. "Okay, I'm good here. I think I've met everyone now. Try to smile once in a while, okay? Practice in your mirror. In a few weeks, you won't even feel it." He turned away to continue talking to the officers, as Grayson made his way to his stateroom.

Was it nighttime yet? Grayson didn't have a clue. Being on a ship warped all sense of time and space. He wasn't sure the last time he saw sunlight.

You won't even feel it.

For the past four weeks, Grayson had repeated that mantra. What a crock. Lance had been so very wrong. Grayson wobbled around nearly bow-legged to account for the ship's roll. Supposedly, sailors had the most difficulty when transitioning back to land, but it was completely backward for him. He couldn't wait for the opportunity to touch solid ground again.

Grayson faked his sanity through the classes he taught and continued to fake it as he discussed new ideas within the reactor spaces, but as soon as he was in private, he hunched over and took deep, calming breaths. As time passed, only one thing seemed to ease his seasickness—stress.

He welcomed the overlapping schedules and nonstop movement of the military. He even assisted with whatever he could when he was allowed on deck. Within the first few days, the ship conducted a man-overboard drill, and Grayson nearly threw Lance off the side of the ship, because he wouldn't stop fixing his hair. This last week, there was training, more drills, and meetings that filled the days, as part of the Carrier Air Wing worked on their planes.

After getting out of his latest meeting with a group of young naval officers, Grayson smiled. They were excited and willing to work. A burst of pride filled his chest, as he checked the dials on his watch. Half a day had already gone by.

Grayson meandered through the hallways and angled his shoulders so a group of sailors could pass him. While walking through the p-ways, he tried to avoid the short kickers sticking out at the base and head of the walls. Those bastards were every ten feet. The death traps had an eye on Grayson's shins.

Outside the dining galley, Lance rocked on his heels, with an expression of delight on his face. His skin practically glowed.

He smiled as Grayson approached. "Hey, you actually look like you don't have a rod up your—"

"Don't." Grayson put up his hand.

Lance cocked an eyebrow. "This is a ship. Full of *sailors*. Are you seriously going to hold lab rules over my head right now? Grayson's rule number fifty-three, no foul language."

"Swear on your own time, but per clause *five* of our company policy, we have an image to uphold while we're here." Grayson's lips quirked in a half-smile. "You were never good with numbers in college."

Lance laughed. "Forgive me." He placed his hand

on his chest in mock concern. "You were never good with people."

"Why do you look so happy, anyway?"

"Unlike you, I really like being on a ship…"

And that was when Grayson started to ignore him. It wouldn't be long until Lance lost his mind, too. The two walked toward the aft enlisted galley, where the sailors dined. With laughter still on their lips, Grayson stood in one line, Lance in the other. They watched each other, as they made their way to the food, seeing who would get there faster.

Thirty minutes later, Lance smirked as he reached his buffet first. Grayson should have opted for the self-serve bar—that would have been much faster—but he didn't want a salad after starving himself in hopes that his nausea would go away. Now he wasn't sure if he was sick or just famished.

Lance grabbed a hot dog and a hamburger and joined Grayson in his line. "Looks like your line has actual food. I'll trade you a hot dog for a steak burrito." Holding out his hot dog, Lance raised his eyebrows. "When we're back in New York, I'll even sort through your emails for you. I'd do anything for a piece of steak right now."

Grayson shook his head and grinned. "Never."

In an instant, Lance was shoved forward a step, and Grayson steadied him. Tossing a dirty glare over his shoulder, Lance thinned his lips to a fine line.

A petite woman smiled at him and put her hands up in defense. "So sorry."

Lance's scowl transformed into a wide grin, and he

stood taller. "Oh, it's no problem at all, ma'am. I'm Lance." He stuck out his hand, but she turned away to cut the line.

Grayson rolled his head back in amusement. "You're losing your touch with the women, my friend."

Huffing, Lance straightened his shoulders. "I think she's just in a rush." He shifted his feet. "Otherwise, she probably would have given me her name. She is pretty, though."

Was she? Grayson saw dedication, passion, loyalty. He didn't notice the shape of her eyes, and he certainly wasn't staring at the girl's rear—Lance couldn't seem to pull his eyes away. Her hair color was nice and shiny, though.

After Grayson grabbed his lunch, they walked to the cafeteria, or what the sailors called the "mess decks." By the time he was used to naval terminology, he and Lance would be long gone for home.

Lance licked his lips and flicked his eyes toward Grayson's burrito. The weight of it in Grayson's hand was daunting. He wasn't sure if he could keep the entire thing down, but he fully intended on eating it slowly and enjoying every bite in front of Lance.

The tables on the mess decks were close together and embedded into the ship's deck. Grayson was getting used to the cramped nature of everything. He sat close to Lance as he ate, their elbows bashing into each other the entire time.

In the back corner, an unusual amount of movement began to creep its way down the line of tables. In the distance, a few women on board yelped with joy, as they held envelopes and walked from the dining galley.

"Sir," a sailor handed Grayson an envelope, "a letter came for you in my division."

Confused, Grayson looked to the sailor, then to Lance. Before he could ask about it, the sailor walked away.

Lance shrugged. "Mail day? Open it. It might be from the lab. I'm expecting a construction update soon."

Grayson scanned the front of the envelope; the return address was water stained and illegible. Grayson doubted anyone from the High Tower would contact him. Not unless it was paperwork for the new laboratory being built on the first floor.

Running his fingers across the worn edges of the envelope, Grayson meticulously opened it and read the letter inside.

I can't believe you're on a ship.

"Neither can I." Grayson ran his palm down the side of his stubbled cheek. He didn't recognize the handwriting.

I wish you were here with me, instead. I miss you so much, I made your favorite meal for dinner last night and set you a plate. Mya is struggling right now, so I'm going to visit her again when work allows. The divorce is just brutal. As for me, everything is coming together, especially with my new apartment...and I think I'm getting a promotion at work! But I won't bother you with those silly details. The only thing missing is you. I'll write to you every day, until you come back to me.

Don't keep me waiting, sailor.

Cassidy

Grayson's heart stalled. "Cassie?" He read the name again in disbelief.

A chill ran up his spine and through his arms to his fingertips. The chattering around him disappeared, and the words became alphabet soup, dancing on the page and recreating images from his past.

"Grayson, come play with me?" Katrina asked. Her head was barely visible from the other side of their white picket fence.

"Not now, Katrina. Lance and I are doing homework." Grayson turned toward Lance and gave a nod. "Let's add one more."

Grayson sat back and adjusted his protective goggles, as Lance gripped the glass tube of Mentos with rubber clamps, tilted the vial, and dropped them one at a time into the liter of Coca-Cola. They crouched low to the ground, expecting an explosion.

Nothing happened.

"Do you think we need more Mentos?" Lance popped one in his mouth.

Grayson lifted his shoulders.

"Hello-o-o?" A small tapping came from the fence. The boys rolled their eyes in defeat and removed their safety equipment. They walked over to Katrina, and she became visible from behind the wooden gate, her little arms crossed in front of her chest.

Lance leaned on the fence and got his face close to hers. "What do you want, Pup?"

With her arms clutched to her chest, she held a red blanket close to her body. All Grayson could see were Katrina's black Mary Janes and the white ankle socks, trimmed in lace, that his mom neatly folded each morning while helping her dress.

Her arms flung out. She hadn't been holding a blanket. It was a cape. And she had it on backward. "I am Princess Cassie from the Land of the Coyotes! You, peasants, is my prisoners!"

"Are my prisoners." Grayson placed his hands on his hips.

"Are my prisoners!" she repeated, her arms still wide.

Lance snorted, undoubtedly holding back a laugh.

Grayson cocked his head and looked down at his baby sister. "Are you watching those cartoons again?"

Her blue eyes begged for attention, as the breeze created an angel-blonde mess atop her head.

Lance tucked some of her hair behind her ear. "Yeah, Pup. Stop filling your head with silly fantasies."

Grayson couldn't help but smile at Lance's ridiculous nickname for Katrina. It was even more horrendous than Princess Cassie, as she insisted everyone call her.

Katrina slouched, and her gaze fell. She began to turn away. Grayson gave Lance a mischievous grin, and they simultaneously jumped over the fence to chase her around to the side of the house.

She transformed from a gentle child to a wild banshee, as the boys hid behind the trees and tried to catch her.

Grayson called after her, "Stay out of the poison oak, Katrina!"

She screamed and yelled in excitement, until they reached the base of the property. Exhausted, the three lay next to the canal, engulfed in wildflowers.

"Are you happy now, sis?" Grayson faced Katrina, lying between Lance and him.

She was sprawled like a snow angel, and her chest rose and fell quickly. She didn't respond. She just turned toward Grayson and kissed his nose.

A call came from the house.

"Better go, Pup. Your mom's calling." Lance rubbed Katrina's back, as she slowly rolled over to her stomach, shoved her face in the wildflowers, and inhaled.

"I am Princess Cassie from the Land of the Coyotes!" she yelled into the dirt. She pushed herself up with ease and brushed off the thistles and grass clinging to her backward cape. "I'm gonna help Mama make dinner." She took a few steps forward. "Don't keep me waiting next time," she threatened over her shoulder.

She quickly made her way up the steady incline back to the house, tripping over her cape and using the long grass and flowers to pull herself up.

Grayson laughed at the memory.

"Don't keep me waiting," he whispered. If Katrina were still alive, she would have written him something exactly like this.

His smile quickly faded.

Every time he thought of his baby sister, he inevitably thought of her funeral. His parents had stopped talking to him then. The only time they ever said anything to him was when he disappointed them.

"I can't even look at Grayson anymore," he had overheard his mother say to his father after the funeral.

Grayson ran his hand down the front of the letter. "Forgive me, Katrina."

He read Cassidy's name aloud, as he traced the swirls and elegant script of her signature. He examined the front of the envelope again and tried to make out the recipient's spattered name and division.

Kyle Greens. How they'd mixed up Kyle Greens with Grayson Daniels, he'd never know. As a civilian on board, and since his name wasn't necessarily recognized by everyone, perhaps the person accepting mail for the division had just assumed it was for him.

Lance looked expectantly at Grayson. "Who's it from?"

Grayson carefully folded and slid the letter into the breast pocket of his jacket. "Wrong person."

Lance nodded and stood. "So, it wasn't from the lab?"

Grayson shook his head.

Lance shrugged. "I guess construction is going well, then. I told you there would be nothing to worry about."

Grayson would find the rightful owner of the letter. But, until then, he would cherish the comfort it brought. Katrina was sending him a message from heaven.

Whenever he'd had the opportunity, Grayson had asked around the lounges and on deck about Kyle. The selfish part of him hoped he wouldn't find anyone by that name, so he could keep Cassidy's letter to himself.

Following procedure, Grayson tried to visit the post office on board. Every time he stopped by, it was closed.

The post office was run by Logistics Specialists, so he expected the hours would be limited.

Grayson's next and last option was to ask someone who *actually* had influence on the ship. He ducked his head, as he entered the hallway below the main deck in search of the captain. He regretted moving so quickly, because his feet barely had traction with the ship swaying under him. Or maybe *he* was the one swaying.

"Oh God, no." A rivulet of sweat trickled down the nape of his neck, as he climbed the ladder to the flight deck. He needed to get to his chambers or the side of the ship—and fast.

His breathing quickened as his suit constricted around his shoulders. This was one of the few times he was topside, the fresh air bombarding his lungs. He saw the edge of the deck and walked straight for it, removing his jacket in the process.

Did I just walk in front of airmen training?

"Hey, idiot!"

"We're trying to get qualified here!"

Yes.

Grayson turned and gave them all an apologetic look. Or, he tried to. He really couldn't make out the difference between a person and a safety cone.

This ship was making him crazy.

He continued to walk backward, and the cool steel of the safety railing touched his lower back. He turned and dry heaved into the crisp, salty ocean air.

The yelling at his back subsided, and Grayson heard the voice of the ship's commanding officer, Captain O'Hare, in the distance. He was likely reassuring his crewmen that Grayson wasn't, in fact, a complete hazard. There was no way the captain could have walked down to the main deck that fast, so he had probably been there the entire time, watching Grayson make a damn-near fool of himself.

Grayson had met Captain O'Hare during the captain's required year at the Navy's nuclear power school. Ten years his senior, Captain O'Hare had no nuclear background or experience. Grayson had been fresh out of college and taught most of the classes as a guest instructor. He respected the captain's passion and, although hesitant at first, the captain began to trust Grayson's knowledge in return. That was the start of their friendship.

When the captain invited Grayson on board to provide training for the Reactor Division during workups and qualifications, there was no way Grayson could have turned him down.

Though Grayson had limited knowledge and experience of the Navy, he knew nuclear energy. And he respected the men and women who devoted their lives to their country. It was honorable. He was important back at his small lab, but his personal accomplishments just didn't compare to this.

Grayson clenched his jacket in one of his fists. He was going to make it through this. His water phobia was better...okay, not really, but he was managing it, just like he managed everything else in his life.

The crinkling of Cassidy's letter in his breast pocket ignited guilt in his stomach for keeping it from one of the men on board. He was going to fix that.

Figuring it would be best to stay out of restricted areas, Grayson weaved to the hangar bay to get fresh air there, instead.

"Dr. Daniels, welcome to the hangars," a low voice erupted from behind, and Grayson looked over his shoulder to see a young man stand in greeting.

"For the love of God, please, just Mr. Daniels. Dr. Daniels makes me sound like my father." Grayson didn't want to think about his parents. Ever.

The man stood close and gazed into the endless horizon. "A few of us are in your classes." He sucked a deep breath into his barrel chest. "Great stuff, Mr. Daniels. When the captain said he'd be bringing a civilian to Ike, we didn't know what to expect, but I swear I've learned more from you than anyone else."

Grayson smiled and shook the sailor's hand. "I'll take that as a compliment. Thank you."

"I'm Patrick."

The shake was firm and strong. Patrick was a burly man with at least two inches on Grayson. Grayson could barely make it through the p-ways without hitting his head on something. He had a hard time visualizing Patrick's enormous frame below the flight deck.

A second man, much smaller in build, walked up behind them. "I wish I could say the same. I can't seem to grasp any of the information."

The first thing that caught Grayson's eye was the name embroidered on the sailor's coveralls. M. Greens. For a split second, he thought he'd found the man he'd been searching for, but the initials weren't right.

After groaning just loud enough for Grayson to hear,

Patrick moved a few feet to his right to allow the other sailor to join the conversation.

Patrick eyed Grayson. "Greens is in the air wing, but he *wants* to be a nuke."

Nodding, Grayson turned to face the sailor next to him. "Why the switch?"

"Well, I thought it would be easier."

Grayson didn't miss Patrick's eyeroll, as he placed an unlit cigarette between his lips that stretched tighter than a rubber band.

Patrick mumbled under his breath and sighed. "Nothing worth having is easy, Greens."

"Easy for you to say. Your life is perfect. You have an interesting girl in your life. You're advancing. I'm stagnant here in the air wing, doing maintenance like an animal." Greens spat the words.

Turning his body, Patrick lifted his eyebrows to Grayson. "I need a smoke. Please excuse me." He bowed his head. "See you in class, Mr. Daniels."

When Patrick was gone, the sailor next to Grayson sighed. "I hate that guy. What a rat. If he weren't here, I'd probably advance faster. He's the reason I'm behind. And, get this, while he's here, his super-hot wife cooks and cleans and travels the world and sends him pictures. My girlfriend isn't adventurous at all. I guess she can cook, but she's nothing like Patrick's wife. Patrick's girl is a solid ten. My girl? Maybe a six." A group of women walked by and Grayson's companion stole a glance. "Did you say something?"

"No. You were talking about your girlfriend and how amazing she is."

"Oh, she's not my girlfriend," Greens clarified quickly. "Fiancée. Anyway, I'm sorry I've missed the last few of your lectures. I saw you talking to Patrick and wanted to come over."

"Things happen, but if you want to do well, you have to apply yourself." Grayson tried not to sound like a life coach. "What's your name, sailor?"

"Petty Officer Mandy Greens."

Grayson almost snickered but settled on a light laugh and lowered his eyes.

"It's the worst name ever, I know," the petty officer continued. "I go by my middle name. Kyle."

Grayson's head snapped up, and he couldn't help but scan Kyle's features. He had beady eyes from squinting in the sun. His posture was decent, but Grayson had a good four inches on him.

"Well, Kyle," Grayson articulated slowly, "it's nice to meet you."

Grayson stuck out his hand and judged the firmness of the shake. It was unassertive. Mediocre. Grayson narrowed his eyes and watched, as Kyle massaged his clean-shaven jaw.

The pain in Grayson's stomach seemed to dissolve after realizing *this* was the man he had been searching for the past few days. "So, why did you join the Navy?"

"I thought it would be cool, you know?"

That's it? "What about your...fiancée? How does she feel about it?"

"I don't like talking about her." Kyle's fists were clenched. Perhaps it was from his bitter interaction with Patrick. Or perhaps Kyle was stressed about staying in the air wing. "I mean, I used to talk about her all the time with the guys. But, after hearing their stories, I realized she just isn't very interesting." He put his hands up in defense. "Don't get me wrong. She's super sweet, and we never fight, but I think the most exciting thing that's ever happened to her is her parents died a long time ago. But I could never say that to her face. God, no. She feels it's her fault. Kinda wish she'd just get over it and do something with her life, like most women do. With time, I'll change her. She's still holding onto the grief. It's silly."

Grayson knew that kind of guilt. Rage burned in his throat, as if Kyle had inadvertently insulted him. It was not *silly*. "I see," Grayson mustered through clenched teeth. "What's her name?"

"Cassidy Thatcher."

"What does she do?" He flung his jacket over his shoulder and held it there with his index finger hooked in the collar.

"She has a bunch of hobbies. She wants to be an archaeologist."

Kyle's answer took Grayson aback. Archaeology was not an easy career. It certainly wasn't a hobby. Maybe it just wasn't interesting to Kyle. If someone had ever called Grayson's career a "hobby," they'd be bound to lose some teeth. "She gave up a big opportunity in New York to spend time with me before this training."

"True love?"

"She's great."

This was where Grayson should have given the letter to Kyle. He could have said the envelope was handed to him by mistake, and he was glad they ran into each other.

Grayson was no master of love—he was married to his job—but he knew a problem when he saw one.

A blanket of protectiveness smothered him. If Cassidy were his sister, he would not approve of Kyle. *You don't join the military to be cool.* He rolled his proverbial eyes into the back of his proverbial head.

Kyle had a measly handshake for a man of his build. He skipped classes that could help him advance through the ranks faster, implied his fiancée was annoying, and on top of that, Kyle had a wandering eye. He was engaged, yet he talked about Cassidy like she was the most uninteresting woman.

Grayson contemplated whether or not to tell Kyle about Cassidy's letter. It was just one letter. In a few weeks, Kyle would surely get a fresh pile from her.

For Grayson to hand over Cassidy's words to someone who didn't deserve them would be like cutting off his right arm. They'd become a part of him. Since he received it, he'd found himself placing his hand over his heart just to see if the letter was still there, surprised by the comfort it gave him.

No. Kyle would just have to wait until the next mail day. From now on, Grayson would keep an eye on Petty Officer Kyle Greens and make sure his mediocre hands stayed where they belonged.

It took fifty-one days of being on Ike before Grayson

wasn't sick. He was, however, thoroughly lost. He went through the map to Lance's room in his head. Usually Lance was the one to come to him, but lately, Lance had been uncharacteristically absent. Grayson hoped that Lance wasn't getting overwhelmed with overseeing the construction project, in addition to training the interns from the middle of the ocean.

Two left turns, one right turn, climb the ladder and watch your head, right turn—or was it left?—then...left again?

Because the ship wasn't at full deployment capacity, Lance and Grayson both had two-bed staterooms. It was the only space where Grayson could stretch his arms without hitting someone. He had started on the 02-level below the flight deck, but he wasn't sure which deck he was on now, after traveling through the bowels of the ship.

He wrapped his fingers around the steel of a door handle. It looked like a closet. He wasn't sure, but he was beyond the point of caring. If there was someone inside, he planned on asking them for directions.

A woman lifted her head as the door opened. She was incredibly fit and possibly a few years older than him. She stacked small boxes and sorted what looked like hundreds of letters.

Grayson stood in the doorway, not knowing if he should stay or leave.

She smiled brightly. "Oh, please come in. I don't get much company here."

"Where is *here*, exactly?" He stepped inside and brushed his hands over the top of the boxes.

"This is the air wing Mail PO. I got a mail call, so

I'm sorting the division's stuff." She lifted a stack of boxes and grumbled, "It's taking me forever."

Grayson cocked his head in question.

She gave an exhausted sigh. "The last rep got reassigned, and I've never done this before. It's just overwhelming. Hopefully, I only have to do this today, before someone else can take over."

"Let me help you." Grayson shuffled through the labyrinth of stacked items. He wedged his feet in the small spaces, and the two of them juggled cardboard boxes of all sizes. He managed to set her handful down on a table to his right, and his eyes wandered. "How are you supposed to keep all this organized?"

"Well, it's all alphabetized, I think. What's your name, sailor? Why aren't you in your coveralls?"

"Oh, well, I'm not—"

"You're one of the captain's guests! I should have known. I'm Mary." She flashed another smile. Her dark hair was pulled into a tight bun at the nape of her neck, and she brushed some flyaway strands back.

"I'm Gr..." He paused. The thought of Cassidy flooded his mind. "Kyle. I'm Kyle Greens. Do you have any letters for me?"

"They'd be right..." She shuffled through her piles. "Here." She handed him a large stack of at least fifteen letters, and Grayson examined the return address on the top few. "Looks like someone special has been writing to you." She waggled her eyebrows.

He lifted his eyes from the stack and blushed. He hadn't blushed since…he couldn't remember.

Mary must have asked a question because she was looking expectantly at him.

"I'm sorry, did you say something?"

She laughed. "I said I wouldn't want your mail to get mixed up with the crew's. Want me to make a note to hold everything for you in here?"

This was wrong on so many different levels, but he wasn't about to let an innocent girl get hurt, when he could prevent it.

Grayson took a deep breath. "Yes."

CHAPTER TWO

CASSIDY PRACTICALLY SQUEALED INTO THE PHONE. "Mya, writing a feature article would be *huge* for me. I think today is the day!"

"Well, you are the best almost-archaeologist in Sidney, Montana. I have no doubt about that." Mya's deep, sultry tone was soothing.

Cassidy needed to relax with all the excitement coursing through her body. "On a side note, I'm settling into my new place." She looked around her small, barely-furnished studio apartment. "I only have, like, two things right now, but this place will be filled soon. I can't wait for you to see it." Maybe she'd even redo the floors, if she could find a way to afford it.

"How long do you have to continue with this unpaid internship at the museum? Does Kyle know?"

"Yeah, I told him I'm getting a promotion."

"But it's not really a promotion…"

"Sure it is! I'm getting promoted from one unpaid position to another. I heard that interns who write the feature articles get a stipend, so I have my fingers crossed. I only have six months more. Contributing to the monthly magazine fills the emptiness for now, until I can finally get my degree. I just wish I could write about ancient civilizations and not ancient latrines."

Mya stifled a giggle. "But I really enjoy your column on toilets."

It wasn't Cassidy's preferred topic, but it wasn't as if she critiqued porcelain thrones and their flush efficiency. Ancient latrines were an important part of history.

Even though this call was to celebrate her inevitable "promotion" at Kline Museum of the Arts, Mya was in the middle of a divorce. Cassidy's heart burned. "How are *you* doing, Mya?"

"I'm just annoyed. When you visited two weeks ago, I was pissed, but now I'm just confused and irritated. I can't wait for you to visit again. This penthouse is so…big."

Cassidy tried to lighten the mood. "You always loved the lavish lifestyle."

"Sometimes I wish I'd just stayed in our small farm town and done nothing with my life. Kind of like…"

"Me?"

Mya sighed at the other end of the line. "No, Cassidy. I wasn't going to say that. And you are doing something with your life. You're just too nice. You need to channel your third chakra and unleash the hell demon within."

Cassidy didn't know what that meant. But what Mya

said earlier held truth. She did stay in their small farm town. She had to make a choice between love or her career, and she'd chosen love. Sacrifices were a part of life, so she gave up her dream job at the Cooper Hewitt to stay in Montana and be with Kyle, her then boyfriend. He had begged her to stay, so they could build a family together. Family. Cassidy was finally going to have one again.

It wasn't like she could have afforded life in New York, anyway. After her parents died, she took out loan after loan to pay her parents' medical bills and was now drowning in debt. As a final slap to the face, not getting paid for her internship at KMA was further killing her credit score. Every time she moved, the place got smaller and smaller. She'd probably be better off living out of her car.

It was Cassidy's turn to sigh as she flopped onto her bed. After a few beats, she sat up. "Mya, what if they don't give the article to me?"

"Well, you can continue writing your toilet column, and once you're done fulfilling that internship, get the hell out of there and come live with me in New York City."

Like that would ever work. Cassidy needed at least a year to plan a big move like that. And without Kyle's permission? She wouldn't. But she couldn't help the grin from spreading across her lips at the thought of doing something spontaneous, for once. She shook the thought out of her head. She needed structure, and that started with getting this promotion at the museum.

Writing the feature article in the museum's magazine

meant one thing—exposure. She could finally show her worth in the industry and prove to herself that settling for a life in Montana was a good decision.

In her heart, she also hoped it meant new opportunities and a job that paid. She didn't want to be one of those people who worked so hard for a degree and never used it. She didn't even have her degree yet. *Augh.* She tossed her head back. She couldn't wait to finally start paying off her student loans.

Jumping off the bed, Cassidy dug through her clothes. "I better go. Boss wants me there early. My car doesn't work, so I have to walk today."

"It broke down again? All right. Call me right after, okay? I need some drama that doesn't involve my own life."

Cassidy briskly walked to KMA and enjoyed the clean bite of the Montana air on her face. The museum was only a few blocks away, so it wasn't a complete inconvenience that her car broke down. It gave her a chance to relish the fact that this morning was going to be the last few moments of her old life.

Taking a deep breath, she walked through the side entrance of the museum. The dimly-lit displays greeted her, and the Navaho jewelry podium she'd set up the night before was ready to be enjoyed.

She could have taken the elevator to the third-floor offices, but instead she took the stairs and savored the tingling in her legs and the light echo of her footsteps through the corridor.

Her heels clicked on the laminated wood staircase that wrapped around the elevator core of the building, and she hummed an unrecognizable tune. She reached the third floor and ran her fingertips over the "KMA" decal on the glass, memorizing it like Braille.

She straightened her nicest silk blouse and black pencil skirt and brushed her hair away from her face. Taking a deep breath, she walked into the office.

Susan, the youngest financial intern, immediately greeted Cassidy with a wide smile. "There is a new kick in your step today, Cassidy Thatcher."

She turned to Susan's desk and leaned forward. "I think I'm getting the feature article." Unable to hide the smile that had been etched onto her face since she'd left her apartment, she squared her shoulders.

"You go, girl!" They gave each other a small high five, and Cassidy continued to her boss's office.

She floated into the ample space. "Hello, Mr. Turner."

The sun was just beginning to rise over the foothills, and silhouettes of Mr. Turner's office decorations danced on the walls around her. Someday, Cassidy would have an office like this. A large window overlooking her hometown, awards decorating her desk, and a lampshade worth more than a small house.

"Cassidy, have a seat." Mr. Turner's eyes crinkled, as he smiled at her.

This is the day. Cassidy sat in the leather chair in front of Mr. Turner's mahogany desk. Her hands shook with excitement, as she placed them on her lap.

"You did an excellent job with acquiring that ancient Aztec bowl. You have given KMA a lot of exposure,

Cassidy. Not to mention the press. *Smithsonian Magazine* even wants to do an article on it."

Would Cassidy get to help write that article? Would they interview her? "I do what I can, sir."

"As you know, we're going through some transitions here at the museum."

Her breathing shallowed in anticipation. "Yes?"

Mr. Turner chuckled, and that eased the tension building in her lower back. A tension that had caused her stomach to cramp. "Cassidy, I have to let you go."

"I accept! Wait, what?"

"I have to let you go."

"Yeah, I-I heard you. So, I'm fired?"

"Let go, Miss Thatcher."

Cassidy's jaw fell open. "But, I'm practically a volunteer." Her voice trembled. "That Aztec piece, the Navaho jewelry…those were *me*." She pointed at herself. *God, what would Mya do in this situation?* Mya would have grabbed him by the throat and demanded a change in this conversation. Or suffocated him with her boobs.

"Yes, and like I said, the team is grateful. But our new partners have a different idea of where they'd like us to go. We just don't have room for you here, anymore."

She couldn't seem to speak, let alone reach for Mr. Turner's trachea.

"You've done a wonderful job on the floor, waving at guests, and contributing to the monthly magazine. Your column is truly inspiring."

She wrote about toilets for crying out loud. "There's nothing *inspiring* about my column. Where am I supposed to go?" Her hands trembled wildly at her sides.

"You know, I want you to be successful. I can make a call—"

She shook her head. The only other place she saw herself was at the Cooper Hewitt, but after bailing on them to build a life with Kyle, the last thing Cassidy needed was her ex-boss calling in a favor. She needed time to think about a new game plan.

She took a steadying breath, and her eyes eventually fell on Mr. Turner's.

Cassidy swallowed. "I'll finish my papers, and then leave."

"You actually need to pack your things now. I'm sorry, Cassidy." His voice was still warm and friendly. The cold-hearted jerk.

She was going to scream at him. Okay, maybe not scream. She hadn't screamed at anyone since she was sixteen.

Her career, her goals, her life. Everything seemed to disappear in slow motion.

Mr. Turner opened his mouth again. "Susan will take over for you. Please leave all files on her desk, so she can coordinate with *Smithsonian Magazine*."

"Susan? But she doesn't even have a degree—"

"You don't either, Miss Thatcher. I'd be happy to write you a letter of recommendation."

Cassidy couldn't help but make a sour face, as she stood and held her hand out to Mr. Turner. "No. Thank you." And to clarify, she didn't have her degree, *yet*. After completing this internship and a few more hours of lab work, she could have finally called herself an archaeologist.

He met her gaze and shook her hand. She left his office just as quickly as she'd entered.

Luckily, her desk was too small for much of anything, especially with three large monitors filling the space. The only thing she had on her desk was a notebook and a picture of her and Kyle on their first date. She checked the time. She wouldn't be able to stand the questioning glances from her colleagues. The urge to get out of there was overwhelming. Grabbing a stack of files from a shelf behind her, she hustled past reception.

She was grateful that Susan wasn't there to ask about her "promotion." Cassidy felt like a fool. A jobless fool. Leaving the files on Susan's desk, she stepped onto the elevator and pressed the button for the lobby. The doors wouldn't close fast enough, so she pushed the lobby button again…and again. The doors closed excruciatingly slowly, and she walked backward until she clashed with the textured wall of the elevator.

Resting her head back, she heard a *rip*. The facade of the wall caught on her sleeve. She pulled her arm away and checked the material in a frenzy. *Just great.*

"Don't get angry." She settled herself and kicked the wall with the back of her heel. "Idiot. Feature article." She snorted. "You stupid, stupid idiot."

For once, she wanted something to go as planned. She wanted to accomplish something. *Be assertive. Find your passion.* What the hell was a third chakra? Instead, every move she made dug her deeper and deeper into a hole. Today was supposed to change her charted path.

She walked back to her place and set her picture frame and notepad on the kitchen counter. Panic racked her brain. She could barely afford living on borrowed money. In four months, she'd undoubtedly be homeless.

Here she was again, doubting every decision she had ever made. If she had taken that job in New York, she wouldn't be broke. If she hadn't run away from home when she was a teenager, her parents would—

She cut herself off before diving down that rabbit hole.

She had Kyle, and he was a good man. He wasn't what she would call her type, but when he was in uniform, he looked just like her late father.

She sighed.

Kyle.

She'd been done for the day they met.

Now, she was just doomed.

Cassidy was in the habit of telling Kyle everything, but she couldn't—wouldn't—tell him about this. He never seemed to understand her career goals. Perhaps that was because he knew how important starting a family was to her. Her heart ached at the thought of him being gone until a "maybe" visit at Christmas. Even though he didn't understand everything about her, his presence was still comforting.

Her phone rang, and she saw it was her cousin. She held the phone to her ear.

"How did it go-o-o?" Mya sing-songed in her usual way. "How's the new corner office?"

Cassidy couldn't make a sound.

"Cassidy? Are you there?"

"Mm-hm." What was that noise that just came from her throat? She choked back a sob.

"Sweetie," Mya crooned, and Cassidy fell apart.

"I...don't...know what happened." Her words were strangled between hiccups. "I walked in and everything was a dream, and then he fired me."

"He fired you? But he's not paying you."

"Yeah, and obviously, he didn't want to start paying me."

"Did you grab him by the throat?"

Cassidy couldn't even find words in front of Mr. Turner. "No."

"Did you tell him you're the best thing that's ever happened to KMA, and he's going to regret firing you?"

"...No?"

"Cassidy, where is your backbone? It's like it has dissolved over the years."

Somewhere along the way today, Cassidy lost her fight.

"Okay. Breathe. Namaste. Always remember there is someone with less than you. Meaning, me." Mya laughed, and the brightness in her giggle made Cassidy smile. "I may have been married to a billionaire, but he's not leaving me anything. *Nothing.* But, together, we'll get through this."

Mya did have it worse, and that small fact made Cassidy feel slightly better, in a weird way.

"We can sell the furniture." Mya's voice was faint. "Before Brian takes that from me, too. I also have some dresses we can sell. Come to New York, and we'll figure this out together."

Cassidy's tears fell in a slow, steady stream down her face. "Not without Kyle's permission."

Mya gasped. "Jesus, you are your own person, Cassidy. You can make up your own mind. And where is Kyle to help you right now? There's no time for planning. You're a mess. I can hear it in your voice. Let's sell some stuff and get back on track. It's decided."

Sighing, Cassidy bowed her head. "Okay, you're right. Maybe we can move into a small apartment together?"

There was hesitation on the other end. "I'm...not ready to leave the penthouse, Cassidy."

"We can't afford it. We come from two different spectrums financially, and we're still broke."

"We can't afford it, *yet*. I'm just not ready to let it go. Just come. We'll figure out what to do."

New York. She couldn't believe she was doing something like this without Kyle's input.

Something shifted in her. A door was opening. Was this her new opportunity?

No, this was her fresh start.

"So...you're just going to kick her out?"

Mr. Whatshisname rudely looked her up and down. Cassidy hadn't even gotten halfway into the lobby before Mya's property manager bombarded her. Whenever

Mya asked her to visit, she often saw him sauntering about, bossing the tenants around.

"Look, lady, my arrangement is with Mya, not you. She said she'd be out after the divorce. It's after the divorce. I want her out."

Cassidy muttered. "Technically, it's not after the divorce."

"Speak up!"

She jumped at the sharp tone of his voice.

She could beg. Perhaps pay him off?

She snorted. She could probably only pay for five minutes in this place.

Be assertive. She could do this. Cassidy blurted the only thing she could think of. "I'll pay her rent until she can find another place to live." She cringed at the thought of applying for a fifth credit card. All her others were maxed out.

The man's dark eyes narrowed, almost as if he were considering her offer. After a stilted pause, he gave a few violent shakes of his head, started waving his hands about and speaking...wait—was that English?

The property manager vented in some indecipherable form of sign language, and her eyes began to inadvertently scan the downstairs lobby. It looked like...well, trash. Plastic wrap covered the countertops and flapped lightly as upscale tenants passed by, their shoes leaving soft echoes as they exited the complex.

Fragments of dust in the air muddled the sunlight. A layer of dirt lined the floor. Or perhaps it was shattered pieces of the ceiling? She looked up and noticed the suspended ceiling was not-so suspended, anymore.

Yup. That pile of garbage on the floor was most definitely the ceiling.

She had been here a few weeks ago, when Mya first received the divorce papers, and many times before that. She'd visited her cousin for whimsical adventures, shopping sprees courtesy of Brian, and to soothe Mya after their fights. In its current condition, Cassidy couldn't believe this complex offered the city's most affluent residents beautiful housing overlooking downtown.

Her curiosity got the best of her. "What happened to this place?"

Mr.—she caught a glimpse of his name tag—Tony abruptly stopped talking, and his expression turned on a dime, sadness creeping in and taking over the anger. It was as if he had a "Depress Me" button on his forehead, and Cassidy had succumbed to the sweet temptation and smacked it.

With a panicked gaze, he looked like he was trying to find something to fixate on, as if he needed support.

His gloomy eyes landed on the giant black splotch fifteen feet from them. "A kid with a little firebomb."

Little? The entire lobby was a disaster.

His arms lay limp at his sides in defeat. "I've been trying to get a crew in here all week. Everyone is too focused on the remodel at the High Tower to mess with this place. Tried every architect, but I can't get anyone in here."

She looked around at the unrecognizable lobby.

"Well, I can't help you there." She lifted her shoulders to her ears. "I'm an almost-archaeologist."

Tony's eyes snapped up and met her gaze. "An architect?"

Cassidy looked from side to side. "Um, no. I said archaeol—"

"I am under a lot of pressure right now with tenant complaints and insurance. If you can get my lobby fixed up…" He paused. "Mya can stay rent-free."

This was her chance. Okay, so she wasn't an architect, but how hard could it be? She was a fast learner. God, who was she trying to kid? She could never get away with that.

Shame washed over her at the thought of deceiving him. She couldn't commit fraud. "No, I'm not an architect. But I'll…um…figure something out. If you *promise* Mya can stay here a little longer."

"Yes, yes. I don't know what to say, Miss…—"

"Thatcher. Cassidy Thatcher."

He nodded and stood in silence, until his black eyes seemed to soften. His hand gestures became less boisterous. He lowered his voice. "Thank you, Miss Thatcher."

Tony didn't seem so wicked in this vulnerable state; he looked hopeful. But Cassidy knew better than to trust this man. He had, after all, made an adamant decision to kick Mya out. And now, Cassidy had to find a way out of this mess.

Cassidy reached into her bag for a piece of scrap paper or an old receipt. "I don't have a card or anything. Do you have a pen? I'll write my cell on this."

Tony handed her an uncapped pen from between the plastic folds atop a nearby counter, the crusty ink globbed at the end of the rolling ball.

Maybe this would keep her mind occupied while Kyle was gone. It would give her a purpose here. It would distract her from the disaster at KMA, until she found another job. She could try to get in touch with the Cooper Hewitt. With some luck, the museum would still be interested in her. She probably should have taken Mr. Turner up on his offer. Maybe, she could still make that work out in her favor.

Guilt churned in her gut. Working in a new city was a decision she would have discussed with Kyle...but Kyle was in the middle of some ocean. This was the best thing for now. She had to accept that he was gone, temporarily. He would understand that she needed to rediscover her passions. She was completely lost. Moving in with Mya, because she'd lost her job, was a choice she had to make.

Tony seemed to gain some composure. "Let's talk again. Say, later today?"

"Okay." She turned on her heel and exited the main lobby. Her phone buzzed in her purse, and she knew it was Mya.

Cassidy clenched her fists and looked around. "What to do, what to do?" She knew what she had to do. She needed to find an architect.

Her feet moved faster than she could have ever imagined, yet she had no idea where she was going. She hummed to herself frantically. Was she hyperventilating?

Specks of colors passed over her eyes, as moving blurs swooshed by in a wild frenzy.

Closing her eyes tightly, she swayed back and forth. What was that thing Mya always told her to do? Find her center, or some kumbaya nonsense. Taking a deep breath, she began to pray, or whatever it was that she was doing.

"Universe?" She groaned. "Please, make my misery go away. Bring me an architect. Show me the light—"

"Miss? Are you all right?"

She mumbled vaguely about being fine, opened her eyes, and everything flashed by in swirls of colors. Cassidy swung around, only to be met with bright, brown eyes. And his eyes were *bright*.

The man's eyebrows pinched together. "I'm sorry, I don't know what you're talking about. Are you having a panic attack?"

She couldn't feel her fingertips.

He reached for her shoulders and guided her toward the nearest storefront. "Sit." At the snap of his fingers, a chair seemed to appear. Or, someone brought it for him. Who was this man?

"Who are you?" Her vision started to clear, and she gazed up at him.

"Colton Albright." His smile was cute. One of his canines was just a little crooked. It made him edgy, but still handsome in a subtle way. He reminded her of her college study buddy.

"I'm Cassidy Thatcher."

Somehow, he had produced a bottle of water and held it out for her. The people passing by didn't even stop to toss her a glance, as they chatted away, and car horns honked as if she didn't exist. This city was too large for her. She accepted the bottle of water, opened it, and took a sip.

Colton towered over her as she tried to relax in a metal chair snuggled up against the glass facade of a storefront. He stood there as if expecting her to say something.

After a few moments, he shifted on his feet and stepped closer. "Is there anything I can help you with?"

Cassidy nearly choked on her water. Now, wasn't *that* a loaded question. She laughed. "Not unless you're an architect." She took another swig of water and rolled her eyes.

It was then that she noticed Colton's attire. He wore a reflective vest that hung loosely over his shoulders. Under his left arm, he cradled a hard hat. Colton wasn't a large man, but he wasn't small either. He was a normal looking guy, with a sweet face.

He cocked his head at her. "I *am* an architect." He said it as if it were obvious.

It *wasn't* obvious. Architects were supposed to wear suits and do art. If she had known all she had to do was beg the Universe for things, she would have started years ago, starting with money.

Cassidy mumbled and rubbed her head. "I obviously don't know anything about architecture."

Colton laughed, and the sound was comforting. Kneeling, he set his hard hat on the ground and leaned close to her knee. "Do you need an architect?"

She needed an architect *and* a job, that's what she needed.

Had she spoken aloud? Her face flushed in embarrassment. This man didn't know her.

His eyes filled with unmistakable humor. "I just saved you from having a panic attack in the middle of a construction zone. I think, you owe me an answer."

Now, it was Cassidy's turn to laugh. "Panic attack?" She waved her hand in dismissal.

"Uh-huh."

She stared at him for a minute. Colton's kind face would be perfect for a Hallmark movie.

Oh, he was talking. "How can I help you?"

This was hilarious. Was he being cute or serious? Did he want to help, or was this just a *"I'll make a call"* type of moment?

Her face fell. She'd already rejected Mr. Turner's offer to help. She wasn't about to make that mistake again. "I need money, Colton. Bad. I have no problem working late nights. I am just off that corner over there. I'm good with my hands. I'll do whatever you ask."

He leaned back a few inches, and his eyes seemed to darken. "Corner? Late nights? Are you...you don't look like...I'm not a...I'm not quite sure I understand what you're asking." His eyes darted back and forth in wild confusion.

"I'm *great* with remodeling. I don't know a thing about architecture, and I can't do art, but I can learn."

An expression of understanding passed over his face. He laughed embarrassingly. "Oh, you need a job?" He moved closer.

She nodded fervently. Hadn't she promised herself she would use her degree? What had she gotten herself into?

Speaking through rough pants, she crossed her hands over her chest. "I've created a mess for myself, and I need help. I'm to the point of desperation. I need an architect. I need a small construction crew. A job. I'll take anything. Please, will you help me?"

She knew that expression on his face.

Pity.

She was going to be homeless, and soon, Mya would be too.

Colton's face softened, and his brown eyes filled with compassion. "Stop by my office tomorrow. I'll see what I can do, okay?"

After composing herself, Cassidy rode the elevator to the familiar penthouse suite. She stared at Colton's business card. He was, indeed, a licensed architect.

Begging a stranger for a job she wasn't qualified for topped the list of her emotional breakdowns. She shook the thought out of her head. She still couldn't believe Mya's advice worked.

The elevator dinged, as she reached the penthouse suite. When the doors slid open, she was greeted by Mya's pleading, dark-blue gaze.

Mya ushered her inside and wrapped eager arms around Cassidy's lithe frame. "Oh, God. I was going to meet you in the lobby, but Tony was right there, going in for the kill. You survived, I see."

Barely. Cassidy didn't even know where to start. "I'm just glad to see you, Mya." Cassidy held Mya's shoulders at arm's length and looked around the nearly empty apartment. "What happened to all of your stuff? I thought we were going to decide on selling things together?"

Pulling away, Mya walked toward the kitchen. "I just sold the big things. I was having problems paying for, you know, other things."

Things. Cassidy knew what that meant. Manicures, shoes...

Cassidy let her eyes wander around the central living space that used to be furnished with oak chairs and mahogany cabinets. The fine china was gone. The Persian rugs, gone. The crystal chandelier hung at a lopsided angle, because half of its crystals were missing —most likely sold.

Mya awkwardly put her hands on her hips. "Did you see how trashed the lobby is?" She was trying to change the subject. "He should have given me a break on rent in this place after that happened. Better yet, you'd think Brian would have left me *some* money to at least buy food, you know? I've never worked a full day in my life, and now...well, I honestly thought I could get by with the money from the photography business I was dabbling in. But, after the press caught wind of the divorce, the clients dried up before I even had my first gig. And the property manager obviously isn't too fond of me." Her voice cracked as she rambled.

Cassidy brushed her cousin's long, blonde hair from her face.

A tear fell down Mya's cheek as she stepped back to collapse on a blanket on the floor in the corner. She looked sickly.

Cassidy opened her arms wide and smiled. "I have good news. You *might* not have to worry about rent for a few months."

Mya's eyes brightened, and she popped back up. "Really? How did you do it?" Mya hugged her cousin tightly, as they spun, laughing in celebration. Mya whispered a sweet, "Thank you, thank you, thank you."

Cassidy pulled away. "Well…" she trailed off, knowing her next words would undoubtedly upset her already vulnerable cousin. "I kind of told him I'd find an architect for him."

Mya covered her face with her hands and shook her head vigorously, groaning. Then she swayed back and forth like a buffalo navigating through the snow. "What have I done?"

Cassidy reached to pull Mya's hands down. "Mya. Stop it. I told you I'd help, so I am. I'm trying to change my tactics a little. And I did find an architect. He's working on that big tower remodel across the street. That place is huge, by the way. I'm meeting him tomorrow. He said he'll see what he can do. I'm hopeful. He seems really kind."

Mya mouthed a defeated "thank you" and shrugged. Her eyes were sad, dull. Like something or someone had extinguished her life force.

They'd get through this together.

Mya led Cassidy into the empty guest room. "Let's get you unpacked, so I can properly welcome you to my humble abode." Mya couldn't hide the cynicism behind her tone.

Cassidy winced again at the thought of Mya having to sell all her furniture. A picture of Mya and Brian sat on a cantilevered bookshelf hanging off the wall. Mya had gotten rid of everything in this room except *that*? Cassidy reached for the frame and turned the picture facedown.

Mya groaned.

Cassidy turned the picture back up. "I'm sorry."

Waving her hands, Mya walked up behind Cassidy and turned the picture facedown again. "No. I should get rid of them. I still have pictures of him. Pathetic, right?" Mya shrugged. "Come out when you're done, yeah? I've got the perfect movie for us to watch on my laptop."

Cassidy leaned over to open her suitcase and when she looked up to respond, Mya was already gone. Before Cassidy could find another reason to feel bad for her cousin, the bedroom window creaked, and an angry wind gusted through the bedroom, reverberating through the walls and slamming the door.

With a startled grunt, she walked over to the window and shimmied the lock. *Of course, it's broken.* Mya couldn't even afford to keep her furniture, let alone fix a broken window lock.

Cassidy pulled a bobby pin from her updo, and her brown locks cascaded down her back. She mangled the pin into an improvised latch and secured the window.

Taking a moment to look over the city, she watched as new leaves rustled in the early spring air. Dark clouds materialized in the distance, as another gust of wind threatened to open the window. *Do your worst, wind.* She gave herself a pat on the back for her window-fixing efforts.

There were no hangers in the closet, which didn't surprise her, but the floors were relatively clean. Strategically setting her blouses, skirts, and shoes into clusters on the floor, Cassidy admired her brilliant color-coding work. She should have gone into freelance closet organizing. Or not. She shook her head at the thought and went through the checklist in her mind—clothes, laptop, phone, chargers, shampoo, lotion...

Once she was satisfied she had everything she needed, she quickly changed into some pajama shorts and a baggy white T-shirt.

Shuffling her feet on the hardwood floors, she left her room to meet Mya in the living area.

Mya held two wineglasses with one hand and *She's the Man* with the other. "Chick flick and wine?"

What woman would ever turn down Channing Tatum and wine? Cassidy nodded with a grin and accepted the wineglass with a *gimmegimme* wiggle of her fingers. The two girls sat close on the blanket Mya had refolded neatly against the wall.

Cassidy tucked a strand of hair behind her ear. "So, whatever happened between you and your landlord to make him hate you so much? I mean, he wants you *out*."

Mya filled her glass as a naughty smirk crossed her face. This was the first time today Cassidy had seen a glimmer of Mya's mischievous personality. In time, Mya would remember where she came from and the person she used to be. She didn't need this fancy penthouse.

"Well. Tony's niece…I married her boyfriend."

That explains a lot. Cassidy closed her eyes tightly and laughed.

"Speaking of marriage," Mya slowly drawled. "Have you heard back from your *fiancé*?"

Cassidy rolled her eyes. "You don't need to say it like that. I know you don't like him. It's only been a few weeks. He's busy, I dunno, being a *hero*? I write to him every day."

"I'm the only family you have. I'm going to be overprotective," Mya defended herself. "I like Kyle. He's great…"

"But?"

"But I feel like you got engaged for the wrong reasons. It's too rushed."

"Rushed? Really? You and Brian got married after a few months. Kyle and I have been together for two years." Although, he had been gone for about one of those. Now he was gone again. Cassidy let her hands fall into her lap.

She looked at her ringless finger and tucked it away under the folds of her T-shirt. Okay, so they had rushed the engagement, but she was not rushing this marriage.

"Yeah, I see that giant *rock* he gave you," Mya retorted bitterly. "Rushed," she confirmed. "You just follow him like a puppy, giving up your dreams. He's controlling. You always have to ask his permission. I wish you could see how toxic that is."

"What's wrong with asking a partner for their support?" Cassidy asked. And, what was with Mya giving all this grand advice that she couldn't seem to take herself?

After a few minutes, Mya looked over. "Have you seen how often he looks in a mirror? When he passes a window, he can't help but check his muscles, which aren't that great anyway. He's just not the guy for you." Mya was treading in shallow water, and by the remorseful look on her face, she knew it. Her expression transitioned to one of sorrow. "I'm sorry, cos. I'm angry at a lot of things right now. I am happy for you, really. At least one of us will be happily married. And I don't want you to think I'm ungrateful for you being here."

Cassidy held out her hand and whispered, "It's okay, Mya. I just lost my job. We're both in a hole together."

They huddled close to one another, listened to raindrops fall over the city, and tried to focus on the movie playing on the small laptop screen.

During the movie credits, the walls shook, and the bathroom door slammed, followed by the guest room door. Soon after, one, two, three, four more doors down the long hallway toward Mya's room slammed with a *bang*.

Mya growled. "God, I hate New York storms. That's the downside of living so high up in never-never land, I guess."

Cassidy rolled off the blanket and slowly stood,

stretching her arms above her head. "I'm going to go check the window in my room. I had to lock it with a bobby pin."

How had Mya gotten into this mess? Oh, right. Brian. He'd cheated on his girlfriend with Mya. Now, he'd probably cheated on Mya to snag his next twenty-something victim. Cassidy only had speculation to go off of. Mya had her suspicions as well, but they'd never caught him.

Cassidy remembered when Brian and Mya had met. She had started with nothing, he gave her the world on a diamond-encrusted platter, and now, she was hiking a switchback trail back to nowhere. Even though Mya wore a mask of calm in the eye of the storm, Cassidy knew her cousin was dying inside.

Cassidy opened the door to her bedroom, unsurprised that the window had found its way open, again, and stepped forward into a puddle.

Puddle?

She looked down and gasped. She was standing in a pool of water and sloppy wet clothing. The wood floor felt sticky under her toes. Red dye floated in swirls around her feet, staining her white silk blouse an arm's length away.

She quickly lunged for her laptop, trying to salvage her electronics. She looked at her clothes and figured everything must have been soaking for at least an hour. This couldn't have all come from the window, could it? *No.*

Her instincts told her to look up and, at first glance, she didn't see any leaks. Then her eyes fixated on a low spot in the ceiling where liquid appeared to be puddling. Water spurted from a crack in the Sheetrock, and slowly, the board peeled away from the nails holding it in place and flipped to the floor, along with all the water pressing against it.

Mya burst into the room and shrieked, "Oh, my God! Your clothes! Your laptop! We can go shopping tomorrow—"

"No," Cassidy said too abruptly. The last thing Mya needed was to shop for clothes and be reminded of everything she had sold. Cassidy couldn't afford it, anyway. The two girls combined didn't have enough money to splurge on unnecessary, material objects. They were lucky to stay in this penthouse Mya was obsessively attached to, even if it was falling apart.

Purchasing new clothes would have to wait. Cassidy didn't need anything extravagant. She could save her jeans. The water had destroyed her blouses, but she could make something work.

Maybe.

Cassidy cleared her throat. "I mean, what for, Mya? It's not a big deal. I'm just going to be hanging out. Do you have anything I could wear?"

A jolt of fear spiked in her stomach. For a brief moment, she had forgotten who she was talking to. After Mya had married Brian, she had become a classy, sophisticated woman. But that version of Mya had disappeared.

Introducing Mya Rivers pre-Brian, former slut extraordinaire.

"Um, n-no. Never mind! I think I can make these

clothes work," Cassidy stuttered, trying to backtrack. She didn't want to prance around New York looking like a hooker.

"I know what you're thinking, dear cousin." Mya wagged her finger at Cassidy, chastising her. "You're, like, three sizes smaller than me, but of course, you can wear anything of mine. They'll be appropriate. I promise!" She left the room to gather some towels and hopefully, some decent clothing for Cassidy to wear.

She grumbled under her breath. After placing her pile of now tie-dyed clothes aside, she looked through the cabinets and opened all the cupboards. She eventually found a step stool in the bathroom closet and brought it back to her room to take a better look at the leak.

With her head stuck in the overhead space, she heard wet footsteps coming toward her.

"How about this?" Mya flung a thick duvet and comforter on the floor to soak up the water. It was most likely what she had been sleeping on. Mya had a smile on her face, and she outstretched her arms to reveal a T-shirt that read "Kiss Me."

Cassidy grimaced. "Is that the shirt you wore the day Jeremy Calhoun spread the rumor that he boinked you under the bleachers?"

"Oh, it wasn't a rumor." Mya laughed and whipped Cassidy across the chest with the cotton T-shirt.

Cassidy leaned out of the way, trying to avoid those disgusting high school memories. She groaned. "I can't believe I'm going to be wearing your clothes."

"Never thought you'd be slumming it like the old

Mya Rivers, huh?" Mya placed her hands on her full hips and cocked an eyebrow. In that instant, Cassidy remembered the young, exuberant Mya. Before Brian had ruined her. Before the fame, the fortune, and New York City.

"Well, no. But how bad could it be? I've always wanted to be a dirty slut." Cassidy grinned, stepped down from the stool, and took the shirt to display it across her chest. "It's so big," she tittered.

"Hey. I'm a curvy girl. And I was chubby in high school, remember?"

"I can't believe you still have all this stuff." She walked over to the box Mya had in the hallway as her cousin removed more clothing from it.

"Oh! I have boxes and boxes. After Brian and I fought, I would go and look through old stuff."

Cassidy hesitated for a moment, nervous the topic of Brian would elicit a sad spell. It didn't. Mya talking about her ex without breaking down indicated progress, and Cassidy exhaled a sigh of gratitude.

She placed a hand on Mya's shoulder. "Thank you for letting me wear your horrendous high school clothing. We'll get through this. We always do."

Mya nodded. "I'm just glad you're here," she said quietly and went inside the guest room to try and clean up more.

Cassidy continued rummaging through the box and held up froufrou shirts the two could laugh about. There was no way she would properly fill them out. Mya rocked some killer curves, with a full chest, wide hips, and a small waist. With brown hair, green eyes, and a lean build, Cassidy wasn't anything extraordinary like her blonde-haired, blue-eyed bombshell of a host.

She scrunched her face, as the duvet slowly soaked up the water in the bedroom, then glanced at the revealing "Kiss Me" T-shirt she'd tossed over her shoulder.

This was going to be an interesting few months in New York.

CHAPTER THREE

IT WAS DIFFICULT NOT TO TEAR OPEN EVERY LETTER AND binge-read the contents. Each one was placed in a crisp, pastel lavender envelope. To anyone else, the color probably would've looked off-white, but Grayson had opened enough to know that these envelopes were purple.

He smiled, as he threw another pillow behind his head and attempted to sort Cassidy's letters in chronological order by the sun-faded time stamps.

This was his second stack of letters from the mailroom. The first had been carefully tucked away once this batch arrived.

He'd stored them all in a small duffel bag full of electronics he had brought with him from New York, with the exception of Cassidy's first letter. He kept that in the breast pocket of his suit jacket.

"Which one will we read today?" He thumbed

through the envelopes and selected the top one, dated a few weeks prior.

He couldn't restrain the burst of laughter that escaped his throat when he took out the contents.

They were random pictures of apartment complexes.

Kyle,

The funniest thing happened after you left. I'll explain everything, once I know what's going on. Here are some pictures of my most recent adventure with Mya!

Grayson flipped through the images and couldn't help his crooked grin from widening. And Kyle said she wasn't interesting. Grayson scoffed.

One image was of a voluptuous blonde posing in front of a cheap apartment for rent. Grayson gawked at her outfit in surprise. He didn't know cotton could stretch like that. At least, by its physical appearance, it looked like cotton. He'd have to take a sample to be sure.

He cocked his head to the side, as he observed her face from all angles. She emanated joy, but there was a sadness hiding in her eyes. Other than her hollow gaze, she appeared happy and vibrant. Her expression shone with mischief, and her posture was playful.

He squinted in curiosity. Was this Cassidy?

Grayson flipped to the next image. It was the blonde again, but she was inside the apartment now. Were they looking for some place to live? He cringed. The floors were scuffed, the walls had obvious water damage, and one of the windows was missing in the background. The vines from outside gripped the inside of the sill.

He continued to follow the girls on what seemed to be an apartment hunt. Each place was worse than the last. The curvy blonde was in every image, smiling like a Colgate model. She was sun-kissed and stunning as she posed next to the sinks, the cabinetry, the floor tiles...no kitchen detail was missed in these photographs.

Grayson had a hard time believing the woman smiling at him was Cassidy. In her last letter, she had described how she wished she owned a garden, and that if she did, she wouldn't be so pasty. He had the words memorized.

A garden for bronze blondie? No way.

Between his fingers, he fiddled with an image of a broken sink. With some work, the porcelain wouldn't appear so damaged. Perhaps the girls were searching for a local remodel project.

There were mysteries behind Cassidy Thatcher that Grayson wanted to explore. The next sealed envelope beckoned him to open it, but he resisted. The temptation to open all the letters and learn more about Cassidy was overwhelming, but Grayson wanted this to last. He was beginning to understand why some of the sailors on board read one page of a book a night. He pushed the entire pile out of his direct sight, returning to the pictures in his hand.

A dark splotch behind the broken sink in the picture caught his attention. In the background, there was a faint silhouette. A reflection in a mirror, he was sure. It looked like the outline of an angel.

"That's my girl," he whispered.

The rays of light from behind refracted off her head in prisms of white and gold. Her hair appeared brown, maybe even gold. She glowed. Grayson brought the picture closer to his face. He could barely make out a bent elbow, holding what looked like a camera or a phone.

Knock. Knock.

He flinched and sat up, only to hit his head on the unoccupied bunk above. "Gah. I'm coming." He placed the photos on the remaining stack of letters and reached the door in two strides.

"Grayson," Captain O'Hare greeted. "May I come in?"

Grayson rubbed his head and opened the door. "I didn't shine my shoes today, Cap."

The captain chuckled. "We'll work on that when you finally decide to join the Navy."

Grayson doubted that. He wouldn't survive a permanent life on a ship. He was already counting the days until summer, when he'd be back on solid ground.

Captain O'Hare stepped forward and met Grayson's gaze. "I can't begin to say how grateful I am you agreed to join us this spring. I can see an improvement in our methods. There's passion, curiosity."

"Thank you, that means a lot."

There was pride in the captain's eyes. They sparkled with life and appreciation. It was times like these that

Grayson lived for. They were small moments that made everything he had worked for worth it.

The captain took a few steps forward. "You seem to be adjusting well. Are you staying out of trouble?"

Grayson tried not to glance at the pile adjacent to him and stilled. Did O'Hare know about the letters? "Uh, what do you mean?"

"Well, as you've seen from the guys that attend your lectures, we have one or two ruffians on our hands…"

Grayson was a ruffian. He was a thief. Every action had a reaction, and he was beginning to realize that taking Cassidy's letters might have repercussions after his adventure on Ike, especially if Kyle somehow found out. Consulting Lance about the matter was a possibility. His chest tightened. What could Lance offer to the situation other than a lecture about how Grayson's interpersonal skills sucked?

Grayson might be able to dodge any fine thrown at him for this inconvenience. The first letter wasn't even his fault. Just the rest of them were.

A deep groan escaped his mouth. Hopefully, an inaudible one.

I should talk to Lance.

"…I came here, because the boys in the airframe shop are about to have a gratitude event to pass the time, and I thought it would be something you and Lance might enjoy participating in. My youngest son is in the air wing. I'd like to introduce him to you. All you do is interact with the nukes, so it might be a good change. It starts in ten minutes or so."

"I…" Grayson hesitated, the troublemaking letters

calling him back to the bed. Lance was definitely going to kill him.

Captain O'Hare's eyes were wide and anxious. Grayson knew that look. The captain wasn't going to take "no" for an answer.

"I would love to join the men. I haven't seen Lance for the past hour, so I can't speak for him, but I'd like to come. Is what I'm wearing fine?" He looked down at his gray sweater, slacks, and Italian leather loafers.

"You're a bit overdressed for the airframe shop, but considering this is casual for you, it'll do just fine." Captain O'Hare held out his hand for a shake.

Grayson smirked and accepted the captain's formality. He stood at an awkward angle to avoid the bunk above.

The captain led Grayson through the entrails of the ship, until they reached the hangar bay on the main deck. The sun was just beginning to disappear behind the endless horizon. The wind was calm, and the air was humid on his saltwater-chapped skin.

An enormous burst of shouting and laughing came from yards away, as they approached the closest airframe shop. The shouting transformed into an unrecognizable chant.

"What *exactly* is a gratitude event?" Grayson asked. By the sounds of it, they were sacrificing a virgin to Poseidon.

Captain O'Hare laughed. "It's different every time. Too bad Lance couldn't join." There was humor in his voice, as he continued to lead Grayson to the sacrificial playground.

"I'm not a virgin, just so you know." Grayson couldn't help but blurt the words out.

The captain turned with his eyebrows raised. He laughed again, and his smile touched his eyes, his weather-worn skin bright.

The main garage door was shut, but there was an aircraft parked outside with the ailerons stripped off, as if someone were just about to start their shift.

Captain O'Hare opened the metal door to the side of the garage, and the noise flooded the outside space like a sonic blast.

"Attention on deck," someone called, and everyone snapped to attention.

The captain lifted his hand. "At ease." Everyone sat back down, and Captain O'Hare towered over the group of seated men. "This is Grayson Daniels. O'Hare," he nodded to a young man in the corner of the shop, "come here for a minute."

The room filled with light chatter, but Grayson still felt like an intruder. He didn't know these men, other than Captain O'Hare. They didn't view him as an equal. He was a guest, an instructor, and not even *their* instructor. He would have never expected any of his associates at the High Tower to treat him as a friend. How was this any different?

He wasn't quite sure what *this* was, but it was certainly unfamiliar.

The captain put his arm around a scrawny boy, who couldn't have been more than twenty. "Charlie, this is Grayson Daniels. Remember me telling you stories about him?"

Charlie's face lit up. "Hi, Mr. Daniels. I've been following your work for years."

Shaking his hand, Grayson was surprised by his strength. The boy looked nothing like his father. His head was nearly shaven, his eyes sunken and dark. But he exuded youth, and his smile was contagious.

One man yelled, breaking the silence. "Well, don't just stand there, Charlie. Let's get this show on the road."

The captain smiled, patted his son on the back, and left. Grayson sat next to a man almost as large as Patrick, from the nuke division.

The men were relaxed and talked to each other in clusters of four or five. Grayson lazily scanned the room and took in the new faces. It was then that he locked eyes with Kyle.

Grayson stared at him. He couldn't help it.

Kyle was in his navy-blue coveralls, the top half wrapped around his waist, revealing the white tank underneath. Tattoos covered his arms and shoulders. He was almost unrecognizable, compared to the last time they had met. Kyle's hair was unruly, and his skin shone with a light layer of fuel and oil.

In this atmosphere, Kyle was an even starker contrast to Grayson. Grayson would choose his desk job over being doused in gallons of that crud, any day.

Kyle waved, and Grayson smiled weakly again. This half-smile seemed to be his favorite expression of the night.

His thoughts were interrupted by a loud, animated voice that echoed between the walls of the garage.

"Gentlemen, gentlemen. I'd like to welcome you to our first gratitude event." Charlie bowed, and everyone cheered.

Grayson leaned forward and rested his elbows on his knees.

"I'm going to pass out these questionnaires. Please, fill them out. But don't forget, you aren't filling them out for yourself." He walked to the center of the room and eyed the crowd playfully. "You are to fill them out for one of your loved ones. And don't lie, because the truth will come out eventually."

A man in the back clapped loudly. "Hand out the papers already, Sticks."

Grayson laughed at everyone's enthusiasm. He turned to the brawny man next to him. "Sticks?"

Grayson was met with a sly grin. "Have you *seen* him? Charlie's the skinniest man on this ship, but the boy's got a way of lightening the mood."

"Shut up, people." Sticks crouched low and smiled. "After you fill out your questionnaire and feel you've done your loved one justice, crumple it, and put it in the bin." He pointed to a large, empty trash can. "Then, we'll each go around and pick one. Your goal is to guess whose loved one you have chosen. I can't imagine it being hard, except for our guest over here, because we all know each other."

Papers and pens were passed around, and the giant, welcoming man sitting next to Grayson tried to take a peek at what everyone was writing.

A collective "sh-h-h" fell over the room as the men began to write. The questionnaire was simple. Favorite color. Favorite toothpaste. Favorite hobby. It was a list of random questions one would supposedly know about someone they cared for.

This seemed like a pointless exercise.

Who was Grayson going to write about? Lance? Lance's favorite color was women, his favorite toothpaste was lipstick, his favorite hobby…easy. But what would these men think if Grayson wrote about his sex-craved business partner?

Jesus Christ.

Maybe Lance was right. Grayson needed to stop being so awkward.

He decided to write about Katrina. She had consumed his mind since their departure. It felt right to acknowledge her. Her favorite color was pink, her favorite toothpaste was *his* favorite toothpaste, and she loved to swim.

He smiled as a blanket of warmth covered his heart. He hadn't thought about his baby sister so often and freely for over a decade.

Ike had broken down barriers in him and unexpected feelings surfaced. Was it his fear of water? That was probably part of it. Was it Cassidy's letters? He wasn't sure, but he didn't feel alone anymore.

Someone was watching over him.

He looked around, and everyone had completed their questionnaires. They must have been writing for a while because as Grayson sat up, a sedentary stiffness pulled at his right hip. People began crumpling the forms and tossing them into the bin that Sticks had placed in the center.

"And now," Sticks spread his arms wide, "it's time to choose!" He struggled to hoist the trash bin under one arm and walked toward Grayson. "You're our guest tonight. Please, pick a loved one."

Grayson smiled as the men around him chanted. He grabbed a wad of paper and slowly unfolded it.

It was...blank. Except for an occasional "N/A" or some form of chicken scratch.

At the bottom of the sheet was something legible.

Hobbies: archaeology

"Kyle," Grayson whispered, and the room fell silent. "Kyle," he said a little louder. "I think I have your fiancée." Grayson displayed the sheet of paper and looked at Kyle.

Kyle's face lit up. "What are the odds of that?" He laughed, and the men around him patted his back in some sort of congratulations for having someone guess his loved one.

The trash bin was passed on to the next person, and Grayson turned back to the paper in his hand. He paid more attention to the few words that were scribbled on the sheet.

Favorite color: orange

He took a deep breath. "Her favorite color is purple, you idiot."

Favorite food: take out

Based on the endless kitchen pictures he had been looking at just a half hour ago, he doubted Cassidy enjoyed splurging on takeout. No woman obsessed with a kitchen sink would prefer takeout over a home-cooked meal.

Grayson was frustrated. Why be engaged to someone you don't know? Someone to control? To change?

Kyle Greens made Grayson sick. To make matters worse, Kyle had an annoying smile plastered on his face. He was giving high fives and laughing with his friends.

Cassidy wouldn't be Kyle's for long, if Grayson had anything to do with it. He tapped his pen against the bend of his knee and stared into space.

"Hey, nice job guessing Cassidy." Kyle's voice came from Grayson's side. As Kyle sat, the smell of crude oil emanated from his skin.

Grayson didn't even toss Kyle a glance. "Lucky guess."

A few people were cleaning up, and there were only a handful left in the garage. He wasn't sure how long he'd been sitting there, staring at the walls.

"Captain needed hands on deck, but I got out of it," Kyle said with a laugh, and placing his arms through the sleeves of his suit, he stood, zipped it, and walked off.

"Good for you." Grayson exhaled a slow breath, and silence fell in the air.

Fire burned in his chest. That same unknown twinge that had started in his stomach now stabbed at random places over his arms. How a man like Kyle had ever ended up with a kind, loving woman like Cassidy would likely remain a mystery.

A *thump* came from behind, and a warm hand pried the pen out of Grayson's clutched fist.

"I've been looking for you everywhere. Jesus, come quick."

Grayson twisted around to see Lance—he had appeared out of nowhere.

Grayson stood. "Where have you been?"

Lance looked like a mess. His shirt was disheveled, and he was panting. "I've been in the control room, trying to get service. Then my stateroom. I was getting worried, because I hadn't received an update on construction at the lab yet. I know how important the success of that is." Lance spoke fast, and there was urgency in his tone. "A few emails came in…"

"And the point?" Grayson urged.

Lance turned and waved for Grayson to follow. "Someone is trying to steal our architect. I mean, that's what the email said. And, they're not just taking Colton. They're poaching part of the crew. I printed it out. Come, I'll show it to you."

It was likely a misunderstanding. It appeared to be Lance's turn to lose his mind on this ship.

"You're doing that thing again," Grayson teased, as he followed Lance to his chambers. "You're walking with your shoulders forward, and you have this hideous pigeon-toed shuffle. You can't micromanage everything. You know that, right?"

Lance didn't turn around. He halted, and Grayson

nearly ran into him. Lance opened the door to his room and beckoned Grayson inside.

Papers were thrown everywhere. A lamp was placed on the floor next to a set of construction plans.

Lance shrugged in defeat. "I'm kind of panicking. What does the dashed line on these drawings mean again?"

Grayson stood in front of his childhood friend and placed his palms on Lance's shoulders. "Go lie down, Lance."

Lance rolled his eyes and retreated to his bed, where he wilted into the sheets.

Grayson laughed. "You always do this. Ever since we were kids you have found unnecessary ways to stress yourself out. For someone so...organized...your life sure is a mess."

"I miss my desk." Lance rubbed his smooth-shaven face. "I used to have a calendar. People to manage."

Grayson stepped over the paperwork and sifted through it, as Lance continued to whine about inconsequential things. Grayson finally saw the email Lance was referring to and pushed the other papers aside.

Lance,

Our architect and part of the construction crew are leaving at 3:00 p.m. every day to work on a lobby remodel next door. I thought we had them until 5:00 p.m. Help? I couldn't get the name, but I have attached the phone number of the main contact...

Someone *was* poaching their architect.

Grayson let out a long huff. "Are you kidding me? What are you *doing*, Colton?"

Lance moaned in agreement.

Folding the letter and placing it in his pocket, Grayson tried to maintain his composure. He had spent years buttering up the CEO of the High Tower to let him and Lance oversee the new lab construction. And the only reason he did *that* was because he wanted his opinion heard when it came to building the second High Tower, a few miles away. Grayson had no interest in infrastructure or real estate, but if this small laboratory rebuild didn't go as planned, his reasons for getting involved in the first place would have been for nothing.

Groaning, Lance crossed his legs on the bed. "I can try to call Colton. I'll get this straightened out."

"No. I'll take care of this." Grayson walked over to where the lamp rested on the floor. "I'll reach Colton and whoever is in charge of this lobby remodel. He has no business taking other work right now."

Lance sighed. "I need a woman. That would fix this."

Grayson chuckled. "What you need is to *relax*. I'll handle it from here."

Lance propped himself up on his elbow. "Actually, what we need is a *secretary*, so I don't have to deal with this crazy influx of emails. I blame you," he pointed at Grayson, "for firing the last two."

Grayson shrugged. "They deserved it. Besides, secretarial work fits you so well."

This is what Grayson wanted to avoid. Ever since

they'd embarked with the crew, Lance had taken on everything while Grayson taught classes and assisted the captain. He'd been treating Lance like a butler, rather than his business partner. Guilt swirled in his gut.

He had put Lance in this position when they were seniors in college and the lab was still young. He'd promised himself he wouldn't ever do that again. He would fix this. Lance was getting overwhelmed. He wasn't ready to manage this much remotely.

Lance flopped on his back. "Soon, we'll be back home, and everything will be normal again." He dug his head deep into his pillow. "Then, you can go back to being *you*, and I can go back to cellular service and my laptop." Lance's breathing deepened.

"Me going back to being *me*?" What did that even mean? There was a calm breath from Lance, and Grayson let his eyes scan the stateroom that was an exact replica of his. "I realize I haven't been as present." He had been distracted. Even at that moment, he was thinking of getting back to his room…back to Cassidy's letters…to see what other horrendous kitchenware she had taken pictures of. "We're a team." Grayson leaned over to turn off the lamp. "I'll take over the construction project at the lab and deal with this confusion."

Grayson turned to face Lance. He had fallen asleep, and Grayson shook his head in disapproval at the awkward position his friend rested in. Lance's head had slid off the pillow, one of his feet was dangling off the end of the bed, and his sweater had crept up his stomach, exposing the white undershirt tucked into his slacks.

"If only your women could see you now." Grayson left the room, the email from the High Tower in his pocket. He had a phone call to make.

He took his time returning to his stateroom. Lance was usually the smooth talker who ironed out messes with clients. Grayson wasn't sure how he would approach this situation. He figured he would treat it in the only way he knew how. He would demand he get his way and close the deal.

He walked to the small duffel bag under the desk is his room and searched for the iridium phone provided by the ship. Worried he had misplaced it, he removed all the contents and re-organized it, not forgetting to place Cassidy's letters in their designated spot.

There was no phone. Perhaps Lance had borrowed it.

He'd talk to the captain in the morning or wait until the ship reached port. That could be days from now.

Growing impatient, Grayson's mind drifted. When they reached port, would Kyle try and reach out to Cassidy? A groan escaped his throat. It wasn't like he could do anything about it from the middle of the Atlantic.

That same unfamiliar feeling from earlier swelled in his blood. He could almost place the emotion.

Grayson cursed.

On his bed were the pictures from Cassidy's letters, and he stopped pacing. He hadn't realized he'd been walking in small circles in the center of his room. He reached for the stack of pictures and flipped through them.

His curiosity took control of his hands. "Come on. Come *on*. Let me see you."

Nothing.

After examining who he thought was Mya in the images, the desire to discover what Cassidy looked like poked and prodded at his brain. He was back to the same place as earlier that night—staring at the stack of lavender envelopes, wanting to feast his eyes on every word.

Cassidy was so similar to his sister. Every day, he looked forward to the peace her letters brought him.

This was a test, and Grayson knew it. The stack of envelopes taunted him.

He took another deep, calming breath. He would wait until tomorrow to read another one of Cassidy's letters. He carefully packaged the pictures and set the stack of letters from Cassidy aside.

In the meantime, he needed to conjure up something to say to the idiot stealing his architect.

CHAPTER FOUR

CASSIDY SWEPT THE SAWDUST FROM HER TABLE SAW. After wiping her goggles to see through them, she grinned and examined her handy work. She wasn't processing data of ancient artifacts, but helping Colton gave her a sense of accomplishment.

One of her crewmen came up behind her and took the piece of lumber from her hands. "That'll do real nice in this wall, Miss Thatcher. You should quit working for that fancy Colton fella and work with the guys." He walked behind the main counter, and a spiral of dust followed in his wake from maneuvering around the shards and scraps on the floor of the lobby.

She turned her head and smiled to herself. Working for Colton wasn't half bad. After showing up to his office the day after her poorly timed panic attack, she told him about her situation, and he didn't turn his back on her.

He offered his help so willingly. When Colton took

her and Mya to drinks one evening, he called Mya's lobby remodel his pro-bono job. Cassidy laughed at the thought. She was Colton's charity case, but somehow that didn't make her feel small. It was nice having someone on her side.

After evaluating her skills, Colton told her she wasn't really good at anything design related, but she did have a knack for building things.

While Colton worked on his main project at the High Tower, Cassidy ran with the interior remodel of the lobby. Painting. Sawing lumber. Things she could redo if she screwed up too badly. She worked most afternoons for minimum wage. It was only enough for groceries, but considering she just got fired from a volunteer position, it was a godsend and one less thing for Mya to try and budget.

The construction was a much-needed distraction from her immediate reality. When her hands weren't busy, her mind jumped to the electric bill that had showed up that morning. They'd sold off a bit of Mya's remaining wedding china, but that wasn't likely to cover the bill for a huge, poorly insulated apartment. That was the struggle, Mya latching on to material objects. She used to be so simple, but she had outgrown the minimalist life and Cassidy hadn't. Between the two of them, with some luck, they'd be able to make a reasonable decision.

She removed her safety gloves and lightly tossed them on the edge of her workbench.

In two months, when this project ended, they'd have to leave the penthouse and find someplace else to live.

That date was creeping up on them.

Helping the guys with small tasks gave Cassidy something to look forward to each day, something to keep her off Mya's tail, pressuring her to pawn some of her expensive knickknacks for extra cash.

Cassidy had yet to call the Cooper Hewitt to ask for a job. Part of her was too embarrassed. What was she supposed to say? *I'm sorry I turned you down, but hey, I decided to sacrifice my dream to be close to my boyfriend. Oh, but I just got fired, and you're my second-best option. When do I start?*

She rolled her eyes. For now, working with Colton was a blessing.

Her heart clenched at the thought of Kyle not being able to support her through this mess of a situation. A letter from him would have been nice. An email, maybe. She didn't know if he had service or not. One time, he didn't have internet for an entire eight months. She hoped that wasn't the case now. Part of her wondered if he could buy a local burner phone when on land, just to call and say hi. Maybe they had pay phones?

Kyle hadn't talked much about the resources available to him on board.

Between her debt, remodeling this trashed lobby, and being nearly broke, she just needed someone to tell her everything was going to be okay.

Cassidy looked at her watch and saw it was almost 8:00 p.m. Usually, she would be showered, dressed, and ready to write Kyle about her day. Just another thing not going as planned.

Her phone vibrated in her pocket. She stepped

outside the work area and pulled out one of her earplugs. "Mya? Hello?"

"Hey! I'm...well, it's expensive...home at...soon?" Mya's voice was broken.

"Where are you? I can't understand you." Cassidy jumped as a nail gun fired consecutive rounds somewhere behind her. There was an office adjacent to where she stood, and she walked the few paces and stepped inside, pulling the door shut. "Mya? Are you there?"

Silence stretched as her phone displayed her home screen, indicating the call had disconnected. She scrunched her face in disappointment, hoping Mya hadn't spent the day in a Dead Sea mud bath, thinking that counted as therapy.

Her cell vibrated again. She expected it to be Mya calling back, except she didn't recognize the number.

She brought the phone to her ear. "Mya?"

Again, the line was static. Cassidy shuffled around the office, trying to get out of any dead zone.

There were hints of a man's voice. It was luxuriously deep. Her heart leaped.

"Kyle?" Cassidy was breathless. "Kyle!" She sighed in relief.

The crackling in her ear continued for another minute, but Cassidy didn't mind. If this was as close to Kyle as she could get, she would take it. The soft hum in her ear reassured her. It gave her hope.

"You're a thief."

She stopped pacing. There was a long delay.

"You're taking my architect, my crew, my time. Who do you think you are?"

This man was not Kyle.

Cassidy didn't know how to respond. "Um. Hello?"

"Yes. *Hello.*" Irritation hardened his tone. "Have you been taking notes on anything I've said?"

Notes? "I'm sorry, I didn't realize this was a lecture." Cassidy scowled, surprised at her sudden outburst. Adrenaline rushed through her body, and guilt encased her chest. She shouldn't be snapping at a stranger. *Everyone is a potential client.* Colton had taught her that. She took a deep breath. "How can I help you today?"

Another delay. "Don't tell me I have to repeat myself."

She was taken aback by his bitterness. "Oh. I...okay—"

"I'd like to talk to the man in charge of the lobby remodel." He spoke slowly, his voice laced with assertion.

"That would be me." Satisfaction encircled her words, and a small smile spread across her lips. Yes, she was proud of being in charge of this remodel. It wasn't an ideal situation, but she enjoyed it nonetheless.

A sound crept through the other end of the line. Was he...laughing? "No. The man in charge. Colton Albright."

Cassidy's smile faded, and that burst of anger she had felt just moments ago was back. She would put this man in his place and not feel guilty about it. "You won't find him, because I am in charge of the lobby."

There was a heavy, annoyed sigh. "You're taking my

workers." His voice was dark, as if it had lowered an entire octave.

His accusation made Cassidy's face flush, and her lips pressed into a firm line. "O-o-oh, you mean, you're one of those lab rats from that High Tower place? Yeah, well, take note of this. Learn how to read, because your contract says you have the crew until 3:00 p.m., and your architect doesn't have to work exclusively on your project." Cassidy raised her chin, although no one was there to see it.

"How much?"

"Excuse me?" She envisioned him pacing in an Armani suit, his smug face permanently set in a glower.

"How much to buy you out? What's your price?"

Cassidy's jaw dropped ever so slightly. She could not be bought. Well, if the circumstances were different... *No.* She wouldn't let this man degrade her and then bribe her. "I don't know who you are, and I don't care. What makes you think your project is more important than mine?"

"Mine is for research." He sounded so matter of fact.

Oh God, was this guy curing cancer or something? Remorse was a thick mucus in her chest. "I'm sorry." She must have sounded so selfish. "What kind of research?"

He groaned. "Why do women always insist on deflecting?" De-*flect*-ing. Yup, he was pissed.

This guy was probably inventing the next Pop-Tarts flavor. It was an honest question. Cassidy pulled the phone away from her face and rolled her eyes. Who was this entitled prick? It honestly sounded like he believed he was king, and she was a peasant, except he wouldn't tell her why.

Her blood pressure reached unexplored territory. "Go research how to screw yourself!" She hung up and growled in frustration. "Augh! Men!" She kicked a nearby trashcan, and the echo filled the room. She kicked it a few more times for good measure.

"Cassidy?" A shadow on the floor crept closer from behind, and she spun to see Mya with round eyes, holding a paper grocery bag in one hand and her purse in the other, standing halfway in the doorway. "Who was that? Kyle?" Mya approached. "Did you two just have your first fight?"

"No. I have no idea." Cassidy let out an exaggerated sigh. "I've never been so angry."

Mya's giant blue eyes filled with confusion. "You've *never* been angry. Period. Where has this beast been hiding?" She placed the grocery bag and her purse on a table.

Cassidy avoided Mya's gaze, and Mya came close to rest her chin on Cassidy's shoulder.

"Let's go make dinner and talk about it," Mya whispered, turning away to grab her things. "And when I say that, I mean you can make me dinner, while we talk about it."

Cassidy stood there for a moment to compose herself. She placed her cell phone on the table to her left and ran her damp palms against the oversized overalls she'd picked out of one of Mya's old clothes boxes.

She just wanted to be home.

But where *was* home? Montana?

She grabbed her cell phone and followed Mya in a slow, deliberate trudge. "I'm coming."

Pots and pans clanged, as Mya rinsed off some vegetables. "...so that's where I think Brian is. I mean, where else would my traitor of a husband be?"

Mya had been talking for at least ten minutes, but Cassidy couldn't find it in herself to actually listen. She sat on the only bar stool in the apartment and gazed at the bowl in front of her.

"What temperature do I set this to?" Mya's voice passed straight through Cassidy's skull. "*You're* supposed to be cooking, by the way."

Cassidy could feel the words dancing in there, but she didn't want to respond.

Mya waved a wooden spoon in front of Cassidy's face. "Earth to Cassidy?"

"I'm here!" Cassidy sat up and slouched once again, giving Mya an apologetic glance. "I'm not in my right mind today."

"I know. First, you yelled at someone. Now, you're staring at that bowl of fruit like you're trying to communicate with it." Mya moved the bowl away from Cassidy's direct line of sight.

Her eyebrows furrowed. "Am not."

Mya cocked her head.

Cassidy decided to change the subject. "What were you saying about Brian?"

Mya turned off the water and rested her elbows on

the counter. "That person on the phone downstairs. Who was it? You know, the one where, after you spoke to them, you went all Mike Tyson on the trash can?"

"I don't know who he was." Cassidy's blood boiled again. "He said he was from the High Tower, and I was stealing their architect and workers. I've never been so insulted. It was like being accused of grand theft auto."

A twinkle illuminated Mya's eyes. "A man? Now, wait a second. You never said it was a *man*. What did he sound like? Blond hair, blue eyes, or dark hair, dark eyes? Was his voice husky and rough?"

"I don't know. It was static most of the time." Cassidy shook her head in frustration.

"You should ask Colton about it. He is working on the building, right? I wonder if it was Grayson. I would die inside if you talked to Grayson Daniels." Mya fanned her face in exaggeration. "I heard he owns the entire High Tower *and* the block it sits on!"

Cassidy hadn't a clue who her cousin was taking about. The rosy flush on Mya's cheeks made Cassidy's lip quirk in a grin. Mya was handling this divorce quite well.

"Don't tell me you don't know who he is. I hear he's going to be the first man on the moon."

"That's already happened, Mya."

"Want to know what else I heard?"

"Hm?"

"He's single! He's the only man in this city who's single! I'm putting him on your cheat card." Mya pointed at Cassidy's chest.

"My what?"

Mya's face became incredulous. "Your cheat card. He's already on mine. You know. If you ever meet a celebrity or something, you have Kyle's permission to cheat on him to have your one day in paradise."

That only sounded like the dumbest thing ever.

Mya stood and continued to fan her face. "Brown hair you just wanna pull, blue eyes as deep as the ocean. He's not handsome per my standards, but he's fascinating and mysterious. Now his partner, Lance? Yummy." She danced around the kitchen island with herself. "He's tall, too." She stopped to look at Cassidy. "Like, six foot four. Tell me you want a tall man, Cassidy."

"Kyle is tall."

Mya prowled closer. "But is he six foot *four?*" She wiggled her eyebrows. "Grayson is tall…"

"Eh, too tall." Cassidy brushed Mya off, but she couldn't help wondering what it would feel like to be in someone's embrace again. The memory of Kyle's warmth was fading.

"Blue eyes for days and nights."

Cassidy raised her eyebrows.

"Large hands that can engulf your face like a basketball!" Mya squealed and placed her hand on Cassidy's face.

"You've gone crazy." Cassidy removed Mya's hand. "You've transformed into a crazy person." She stood and took control of the food, as Mya sat.

"They didn't call me wild back home for nothing…"

The two burst into fits of laughter.

Mya reached for an apple and rolled it between her

hands on the counter. "I just want you to keep your heart open in case someone better comes along."

Cassidy groaned. It wasn't a matter of someone *better* coming along. Cassidy had chosen Kyle, and he'd chosen her. "Not this again. You know what? Kyle never makes me angry. He's kind. He's brave. He's in the military. Aren't you grateful he's fighting for us?"

"Speaking of fighting, you two never argue. You only fight with me, yet I'm the one person who wants to help you. When I saw you downstairs earlier, I was hoping it was Kyle you were yelling at. Of course, he had to screw up all your hopes and dreams. Remember when you were seven? You wanted to help Uncle Rob dig that trench around your farm. You loved playing in the dirt. How we're related, I have no idea, but you've always dreamed of working with the Smithsonian Institute...or is it Institution? You know what I mean—that Cooper Hewitt Museum. Except, doesn't that museum have more architecture-related stuff? Whatever. A museum is a museum. Then one day, you just gave it up. You quit. And it's because of Kyle."

She didn't quit.

Mya lifted her arms above her head to stretch. "I want what's best for you. I like Kyle as a friend, but he's a fake. He emanates Gumby."

"Gumby the cartoon?"

"Yeah, that happy, little piece of clay that has a smile on his stupid green face all the time. He's fake. He doesn't challenge you. He makes you feel like he's taking care of you, when really, you're the one taking care of him. Think about it."

Cassidy didn't want to talk about this. Every time they spoke about Kyle, it was a battle. "Can we please talk about something else?" Tightness gripped her chest. "Did you find an apartment for us? You were saying something about Brian earlier, too."

Mya avoided eye contact. "Why can't we just take advantage of living here longer?"

Cassidy knew that Mya was terrified of going back to living an ordinary, penthouse-free life.

"I think Brian is in Dubai. God, he's probably shacking up with princesses and dining with sheiks." Mya rolled her eyes and continued, as if they hadn't just had tension between them. "I want to dine with a sheik…"

Her words blurred together, as Cassidy fell deep into her own thoughts. It was easy for Mya to move from one conversation to the next, but Cassidy dwelled on Mya's last words. *He makes you feel like he's taking care of you, when really, you're the one taking care of him.* Cassidy could list a thousand times Kyle had made a sacrifice for her. Not one in particular stood out in that moment, because she was flustered, but when her mind settled, she'd reassure herself later. She sliced some fresh beef and placed garlic in the pan, as the butter sizzled.

Mya paced the dining room. "…I have to cook for myself. Do you realize how dangerous this is for me?"

Cassidy's thoughts were broken by a loud *pop* of butter, and she nodded, but she had nodded at nothing because Mya's word vomiting stopped. Cassidy turned to see Mya strutting down the hall and continued to prepare the snow peas for their stir-fry meal.

Mya emerged from her bedroom moments later with her laptop in hand. Her footsteps came up behind Cassidy, and she held the laptop to Cassidy's face, so she could read while stirring the beef into the butter garlic sauce. "See? He's in freaking Dubai."

There he was. Brian Wittington, as handsome as ever. His wavy honey hair was slicked back, and he wore a tuxedo. He had a wide smile on his face—one of pure joy—and Cassidy wanted to smile herself.

"Don't smile," Mya demanded. "I almost did when I first saw the picture. I'm a traitor. He makes us sick, remember?"

"Yes, he makes us sick." Cassidy had her own reservations about Brian and Mya's relationship, but there were so many unknowns, it would be best for their relationship to be left to fate.

Cassidy cooked their meal, as Mya continued to stalk her soon-to-be ex-husband's whereabouts. Cassidy wished her laptop hadn't been destroyed a few weeks earlier. Then she could have done some stalking of her own on the High Tower, and maybe locked down a name for her mysterious caller.

She grabbed two plates from the cupboard and dished each of them some food. She placed a plate in front of Mya, but Mya's eyes were glued to her computer screen.

She picked a snow pea off her plate with her fingers and hummed in satisfaction. "You know, this whole divorce thing would be easier if I saw some terrible pictures of him. All I see is his handsome face, smiling at me. It makes me want to shape-shift into a bear and claw at his guts."

Cassidy couldn't help the small giggle that passed through her lips. "Let's just eat, yeah?" She pointed toward their makeshift couch on the living room floor.

Mya lifted a snow pea between her thumb and index finger. "How many calories are in a snow pea?"

"Will you stop? You are beautiful, Mya."

She picked another snow pea off her plate, and a loud *crunch* escaped from between her teeth.

They ate quickly, relishing each other's company. That was until Mya decided to conjure up some more "what if" theories about Brian and why he wanted a divorce.

Cassidy should have been a good friend and talked about Brian with Mya, until she decided to go to sleep, but Cassidy was distracted. She wanted to know who this man was from the High Tower. Some administrative jerk, probably. One of those people who always thought about billable hours and screwing people over.

She sat and listened as Mya chatted on and on, washed the dishes, and continued chatting, as she walked into her bathroom down the hallway.

When the door at the end of the hall shut, Cassidy took a breath and rested her back against the wall. Her eyes fell to Mya's laptop, still sitting on the kitchen counter. She stood and shuffled to it, bringing it to life with the tap of her finger.

Brian's face popped up, and it was the same smiling image she had seen before. Cassidy closed the window and opened up a new search. She typed in "High Tower NYC."

The High Tower is located in downtown New York City. The prestigious building is home to thousands of patented nuclear energy creations. The owner of the laboratory, thirty-three-year-old Grayson Daniels, recently won a national award for his research on nuclear fission.

"Nuclear fission." She annunciated every syllable. *Whoa. Okay, so maybe this place is a big deal.* Was the entire building a lab? This Grayson guy really did own an entire skyscraper.

Cassidy scanned the screen, but instead of clicking on the next link for the High Tower, she continued reading about this six-foot-four Grayson Daniels Mya was obsessed with.

Grayson Daniels High Tower Lab
Grayson Daniels Sexy Geek Blog
Grayson Daniels Background

She selected the last hyperlink and found nothing. There was a blank canvas on this man, other than his impressive list of degrees. And boy, was he intelligent.

He had a bachelor of science in nuclear engineering from NYU, a master of arts in business from Harvard, and another master's degree as well as a doctorate in science topics she couldn't even pronounce.

Dr. Daniels. It had a nice ring to it.

Smart—check. Admirable career—check.

Tall…check.

Cassidy was in awe. Maybe, she would ask Colton about the High Tower tomorrow. The block practically belonged to a single man. The structure itself was an empire. Yet, there wasn't any information on Grayson's personal life. He screamed mystery.

Then she reread how many people the High Tower employed. Thousands.

She sighed. "How am I ever going to find out who called me?"

She would continue the lobby remodel as planned. If the nameless man truly felt his project was more important than hers—and she was beginning to think that it *was*—then he would call again. Perhaps this time, he would be nicer.

As an image loaded on the screen, Cassidy walked over to the sink to grab a glass of water and sat on the bar stool.

The image cleared up one pixel at a time, and Cassidy put her face close to the screen as it condensed and the title came into view.

The caption read, *Grayson Daniels at High Tower Lab*.

The blue eyes came first.

Then the perfectly sculpted brown hair.

He did have nice hair.

Grayson Daniels was a sight to behold. He stood in the middle of what appeared to be his office. Awards and degrees flooded the wall behind his desk. Cassidy tried to zoom in to see what they all were.

His shoulders filled out his white lab coat, demanding the space. He was thirty-three, although his experience gave an illusion that he was much older. There was another man in the image as well, sitting on a black couch with his legs crossed. He, too, wore a lab coat.

Lance, maybe?

Grayson's skin glowed. He had angular, strong features. He wasn't handsome in a conventional way. He was just dominating. Her eyes followed the line of his clenched jaw, a wickedly charming half-smile on his lips.

She leaned her face even closer to try and see if there was a splotch on the image, or if Grayson had a scar on his chin right under the left side of his bottom lip.

Cassidy took another sip of water, unsure of why there was an unquenchable thirst in the back of her throat. She looked at the time. It was almost midnight. Had she been reading about Grayson Daniels this whole time?

There was something alluring about him. Comforting, almost. Perhaps it was just curiosity about how a man so young could have created such an incredible life for himself.

She envied him.

Maybe he had a book on how to make money.

She laughed at herself. "Look at what you've become." She closed the laptop and backed away slowly. "You're a mess."

Glancing at the blank paper and envelopes on the kitchen counter, she rubbed her tired eyes and retreated to her bedroom.

CHAPTER FIVE

DID SHE...HANG UP ON ME? GRAYSON PRACTICALLY growled. Animosity coursed through his veins, and he rubbed the back of his neck. Again, he wished he was back home where he had authority. He'd have walked straight up to that savage woman and showed her who was boss. About to combust from frustration, he clenched his teeth so hard his jaw ticked.

The echo of footsteps approached from the other side of the main office door, and Lance opened it.

Grayson exhaled. "Do you ever knock?"

"Oh, hi Grayson. I'm doing fine, thanks for asking." Lance closed the door and strolled inside. "What's gotten in to you?"

Grayson held out his phone. "I just got hung up on."

"Probably the spotty service. They'll call back." Lance shrugged and sat on the lounge chair in the corner of the office.

"I'm pretty sure when someone says, 'go screw yourself,' and the line goes dead, it's not spotty service."

Lance smiled.

Why was he amused by this?

He leaned forward on his bent knees. "I don't think I've ever seen you so...so..."

Grayson put his hands on his hips. "Flustered?"

"No. This is a new emotion for you. We'll leave it unnamed for now." Lance leaned back and cocked his head.

Go screw yourself. Grayson couldn't believe the woman had yelled at him. Had she not heard him thoroughly introduce himself and explain his reasons behind calling? She hadn't even given him her name before yelling at him. She had acted like he'd immediately insulted her or something.

He could get this turned in his favor, even if that meant playing nice.

He'd have to think about his strategy. He wasn't used to dealing with uncooperative women. He could try and use his charms. Although rusty, it wasn't like women ran at the first sight of him.

Lance had been talking. "...so, tell me how you feel, Grayson."

That was a stupid question. He was angry. Obviously. Two decades of friendship, and Lance was still blind.

And what was this, a therapy session?

It crossed his mind that talking to Lance might ease some of his worries. Worries that had nothing to do with the High Tower. He didn't know what Lance would say when—correction, *if*—Grayson told him about hoarding Kyle's letters. Grayson's instincts told him he was justified in his actions, but Lance might not see it that way. A courthouse might not see it that way.

Grayson didn't do small talk. *Hey Lance, I'm committing a felony. Surprise!*

It wasn't supposed to feel like this. The mix of emotions overwhelmed him, and he fixated on a spot on the ceiling. The construction not going as planned upset him, but he couldn't help the part of him that worried about Cassidy. Was she still in New York visiting Mya? Were they looking for apartments, or had they found one? There were too many unknowns.

Then, there was Kyle. They were close to port. Unless Kyle wandered off with one of the women he'd been eyeballing constantly, he would probably contact Cassidy. The Reactor Training Division had internet access every other day, but Grayson wasn't sure about the airframe shops.

Lance's voice hung in the air like an afterthought that wouldn't disappear. "Are you okay there?"

Grayson needed to determine if Kyle had contacted Cassidy yet. He did the math in his head. Cassidy's letters had found their way onto his nightstand for weeks. If Kyle had written to her, Grayson would learn in the batch of letters he had now. The next opportunity he had, he would read them all. There would be no more waiting.

Cassidy. The woman he'd vowed to protect.

Vowed to protect? Grayson shook his head. He needed to slow down. He hadn't vowed to anyone, let alone a woman he hadn't met. He was merely protecting a sweet girl from getting hurt.

Grayson rolled his upper lip between his teeth. "I just got off the phone with the person poaching Colton." His eyes remained fixed on the ceiling.

The leather cushions creaked under Lance's weight as he readjusted. "And he speaks!" He laughed. "You really took care of business." There was sarcasm in his voice. "Did he actually hang up on you?"

Grayson suppressed the urge to scoff and let his eyes fall to Lance. "She."

Lance stood, that smug smile still on his face. "And?"

"I've never met someone so...so…"

Lance's eyes darted around the room. "Impatient?"

Grayson began to pace. "Jesus. So—"

"Compulsive." Lance waved his hand in an exaggerated circle, as if entering the word in a game show.

Grayson glowered. "What was it you needed, exactly? Or did you just come in here to give me a hard time?"

"Well, I'll take that as my cue to leave." Lance ran his hand through his hair and took a step backward. "There's an article about us in *New York's Eye*, and I thought you'd want to read it."

This was the first time Grayson noticed the magazine in Lance's hand.

Lance placed it on the couch to his right. "We're close to port, so I'll have full service soon. I've got finances to go through, and you're taking care of the construction at the lab. Oh, and what I wanted to tell you is that I'm going to hire a new secretary. I've decided you've given me permission."

A rumble developed in the back of Grayson's throat. When he turned to face Lance, he had already gone. Grayson's feet clomped on the metal floor as he reached for the magazine Lance left behind.

He skimmed through the garbage they wrote. Everything was always so exaggerated. Lance had tried to convince Grayson to do an actual interview, but Grayson knew they'd just twist his words into something else.

He read a few sentences out loud. "Lance and Grayson take over New York City with their High Tower research." He scoffed. They weren't even in New York. Where did these people find their facts? He looked at the date. The magazine was published a few weeks ago. "Grayson has big plans for his High Tower."

There, they did it again. *His* High Tower. They always did this. Grayson didn't own the High Tower. He ran the laboratory on the first two floors. He slammed the magazine shut and tossed it in the closest trash bin. Stupid magazines never got it right, and Lance never seemed to find the time to correct their ignorance.

Grayson exited the main office and hurtled to the deck. Everyone he passed looked so happy. His lips formed a thin line as he continued to fly down the p-ways of the ship, bashing his shins on every other kicker at his feet.

He wasn't sure where he was walking, but he needed

to clear his head before retreating to his room. The highly exaggerated article on the High Tower…Cassidy.

A group of sailors jogged past him, probably late for something. Two of their strides matched one of his.

"Hi, Dr. Daniels!"

"Good morning, Dr. Daniels!"

He hated being called that. After Katrina's accident, Grayson wasn't allowed to call his father "dad." It was always Dr. Daniels. The thought of his father fueled his anger even more.

Grayson shot his eyes to the right as they passed. "Good morning." He had to figure out what to do about this woman back in New York. No wonder Lance had ripped his hair out over this construction job. It was a managerial mess.

He made a mental note to ask Lance to retrieve their most recent contracts for him.

The PA system came on, interrupting Grayson's thoughts. *"Abandon ship. This is a drill. Abandon ship."*

His immediate thoughts about Cassidy were paused as he turned on his heel and mustered with the nuclear division in the hangar bay.

Anxiety swirled in his chest at the thought of possibly having to jump in the water. Being crammed on a boat with fifty other people didn't help the claustrophobia that closed in on him.

Patrick waved at Grayson to stand next to him. "You look sick, Grayson."

Grayson hoped his hesitation wasn't obvious. "There's no swimming involved in an abandon ship drill, right?"

"Only if you fall in." Patrick's smile reached his eyes.

After putting on his uninflated lifejacket, Grayson stood in formation. It only took a few minutes for Lance to arrive and follow suit.

"The distance to nearest land is 173 miles, land is friendly, wind is negligible, and the water temperature is thirty-one degrees. Your life rafts are located on the starboard side and will inflate automatically once submerged ten to forty feet. They may also be deployed manually. There are safety kits in each raft..."

A snide remark carried to the row that Grayson stood in, and it was unmistakably Kyle's voice. "I hope the air wing gets to abandon ship before anyone else."

Patrick turned his head. "Will you shut up, Greens?" Leaning close to Grayson, he whispered, "If I throw him overboard, do you think anyone will notice? Except, I don't know if Kyle would be terrified to swim with sharks or relieved he's the first one off the ship."

Grayson shook his head in disgust.

The drill lasted fifty minutes, and luckily, Grayson didn't have to demonstrate his swimming capabilities or play buddy-buddy with a raft full of chatty sailors.

He just wanted to get back to his room, where he could think clearly.

Shuffling through the bodies that were trying to return to their stations, he yanked at his lifejacket in an effort to remove it. He pulled at the clasp only for the jacket to inflate.

He cursed under his breath and dropped his chin to his chest in defeat.

"Looks like I caught you at a bad time."

His teeth clenched at the familiar voice. "Hello, Kyle." Grayson ran his hand down his face.

"Can we talk?"

"I'd prefer if you waited until our next class." He pulled at his lifejacket again.

Kyle walked in front of Grayson. "About that. You failed me. Why?"

"This isn't the appropriate time, sailor." Grayson's arms fell to his sides in exasperation, as he turned to walk away, but Kyle moved to block his way.

"I was on track before you got here. I was advancing." He scowled. "Slowly, but still, it was something." Kyle took a few steps backward. His entire body, from shoulders to toes, was drenched in oil. He looked as though he hadn't shaved for days. "Then, you come on board, and the cap goes nuts, bows at your feet, and requires us to take your ridiculous classes. I was banking on this. Why did you fail me? I'm supposed to be in the nuke division."

Grayson took a deep breath and stepped forward, towering over Kyle. "Actually, Kyle, you weren't *required* to do anything." He found the deflation button on his jacket, removed it, and hung it up with finesse. "To me, it appears you are just looking for an easy way up," Grayson stepped closer, "and you won't get there through me."

He wasn't sure if he was talking about Cassidy or Kyle's advancement, but that statement held true for both. Kyle would only get what he deserved.

Kyle scoffed and waved his hand as if swatting Grayson's statement aside. "Come on, Grayson."

"It's Dr. Daniels to you."

Kyle's eyes fell, and his shoulders hunched forward.

A shout came from the airframe shop. "Greens! Get back to work."

Kyle rocked his head from side to side and grabbed a dirty rag from his back pocket only to wad it up into a tight ball in his fist.

Grayson didn't want to interact with any more people, if he didn't have to. He strode to his chambers, unlocked the door, and his eyes immediately fell to Cassidy's stack of letters next to his bed. They had their own gravitational field, drawing him closer.

He sat on his bed, his head skimming the underside of the bunk above. Sifting through the stack, he set aside the few letters he had already read. The remaining rested on his lap, as he removed his jacket, tossing it across the back of the desk chair. It fell to the ground, but he didn't bother to pick it up.

One by one, he opened the envelopes. The tension in his back released. His shoulders settled into a natural, comfortable position.

There were more pictures of Mya and notes about Cassidy's daily activities.

Cassidy seemed happy, though each letter seemed to get shorter in length. She made no indication that Kyle had contacted her in any way. Grayson could only assume she would have said something about it.

The vice around his lungs disappeared.

She was safe.

He unfolded the final letter in his pile.

Kyle,

I've been avoiding telling you this, because I didn't know how. I got fired from my internship. I thought I was going to get assigned the feature article in the magazine, but Mr. Turner let me go. I had to move out. I'm with Mya, so please don't worry about me. Forgive me for not telling you sooner. I just wanted to have a plan…and I don't. Not yet, at least. My mail is being forwarded, so know that I'll get whatever you send me.

Cassidy

I got fired. He read the words over and over.

So, Cassidy *had* been looking for an apartment with Mya. Grayson's mind wandered to the worst. His girl could likely be meandering around NYC homeless.

He frantically searched for the envelope the letter had come in, except he had managed to shove everything on the floor during his frantic binge-read. He stacked each piece of paper and sorted through them for the most recent date.

It was dated four weeks ago. Cassidy had lost her job at least four weeks ago. Probably even sooner, since she had visited Mya in one of the first letters he received. His heart fell into his stomach.

He recalled her words from weeks prior and concluded she lost her job when Grayson first left port. Two months ago.

He needed to do something…but what?

The doorknob of his room jiggled. *Lance.*

"Grayson, are you going to let me in?"

Grayson piled all the paper that had been strewn about and placed them in the small drawer of his nightstand.

There were two knocks.

He smirked and walked to the door to open it. "So, he *can* learn."

Lance was undoubtedly going to say something snide, but then his eyes descended to the floor behind Grayson.

Had he forgotten to put away some of the letters?

Lance strode in and bent over. "What happened to your jacket?" He lifted it by the collar with his index finger. "It's not like you to throw clothes on the floor like that."

Grayson sighed in relief. He wasn't ready to explain himself when it came to Cassidy. He didn't need Lance mocking him and his inability to have normal relationships outside of work.

"What happened to your shirt? You look like you were just in a fight." Lance tossed the jacket to Grayson and sat on the bed.

Grayson hung his jacket in the closet. "Why do you care so much about my wardrobe? I've had a rough day." He was grateful Lance wasn't the prying type. "By the way, the next time *New York's Eye* does an article on us, will you make sure they get the facts right?"

Lance shrugged. "I don't know what the big deal is. So they spun a few misleading facts. It'll only bring the lab more publicity."

Publicity. What they needed was an article that was interesting.

Shaking his head, Grayson sighed. "That article made it sound like we own the entire block, Lance. We only occupy the first two floors of the High Tower. We're the High Tower *Lab*, not the High Tower. It's different."

Standing, Lance adjusted his sweater. "Yeah, but our lab contributes to the High Tower's success. We're the twenty percent that brings in eighty percent of the profit. We're the main research facility. Trust me. It's good if people think we're powerful. We can talk about it later, if you like, but we can't do anything about the article now. Look, we're a few miles from port. How about we get off this ship and get some work done?"

Grayson couldn't agree more on that front. He could also set a plan in action to help Cassidy. "I second that. Also, can you get me in touch with Marley at the office?"

"The new redhead?"

With an eyebrow raised, Grayson shrugged. "She's not new, and she doesn't have red hair."

"No, we're talking about the same girl. The slim girl with the vibrant red hair. Long fingernails that would feel amazing on your scalp." Lance groaned, either in longing or a gargled mating call. "Okay, when we're on land, we'll get her on a conference call."

Grayson unbuttoned his shirt. "I'd, uh, it's kind of personal. Not work related, I mean. I'd rather talk to her privately."

"You know, I can take care of anything like that for you—"

"No. It's quite all right. I'd like Marley to take care

of it. She's," *think of something, think of something,* "soft spoken."

Lance's eyebrows furrowed. "Right. Soft spoken."

Grayson would fill Lance in on the details later. Maybe.

CHAPTER SIX

Cassidy swooshed her hands back and forth at her sides, the bubbly water leaving a swirling trail of turbulence down her legs. She used her foot to turn the dial to "hot" and steaming water escaped the faucet.

"...so those are the basics of nuclear fission." Grayson's voice echoed in the luxurious bathroom.

"Nuclear fission." She articulated the words every time he said them. While turning off the hot water, she simultaneously reached through the mass of bubbles and dried her hands on a towel next to the tub. "Let's see what's next, Mr. Genius."

This was her fifth episode of *Science with Grayson*. At least, that's what she called it. They were recordings posted on the High Tower website, each about twenty minutes long. She scrolled to the next lecture on the list and selected it.

His speech resumed, and she closed her eyes. She felt smarter just listening to the man. She needed some of that brilliant logic to help her figure out what she was going to do with her life.

Grayson's deep, melodic tone bounced off the tile walls. She was transported to an amphitheater where he was on display, with his giant microscope, giving her a private demonstration.

Was there a difference between fission and fusion? She would have to research it. She'd never been so interested in science before. No one had ever inspired her to be. Archaeology had just become her passion.

Grayson laughed in the video, and she opened one eye, catching a glimpse of his finger getting stuck between two dials. *How adorable.* He could have edited that part out, but Cassidy admired how he hadn't. It was pure and honest.

She closed her prying eye once more and rested her head back. The smell of lavender and vanilla engulfed her. Her sore, blistered hands finally relaxed. The ache in her lower back melted away.

"I'm going to show you the atomic structure of—"

"Nuclear fission," Cassidy whispered with a smile on her lips.

It was as if Grayson, himself, were sitting at her bathtub's edge, reading her a book. A geeky book, but still, a magnificent piece. His tone oscillated and crescendoed at intervals, and when he paused, Cassidy cracked open an eyelid once more, so she could see what he was doing.

Usually, he was poking and prodding something. In this lecture, he was drawing circles and lines. There were positive and negative signs everywhere. Even his handwriting was perfect. Were these mini-lectures supposed to be for kids? Cassidy was one hundred years behind, if they were. She had only just mastered how to pronounce "fission," mimicking the sweet curl of Grayson's lips.

Why had she been so drawn to watch these videos in the first place? She figured it was the same desire she had after finding a new actor she enjoyed. She'd search for content and try to learn about them. There wasn't much to learn about Grayson. His personal life seemed under lock and key, but there was an abundance of material available on his research. So, she'd decided to binge on that.

His words were hypnotic. It was inspiring. His passion filled the space, and his lectures gave her motivation to take charge of her life. She'd never felt so empowered before. She didn't need anyone to recommend her or make a call. She was Cassidy Freaking Thatcher.

Newly inspired, she decided that she'd contact the Cooper Hewitt and ask for a job. This little gig with Colton would only last so long. She could manage one phone call. They had wanted her before, and if she was lucky, they'd consider her again. No, if *they* were lucky, she'd join their team.

The video randomly paused, and Cassidy examined Mya's computer screen. There wasn't any internet connection. *Seriously?*

A knock came from the door. "Do you have my laptop? I can't find it anywhere." Mya's fingernails clawed the door up and down.

"Yeah, I was watching videos, but," Cassidy leaned over to press the Wi-Fi button a few times, "the internet is out."

"Okay. I thought I'd lost it. No biggie. Have you written to Kyle, yet? Your stuff is all over the kitchen, and I almost started a fire making lunch with all that loose paper everywhere. Anyway, I need to go talk to Tony. The power just went out, too. We still have a few more weeks here, so I don't know what's up." Mya's footsteps receded into the hallway and disappeared.

A few more weeks and nowhere to go after. Cassidy groaned. They still hadn't found a reasonable place to move after leaving Mya's penthouse. She'd hated every option Cassidy had presented. It all boiled down to Mya not being ready to give up the glamour, and Cassidy didn't know how much or little to push back.

She stood, making sure her feet had traction, and reached for a towel. It was mid-day, and the sun shone vibrantly through the lace curtains. She lifted one leg out of the bathtub and stilled, as tension yanked in her hamstrings. She was sore and grateful it was Saturday, so she could have the day off to rest—meaning watching more inspiring videos of Grayson Daniels. If only the internet would turn back on.

After dressing, she grabbed Mya's laptop and headed for the kitchen. The laptop was still frozen, and an image of Grayson leaning over a microscope filled the screen. She could do this. She reached for her phone and dialed.

Ring. Ring.

She paced.

Ring. Ring.

"Cooper Hewitt, how may I direct your call?"

The words stuck in her throat. Her body froze in time, just like Grayson when the internet connection had died. No oil would save her tin-man frame. This was a yellow brick road to nowhere.

"Cooper Hewitt, how may I direct your call?"

Cassidy couldn't breathe. What was wrong with her? She couldn't move, *and* she didn't have a brain. All she had to do was ask for Dr. Pinkerton, and that would be the end of it. Part of her told her not to do it while her inner consciousness taunted her. *You need money. Colton can't save you forever.*

She stood taller. "Yes, I'm Cassidy Thatcher."

"Who?"

Her heart sank and so did her shoulders. "Um. Cassidy Thatcher? Is Dr. Pinkerton available? Dr. Pinkerton from the Cooper Hewitt?"

"Dr. Pinkerton retired a year ago. Is there anything I can help you with?"

Her only contact wasn't even there anymore. Cassidy was ready to change her stars, but her stars just weren't close enough. "No. Thanks."

She couldn't explain what happened. Her light had extinguished. She looked to the ceiling and wanted to cry. She was never going to finish interning at a museum and get her degree. Maybe archaeology wasn't her calling.

Her phone buzzed in her hand, and there was no caller ID. She found it hard to add life to her voice as she answered. "Hello?"

"Hi, Cassidy Thatcher?"

She meandered toward the floor-to-ceiling window that overlooked the city. She spotted the High Tower, and a surge of envy spiked in her chest. "That would be me."

"My name is Karen Joseph." The woman's voice was piercing. "I would like to talk to you about a potential commission. Are you familiar with *New York's Eye*?"

Cassidy was taken aback. "Yes, I know that magazine. You publish a wide variety of articles every season." The oxygen seemed to have come back into the room. "How can I help you?" A jolt of confusion coursed through her.

"We'd like to commission you for the feature article. The article is on spec, the topic will be Mesoamerican culture and how we've maintained that lifestyle in New York City."

Had her ex-boss referred her? No way. He didn't know she was in New York. The only other person who knew she was in New York was Kyle. Her heart fluttered. Kyle must have received her last letter confessing her and Mya's situation. *He* was the one who had arranged this. Kyle deciding to support her career made her fall in love with him all over again. He was behind her on this.

Cassidy's answer came almost immediately. "I-I accept. Oh my God, I can't believe this. Thank you." It wasn't *Smithsonian Magazine*, but it was her own feature article.

The next few minutes passed by in a blur. Contact

information was exchanged, due dates were thrown all over the place, and Cassidy couldn't find anything to write them down on. Mya must have moved Cassidy's stationery out of the kitchen.

Moments later, she stood in disbelief, staring down at her phone. "What just happened?"

Mya drove her soon-to-be ex's Lamborghini up Laramie Hill. "I can't believe this magazine just called you out of nowhere. Talk about good luck. And it's not about toilets. Yay, you!"

Cassidy couldn't get rid of her smile, as they continued the ride to the address Colton had given her. She wanted to explain her theory about Kyle and how he was the one who set up the gig with *New York's Eye*, but every time she brought up his name, Mya seemed to recoil in disgust. They were having such a wonderful day. She'd find time to tell Mya later.

Colton had texted Cassidy that he needed her help with the interior design of one of his friend's homes. Her money situation was becoming less of a burden as the days passed. Ever since he'd come into her life, opportunities seemed to zoom by, and all she had to do was reach out and take them.

Mya gawked at the stunning houses. "And what about this gig with Colton? Are you going to continue working with him?"

To be honest, Cassidy didn't know what she was going to do about Colton. She hadn't really talked to him about what would come next, since they agreed she would help him and he'd hire her on a contract-by-contract basis.

Her phone rang, and she answered. "Hey, boss."

"Cassidy, are you on your way? I'm running short on time. I want to show you the house, before I have to head back to the High Tower. My *client* is getting moody." The way he growled the word "client" didn't sound good.

"Yeah, we're right around the block." She hung up and pointed to the right. "Oh! Turn here. It's here, Mya."

Mya made a sharp turn onto a gated property. An awning of trees encased the road. It was surreal. They drove for a few long minutes until the tunnel of thick branches opened, revealing a magnificent mansion.

Mya's jaw dropped, and Cassidy's eyes bulged.

Mya checked the number on Cassidy's scratch pad. "Are you sure this is it?"

Colton stood in the middle of the driveway.

Cassidy nodded. "I'm pretty sure."

Mya licked her lips and cocked her head to the side. "Colton is kind of cute in a suit."

Cassidy and Mya exited the car and walked side by side up the pebbled driveway. Colton was impeccably dressed. He wore a black suit with a white button down and no tie.

He waved. "Hi, ladies."

"I want to eat his face," Mya mumbled into Cassidy's ear, and Cassidy elbowed her in the side. "Ow. Troll."

Cassidy stepped up first. "Hi. We aren't late, are we?"

He shook his head and guided them to the side of the house. "No, I'm just in a rush. I wanted to make sure you had the keys, before I head back downtown."

Mya danced over the brick walkways and examined the ivy that decorated the sides of the enormous home. She spun in a big circle with her arms outstretched and inhaled deeply. "Can you imagine living here?" She turned to face Colton. "We'll take it."

Cassidy shook her head. "Can you give us a moment?" She pulled Mya aside, as Colton fiddled with some keys. "Mya," she hissed. "You aren't making sense right now."

"Sure I am. I say, we take it."

If Cassidy's shoulders slumped any lower, she might as well lay on the pavement. "This isn't *our* house. I don't even know if I should take this job. Every contract I sign with Colton is another few weeks...or months...and I can't get tied down into anything long-term right now. This place is freaking huge. This could be a forever job, and I need to get my degree. You know, my *archaeology* degree. This place is incredible, but it's a forty-minute drive from the nearest place we can afford, and it's too far from the city."

Mya's hollow eyes pleaded. "We can find an apartment close to this place while you work. It's nice up here. I can lay out in the yard, while you paint and stuff."

There was no way they'd find a reasonably priced

apartment in this area. The house they were standing in front of was even nicer than Mya's penthouse.

"Ladies." Colton's voice interrupted the energy, and both girls snapped their heads toward him. "This way." Colton led them down the driveway and to a tall hedge.

"Where is he taking us? The house is behind us…" Mya's voice wavered.

Elbowing Mya lightly in the ribs, Cassidy stayed close to Colton. He reached inside the dense bushes, revealing a worn archway in the shrubs just big enough to walk through. He gestured with his free hand for the girls to enter.

What the…

Cassidy went first, and Mya followed.

It was a small, quaint cottage. Cassidy was thoroughly confused.

Mya put her hands on her hips. "Where are we? What about the mansion back there? This place doesn't even have a sidewalk." Mya had no problem asking what Cassidy seemed to be thinking.

There was an uneven, narrow gravel path that led from the hedge to the front door. The walkway didn't even start where Colton had magically revealed a hole to pass through. He sauntered on the pebbles like this was completely normal and waved at the girls to follow him. This wasn't normal. The grass was unkept, but the house mirrored the same style as the mansion on the other side. Ivy climbed up the east elevation. Stone veneer decorated the walls, and the wood detailing was old, but it held charm.

Mya's expression was of fear and disgust.

Colton inserted a key into the lock of the front door and swung it open. "Cassidy, this is the home I was telling you about. It belongs to my friend. He's on an aircraft carrier right now. I go through stages of doing things right with him and then unintentionally screwing him over. Remodeling his house is me trying to make things right, after having screwed him over."

Her voice came out in a whisper. "An aircraft carrier?"

Cassidy stepped forward. She wanted to ask which aircraft carrier. Was his friend on Ike? Maybe he was deployed with Kyle.

God, it never seemed like the right time to talk about Kyle.

Mya huffed and crossed her arms, obviously displeased. "There isn't a driveway."

Colton nodded. "I know. He likes his space. When you meet him, you'll understand. It's not like anyone wants to come visit him, anyway." He laughed, but it didn't really sound funny. It was actually quite sad.

Cassidy eyed the small kitchen space in front of her. "Okay, so, to access the house, I have to crawl through the bushes like a bandit?"

Colton nodded again.

Mya didn't even want to come inside. "I'll just stay out here. You two talk amongst yourselves." She waved her hand back and forth.

Colton shrugged and followed Cassidy inside.

Looking at Colton, Cassidy lifted her hands in question. "This place is cute. It's furnished. I see there's a loft. I'm guessing the bedroom? What exactly does this place need?"

He nodded. "It needs a facelift. New paint, maybe polish up the floors. The kitchen is way old. That entire corner should be redone. You're my girl, Cassidy. You draft it up, I'll approve it. The usual. We'll get an engineer involved if we have to, but I think this will be an easy fix for you to manage. I can pay you a few thousand dollars up front."

A few thousand dollars? Her jaw nearly dropped. Smiling, Cassidy took a few steps forward. "Why me, Colt?"

Standing beside her, he nudged her shoulder. "I'm swamped with the High Tower Lab, and now that Mya's lobby is almost done, I thought it would be something we could do together. It's a small job. It won't take long. I *need* to focus on the lab, so why not let you take a stab at this? You're ready."

Warmth spread through her chest. "That means a lot to me. Thank you." For once, someone was giving her a job, because she was qualified to do it. Even though she was a glorified housemaid.

He smiled that sweet, crooked smile.

Cassidy turned to face him, and his gaze was warm and intense. "I've been meaning to ask you, why are you helping me? Out of all the people in this city who are actually architects, why did you choose to help me with the lobby and continue to help me now?"

His smile faded ever so slightly. "There have only been two times in my life that someone has asked for my help. The first time was in college. And the second time was you. What can I say? I can't resist a killer smile."

She couldn't help but snort. "Oh, you're smooth." She tossed a glance over her shoulder and made eye contact with Mya. Taking another deep breath, she looked up at Colt. "I don't know, Colton. We could use the money, but it's so far away from where we're staying now…"

Through the open front door, Mya waved at Cassidy to come outside.

Mya's arms flailed, until Cassidy stepped onto the gravel path. "I think you should take the job. For the last few minutes, I've been thinking. I know this little cottage is a dump compared to the stunning house over here to our left." She circled her hand for emphasis. "But everything has led to this moment. The Universe is trying to give us something. I think we need to listen."

Oh, God. Not this talk again.

Cassidy leaned forward. "We'd have to move closer. If we sell Brian's Lambo, which I'm not even sure is yours to sell, let alone *drive*, maybe we could live around here for a few months. But, then what? We'll be right back where we started." She paused. "We have to be reasonable. We can't live out here just to feed your fancy desires and be around rich people."

"Hey, I'm getting better with my spending. I'm trying to contribute. I just…can't…" Her gaze flickered to the left, and she stuttered over her words. "No more eating out, no more yoga. We can do this together. You need to take this chance. I'm just getting these really good vibes right now, Cassidy."

Cassidy scrunched her nose and looked back at the small cottage. In her book, "chance" and "five-year plan" weren't on the same page, but Cassidy was going to determine her own fate. She channeled her inner Grayson Daniels for strength. "Okay. I'll do it."

CHAPTER SEVEN

THE WIND WHIPPED AROUND GRAYSON'S FACE, AS THE helicopter soared over the water. It was a black abyss at sunset.

The pilot in command turned to Grayson. "We'll head back after this last round of tests. You doin' all right?"

Grayson was having such an amazing time, he wasn't sure if he wanted to go back to Ike. Hovering above the nuclear submarine, rather than being inside it, gave his insides a much-needed break.

"To be honest, I like this much better."

"Me too." The pilot laughed. "You afraid of water?"

Grayson looked out into the horizon where the sea and sky blended together. "I guess you could say that."

"Well, you and Lance are heading home tomorrow. You'll be back on land soon."

Grayson was anxious to get home and see what his team had been working on in his absence. Spending the last week in the sky, rather than in a cramped submarine or on Ike, had made the days go by faster.

He was going to find a way to meet Cassidy. He couldn't help the smile that crept over his lips. He hadn't heard back from *New York's Eye* on whether or not Cassidy had accepted the commissioned article, but he hoped she had. He wanted to give her some type of security or some reason to stay in New York. The urge to see her in person sent waves of excitement through him.

When Grayson got back to Ike, he walked straight to where Mary typically stacked Cassidy's letters for him.

The door was open, and he stepped inside.

Mary handed over a small bundle of envelopes bound together with a thin, blue rubber band. "Hey, stranger. This is all I've got for you."

He fingered the pile. Although, it could hardly be considered a pile. There were three letters. "Are you sure this is it?"

Mary nodded and shrugged. "Sorry, Kyle. That's all I've got."

Grayson rolled his lips between his teeth. "Thanks for these." He held up the stack and smiled. "I'm leaving tomorrow, so you be safe this summer, okay?" He leaned forward and kissed her cheek.

"Now, you stop that." Her face turned a shade of crimson.

Grayson still had some charm. Lance had no idea what he was talking about, saying Grayson couldn't have normal relationships. It warmed him, having made a new friend. Except she didn't know his real name.

He beamed and stepped backward. "Red's a good color on you." He winked and retreated into the hallway.

"Until we meet again!" she called from inside the mailroom.

Grayson hoped they would meet again. Mary had been vibrant and kind his ninety days on Ike. But now it was time to go home.

He passed a group of men he didn't recognize and continued through the p-ways to his room. After closing the door, he pulled his suitcase from under his bed and began packing his things. His bag of electronics laid under the desk, and he crouched low to bring that to his bed as well.

Cassidy's letters filled a quadrant of the duffle bag. The edges of his favorite notes from her were worn, the pastel envelopes faded to a creamy white.

He examined the small stack in his hands, snapping the rubber band a few times before deciding to remove it.

The doorknob behind him jiggled, and Lance barged in. "I have your fancy satellite phone." His eyes fell to Grayson's hands. "What are those?"

Grayson shoved the letters into his bag and zipped it shut. "Nothing."

"Nothing?" Lance voice practically jumped an octave.

"Yeah, it's nothing."

Lance raised an eyebrow. "You sure shoved them in your duffle bag quickly." He handed Grayson the satellite phone. "Are you seeing someone?"

He scoffed. "No. I'm not *seeing* someone." Heat enveloped his skin, and he caught a glimpse of his rosy complexion in the small mirror inside his open closet door.

"Then who are those letters from?"

Jesus Christ. Lance was usually so nonchalant about personal things. But as soon as a woman was involved, there was no hesitation. He would undoubtedly attack with no shame, want to know what she looked like, and most importantly, if she had any attractive friends.

Grayson held his breath. On a quick exhale, he said, "Her name is Cassidy."

Lance clapped his hands together and sat on the empty side of Grayson's bed, grabbing the pillow on the far end and fluffing it before placing it behind his head. "I knew it. What's she like? Tall, short, redhead…blonde?"

Grayson stared at his closed duffel bag. How was he going to explain this? "I don't know."

"You don't *know*?" Lance lifted to rest on one elbow. "Don't tell me you're in a relationship with a woman you don't even know."

"I know her." Grayson raised his eyes. He knew her passions, her goals. So, what if he didn't know what she looked like? He would eventually. "But, we're not together. Not like that."

"Oh? That stack of letters says otherwise." Lance smirked and rested his head back down, his dark brown hair smashed against the pillow.

A lump formed in Grayson's throat, and he beat his fist against his chest in hopes of clearing it. "Those letters weren't sent to me." He reached into his breast pocket and retrieved Cassidy's first message to Kyle. He handed it to Lance.

Lance read it and eyed Grayson. "What is this?"

"It's a letter to a man named Kyle Greens. Cassidy's fiancé."

"I can see who it's for. But why do *you* have it?"

Grayson snatched the letter back and put it into its safe place. He couldn't seem to formulate the right sentence. "Remember a few weeks in, I received a letter at the mess decks?"

By the slight roll of Lance's green eyes, he didn't remember.

"We thought it might be something from the lab or Colton, but it wasn't. It was this." He pointed to Cassidy's words that were pressed against his chest.

Lance rested on his elbow again, an incredulous look on his face. "And you didn't even think to find this Kyle guy?"

"I did. I searched and asked around. And then I met him and—"

"Why do you still have the letter?"

"Damnit, I'm getting to that." Grayson ran his hand through his hair. "Just give me a second to explain."

Lance's jaw tensed, as if he were about to say something, but he sighed and nodded.

"Kyle is a real piece of work." Grayson's hands flew all over the place, trying to draw a picture. "The things he said. I just couldn't get myself to give it to him. Then, I started getting all of her letters from the mailroom."

Lance's eyebrows rose. "Like a collection?"

"No, not a *collection*. It's not like your collection of women. Give me a break. This…is different." Grayson winced at his explanation.

Lance had a blank expression on his face. He finally spoke. "It's different, because you love her?"

Grayson rolled his eyes. What was with the questions? He didn't love Cassidy. He didn't know Cassidy. Well, he *did* know her, but not like that. "Of course, I don't love her."

"We're leaving tomorrow. You're going to stop getting these letters, right?"

He nodded.

"Good. Then we can put this Cassidy thing behind us." Lance slid Grayson's bags down the bed to make room for his legs. "Is this phase of yours done?"

It wasn't a phase, and technically, there was more of Cassidy Thatcher left to explore when they returned home. Grayson avoided eye contact.

Lance rolled over and stood. "What have you done?"

Grayson rocked back and forth on his feet.

"I know that look. You're plotting something."

"I called *New York's Eye*." Grayson slowly lifted his eyes to Lance's. "Cassidy is in New York right now, and I told their editor that if they gave her the feature article in the winter edition, I'd let them write an exposé on us and the lab. An honest exposé. None of that garbage they've been writing thus far."

Lance's jaw dropped. "You what?" His hands shot up. "Wait, so first you steal this soldier's letters. A felony, by the way. We need to come up with a plan there—"

"I know—"

"Next, you talk to a magazine that you hate and get this fantasy girl of yours the feature article? That's ridiculous! And our image is doing just fine. There's nothing wrong with people thinking we're rich." Lance stood there with his hands out. "This is typical you," he seethed. "You *would* fall in love with a random girl's letter to someone else. Did you hear that? Someone. Else. Do you see how incapable you are of having normal relationships?"

"I have normal relationships."

"Yeah, with Poppy, your new microscope? Who names their microscope?"

"That's actually the brand…"

"What if this gets out? What if there's a lawsuit? It'll tarnish the lab's reputation for good if your stupid exposé includes this little stunt. We'll be the laughing stock of the city. I can see it now, plastered in *The New York Times*." Lance was exaggerating. "If you get into trouble again, I can't run the lab by myself. And who will I end up promoting? The staff is far too young and inexperienced right now. We don't even have a dozen associates yet."

"Nothing will happen to the lab." Grayson's words were firm.

"You need to let her go."

The thought made his heart flip, and he shook his head once. There was unfinished business to be sorted out.

"I'm not just saying this as your friend, Grayson, but as your business partner. You *need* to let this go." Lance remained at Grayson's side, seemingly waiting for a response. "She's just a woman, for Christ's sake. You don't need to play savior. Why is this so hard for you to see?"

Cassidy wasn't just a woman. She was a reminder that good things could still happen to people who didn't deserve it. Grayson finally managed to look at Lance and the domes staring back at him softened.

As if Lance had read Grayson's mind, he placed his hand on Grayson's shoulder and squeezed. "Katrina." His voice was nearly a whisper. "I lost her, too. But we aren't teenagers anymore. If someone presses charges, you could be locked up for months. The lab can't afford this."

Grayson stepped away from Lance and moved his packed bags to the floor. "I failed as a son and as a brother. This is my second chance, Lance. I know it sounds crazy, but I need to see this through."

Lance's chest expanded, and he blew a slow, steady stream of air. "Okay. What's our backup plan?"

"If Cassidy doesn't accept the article," Grayson's eyes fell to his small duffle where Cassidy's letters were packed away, "I'll let it go." He was surprised how easy that lie came out of his mouth. He knew one thing for sure.

He wasn't going to let Cassidy go.

Mya reached for a cardboard box. "It's not the penthouse, but I kind of like this place."

Cassidy smiled to herself, as she opened a new box of silverware.

"Do you know anything about Colton's mysterious friend? Do you think we should cook him a meal or something when he arrives? I mean, Colton said he's been God knows where for God knows how long."

Wiping a spoon clean, Cassidy placed it in a drawer. "He hasn't told me anything. He's been too busy on the High Tower remodel. But, that's not a bad idea. Do you think that would be weird, though? I'm already working on his house. I feel like cooking for a stranger would be weird." She grabbed a dinner knife and swirled it in the air. "We don't know him, and we're making him food."

Mya shrugged. "I don't think so. Colton knows him. He's been deployed, or whatever you call it, and I'm sure he'd appreciate a home-cooked meal. It's not weird at all. When he returns, we'll have a feast waiting for him."

Cassidy's lips quirked to the side, and she nodded. It was decided. He was kind of their hero, in a way. Now Cassidy didn't have to worry about being homeless, at least for a little while. The check Colton wrote was enough for a down payment on a new apartment and two months' rent. They didn't have much of anything to move over from the penthouse, but they did have some spare cash to buy dishes and silverware.

The lobby remodel at Mya's apartment complex would be finished in a few days, and they would officially move into their new place thirty minutes away from Laramie Hill.

Mya stood and walked to Cassidy's side, helping her

put the silverware away. "Thank you for taking this risk." She rested her chin on Cassidy's shoulder. "I know you still have doubts about living here with me."

And boy, was this a risk. This move felt permanent, and it made her belly squeeze with uncertainty.

Cassidy's chest rose and fell, and a light hum escaped her mouth. "To be honest, I don't like not having a solid plan—especially without talking to Kyle—but I think this could *possibly* work out. I trust Colton. I'm sure his friend is awesome, if he's a soldier, right?" Doubt still managed to encase her words.

Mya lifted her head and nodded, walking back to her stack of boxes and kneeling. "I wonder what Kyle thought when you told him about this place. He probably freaked out."

Well, Cassidy hadn't told Kyle *everything*. But she would when the time came. She just needed to get her life on track. Part of her feared that Kyle would eventually make her feel bad about her decision to work on the east coast again. It was fine while he was overseas, but when he returned…then what?

She could hear his voice now. *Remember the last time you banked on New York? You still ended up in Montana. Spare yourself the heartache.*

Cassidy couldn't help but scoff in disbelief. Thinking about Kyle in that moment pissed her off. He'd never understood her desire to work and make a living. Although, he certainly had no problem letting her pay his bills.

"Ow!" Mya shook her hand in the air and stuck her finger in her mouth. "Paper cut."

Guilt rose in Cassidy's chest as Mya's exclamation brought her back to the present. She shouldn't think bad things about Kyle. He was an honorable soldier fighting for her freedom, and she was complaining about him merely wanting the best for her. After all, he had been the one who managed to set her up with a feature article in a major magazine. Not hearing from him was messing with her mind.

Other than Mya, Kyle was the only person who cared enough to express his thoughts. And deep down, Cassidy knew he was trying.

Not trying hard enough to contact me. She shook her head. "Stop it."

"Are you okay?"

Cassidy lifted her eyes to see Mya's sideways glance. "I'm just thinking."

"So, what kind of food do you think a sexy soldier would want?" Mya sing-songed.

Cassidy snorted. Mya had dreams of this man being her knight in shining armor. "What if he's, like, eighty?"

Mya looked to the ceiling in thought. "Maybe I need that, you know? What does your Grayson Daniels always say in his little lectures you're obsessed with? 'Poke and prod the specimen.' He can poke and prod me."

Cassidy flushed a hot pink, a tingling sensation spreading through her fingers.

Mya's wicked smile was on full display. "Yeah, I see you watching those."

Embarrassment was cast over Cassidy's face. She wasn't sure why Mya talking about *Science with Grayson* seemed so intimate. It was like Cassidy had just been caught making out with her high school crush and sent to detention.

She waved her hands in protest. "First of all, that's not what he says."

Mya rocked her head from side to side, a Cheshire cat grin dancing on her lips.

"And, if he *is* eighty, we had better make something that won't pop his dentures out."

They shared a laugh and continued unpacking boxes of sheets and picture frames, the only things they really had left after selling most of Mya's furniture.

They had rented a small apartment above a pole dancing studio just barely outside the city. Mya was excited for the possibility of taking free classes.

There was one bath, a kitchen, somewhat of a living area, and a small room to the side they planned on using as a bedroom they'd share. It was comfortable and small —just what they needed.

Mya opened another box. "Let's have a barbecue. A good one. And, maybe you can make a casserole or something, in case he is old and can't nom on a rack of ribs." She stood and walked over to the kitchen counter to get her wallet.

"Where are you going?" Cassidy pointed at the few boxes they had yet to unpack.

Mya sighed. "I have to go to the DMV, remember? I can pick up some groceries, too. Selling that crystal chandelier was the best thing that ever happened to me. I'm actually not worried my card will scream 'rejected' when I pay for things."

Cassidy smiled. Mya wasn't doing as bad as Cassidy had thought she would. Mya had downgraded her lifestyle considerably and was transitioning surprisingly well.

She swung the Lambo keys around her right index finger. "But I have to go to the DMV because they put down that I weigh 165 pounds on my driver's license."

"But you do weigh 165 pounds."

"I can't have that on my public record. I'm going to convince them to lower it." Mya walked out the door.

Okay, so Mya still had a ways to go in terms of living an ordinary life with normal expectations.

Before she had a chance to shut the door, Cassidy called, "Did you have the mail forwarded?"

Mya's echo trailed into the stairwell, but Cassidy could have sworn she heard Mya mumble, "Yeah, yeah."

Cassidy didn't want mail forwarding to be another wall between her and Kyle. With Mya gone, silence consumed the space. Cassidy looked around and stood there for nearly a minute. At least, that's what the long second hand of her watch said.

She inhaled the scent of fresh lemons from the cleaning agent she had used before unpacking. A few moments passed. Sultry music blared from the studio below, and she laughed.

Her giggles disappeared when doubts crept into her mind. She wished Kyle was there to experience this with her.

Thoughts of Kyle at war clutched her throat. *Is he hurt? Is that why he hasn't written?* With nervous hands, she searched through Mya's leather tote and pulled out the laptop.

She sat on the floor and frantically searched for Kyle's unit on Facebook. She checked her messages. Nothing. She looked through the unit's page, but there were no updates. Her email inbox was empty as well, and the ship's bi-monthly newsletter hadn't been released yet.

She leaned back against the crème-painted wall. Fear and anger collided in her chest. She wanted to tell Kyle everything, to confide in him. Even if he did have some snarky comment about New York, it would be better than this silence. She had not been completely honest with him in her letters, and it was eating away at her conscience.

Frustration ping-ponged off the walls of her mind. Doubt encircled her thoughts. Most of all, guilt was what brought her to open a new email to Kyle and spill her heart out about everything that was going on.

Her fingers danced on the keyboard, the tapping muting the music downstairs. A tear fell from her cheek as she described her hesitation to stay and not go back home. She'd promised Mya they would get through her divorce together, but she still had doubts about their future. She wrote about Mya and how they were living above a pole dancing studio, something Cassidy never would have found appealing just months ago.

She even wrote about how Grayson Daniels was her new inspiration, his advice challenging her to see life in a new way.

Lastly, she begged Kyle to give her a sign he was okay. She took a breath of relief, all of her mixed emotions coming to a singular focus. She was calm but energized. She'd held nothing back, and a small smile spread across her lips. Yeah, Kyle would likely complain about her choices—that was inevitable. Being completely honest with him felt right, no matter the consequence.

Besides, if Kyle *really* wanted them to live in Montana, she would take that into consideration. She always took Kyle into consideration.

After long minutes of debating, she decided to wait and talk to Kyle before signing any more contracts with Colton. It was the right thing to do, and if their marriage was going to be successful, they had to make decisions together.

She moved the cursor to "send," but a notification caught her attention.

It was from Kyle.

"Oh my God," she squealed and clicked on the little icon that brought up Facebook. Kyle was okay. He had Wi-Fi, apparently, the green circle next to his name indicating he was online. Cassidy copied her email and pasted it into a private message.

And then she saw it. The notification from Kyle wasn't for her. Rather, it was him liking a picture of his ex-girlfriend.

Her hands trembled once more but this time, for a different reason. The circle adjacent to Kyle's name turned gray. He was offline.

She slammed the laptop shut. Kyle had taken the

time to "like" his ex-girlfriend's picture instead of sending his actual girlfriend—no, *fiancée*—a message?

Cassidy must have been seeing things. Kyle had told her he wasn't sure if he'd have any service, which is why she had vowed to write to him instead. She was certain it was one of Kyle's friends who logged into the wrong account somehow. It had to be. She stared at the wall in front of her. Hours seemed to go by like the blink of an eye. The front door opened and closed, and Mya's footsteps approached.

She crouched down. "What's wrong? Are you having second thoughts about being in New York?"

Cassidy didn't hesitate for a second. "No, Mya. I'm staying."

CHAPTER EIGHT

WALKING ON SOLID GROUND HAD NEVER FELT SO GOOD against the balls of Grayson's feet. The world didn't spin, his stomach didn't summersault, and a relaxed smile formed across his lips.

Today was his first day back at the High Tower.

He strolled through the main entrance and was greeted by the lab's security team.

"Welcome back, Mr. Daniels."

"We're glad to see you, Grayson."

He nodded and continued to the sanitation area. On the way to the elevator, he saw the crew working on the new lab. It was making progress. More progress than he thought they would have, considering they were leaving early every day. The plain gray walls of his building were comforting. Familiar. He was anxious to get to his desk and see what paperwork there was to fill out.

Paperwork. His mind flipped from work to Cassidy. Concern grasped his lungs, and it seemed more difficult to take a breath. He wasn't sure if she'd accepted that article commission yet. Marley hadn't given him an update either. She was supposed to have called Karen Joseph and set that up.

Grayson's mood exponentially plummeted.

It was 7:30 a.m., later than he usually got in, but his plane had landed in New York merely two hours prior. It was just enough time to run to his house to shower, change, and come straight to the office. While at his place, he was pleasantly surprised that Colton had started to remodel the kitchen. Colton was getting a lot of work done.

Grayson turned to the left and climbed the staircase to the second floor. He stepped out and walked to his lab at the end of the hallway. The glass walls were spotless, sunlight from the rising sun casting a glow over the desks. The empty desks.

He yanked on the steel handle of the main door and walked inside. He scanned the rows of tables, filled with equipment. His pride and joy, Poppy, stood immaculate and tall in the corner beside his office. He had brought home some samples from his time spent with the navy and hoped to have a minute today to examine them… that was, if he didn't have to catch up on all the work his associates were slacking off on. Where was everyone? Usually people trickled in around 6:00 a.m.

He continued to his office, and Lance appeared from behind a partition wall. "Lance, you beat me."

Lance sported a smug smile.

"I don't know what you're smiling about." Grayson

nearly grumbled the words. "I should just fire everyone—"

"Surprise!"

Behind the wall were all eight of Grayson's associates under a banner that read "We Missed You!"

Grayson swallowed hard, and everyone looked around, waiting for his reaction.

Lance elbowed him and brought his lips to Grayson's ear. "This is where you say, 'thank you.'"

He paused. "Thank you? Now, it's time to get back to work." He nodded, and everyone shuffled to their workstations, leaving behind card stock hats, paper streamers, and an untouched cake.

When the area cleared, Lance glared at him.

Grayson shrugged.

Lance turned away and looked over his shoulder. "Well, at least you said, 'thank you.'" He then retreated to his office down the hallway.

Yes, Grayson was a very appreciative person. Lance was in a mood today. Grayson turned sharply and met eyes with Marley. Her gaze filled with terror when he waved at her to join him in his office.

He held the door open as she entered, swiftly closed it, and walked to his cherry desk.

Marley wrung her hands. "I'm sorry, Mr. Daniels. This was my idea." She paused. "Are you going to fire me again?"

Grayson sat in his leather chair and nearly sighed as the hinges succumbed to the weight of his body, the cushions cradling him. "Sit down, Marley."

She stepped forward and sat awkwardly in one of the two chairs in front of Grayson's desk.

"Tell me about *New York's Eye*. You didn't update me yesterday."

Marley's posture relaxed a little. "Oh. I haven't checked my email yet, Mr. Daniels. I don't know if Cassidy has accepted the feature article or not. It's so nice of you to take on another charity project."

Cassidy wasn't a charity project. He tapped on the wooden ply of his desk, Marley's eyes following the oscillating movement of his index finger. "And? Why haven't you checked your emails yet?"

"Well...um...because I was on vacation the last two weeks? And yesterday was Sunday?"

Grayson inhaled sharply, and Marley leaned backward, straightening her back.

"I'll check right now." She stood and waited for Grayson to give her permission to leave.

He nodded, and she hustled out of his office to her desk.

Now that his main concern was being addressed, it was time to check up on the little thief interrupting his construction.

By the looks of it, the laboratory was still making progress. He had yet to see the actual contract stating the working hours of the crew.

He pulled up an email to Lance and requested that any construction documents be brought to his office immediately.

Lance's response was quick.

—

From: Lance Romero
To: Grayson Daniels
Subject: Communication Skills

You have a phone…not all communication has to be impersonal.

—

What was that supposed to mean? Grayson leaned past his desk to peek into Lance's office and saw Lance on the phone, his feet propped comfortably on his desk. He had a smile on his face, his phone blinking a wild collage of red, several calls on hold.

Grayson grunted and reclined, enjoying the silence and the foggy view outside his window.

Taking Lance's advice, he picked up his phone and dialed a number he had only used once before.

"Hello?" There she was.

"So nice to hear your voice again."

She groaned. "Oh. It's just *you*. How can I help you today? Ready to insult me some more? Maybe accuse me of identity theft?"

That reminded him. He still needed to research the penalty for mail theft. He brought up another email to Lance, requesting they meet and discuss New York state laws.

"Hello-o-o?" Irritation infiltrated her tone.

Grayson stood and paced to the center of his office. "I'd like to discuss business."

"Okay." She sounded surprised. "I'd be happy to discuss this like civilized people—"

"9:00 a.m. High Tower. Second floor. Don't be late." He ended the call and replaced his phone. "That went quite well." He sauntered to where his lab coat hung next to his office door and whipped it around his shoulders. "God, it's good to be back."

9:00 a.m. came faster than he anticipated, and he was stuck in an interview with Lance. A small film crew hovered over them and interrogated them about their trip on Ike.

During a short break, Grayson turned to Lance. "I have a nine o'clock with that...person." Grayson still didn't know her name. How rude of her to never have introduced herself.

"Go ahead. They'll be forced to ask me a question now. I swear, they've been ignoring me. I don't know why. I'm the one who looks better on camera." Lance turned to the film crew while Grayson gracefully excused himself and went back to his office.

He expected someone to be waiting when he got there, but there wasn't anyone. He looked to Marley, her eyes the only ones looking up from a monitor, and she darted her gaze away.

9:01 a.m.

Late.

A rumble stirred in his chest. Grayson walked to his desk and leaned his hip against it, his lab coat unbuttoned and casually draped around his shoulders.

It was then that he saw a woman walking down the center aisle of microscopes. She looked entirely out of place in baggy overalls and practically covered in dirt. At least her face was clean. Her hair was tied in a knot on the top of her head.

She had no idea where to go, and it was obvious by the way her gaze darted around.

The girl must have been late twenties, but he wasn't sure. She appeared younger as she approached. Then she hesitated, turned, and walked back to where she'd come. Her hands skimmed the steel tabletops, and she paused at every other microscope to examine it.

She touched a dial, looking around to make sure no one was watching, but Grayson was. The delicate curve of her wrist flexed as she twisted the knobs and peered through the scope.

It almost seemed as if she knew what she was doing.

Until one of the dials fell off.

She stepped back and shoved her hands into her pockets.

He held back a laugh as she stood there, aloof. She had been playing with one of the intern scopes—that piece of crap wasn't good for anything other than taking it apart and putting it together again.

Grayson's breath caught when she looked in his direction. He could see the emerald of her eyes from the back wall of his office where his desk sat. She had a soft gaze, an innocent stare.

She was heading his way. He adjusted the lapels of his lab coat.

He waited for her to knock on the semi-translucent glass of his office door, but she stopped a few feet away. It was clear in that moment she had no intention of seeing him. She was fixated on something else entirely. She walked closer to Poppy, her arm outstretched.

He lunged forward. "Oh no, you don't." He didn't mind her messing with the intern scopes, but no one—*no one*—touched Poppy.

He opened his office door and waited for her to face him. She didn't. She whispered something that sounded like, "nuclear fission."

He waited another few seconds before speaking. "I'm going to have to call security if you touch that."

She yelped and faced him, a small smile tugging at the sides of her mouth.

Grayson motioned with his palm for her to enter his office.

She hesitated before entering, walking slowly to one of the chairs at his desk. She stared at the degrees and awards behind his chair, her face glowing with curiosity. "I got kind of lost. I wasn't sure where to go, really." A rosy pink flushed her cheeks, a color similar to her lips.

Sitting down, he eyed her. She was rather calm for such a feisty woman on the phone. "You're late."

Her expression dropped and was replaced with a single raised eyebrow. "You're...*him?*"

"If by 'him,' you mean the person you're stealing from, then, yes. That would be me. I'm—"

"I know who you are." She stood, and a look of disappointment crossed her face. She huffed and slapped her hands on her thighs.

Dust flew from her overalls, and little particles of who knew what scattered all over his office.

Grayson put his hand up, trying to get her attention. "Please, don't do that."

She mumbled something and pinched the bridge of her nose. She turned in a slow circle and spun to face him, more dirt flying off her clothes.

"Will you stop moving? Jesus Christ." Grayson stood and removed his lab coat, walking toward her and placing it over her shoulders. "You're contaminating my office."

She stood there with a blank expression on her face. The sunlight from behind her created a familiar halo around her head.

His hands rested on the top of her arms, and he couldn't help but gaze into her eyes. Why did she look so sad? It wasn't like he had said anything offensive other than she was dirty. By the look on her face, he might as well have cut her heart open with a rusty scalpel.

Grayson realized he had been holding her a little too long and released his grasp. He stepped back. "Are you mute?"

She exhaled, and he knew by the demon in her eyes, her wrath was about to be freed. Reaching into her pocket, she unfolded a piece of paper and dropped it to the floor, not giving him enough time to retrieve it from her. "I have the crew at three. But it doesn't matter, because today is their last day. You won't ever see me again."

Grayson cocked his head at the piece of paper lying on the floor. "I can agree to that."

She stuck out her hand, and he accepted. His hand

enveloped hers, and a bolt of something shot through his arm—static, probably.

After releasing his hand, she moved to take off his lab coat.

He shook his head and scrunched his face. "Keep it. It's filthy now."

A twinge of hurt glinted in her eyes, but what else was he supposed to say? She was a walking dust devil.

She wrapped the lab coat tightly around her body, and even through all the layers of material, he realized she wasn't as shapeless as she had first appeared. An unfamiliar heat rose from his feet to his chest. He diagnosed the emotion as frustration, but that still didn't seem right.

She turned and stormed out of his office, but unfinished business lingered in the air. She still hadn't introduced herself. She walked toward the main doors by the lobby, and Grayson caught up with her.

He held the door open.

Did she just roll her eyes? He was trying to be a gentleman. Something was wrong with this woman.

"Thank you for the coat. Now, I have a meeting with my boss and his client this afternoon. I should get going. I want to head home and dress appropriately so, you know, I don't *make a mess.*" Head straight and shoulders back, she marched toward the elevator, the gentle sway of her hips causing the bottom of his lab coat to dance.

CHAPTER NINE

"*Eww*. YOU'RE SO DIRTY," CASSIDY MOCKED. "PUT THIS on. You're *contaminating* things."

She knew Grayson was staring at her. She could feel the heat of his gaze on her back, as she waited for the elevator. He probably wanted to make sure she didn't leave a trail of mud behind.

Argh. Where were the stairs? All the doors looked the same. She was only on the second floor, so maybe she could just jump out the window instead. Anything to get out of here.

This meeting did not go as planned. It wasn't even a meeting. She basically threw a contract at Grayson Daniels, a man she had come to admire. A man who turned out to be a complete jerk.

The elevator dinged, and the doors opened. She waited until she was inside and the doors fully closed, before letting her shoulders slump. She rested the front of her head against the steel facade of the back wall and hit it lightly on the surface.

Her throat had closed up as he towered over her. The man she had been watching endless videos of, the man she'd gained strength from, was an imposter. He was nothing like the passionate man she'd thought he'd be. Instead, he was rude and conceited.

Yet, he was oddly sweet, in a barbaric way. He *had* escorted her to the door.

She snorted and moaned. "Boo, get out and keep my coat. It'll help keep your dirt off of things." Her voice echoed, and she continued to beat her head against the elevator wall.

Just like when he'd first called her a thief, he'd awoken an unfiltered emotion within her. She had never been this vocal toward another person or expressed her anger so freely. She usually kept herself from getting upset altogether, but Grayson Daniels knew just the right things to say to tick her off.

Her arms were tucked around her, holding his lab coat snug against her body. God, no. She ripped it off, threw it to the ground and brushed all the dirt off her overalls. "How's that for contamination?" She vigorously rubbed her clothes, leaving a thin cloud of dust in the air.

The elevator beeped, and Cassidy stilled. As the doors opened, two young construction workers stared at her like she was a specimen. Their eyes widened, watching as her force field of filth dissipated in their direction.

She brushed loose strands of hair away from her

face and smiled. Grayson's lab coat remained scrunched at her feet, and she gracefully bent to pick it up and exited the elevator.

When the coast was clear, she shoved his coat into the nearest planter.

She didn't have to walk through the giant laser-zapping machine on her way out—supposedly that was for contamination. She had already walked through when she first arrived. Obviously, it wasn't good enough for Grayson.

Her phone buzzed, and she ignored it. All she wanted to do was get to Laramie Hill and prepare for her meeting with Colton and his client. After finding out the jerk who had heckled her and called her a thief was the one and only Grayson Daniels, her heart needed a pick-me-up.

"That bastard." Cassidy slammed the door behind her, and the entrance reverberated. The walls jiggled, and prisms of colors bounced off the dull walls and wood ceilings. Emotions from her earlier encounter with Grayson still tore at her chest.

She brushed flyaway hairs from her face with shaking hands. The strands fell back down and poked her eyes. Blinking furiously, she didn't know if she should be angry or disappointed. She leaned her back against the front door and sighed.

The man she'd been researching, admiring, and

practically stalking online with little luck for the past few months was a giant disappointment. Just great.

The deep beat of her heart pulsed through her ears. No, that was a knock at the door. Cassidy swung around and grabbed the door handle. She pulled the timber ply open to find two burly men with sheepish grins on their faces, holding what looked like a steel bed frame.

The tall blond closest to her blushed and looked away shyly. "You locked us out, ma'am."

Cassidy raised her eyes to God and cursed herself. She hadn't noticed anyone, let alone a truck in the neighbor's driveway. In her heated rage, she'd stormed inside without even noticing her surroundings. "I'm so sorry. If only this guy had a driveway." She stepped aside and let the men pass.

They looked like they had just been dragged through hell—twice. Leaves stuck out of their long-sleeved shirts, and the guy in the back had a cut on his cheek...unless that was from a bar fight or something.

Smiling weakly, Cassidy shrugged. "I guess you guys didn't see the hole in the hedge about four paces from the sorry excuse for a pathway..."

Turning their gazes back to the bushy foliage, they simultaneously blushed.

Mya revealed herself from behind the corner. "Hello, gent-le-men. Follow me to the bedroom." She dressed to impress in a low-cut tank top and black booty shorts.

Cassidy coughed lightly, and Mya shrugged as if to say, "what?"

Cassidy tugged on Mya's elbow, pulling her into a

small nook. "What are you *wearing*? We're about to meet Colton and his client. You look like you've just filmed a dirty car washing video."

A huff of offense escaped Mya's throat. "You're one to speak. You look like a sewer rat." She leaned closer. "And you smell like one, too. I had a pole dancing class and no time to change. I just got home."

At least Cassidy was fully dressed. "This *isn't* your home."

Mya's eyes were focused on the men in the small foyer. "Yeah, whatever. Where were you this morning? I tried to call you ten times. I didn't understand the checklist you left me."

A slight panic ripped through Cassidy's body from her toes to the ends of her hair. "Did you get all the food? I left precise instructions on spices, brands, and I left a ton of cash on our kitchen counter. You saw all of it, right?"

Sighing, Mya's gaze dropped to the floor. "Yeah, I saw it." Her eyes briefly met Cassidy's. "But what's McCormick? And in the vegetable section, I couldn't find any lemon peppers."

A loud, breathy sound escaped from the pit of Cassidy's throat. "I wrote out everything, Mya."

In the background, the two men waited for instructions.

Leaning closer to Mya, Cassidy whispered, "Don't tell me you ordered furniture for this place. It's already furnished." The words came out as a wavering hiss.

Mya avoided eye contact and pointed upstairs, indicating to the men where the bedroom was.

Cassidy waved her hand in front of Mya's face. "Don't do this, Mya." Cassidy groaned and rubbed her eyes. "This day has been a disaster."

First, her idol turned out to be a jerk. Next, she visits the site of her next remodel, and Mya seems to think she lives here. Lastly, their boss's client was coming over in a few hours, and neither of them looked professional.

Mya lifted her chin. "*You* don't do this. I'm sorry I'm the only who seems to answer my phone. Apparently, the man got a new bed, and it was scheduled to be delivered today, okay?"

Cassidy stilled and dropped her hands to her sides. "Who called you? They should call *me*. Wait. You didn't order this stuff?"

Mya reached one hand up, checked her nails, and grunted. "I tried to call you this morning around nine, but I didn't know where you were. Then I went and got most of the things you wrote down. I took a cab here, like we planned, and here we are."

Most? Hopefully, they'd have enough time to pick up everything Mya didn't get.

"Anyway, *Colton* called and said his client would be here a little early, like 2:00 p.m., and that some movers were going to bring a new bed, because, you know, the guy *lives* here. That's all. It was a one-minute conversation. And Colton said he would come as soon as possible. I gave him my number the last time I saw him. I can't blame him for wanting to use it, especially when you're totally distracted."

Cassidy looked at the small clock display on the kitchen stove—if it even read the correct time. "It's almost 1:30 p.m. We need to start cooking." Her eyes darted around, the panic secreting through her skin causing more fog to surround her. There were no groceries anywhere. She looked to Mya and outstretched her hands to her sides in question. "You've hidden the groceries, right?"

Raising one of her eyebrows, Mya sighed. The expression plastered on Mya's face was the same annoyed look Grayson Daniels had earlier.

Tension pulled in Cassidy's gut. Even thinking about her encounter with Grayson made her want to throw up. He had looked at her with such irritation, like she was beneath him. When he wrapped her in his white coat like a mannequin on fire, then swept her out of his office, she knew he had watched her until she reached the elevator at the end of the hallway. His radiation eyes burned a hole through her skull. What a joke. He was nothing but selfish and coldhearted.

Mya's eyes softened, and she brought her hands together in front of her chest. "Namaste, Cassidy. Namaste. I started barbecuing a second ago, and everything is set up in the back yard."

The two movers walked past empty-handed, shamelessly admiring Mya's backside before heading back outside.

Men were pigs. All of them.

Cursing again to the air, Cassidy cocked her head to the side. "And what did the *Universe* tell you to barbecue?"

"I don't know about the Universe, but your list said baby back ribs, so that's what I got."

Regret frayed the ends of Cassidy's breath. It was then that she saw the look of satisfaction on Mya's face. Her bright eyes. Her confident stance.

Cassidy smiled. "You cooked all that? Thank you, Mya. I'm proud of you. I shouldn't have been so mean. I'm sorry."

Cooking something from scratch and not destroying it was a miracle for Mya.

Moving to the sliding door in the kitchen, Cassidy caught a glimpse of the built-in grill next to the fire pit.

Mya walked forward. "About that…I picked up the food from a restaurant and slapped it on the grill to keep it warm. Took me forever to get the thing started, but Uncle Rob showed me one time."

Robert Thatcher. Cassidy's father was still watching out for her from heaven. More like watching over Mya, but Cassidy would take that.

This influx of foreign emotions was throwing her out of whack. She resented Kyle, she was annoyed with Mya's frivolity, the two men outside made unnecessary banging noises, and even the birds out back wouldn't shut up.

Finally able to take a full breath, Cassidy tried to find something good to think about. This wasn't going to be the extravagant home-cooked meal she had planned to the fifth decimal, but hopefully it would be enough to show their gratitude to Colton and his client. Cassidy was just grateful that her cousin improvised and managed to save the afternoon.

Mya held her hand out for Cassidy, and she accepted.

She dragged Cassidy into the living room. "You aren't your usual self. I have just the thing to cheer you up."

"Yeah? What's that?"

Mya's face lit up with joy. "Your Grayson is on channel eight, talking about his most recent trip." She bounced up and down. She swooned like a peacock, her hair floating around her shoulders in huge tendrils. "Look at his piercing blue eyes. I told you they were blue. You can see it so well here on the screen. And let's not even talk about Lance. Rawr. Isn't Grayson gorgeous in a rugged kind of way?"

"No." And he wasn't *her* Grayson. Cassidy couldn't even bear to look at him.

Mya exhaled, and her smile dropped at the same time as her shoulders. "Wow, not even GrayGray can cheer you up, today? You really did have a bad day." She rubbed Cassidy's back, kissed her cheek, and left to talk to the movers who had peeked through the front door. They seemed to want to ask something.

"You don't even know the half of it." Cassidy cringed as one of Mya's butt cheeks played peekaboo from under her shorts. Looking down at her own attire, she winced. She needed to change into something more appealing than dirty overalls, and fast. Knowing today would be hectic, as it was for the last day of the apartment remodel, she had packed clean clothes in the Lambo and could freshen up quickly in the restroom.

Cassidy glanced back at the TV. Grayson's face was paused on the monitor. He was in his lab coat. The same lab coat he'd placed on her shoulders. The same lab coat she'd thrown to the elevator floor and stomped on like an enraged elephant.

How could he look so content on the screen?

The pixels didn't do his features justice, though. In real life his nose was straighter, his jaw harder, his eyes meaner.

And it had been a scar on the left side of his chin below his bottom lip. Probably from someone punching his daylights out for being such an arrogant pig.

She glared at him. "You think you're so smart, huh?" She held her arms out, bent at the elbows and palms up. "Looking at me all smug-like in your stupid coat. What do you do all day? Look gorgeous and insult people?" Scoffing and rolling her eyes, she turned on her heel, fully intending to leave the room.

Something held her back. A force latched onto the base of her spine and stopped her. Instead of heading back toward the kitchen, she faced Grayson to speak her mind. She hadn't had the guts to defend herself when her ex-boss fired her, and she wasn't going to live life hiding behind her timidity...even though she was talking to herself in the middle of the living room.

Opening her mouth, she expected a slew of foul words to spew out. Words that had billowed in her mind the entire drive up Laramie Hill...but his eyes. They were a penetrating blue. More vivid in person, but equally as captivating on the screen.

She squinted at him. Could he see how disappointed she was in him? Her doubts?

This man on the TV was not the same Grayson from earlier. This Grayson looked excited and anxious.

For what, she didn't know. He had his hand over his heart—a gesture she hadn't seen him make in any of the videos of him she'd watched. After viewing endless hours of him talking, moving, she thought she could read his every intention just by the orientation of his feet, his stance, the direction he angled his shoulders—until today.

Earlier, she hadn't recognized Grayson Daniels, at all. He aggressively towered over her. He had been close enough to breathe the same air as her.

Maybe he just had a bad day. Like her.

She laughed at herself. She wouldn't make excuses for him. She had already used every excuse in the book for Kyle's strange Facebook behavior the weekend before. Emotionally exhausted, she slouched so deeply her overall straps nearly fell off her shoulders. Defeated, her once bright stars dulled around her.

Everything seemed so lifeless. The scuffed floors were filthier than her last visit. The ceilings closed in on her inch by inch. Running out of objects to look at and criticize, she turned to Grayson once more.

Even in the emptiness of the room, he radiated hope. Cassidy mirrored his posture and lifted her chin, gaining strength from him just like she always had after *Science with Grayson*.

Stepping forward, she reached for him. "You look at me, like you know me." She examined him with intensity.

She must've looked ridiculous in the living room, reaching for the screen with one hand like Grayson was there in the flesh. She put her hand down and looked over her shoulder, checking to make sure no one saw her groping a TV.

Turning for the kitchen, she headed toward the backyard to check on Mya's masterpiece of a meal.

On the small stone tabletop next to the grill lay sheets of newspaper Mya must have placed to keep the surface relatively clean. Although, there couldn't have been a mess, since she shoved the entire aluminum foil container under the lid.

Cassidy reached for a fork or a knife or anything to poke and pry the hot foil and check that the ribs weren't completely fried, but there were no utensils anywhere. "Mya," she growled, wadding newspaper around her hands and reaching inside the grill.

Once the container of ribs was freed, Cassidy tossed her crumpled sheets of newspaper to the grass by the small, dirty swimming pool that—for some strange reason—didn't have any water. It looked as if it had been unused for decades.

She lowered the coals, so they could burn off. On one of the dirty wads she had flung to the ground, Grayson's name caught her eye next to a colored rendering of a building that resembled the High Tower, but it was much larger and had a helical twist to its glass facade. She reached down to pick it back up.

She unwrinkled the piece of paper and wiped away some lingering char and barbecue sauce. By the looks of the article, her hero-flop was going to be involved in a massive project demolishing an entire block, including the city's last children's home.

Hearing footsteps behind her, she quickly scanned the text.

Children's home on historic block to be demolished first.
Second High Tower to be built on existing block.

Why would anyone ever support the destruction of a children's home? Surely, there was some kind of organization that protected historic buildings. She'd have to ask Colton. Grayson already owned his own block. He didn't need a second one.

Every nerve in her body ignited in flames. These children needed stability, not some selfish man looking for a new building to plaster his name on.

Frustration from earlier came back in violent waves. She couldn't smother the visions of Child Protective Services coming to get her when her parents had died.

Her stomach somersaulted at the thought of some rich scientist destroying any kind of familiarity around these kids. Cassidy would have ended up in a similar place after the death of her parents, if Mya's family hadn't taken her in until she left for college.

Those poor *children*.

Her lips formed a tight line. There certainly was more to Grayson Daniels than what met the eye. He may have been passionate, but he was ruthless, heartless. A rich, entitled jerk.

A light cough cued Cassidy's spin, and she met Mya's gaze. Mya stood in the doorway, her hair perfectly tousled and her eyebrows high.

She mouthed something to Cassidy.

"What?"

Mya flapped her hands in front of her chest as if trying to speak...or something.

"What are you *saying*?"

"He's here," she hissed. "He's coming this way. You are going to *freak* out."

Jesus. It couldn't have been 2:00 p.m. already. Cassidy hadn't changed yet. Mya hadn't changed yet, although Mya likely had no intention of changing. Cassidy was still in her baggy, filthy clothes, her hair piled on top of her head. Her hands were covered in barbecue sauce and gray newspaper residue.

Cassidy's savage eyes couldn't settle on anything. "Do we have utensils? Where is the pasta? Do we even *have* pasta?"

Soft, confident steps drew nearer, and Cassidy held her breath.

She needed to get herself together.

The aroma of slow-cooked meat bombarded Grayson's senses, and his stomach rumbled just at the thought of a homemade meal.

He wasn't sure who was in his house, but considering he was supposed to meet Colton, it must have been him in the back barbecuing. It was about time Colton did something right. They had a thing or two to discuss about the High Tower and Colton taking part of the crew to work on another project without his permission. They had an agreement.

Before he could reach for the handle, someone opened the door. Grayson was taken aback. It was Mya.

"Hi, boss. Well, not my boss. But whatever. I'm sure Colton has told you all about me." She stuck out her hand in greeting. She was just as stunning as in the pictures Cassidy had sent to him—to Kyle.

He missed receiving Cassidy's letters, and now he was seeing things.

Mya took a few paces back, her hand still extended. "Colton is running a little behind, but we have a late lunch started for you. I hope you're hungry."

We? And what in God's name was she wearing? He twitched in hesitation, as he stepped inside.

"Wow, you're even taller up close." She stepped backward. "Huh, you don't talk much, do you? Colton said you are socially awkward."

Colton had *a lot* of explaining to do. "Why are you in my house?"

More nervous than when he'd first set foot on Ike, Grayson roamed into the kitchen. The TV in the living room was turned on, a blue blob for a screen saver on display, moving around each quadrant.

He didn't see any signs that his new bed had been delivered. After sleeping on a bunk bed for three months, he wanted a king-sized mattress to sink into. He was tempted to ask about it but considering he didn't know what the hell was going on, he decided to shut up.

Mya waited for him in the doorway separating the kitchen from the backyard. She had said a multitude of things to him since he'd arrived, but he couldn't for the life of him recall the words.

All he could think about was Cassidy.

Uncertainty coursed through his body.

Putting his hand over his heart, the faint sound of weathered paper in a sleeve of silk gave him the courage. He could do this, whatever craziness this day brought.

Mya stood expectantly, leaning her hip against the door jamb. "Cassidy?" Stepping outside, Mya walked past the pool and veered left.

Just hearing her name was enough to send his senses into overdrive. She was here. Grayson followed to the patio, and his eyes fell on her. The breath left his chest.

Her.

The same girl from the lab. The thief on the phone.

He shook his head. "No, this is a mistake."

"Mistake?" Mya questioned, lifting her hands up in confusion.

Grayson headed back for the house, but halfway through the opening, he turned and made eye contact with Cassidy. "Why are you here?"

She had a dumbstruck look on her face.

Mya stepped back. "Uh." She looked around, gazing at everything but him. "Because she works for Colton? This is her project? And, I'm her cousin. We're a package deal. Didn't Colton tell you?" She was shoulder to shoulder with Cassidy. One girl a flirtatious thing, the other a mess.

Cassidy still hadn't said anything.

Once his eyes fell to her, he couldn't take them off even if he tried. He couldn't figure her out. She wore those ugly overalls that swallowed her whole, her hair was an even nastier nest than earlier, and she had something on her face that looked like an eagle had used her head for target practice. After taking in her degrading appearance, he met her gaze. "Where is my lab coat?"

Mya looked to Cassidy as well. "What is he talking about?"

Cassidy crossed her arms. "I don't have it."

Huffing, Grayson strode forward, one of his steps equaling half of the back patio length. "You don't have it?"

Taking a deep breath, she nodded. "What, you want me to dry clean it? If you want it so badly, I shoved it into the planter by the elevator on the first floor."

Mya gasped a breath, and from his peripheral, Grayson watched her ease away.

The roaring hunger in his stomach was suddenly replaced with disappointment. "This is clearly a mistake. I don't know why you're in my house. Colton should be here. I have to get back to the office." This hellcat of a woman was nothing like the sweet Cassidy he thought about every day and night. He turned and re-entered the house. Mixed emotions stirred deep within him. Colton hadn't mentioned anything about this, which pissed him off further.

There was a snort and two heavy footsteps behind him. "Of course you do. Go run to your little science project."

Turning to confront her, he raised an eyebrow. Her rigid body was only a few feet away from him, her arms still crossed.

He was about to argue with her, until a ray of light shone through the back window and fell on her hair. The image of her stole his breath. Standing in front of him was the angel from the photograph. The silhouette in the mirror's reflection he had craved to put a face to.

Her skin glistened, and her mouth parted. He wanted to be angry, but all he could do was stare. He had found her.

The brown glob that looked like barbecue sauce had slid from her eyebrow to the top of her cheekbone. Freckles that he hadn't seen earlier dusted her nose.

Disappointment mixed with longing stirred wildly in his chest—and guilt.

Seeing the frustration on Cassidy's face, her scrunched nose, her furrowed brows...he had been a little harsh to her on the phone. She was the one person he didn't want to hurt, yet here he was, unable to have a civil conversation with her.

She placed her hands on her hips. "Suddenly speechless? Didn't have enough of me this morning and decided to show up here and put me in my place?" She wiped her hands on her overalls and gray flecks of dirt flew in projectiles off her body. They leaped so quickly, they seemed to fall in orbit around her head like satellites around the Earth.

He swiped his hand back and forth, dispelling the atmosphere of dust.

Mya rushed to Cassidy's side and placed a palm on Grayson's shoulder. "Excuse us for a minute—"

Brushing Mya aside, Cassidy took a step closer to him, glowering.

He understood the reasons behind both of their frustration. She wasn't what he expected, and from her mannerisms, he had a hunch that he wasn't what she expected either. Hurt flooded her eyes, as if he had betrayed her. That realization stung.

She was close and red-faced.

Crimson covered Cassidy's chest and face. One more look at her disheveled hair, and he couldn't help himself from smiling. It was as if she had just dipped her head into a hole like an ostrich and hired a gopher as her hairdresser.

The she-devil leaned backward. "You're crazy. Why are you smiling at me? You're completely incapable of having a normal conversation."

And she was?

Mya's deep breaths could be heard from the corner she had pressed herself into.

Cassidy's flush somehow managed to recede to an adorable shade of pink. "So, yes. You go run to your Bunsen burner and little drippy, glass syringes."

Grayson raised an eyebrow. "Those are actually called pipettes."

Inhaling a loud breath, Mya marched up to the both of them. "Let's break this up, shall we?" Her voice was light and playful, and she moved closer to Grayson. "We don't want to keep you from work or anything. We're being selfish. We aren't the center of the Universe."

For the first time, Grayson took his eyes away from Cassidy. "The Universe doesn't have a center, so that statement is highly inaccurate."

Blink. Blink. "Okay." Patting his arm, Mya gestured

with an outstretched hand for him to go to the backyard. "How about a delicious lunch, instead? You must be hungry."

He had been hungry earlier, famished, but his disappearing appetite was accompanied by the need to get back to the office. It was the only place he could think without any distractions, and he needed to get ahold of Colton to find out what was going on here.

"Thank you, but I'm going to go back to work. I have things to do." He placed his hand on the kitchen counter.

Cassidy's gaze darkened. Grayson couldn't help but lean forward, even if it was to see if her eyes were a sea green or emerald.

Mya waved her hand in-between their faces. "Do you two know each other?"

"No," Cassidy whispered.

"Yes," Grayson said at the same time.

Inches apart, he could smell her sweet scent. The aroma of lavender and vanilla challenged his senses.

"No?" Grayson asked. "We've only argued on the phone incessantly two times."

There was a twinge of something Grayson couldn't peg that crossed Cassidy's face. She was frustrated, no doubt because of their earlier meeting, but there was more behind her eyes. It was as if she wanted to say something but was holding back. She had already lashed out at him, why couldn't she just say it?

This was a mess, but he hadn't come this far to turn his back on her now.

First, he needed to find Colton, then he would fix this.

"Colton, I think it's time that I fire you."

Colton's brown gaze was expressionless as he looked up at Grayson. "That's what you called me to your office for? You say that every other week, Grayson. I'm in the middle of construction, you can't fire me."

Grayson ran his hand through his unruly hair. "You just don't listen to me when I fire you, but I'm firing you —officially—now." He pointed at the ground for emphasis.

Standing, Colton took his sweet time to respond. He licked his lips, straightened his suit jacket, and unbuttoned it. "Do you remember in college when you asked for my help?"

Not this again. "You won't seem to let me forget."

Colton paced Grayson's office. "That's because you owe me. While you were in prison after..." Hesitation lingered in the air.

"Just say it."

Licking his lips again, Colton took a deep breath. "... after running over that little girl, Lance and I kept your reputation spotless. You promised me you would repay me, and you've got a good start with this High Tower Lab and your house renovations. And, hopefully, you'll put a good word in for me with the second High Tower that's being planned?" The optimistic inflection in his voice was

undeniable. "So, don't even think about backing out on this. I saved your career, and in exchange, you were going to help me start off right when I got licensed."

The past just wouldn't seem to go away. Ghosts lived in the present and occupied the same space. Grayson swallowed hard. "I want to honor my word, but in order for me to do that, I need you focused on the laboratory downstairs. Do you see all this equipment?" He pointed to the workstations that cluttered the tabletops. "I need a place to put this stuff. And if this fails, there's no chance either of us will be involved in the new expansion project. And what the hell is going on at my house? I was impressed you were juggling all these jobs and still making progress, but then I come to find out you're pawning your work off on someone else. I need your focus here. Why didn't you tell me about Cassidy?" He couldn't seem to peg his own emotions. He was upset with Colton for not focusing on the progression of the lab, but Cassidy being in the middle of things sent an uneasy gust of air between them.

Colton's face lit up at the mention of her name. "My new intern? So, you did meet her. I was going to introduce her to you today. I thought maybe you hadn't made it up there, yet, when you called me to meet you here instead. Sweet girl, huh?"

Yes, very sweet. Cassidy had a spell on everyone from the east to west coast. Grayson didn't know how long he could keep this up.

Taking a shallow breath, he gestured with a sweep of his hand for Colton to sit down, and he did. "When I fire you, what will that do to her?"

Colton drummed his fingers on his knee. "You aren't firing me, but if you did, it would screw her over. You promised me this. And, I promised her that I'd have her back. She's broke. She's trying to finish her degree, but she doesn't have enough internship hours or lab experience."

Grayson didn't know the intimate details of her career in archaeology. She never wrote about it to Kyle, and part of Grayson didn't like that Colton knew these things.

"She asked for my help a few months ago. So, I offered my services, got some of the guys, and we helped her out of a little situation. It didn't interfere with construction here. I know you're hellbent on that. She actually did a really great job when we worked together. So, I assigned her your house. We can do both jobs at the same time. I'll focus on the lab. Just let her work on the house. It's all she has right now."

Grayson stood over Colton and examined him. Grayson wouldn't fire Colton today, but not because he owed him anything. Grayson would do this for Cassidy.

As if reading Grayson's unspoken agreement, Colton beamed. "Believe me, you won't be disappointed. She's absolutely *incredible*."

He didn't have to keep complimenting her—it was unprofessional.

CHAPTER TEN

WITH HER HANDS ON HER HIPS, MYA SCOWLED AND stepped closer. "There is an entire background story here, and I'm being left in the dark."

Cassidy rolled her lips between her teeth and let her eyes fall...to what? She didn't know where to look with Mya right in her face. If Cassidy could turn her head just a little more, Mya could be erased from her field of vision.

Crossing her arms and tapping her manicured fingers, Mya shook her head. "When did you meet Grayson? How do you know each other? He *gave* you his jacket, and you didn't even think for a second to tell me? Fill me in. Now."

Cassidy lifted her eyes. "He was the one who called me that one time, saying I was stealing his construction crew."

Recognition processed on Mya's face. "The man you

yelled at? O-o-oh, the plot thickens." She leaned forward, her elbows on the kitchen counter.

Cassidy had barely moved since Grayson left. She just stood there like a collision test dummy, waiting to be slammed into a wall. "Then, this morning, the same caller asked me to meet him in his office, with not so much as an introduction. Turns out it was Grayson."

"Let me guess. It didn't go well?"

"Gah, it was terrible." Cassidy flung her hands in the air. "Then everything just went downhill from there. He's going to tear down the historic district, Mya. Did you know that? And a *children's home*. How heartless can one man be? He's the devil. And you need to see how impeccably clean his office is. He's probably so OCD he alphabetizes the vegetables in his fridge."

Mya shuffled to where Cassidy stood. "Stop making excuses. You've already signed the contract with Colton."

"That was before I knew it was *his* house." As if that explained everything.

Mya's bouncy curls swayed, and she lightly smacked Cassidy on the shoulder, frustration in her eyes. "We have no money." *Smack.* "Colton is a godsend." *Smack.* "Grayson is rich!"

"Ow. Will you stop it? Grayson was so upset." And if Grayson was rich, why was he living in a cottage with no sidewalk? Cassidy gazed at Mya. "Let's just wait to hear from Colton. This is Grayson's house, and he'll know what's best."

Mya tossed her head back. "Please. He said the Universe has no center. He obviously knows nothing."

Cassidy bit her lip to stop a giggle from escaping. "I love you, Mya."

Smiling, Mya dragged Cassidy to the living room. "Yes…" she whispered. "I know…now look at Grayson's face." She unpaused the TV, the screen saver disappearing, and Grayson's deep voice infiltrated the room.

Mya waved her hand in front of Cassidy's face to get her attention. "Stop being wishy-washy like me, and take charge of your life, Cassidy Thatcher. So, what if this isn't archaeology? You've got the feature article in *New York's Eye* to feed that passion until you're back on track. You need to think about yourself for once."

She had almost forgotten about the article. Being wrapped up in the world of architecture was distracting. And for the record, she did think about herself. *Take charge of your life.* Isn't that why she came to New York? To redefine herself after getting fired? To help Mya?

Mya shook her head as if reading her mind. "I know what you're thinking, and the answer is no. You came here for me. You didn't come here for you. But now, you have a chance to change that. I've never seen this fiery side of you. It's like, you're growing a backbone. I sense change coming for you. Seize the moment."

With an ache in her eyes, Mya seemed to search Cassidy for an answer. Again, Cassidy was presented with the decision she thought she'd already made…and remade. She couldn't go back to Montana, not now. Not until Mya was back on her feet, and certainly not until she closed her open ends in New York.

Cassidy's phone buzzed, and she reached for it.

"Colton?" She groaned. "I just met Grayson. He was so angry and confused." Her breath caught in her lungs.

"It's okay, Cassidy. I just spoke to him."

She released a steady stream of air. "What do you mean 'it's okay?'"

A car engine started on the other end of the line. "I hadn't had a chance to fill Grayson in on all the details. Meaning, he had no idea you were going to be working on the house, while I was at the lab. He just kind of assumed that I was doing everything. He didn't like that. I think you caught him off guard today. I told you he's bad around people."

That was obvious. "So, what's the plan?"

"He's hellbent on me finishing the lab, so that means I can't supervise you as much, but we already knew that. I'll still be here for you, of course, but I'm going to rely on you to do the heavy lifting. Keep me updated, and don't be afraid to talk to Grayson directly if I'm unavailable."

She could temporarily deal with Grayson Daniels and his bad manners. She wasn't so sure she'd be able to manage her own manners, but at least Colton could act as a filter. She would not let her emotions get in the way of making this decision. That always seemed to get her into trouble.

Logic, that was her plan. Logic with a touch of spontaneity. She nodded.

Mya's expectant gaze, Grayson's voice in the background, Colton on the phone.

This was her future.

CHAPTER ELEVEN

GRAYSON THOUGHT HE'D BE ABLE TO SLEEP AFTER BEING on a ship for three months. He couldn't. Not even his king-sized mattress was comfortable enough.

He showered lazily, dressed in his usual charcoal-gray suit and white button down, and wandered into the kitchen. The scent of Cassidy's perfume lingered in the hallway. His blood swirled with emotion. He couldn't stop visualizing her silhouette by the window with the sun glistening over her wild hair.

This house was supposed to be his sanctuary away from people, but the longer he stood there, the more potent her presence became.

He didn't know what time it was, but he skipped whatever meal came after waking up in the middle of the night. After passing through the worn opening in the hedge with a box of equipment in hand, he climbed into his black Jeep, parked in the small alley between the unoccupied house next door and his small cottage.

He sat for long minutes just staring at his dash. Where was he going, again?

He was completely alone in his car, yet Cassidy still managed to distract him. Lightly tapping the back of his head against his head rest, he sighed. The urge to stay home, when work taunted his every sense, perplexed him. He typically couldn't wait to get to the lab, but now he craved to surround himself with the shadow of her presence.

He drove to the High Tower quickly, hoping that would divert his thoughts from Cassidy.

When he arrived, he gave himself a pep talk. "Go straight to your office. Do work. Don't think of her lips or her emerald eyes or the sway of her hips."

One of the security guards nodded to Grayson. "What was that, Mr. Daniels?"

He strolled toward the elevator. In his hands was his large box of vials and test samples. He just wanted to get upstairs and fondle his microscopes. He couldn't help but let his eyes wander to the planter to his left. He snapped his head away as the elevator doors opened. "Don't think about her."

Don't.

As if Cassidy were there herself, his eyes descended to the planter once again. As promised, his lab coat had been shoved between the ferns on display. He hadn't even noticed it yesterday, in his haste to fire Colton.

Frustrated he couldn't reach for it without making an awkward scene, and with the security guard's eyes on his back, he let it go. Jesus, that woman had a temper that challenged his own.

Once he reached the second floor, he finally gathered himself. Other than his home, his office was his place of seclusion. He could be himself here. He could do what he loved to do, without the hum of people talking in the background and generally sucking the energy out of him.

There was no one at the office. Gleams of moonlight reflected off the steel work stations. His stomach grumbled in a roar, and he walked toward the break room in the back. He left the lights off, only the emergency exit sign illuminating the space. He set his equipment aside to open the fridge, in hopes that someone left him a piece of cake from his welcome home party. Empty.

With no one to hear him, he swore like a sailor, as he lumbered into his office—unfiltered and unabridged.

He placed his box of lab equipment in the far corner and slammed the door behind him. He could smell the bitter rust-like odor of sawdust and earth. Even the dirt that flew off Cassidy yesterday had a scent, and it loitered on every surface. He ran both hands through his hair and down the sides of his unshaven face.

"Wow, Grayson."

He clenched his jaw at the familiar voice and turned to face his black leather couch. "What are you doing here?"

The silhouette of a neck and head were visible above the backrest of the couch. "Drinking."

"In the dark? In *my* office?"

Lights from down below danced on the large glass window overlooking NYC. Lance's yawn was long and drawn out. "Your office has alcohol, and I dozed off for a little bit. Nothing wrong with a man spending time alone in his friend's office."

He always had an answer for everything.

Grayson unbuttoned his coat. "How long have you been here?"

"Long enough." Lance stood and stretched, the outline of his body a shadow against the illuminated backdrop. "You'd better get rid of that temper you've been sporting all day or—"

"Or what?" Reaching for the light switch, Grayson turned it on.

With his shoes off, Lance extended out his hand to pick up one of Grayson's tumblers, gripped the whiskey from the side table, and poured himself a hefty serving. By the looks of it, Lance was ready for a heart to heart.

A drink sounded like a great idea, though. With finesse, Grayson reached his arm for the whiskey in Lance's hand and poured the elixir into another crystal tumbler, watching the amber liquid form patterns as it settled. He could see his polished shoes through the glass as he lifted it slowly to his lips and tasted the kaleidoscope of translucent swirls.

Lance looked outside the window, while Grayson meandered around his desk.

Turning to face Grayson, Lance's cool gaze disseminated judgment. "You're not usually... I still can't find the word for it."

Annoyed? Irritated that he couldn't get a moment to himself?

Grayson kicked his own shoes off and sat behind his desk, crossing his feet and leaning back in his chair.

Settling in "his" black couch, Lance raised his glass to the light and turned it every which way, watching the whiskey gyrate inside. "How is it going with Cassidy?"

Where was Grayson's briefcase? He could have sworn he left it by his desk. Sitting upright, he looked to either side of him, but it wasn't there.

A groan echoed from Lance's general direction. "You promised me that if she didn't accept the article, you would let her go. Is that what happened? Did she turn it down?"

In the depths of Grayson's throat, he hummed a growl. He came to the office to work and distract himself from Cassidy, not think about her more. He placed his whiskey on the center of his desk. "She works for Colton now, Lance. And before you think the worst of me, I didn't orchestrate that. She's not going anywhere."

"Grayson..." Lance's voice held warning. "This is only going to end badly."

Things weren't going to end badly. Grayson removed his suit jacket that seemed to constrict his every movement and stood to hang it on his coat rack. It was suffocating him. This room was suffocating him. Where in the hell was his briefcase?

Moving to stand in front of him, Lance placed his drink on the edge of Grayson's desk. "Why can't you hook up with an unattached girl? A girl like, I dunno, Isabella." His palms were outstretched in question.

Grayson's shoulders stiffened. He finally looked up to meet Lance's troubled expression. "Isabella? You mean the best friend of the woman who practically ruined my life?"

Lance inhaled so deeply the button at the center of his chest looked as if it were about to pop off his dress shirt. "Okay, so that may have been a bad example. I didn't mean to bring up Veronica's circle of friends."

Veronica was one of many Grayson didn't want to think about. "And of course, Isabella is unattached. Does that honestly surprise you? It's not like anyone in Veronica's posse screams, 'take me now, I'm marriage material.'"

Lance scoffed. "Because *you* want marriage? How many times have you told me, you'd rather elope with your research and work remotely from a private island? And you hate kids." Lance was doing that thing with his hand he always did when he wanted to make himself clear, chopping the air to emphasize every word. His hand movements were giving Grayson a headache.

Grayson didn't hate kids, he just didn't like being around children that reminded him of his past. Grayson placed his hand on Lance's shoulder. "Call a cab to take you home and let me work."

Lance stepped back, reached for his tumbler, and tipped all the contents in his mouth before placing the glass down and turning on his socked heel. "Your briefcase is at your desk, by the way," he called out from over his shoulder.

Grayson looked to his left. For the love of God, why hadn't he seen it before? Right under his nose.

Smirking, Lance sauntered toward the door, grabbing his jacket from the backrest of an armchair. He looked back at Grayson and swung his jacket onto his shoulders. "Since it's technically morning, you have dinner tonight with Jason. You have reservations, and he already called to confirm. I forgot to tell you because, well, we're *supposed* to have a secretary who does that."

Was that bitterness in his voice? What time was it, anyway?

Leaning over, Lance picked up his leather loafers that were placed just to the right of the door jamb. "He wants to talk to you about the children's home, because they're planning demolition soon. And, before you say anything, I know what you're thinking."

"I didn't realize you were psychic."

"He's going to ask you about that camping trip he sets up every year, and I highly suggest you say yes, because we've said 'no' since the day we met him. We need to build a better relationship with him. It's called networking."

Grayson waved Lance off. Lance could go network all he wanted. They had just gotten back from the middle of the Atlantic Ocean. Grayson had better things to do than think about another trip of any kind.

A loud grumble erupted in his stomach. Cake would have held him over, but he couldn't even have that. Nodding, Grayson sat behind his desk and watched Lance navigate through the labyrinth of tables, and out the main exit.

He finally looked at the time. 2:00 a.m. He had four

hours of peace and quiet to himself before his junior associates started to trickle in.

He reached for a stack of papers on his desk.

Where had he put his pen? He patted his chest and stood to reach into the breast pocket of the jacket he had hung up. All he could find was Cassidy's first letter to him. He removed it and read it.

Warmth flooded his veins every time he scanned her words. A reel of images flashed before his eyes. Teaching Katrina how to swim backstroke, her two front teeth missing. Lance, Grayson, and her at the state fair. Katrina sitting on their shoulders, holding a small stuffed panda above her head.

He tried to remember all the times he had been a good brother. But there was only an instant—one minute—that he hadn't been there for her and *poof*. For years, he had begged for a do-over. He had focused on work and the High Tower, until Cassidy's letter brought back all those emotions.

She was a complex formula that he wanted to solve. The permanent scowl confused him, yet the determination behind her eyes enthralled him. Each coefficient of her life was another part of Cassidy he wanted to unveil, but it seemed that her fire unburied his past regrets, and he didn't know if he would be able to catch her flame.

An ache jabbed at his sternum. Looking to the ceiling, Grayson rubbed his tired eyes with his palms, Cassidy's letter hanging loosely from his fingertips. "I hear you, sis."

If second chances really did exist, helping Cassidy was as close as he was going to get to righting his wrongs. Tucking Cassidy's letter back in his pocket, he knew what he had to do. He would acknowledge Lance's warning, but he'd see this through no matter what.

The Jamaican was Jason's favorite restaurant downtown. Grayson didn't care much for the eclectic food and casual attire, let alone all the people, but Jason had insisted they meet there. Grayson had barely eaten all day. He was swamped with deadlines and consumed with coordinating with Colton to make sure construction was going as planned.

Grayson checked his watch, and it was almost 8:00 p.m. He waited patiently in a booth on the second-floor loft of the space, his eyes scanning the lower dining room area for a familiar face.

A waitress came over and handed him a menu. He ordered a Coke, and moments later a different waitress brought it to him. "Welcome, Mr. Daniels. Your guest is in the ladies' restroom." She turned to walk away.

"Excuse me?" He smiled at her. "You mean the men's restroom?"

She giggled. "Why would she be in the men's restroom? That's so silly of you. You're so funny." She giggled again before sashaying off.

He sat back in confusion.

A few minutes passed, and a hand wrapped around

Grayson's neck, followed by a kiss to his cheek. "Hello, darling."

Grayson blew a steady stream of air and reached for his glass of water. "Veronica." He avoided eye contact for as long as possible.

Veronica's long, bare legs crossed, as she sat in front of him. Her shoulder-length, cobalt-black hair shone in the dim light. Her bright blue eyes were as show-stopping as he remembered.

Grayson raised an eyebrow. "I'm waiting for someone."

Pouting her dark maroon lips, she leaned forward on her elbows. "Jason isn't coming. I met his wife today for lunch, and she mentioned that he was meeting you here tonight, so I told her you were sick."

Anger took the reins of his mood. He leaned back in his chair. Why did Veronica have to do this? Why now?

"I wish you wouldn't talk about me like you know me." Reaching his hand up to the waitress, he mouthed "check," and she nodded from half a room away.

Veronica extended her hand to his and placed it back on the table, her fingers intertwining with his. "Tell me, why do you care so much about that silly children's home? Jason is going to tear down every other building on that block. Why not that one, too?"

He yanked his hand away from hers.

Veronica's eyebrows shot up in surprise. "Don't do this. I *do* know you. I've known you since high school. Please, just talk to me. I'm trying to have a conversation. I know we haven't seen each other in years, but don't be unreasonable."

"Really, I like it better that way." He tapped his foot under the table. "I had important business to discuss with Jason. I have a lot banking on this. If you wanted to meet with me, you could have—"

"Called your office? I've done that. Called *you*? You changed your number, remember?" Her long, sculpted, red fingernails raked through her hair. The strands glistened and gleamed only to fall back into a perfectly coiffed position as she pouted her lips once more.

Standing, Grayson waved to the waitress again and pulled out his wallet.

Veronica gasped and patted the center of the table. "Grayson, sit down. You're making a scene. I need you to sit down, *now*." She smiled weakly at the other guests surrounding their booth as if to apologize.

Grayson didn't want to sit down. He bent forward, leaning over Veronica's slim frame. "You know, when I needed you, you lied."

Her bottom lip quivered, and her glassy blue eyes hollowed. "That was over ten years ago, Grayson. I lied to protect myself, my family. Haven't you ever lied to protect someone? We were inseparable. We know everything about each other."

He couldn't even look at her. "Not everything." Grayson straightened. "Second chances don't exist, Rony."

The waitress came over, thank God. He paid for the Coke he'd ordered, tipped her well, and left The Jamaican.

Walking out the exit, he didn't turn back to see if

Veronica was still there. He was certain she was trying to act calm and collected—her fake facade.

He reached into his pocket for his phone to find a text message from Jason.

Jason: Sorry you're sick. Let's reschedule.

Grayson walked back toward the High Tower rather than taking a taxi the short distance. A grumble ripped through his chest as he approached the parking garage.

A security guard nodded as he walked by. "Good evening, Mr. Daniels."

Smiling weakly, Grayson bowed his head and proceeded to his Jeep.

The drive back to Laramie Hill took longer than anticipated. It was late, so there was no reason why Colton, Mya, or Cassidy would be there, but he was nervous to confront the girls again. He hadn't been in the best mood after arriving back in the city the other day, and now, after seeing Veronica again and opening old wounds, he wasn't sure he wanted them to see this broken side of him.

He assured himself that tomorrow would be better. If only he could get some sleep. After he ate, things would definitely be better. Maybe he wouldn't be so grumpy and toxic.

Finally home, he parked his car and walked toward his hermit hole in the trees. The first time he'd passed through this hedge, he'd been a teenage boy looking for a place to live.

Lance had told Grayson about rich man Parker's

pool house when he got kicked out of the house. He snuck in every night. He had gotten caught creeping out of the hedge one morning, and rich-man Parker sat him down, only to give him a three-hour lesson in responsibility. The next day when Grayson was caught again, the lesson was about managing money. Parker taught Grayson how to start a business, how to sculpt a rewarding career, and how to take care of himself. They talked every day for a decade, until Parker passed away, and Grayson continued to live in the pool house.

Now, the mansion next door just sat there. It had been for sale off and on, but it seemed like every time a prospective owner took a tour of the property, they were startled by Grayson bouncing back and forth through the hedge.

When potential buyers requested to see the pool and the pool house, that's when house showings got awkward. Every real estate agent seemed to have difficulty describing Grayson's deal with Parker and the fact that the pool house wasn't exactly a part of the house anymore.

It was Grayson's now. The only thing he didn't like about the pool house was the large swimming pool in the back. Now that he was finally fixing the place up, he could get rid of it. He'd have Colton fill it with dirt.

He marched down the narrow gravel path and tugged on the front door, surprised to find it was unlocked. He never left the door unlocked. He looked around cautiously and quietly stepped inside. Listening for a few moments, he waited for sounds of movement inside the house.

Striding up the stairs to the loft, he checked the bedroom. He moved within the narrow spaces and crouched uncomfortably under counters to check everywhere.

He strolled into the kitchen and flipped the far light switch on. The kitchen illuminated in a soft glow. Sighing, he walked into the living room, almost tripping over something firm and small. Was it an animal? The thing clutched his ankle, and he tried to kick it away with no luck. It was like a miniature bear trap clutching his foot.

Grayson leaned over for the light switch to his left and turned it on. Around his right foot was a beige purse. His foot had slid inside the handle. He chuckled lightly. One of the girls must have left it here by accident. A good sign of them returning? Perhaps.

Except, what an odd place to put it. Right in the middle of the room. He examined the purse then scanned the living room space. He halted when he saw Cassidy asleep on his couch that had been pushed into the corner. She was wearing a plaid button-down blouse and a worn-out pair of jeans. A thin layer of dust covered the far end of the room where it looked as if she had started replacing old floor boards. The blood-red leather encased her, swallowing her whole.

Not wanting to wake her up, Grayson crept back to the light switch and slowly turned it off. Letting his eyes adjust to the darkness, he approached her.

"What are you still doing here?" he whispered to himself more than her, but even he could hear the confusion in his voice.

Leaving her purse upright on the floor, he knelt beside her. Cassidy's mouth was slightly parted, and the moonlight followed all the carvings of her face. Her eyebrows, cheekbones. She looked different when she wasn't smothered in dirt. A sleek ponytail freed her face from flyaway strands, and a thin gold necklace conformed to the dips at the base of her neck. He skimmed her shoulder with his index finger.

A low moan escaped her mouth.

He brought his face close to hers. "Where's Mya?"

She mumbled something about an interview and taking a taxi home. Cassidy took a deep breath, and Grayson stilled yet again, as if she controlled his every move. "Kyle? You haven't written to me. Why?"

She was talking in her sleep and, damn Grayson's heart, it was the most endearing thing he'd ever seen. Everything else in the world was inconsequential at that point. "I've been busy, that's all."

She took another deep breath. "You smell different."

Quickly leaning away from her, Grayson gave her space. Stiffening, he didn't know where to go or what to do.

"I like it."

He smiled and leaned forward once again, closer to her. His phone dinged wildly in his pocket, and he reached to shut it off. There was a text message from Jason.

Jason: Are you going to my company camping trip next month?

Jason had the worst timing. Grayson put his phone

on silent and placed it back in his pocket, only for it to go off again and *again*.

"Jesus Christ," he hissed. "Will you leave me alone?"

Jason: I won't take no for an answer this year.
Jason: Don't say you're going to be sick.

Grayson quickly pulled up a new message.

Grayson: Yes yes il go gnight

He cringed at his grammar. There was no time for punctuation, Jason just needed to go away. Grayson pressed "send," and the vibrating in his pocket ceased. He looked back at Cassidy, and her head was tucked in her arm at an awkward angle. He didn't have the heart to wake her. Instead, he stared at her.

She was much smaller than he originally thought. Her baggy overalls had swallowed her yesterday.

Grayson's eyes absorbed her every breath as she slept, the burning rage from all their arguments before dissolving. He mirrored the cadence of the rise and fall of her chest. In that moment, with just him and her in the room, he finally felt like he had privacy. He could breathe. His thoughts weren't muddled or fogged.

Leaning forward, he placed the back of his index finger at her left brow and traced a line to the corner of her lips. "Now that I've found you, tell me, how do I stay away from you?"

Who was he trying to kid? The idea of focusing on

work was laughable. He was completely bewitched by her. *This* was the girl from the letters.

Pulling away, he stood. Before retreating to the kitchen to turn off the dim lights, he turned to catch one last glimpse of his second chance.

CHAPTER TWELVE

CASSIDY HAD NO INTENTION OF TELLING MYA SHE SPENT the night at Grayson's house. She didn't hear anyone come home, so she was sure she was in the clear. But still, she couldn't explain why that had happened...let alone explain it to Mya.

She had jolted awake with the sun in her face, called a cab, and bolted out of the house in a panic. Colton hadn't been kidding when he said, "You'll understand when you meet him." Grayson was awkward as hell and a workaholic. Did the man ever sleep? Even when she woke up, his car was gone.

If she had seen him, she would have been tempted to ask about the children's home and if he really was a demon who ruined little kids' lives. She paused. She didn't seem to have a filter around Grayson, and that was dangerous. She would need to watch her tongue around him.

Nonetheless, she was grateful he hadn't come home to see her sleeping on his couch—the science slave.

Her mind couldn't even comprehend the amount of work he had to get done after being away for so many weeks. Guilt swarmed her chest at the thought. He probably hadn't slept for days, maybe even longer. No wonder he seemed so grumpy. That didn't give him any reason to be vile, but at least she could see why.

Cassidy poured a fresh cup of coffee for Mya, who was just waking up.

Yawning, Mya rolled her eyes and sat at the kitchen counter. "When did you get home? I didn't hear you. You look nice in plaid."

No one could hear anything with that stripper music playing downstairs 24/7. "Oh. Pretty late." *More like five minutes ago.* "It was a long day, so I'm glad you got your rest."

Rubbing her eyes, Mya groaned. "Waking up gets harder and harder when I have nothing to look forward to each day. Every interview I've had this week has been a flop."

Pouring herself a cup of coffee, Cassidy stepped toward Mya. "I know, but you have another interview on Monday, right?"

"They canceled."

Cassidy couldn't think of anything to say. "We'll figure it out. We have some money for a little while. You don't need to look for work right now." She tried to sound hopeful, but Mya's permanent frown broke her heart.

Flinging her arms in exasperation, Mya turned to

Cassidy. "That's *just* what I need. To mooch off my cousin. Isn't that what I did my entire relationship with Brian? Depend on him? I need to do something for myself. What about when you leave?"

Cassidy laughed. "I'm not leaving, Mya. What makes you think that?"

"I'm just saying. I can't have people think my husband left me, and now I can't take care of myself. That's worse than getting divorced." Mya stood and walked to the refrigerator. She wouldn't find anything in there. The only food they had were leftovers at Grayson's house. Mya had insisted they wrap it up and leave it for him in case he got hungry. In hindsight, Cassidy should have fought her about it, because her stomach roared like thunder.

Cassidy would go shopping for them today. Walking back to the bedroom, Mya lightly closed the door, and Cassidy was once again left alone with her thoughts.

Her phone rattled. Assuming it was a notification that her battery was low, she found her charger, plugged it in to the back wall, and walked to the bathroom.

She looked pretty decent for having slept in her clothes from yesterday. Heading back to the kitchen, she searched for any kind of sustenance.

Cabinets, bare.

Cupboards, nearly empty.

In the freezer, however, were frozen grapes. Bless Mya for being obsessed with freezing fruit. Cassidy shoveled the fruit in her mouth and reveled as they slowly melted. "So good." She was about to take another handful when her phone vibrated again. "It's 7:00 a.m., people. I don't work until the afternoon."

She took a few strides forward and reached for her phone to open her email.

Her lungs constricted at the sight of Grayson's name.

—

From: Grayson Daniels
To: Colton Albright
Cc: Cassidy Thatcher
Subject: Contract

Colton,

I've been trying to reach you since yesterday.

I need you to be more responsive. This is unprofessional, and I expect more from your team.

You were supposed to be at my house at 7:00 a.m. this morning.

Grayson

—

Cassidy didn't know if she should respond to Grayson or not, but she didn't like the tone of his email. She scrolled to the next one.

—

From: Grayson Daniels
To: Colton Albright
Cc: Cassidy Thatcher
Subject: Anyone there?

Colton, if you're so busy, please send Cassidy to the house immediately.

—

She stared at her phone, waiting for the next demand to come. This man was terrible at email etiquette. But isn't this what she had expected?

—

From: Colton Albright
To: Grayson Daniels, Cassidy Thatcher
Subject: RE: RE: Contract

Grayson,

Cassidy will be at the house by 8:00 a.m. Sorry, just swamped at the lab. We'll be better with communicating.

Colt

—

Just then, Colton called in a panic to talk to Cassidy about her schedule, wanting to bump her hours up.

"Whatever you need, Colt. I'll be at the house by 8:00 a.m." She scribbled a note for Mya and taped it to the fridge. Taking the keys to the Lambo, her purse with her overalls shoved inside, the mail on the counter, and another mouthful of grapes, she left their apartment.

Grayson's Jeep was parked outside the hedge when she arrived, and she parked next to him. Her hands shook as she turned off the engine. She took a deep breath and rubbed her palms against the jeans she still had on from the day before. Grabbing her purse and leaving her mail on the passenger seat, she gave herself another mental pep talk.

Each step toward the front door was torture. Grayson's emails were so cold, she was certain he wouldn't be in a good mood. She took a few calming breaths when she reached the front door and knocked.

Moments later, Grayson opened the door dressed in jeans that hung low on his hips and T-shirt that hugged his torso. This wasn't his usual attire. Not that she knew what his usual attire was, but every time she had seen him, he looked like he couldn't move his arms in fear of ripping his suit. That, or he had a rod up his spine.

He observed her attire with equal scrutiny, but was that a small smile? She couldn't tell. She could change into her overalls, and maybe Grayson would stop eyeing her with a pretty little smirk on his face. His permanent half-grin was making her uncomfortable.

Opening the door wide for her, he stepped back.

The smell of bacon and eggs wafted toward her, and she moaned.

She walked inside and wandered to the kitchen, the savory scents making her mouth water. "That smells delicious."

The kitchen was as she had left it that morning, dusty yet organized. She would rip the floorboards out and put in Italian tile, and the walls definitely needed a fresh coat of paint.

She turned to face him and leaned against the kitchen island. "Do you have a busy day today?"

His back was to her, as he stirred the contents in a variety of pans. For someone so insistent on working, he didn't seem like he had anything on his mind other than eating.

Cassidy drummed her fingers on the counter and placed her purse on the corner of the island separating them. If he only told her to come over, so she could stare at his backside all morning, he was mistaken.

Don't look at his muscles. Don't look at his muscles.

Her eyes raked his muscles. His biceps flexed as he tossed eggs. His back was sculpted and strong. His legs were lean, long. His shoulders...

Snapping her eyes away, she cleared her throat. "Are you always this demanding? I mean, in your emails, you certainly didn't have any problem ordering my presence."

Grayson spun and pointed to his left ear. He had a Bluetooth headset in.

She had just managed to look like a fool twice in one

hour. She cringed. "I'm sorry," she mouthed, and he returned to his stupid bacon.

Watching Grayson on a phone call seemed... intimate. She imagined him being rude and incessantly smug like he had been to her the first time they spoke. Now, he was silent.

Setting an empty plate between them, Grayson grinned.

This was unexpected. Was he making her breakfast? Wow, this man was bi-polar, and at that moment, her stomach rumbled in gratitude that he was.

She tried to gesture a "thank you" and ended up bowing to him in namaste.

Grayson lifted an eyebrow. "My call is over. You can use your words."

Cassidy's face flushed. "I thought you were...never mind. I wasn't expecting this surprise."

Reaching for the pans, Grayson gave her generous servings of bacon, eggs, and potatoes with onions and red peppers. She couldn't help the small laugh that escaped. She and Mya had planned an epic home-cooked meal for him that turned out to be a complete fail, and here he was, making her breakfast.

Cassidy's face grew warm. Grayson was confusing. Hot one moment, cold the next. In time, she would understand his unusual behavioral patterns. Maybe.

As soon as Grayson placed a fork on the plate, she pulled the dish toward her and dug in, not even waiting for him to serve himself. "This is so delicious, Grayson." With a mouthful of eggs, Cassidy swung her fork around. "Are you going to set a plate for yourself? Or does math sustain you?"

Grayson leaned forward on the kitchen island. "That *was* my plate."

What? But he smiled. He had never smiled at her before. Not like that.

God, she was reading him all wrong. This was awkward. So, so awkward. She put her fork down, and Grayson laughed.

He turned and reached into the cabinets. She caught a glimpse of the small of his back as his T-shirt lifted when his arm outstretched. He was toned there, too.

He set a plate down in front of himself. "Eat."

Okay, caveman. "Um, I wanted to talk to you about the kitchen. I'd like to start here first. I have some great ideas I want to run by you."

Grayson served himself the remaining food, and Cassidy watched as he leaned forward on his elbows to eat and, hopefully, listen to her talk.

"I would love to replace these floorboards with tile. This kitchen island needs to go, and we'll replace the top with glass. Something elegant and classy." She stood tall. "Then, I was thinking of painting the walls a nice seafoam green. Thoughts?"

He nodded.

"So, you like the ideas?"

His eyes bore into her with intensity and he nodded.

Cassidy smiled. "That didn't answer my question, but great. I'm going to be in here all day, so you just stay away. Sound good?" The silence was killing her. Cassidy avoided his gaze. "Or maybe a blue for the kitchen walls? I'll send you some color swatches."

Grayson turned to face the sink, and she shamelessly admired the view. He seemed in a relatively good mood, except Cassidy didn't know if he was listening to her or not.

She couldn't get the tumbling feeling out of her stomach every time she thought of Grayson tearing down part of the historic district, including the children's home. Maybe with him not yelling at her, she could get some answers and stop assuming he was a terrible person. "I was wondering...maybe we could enhance some of the *historic* aspects of the house?"

He looked over his shoulder and brought his eyebrows together.

"I mean, you're passionate about *history*, right?"

Grayson squinted, as if she were speaking another language.

"You just...seem like the kind of man who cares about preservation. I dunno, you...like children, right?"

His shoulders stiffened, and he turned to face her. His chest expanded, nearly filling the room. "Not particularly, no."

Well, there went her theory. All this conversation concluded was that Grayson Daniels was a prick. A prick who made killer eggs over easy.

He put the two dishes away and started walking toward the foyer. It was hardly a foyer, but that's what Colton had called it, so she would call it that, too.

Cassidy followed. "Wait. Where are you going?" She

had told him to stay away, but she didn't mean literally leave the house.

Grayson pulled on some aviators, and Cassidy's breathing ceased. He was immaculate.

Looking away, she scolded herself. She was an engaged woman. Even thinking a man was attractive was betraying Kyle.

He reached into his pocket and pulled out a set of keys. "Work. I dropped my suits off at the dry cleaners yesterday. I'm going to pick them up. I don't usually dress like this. It's far too casual." His teeth clenched, and Cassidy cocked her head to the side.

"Why would you say that? Jeans definitely agree with you."

Cassidy noticed the abrupt swallow in Grayson's throat. It was as if he were swallowing his words...if he ever said any to begin with.

He turned the doorknob to the front door. Before leaving, he reached into his back pocket, pulled out a thin leather wallet, and gave her a credit card. "Spend as much as you need."

She gaped at him. "All this rush just to give me a credit card? You could have easily done that through Colton. Is there a reason you demanded one of us here first thing this morning? On top of that, you haven't said much of anything to me since I arrived."

He grunted, but that wasn't anything new with him. What was his problem?

Sighing, he continued to hold his credit card out for her. She wasn't going to take it, not without answers.

She crossed her arms and eyed his credit card. "If

you think you can walk all over me, you have another thing coming, Grayson Daniels. Respect goes both ways."

He lowered his hand. "I respect those who keep their word, Cassidy. When someone says they'll be here at 7:00 a.m., I expect them here at 7:00 a.m. Not 8:00 a.m. If you had been here on time, as Colton had promised me, we would have had an hour to discuss the new kitchen you're going to install for me."

Cassidy stepped back. "I didn't realize—"

"Your ideas seem to be in line with what I envision." He paused. "Colton trusts you, so I trust you. But now, I'm about to be late for another meeting, so take my credit card and get to work."

She did as she was told this time. If she was going to be working this closely with Grayson on a day-to-day basis, Colton needed to better communicate the commitments he had made on their behalf. She was on the losing end of this battle, and Grayson had every right to mumble and groan, as she yapped his morning away.

She stood there for long moments after he left, until the crunching of his Jeep's tires against the gravel outside faded.

Her gaze followed the textures of the front wall, observing how the small skylights created patterns on the hardwood floors as the clouds passed by. Or, what had once been hardwood floors; they were severely scratched and aged.

She would refinish them after the kitchen was fixed up.

With a renewed sense of creativity, she pulled her keys out of her purse and headed out the door to buy supplies.

Home Depot was busy, and Cassidy bustled through the crowds with her cart to the paint aisle. Seafoam green, cobalt blue…

Jesus, there were a lot of shades of seafoam green. Which one would Grayson like most?

She took pictures of the wall of sample colors, emailed Grayson, and grabbed a booklet of colors to bring to the house too.

—

From: Cassidy Thatcher
To: Grayson Daniels
Subject: Home Depot

Grayson,

I'm picking paint colors. Which green speaks to you?

Cassidy

—

Immediately, she received an email back.

—

From: Grayson Daniels
To: Cassidy Thatcher
Subject: RE: Home Depot

The one in the middle.

—

That wasn't helpful at all. There were at least two hundred cards in front of her, displaying endless shades of green. Sighing in disbelief, she put her phone away.

"Can I help you, miss?"

Cassidy spun to see a young gentleman, probably in his twenties. "Yes. So, I'm dealing with a difficult man here."

His smile touched his eyes, and he chuckled in amusement. "Husbands are like that."

Waving her hands full of color swatches in front of her face, Cassidy shook her head. "No. He isn't—"

"This paint selection is popular this season. It goes on smooth, and you won't need a clear top coat." He reached past her and pulled out a different booklet showcasing a different brand than what she had been looking at.

"He's not my husband."

Uninterested in her declaration, he finally made eye contact with her. "Which room?"

"Kitchen. I'm thinking a nice green, but his

personality is sometimes cold and bitter, so a gray or blue might be fitting. What do you think?"

"I like vibrant colors. Purples, yellows. BEHR has a fantastic line of semi-gloss bases, and we can mix any color you like. BEHR is also great for accenting a kitchen backsplash. They're buy one, get one one-half off right now."

Would Grayson kill her if she painted the kitchen yellow? "Um, how about something not so..." she outstretched her palm, "eclectic? Think polished, refined, and professional. That's what we're going for here."

"Glidden has their Diamond Interior Paint line. We have a sale for a ten dollar can after the purchase of fifty dollars or more. A polished purple would be stunning."

"I don't want purple—"

"Over here, we have a new shipment of Ralph Lauren interior paints. Huge array of finishes that accent all wall textures. And here we have a local brand," he swung his hand toward the middle of the aisle, "that mixes their colors using clays from Arizona. Very innovative. Although the spectrum is limited since they're pre-mixed. And here—"

Her phone rang. "Thank God. Excuse me, please."

She lifted her cell to her ear.

"Hey, hooker. Guess what?"

Cassidy smiled. "Mya, Gaawd, I'm so happy you called. I was just about to be taken on a field trip in Home Depot." She looked behind her to make sure Purple Rain wasn't following.

"Oh, that's where you went. You disappeared this morning." Mya sounded chipper.

"You're in a better mood than earlier. What's up?"

"I have an interview today!" she squealed, and Cassidy could only imagine Mya jumping up and down. "It's a bookkeeping job at a local law firm."

Meandering farther down the paint aisle to where the brushes were, Cassidy stacked some rollers and painter's tape in her cart along with the array of color cards she had been carrying. "But you don't know how to manage your own money, let alone write financial reports for an entire company."

"Oh. Will I have to do that?"

Cassidy laughed. "Yes, Mya. That's likely something a bookkeeper does. When is the interview?"

"It's actually today at 3:00 p.m. They're looking for someone immediately."

"Just be yourself. I'm so happy for you. Did anything else exciting happen this morning?"

Mya sighed. "Well, I had a little online battle with Isabella."

"The one who's always trying to compete with you?"

"The one and only. Her and her best friend make me gag. She heard from Tony, the landlord from hell, that I moved to the dumps. On Instagram, she's been posting these quotes about how crazy it is that people from your past end up nobodies living in the slums, and she tagged me in it. She's trying to make me look like a fool. I mean, I knew the day would come that she would outshine me in her Prada heels, but I just wasn't ready for it."

Her shoulders slumping, Cassidy rested her elbows on the cart. "It'll be okay. And we aren't in the slums. I thought you liked our new apartment."

"I love our new apartment. But Isabella's Insta-face just wouldn't shut up, so I kind of told her a lie."

Oh, God.

"I told her…well, I left a comment saying that I moved to that mansion on Laramie Hill. The one next to Grayson's little hobo shack."

"You *what?*"

"No, it's okay. She has no idea Grayson's home is right next door. I just told, you know, a white lie, so I wouldn't look like trailer trash online. And she deleted her post anyway, so it's gone."

Cassidy's heartbeat was on fire. "You can't tell people that, Mya. Just because you deleted the comment doesn't mean it didn't happen. You can't lie about silly things. This is only going to come around and hurt you."

For a minute, Mya's labored breaths sounded through the speaker. "I'm sorry?"

"We'll deal with it like we do everything else. Just don't tell anyone else you live in that house. That wasn't smart."

"I promise." She took a long pause. "On a side note, I'm guessing Colton bumped up your hours?"

A loud, drawn-out sigh escaped Cassidy's chest. "Yeah. Don't even get me started. First of all, Grayson just grunts and groans and never talks to me. He literally gave me his credit card and told me to do whatever I want with it. I didn't know it worked like that."

"It probably doesn't, but Colton is his friend, and

this is his house, so it's more relaxed. Go with the flow."
Mya was making more and more sense every day.

"I'm trying to go with the flow, but he doesn't talk to
me like a normal person. If it's not work related, I bet he
just clams up like a…a…"

"Clam?"

"Yes, exactly. He's either moaning in annoyance or
smirking, lifting his arms, and showing his muscles—"

"What, now?"

Plucking some tools from the end of the row, Cassidy
threw them into her cart before continuing down the
aisle. "Yeah, like, pull your shirt down, Dr. Thunder
from Down Under. And on top of all that, I don't feel
like I'm communicating with him. He told me he
wanted the middle color. Out of hundreds. I don't
understand him." Huffing, she released her death grip
on the cart handle.

Mya laughed again, loudly. "Wow. And I thought my
life was rough. Speaking of sexy men, do you think
Grayson can introduce me to Lance? I've been reading
this book about finding your soul mate in six months.
You would actually like it."

Not this again. *Kyle* was Cassidy's soul mate. The
whole Facebook thing really threw her off the other
week, but they'd get through it…if only he'd write her a
letter. The stack of mail was still on the passenger seat
of the Lambo. She'd check when she got back to the car.

"Per this book, if the Universe feels that Lance and I
are a match, then him and I would ignite instantly.
Bonded like two particles in space. I learned that from
this book. I'm sure I'm saying it wrong, but you know

what I mean." Mya was worse than the sales clerk in aisle thirteen. Cassidy knew how much Brian meant to Mya, and here she was trying to mask her pain with the affections of other men.

Cassidy didn't know what to do. "For the love of all things green, if it makes you feel better, the next time we see Grayson, we can ask him if Lance would like a taste of your buns. And for the record, I don't want to read your silly book, and Grayson isn't my husband, for Christ's sake!"

Everyone's eyes were on her. This day was just fantastic.

Grabbing handfuls of random items from the shelves, Cassidy dropped them all into her cart. "Bleh, go away. Leave me in this hell."

"Toodles! Love you, too." Mya shuffled in the background, and the line deadened.

Cassidy sauntered back down the aisle. Gratefully, another sales rep was manning the station. Turning to the BEHR paint cards displayed on the wall to her left, she eyed the fern green, the spring colors, and the forest greens. Quirking her lips to the side, she put her hands on her hips.

Grayson wanted the "middle" one? He'd get the middle one. Walking forward, she closed her eyes and blindly grabbed a color somewhere in the middle of the stack. She handed the color card to the clerk, grabbed a few cans of base and primer, and smiled as the man at the counter mixed the color for her.

Rushing back to the Lambo, Cassidy stacked the cans of paint in the back passenger seat. She giggled to herself, eager to get back to Grayson's place and fulfill his wish of redoing his kitchen.

Cassidy plopped the roller into the creamy yellow paint and rolled it on the kitchen wall next to the sink. It actually looked amazing; the subtle color lifted out the warm hues in the cabinets. When she finished, the soft pastel would complement the—what did Colton call it? —chatoyance...chatoyance of the wood, so nicely.

She hummed loudly to herself, completely devoted to the single task of brushing paint on the wall. Up and down. Side to side. Up and down.

"That's the most hideous color I've ever seen. Mother of Pearl. Grayson agreed to this?"

Nearly squeaking in surprise, Cassidy spun to meet the green eyes of an incredibly handsome man dressed in a sport coat and beige khakis. His Italian, olive complexion and perfectly groomed hair looked familiar, but she couldn't be sure.

She beamed. "Grayson picked the color."

His face was expressionless, but his tone was slightly aggravated. "That doesn't surprise me, whatsoever. I didn't mean to startle you. I let myself in through the back. Grayson said to come in if he wasn't home, but the front door was locked. I was out there for five minutes knocking."

"Sorry, I didn't hear you. I'm Cassidy Thatcher."

Again, his face read no emotion. "Lance." He stood there with blueprints in his hands, looking around, cringing at the wall behind her. At least he could move his mannequin face, although a smile would have been nice.

The color really wasn't *that* bad. These men were intolerable.

Cassidy tried to get his attention by waving her hand. "Okay, Lance no-last-name. How can I help you?"

Lance faced her, placed the rolled set of drawings on the kitchen counter along with a small stack of papers, and took a deep breath. "Can you make sure Grayson gets these?"

"What are they?"

"Old stuff on the historic district and some paperwork he asked me to pick up for him."

A twinge of disgust poked at her gut. "Yeah, I heard about that project. The second High Tower."

Looking at his phone, Lance ran his fingers against the screen.

"I said, yeah, I heard about that," she repeated a little louder.

"I heard you the first time, doll." He didn't lift his gaze.

Doll? Who was this player, and why did he think he had the right to call her any pet name? Because she was underdressed in a tank top and overalls while he was all spruced up and smelling like fresh pine and expensive leather?

This Lance guy was not welcoming.

He turned his head and wandered toward the front door and back. Cassidy remembered his face now. He had been in a picture she saw of Grayson weeks ago after having been called a thief—not one of Grayson's finest moments. It all made sense. Lance was Grayson's partner. They complemented each other in every way.

After straightening the drawings he had just placed on the counter—to Cassidy, they already looked straight —he finally met her stare. "Do you know where Grayson is?"

She snorted. "He hardly speaks to me."

"Good."

What was that supposed to mean? Suddenly feeling protective of her yellow wall, she wanted Lance to go. The longer he stayed, the more she disliked him.

His casual demeanor depicted he had no intention of leaving anytime soon. Scanning the ceilings, the floors, the walls, her, his eyes on her made her feel dirty. They were accusatory and mean.

Brick by brick, her walls came up around her. "So, tell me, Lance—it is *Lance*, right?—would you like a tour before you leave?"

He looked at his watch. *Good grief, just leave.* "No, thank you. There's only a kitchen, a living room, and a bedroom upstairs." He put his free hand in his pocket and spoke to the empty walls. "You know, the High Tower's reputation is important to us, Cassidy. We've worked years to get where we are, and we...*Grayson*... can't afford to be distracted right now."

"I understand."

He snapped his head toward her. "Do you?"

"Yes. I promise this remodel won't distract Grayson

from your work duties. Colton has made it clear that the High Tower Lab comes first."

Lance turned his back to her and took a few steps toward the living area, leaving Cassidy swaying back and forth on her heels. Rude!

She stared at the blueprints in front of her and couldn't help the surge of curiosity from exploding. "Are you really going to tear down a children's home? Seems kind of heartless, don't you think?"

His back was still turned to her. "Nothing is official, yet."

"But I read in the paper that the children's home is on the block that the second High Tower is going to be placed on."

He sighed and slowly pivoted on his heel. His eyes were so intense and steadily increasing in potency the longer he looked at her. "When it comes to Grayson, know that he tries to do what he thinks is right. I support all—well, *most* —of his decisions." Why did he cringe when he said that?

Cassidy raised her eyebrows expectantly. "And the reason behind him wanting to ruin children's lives is…?"

Lance's phone rang. He swore under his breath in aggravation and walked back toward the foyer. "He doesn't want to tear it down. Will you just let him know that I dropped these off for him? I have to go."

Then he walked out the front door. She could finally breathe with him gone. Blueprints and the small stack of paper lay on the kitchen counter. She wanted to throw them in the direction Lance had just left.

So, Grayson didn't want to tear down the children's

home. She wasn't convinced. Why on earth was he even interested in the place? Eagerness to learn more about Grayson consumed her. She leaned forward, grabbing the stack of papers to sift through.

A twinge of nausea stabbed at her stomach. She shouldn't be looking at this stuff. But Lance had left it on the counter. It wasn't like it was confidential, right?

Cassidy's heart ached when she saw Grayson's name —a wildly different emotion than the possessiveness of the space that consumed her just moments ago. These were photocopies of adoption papers.

Grayson's adoption papers.

He had been an orphan.

God, she had gotten his intentions so backward. Was he trying to protect the place? Did he feel like he had to prove something to the world, to himself? There were so many unanswered questions.

And here she was, painting his wall a color he was probably going to dislike. She put the stack of papers down.

The creek of the front door echoed in the silence, but she didn't turn around. Maybe Lance wanted to come and roll his eyes at her one more time.

She jumped when the door shut with a *bang*.

"Didn't I make myself clear?" Grayson's hiss was vicious from yards away. Maybe if she stood in front of the wall, he wouldn't see the color. She didn't want to disappoint him. Not after discovering something so intimate about his past. She felt as though she knew him on a deeper level.

Cassidy groaned in despair. Guilt disbursed through

her. She could turn this around. "What, you don't *like* the color?"

"Colton said you were good at this."

Okay, he was unhappier than she would have preferred. "If you had given me better instructions…"

"I told you to get the middle one."

"Yes, and I did-*ish*. See, it's perfect. You chose the perfect middle color." She shrugged and smiled wide.

Grayson didn't smile. Instead, he rolled his shoulders. He had changed into a suit. Where had the casual, nice Grayson gone? Cassidy wanted him back. That Grayson would have laughed at this…or not said anything. Except the man from earlier had expired, and *this* Grayson did not look amused.

His teeth were clenched. "In the image you sent to me, the cards were stacked twenty-one by thirteen, that's 273 samples. I asked for the middle one."

Oh. He literally meant the middle. Who used such a general term to describe a specific object? Who was she trying to fool? She misunderstood him. "I'm sorry, I don't speak in matrices. You might as well have spelled it out in an algorithm." She laughed nervously.

He ran his hand down his five-o-clock shadow, his large fingers massaging his jaw. It was probably sore from him clenching his teeth all the time. Steam might as well have been spouting from his ears, as he examined the wall behind her. "I can barely look at this color for more than a few seconds without wanting to tear down the wall. I want it off, or we are going to have a problem."

What was she thinking, just grabbing a random

color? Especially after he lectured her that morning about punctuality. This man was her boss's boss. Not only that, but her boss's friend. She would have never pulled something like this with Mr. Turner at KMA. Grayson had every right to be upset with her.

But Mr. Turner had also never made her breakfast. And, even that had been a misunderstanding.

Knowing anything that came out of her mouth would upset Grayson more, she just rolled her lips between her teeth and waited for him to speak.

He sighed, and from the exasperated undercurrent in the air, she knew this discussion was over. Grayson stepped forward, and she stared at his shiny, black leather shoes, as they inched toward her. Her feet were so small compared to his. His hands were in his pockets. Hers were at her sides.

She couldn't get herself to look at him. His scrutinizing gaze from feet away was horrible enough.

Keeping her face turned down, she examined her dirty overalls in contrast to his trousers. If he only bent his knee, he would touch her.

Grayson lifted one hand and brushed a flyaway strand of hair from her ponytail. "I'm not upset. Look at me."

She lifted her head but looked past him. Even in her peripheral, his eyes were soft and comforting. As bright as the sky on display through the front windows.

"It's a hideous color, but I should have explained better. I'm told I'm a little intense sometimes. I'm just not used to people not listening to me."

With a sigh of relief, Cassidy caught a glimpse of his expression, but he was looking past her too.

She lifted one of her shoulders. "I should have listened better instead of being impulsive. I accept your apology. And, I'm sorry, too."

Grayson's eyebrow cocked in bemusement as he continued to fixate on something behind her. "That wasn't an apology. It was a statement."

She smiled weakly. Of course it wasn't an apology. Because Grayson Daniels didn't apologize. Following the line of his textured black tie, her gaze fell on the space between their shoes.

Something unfamiliar tugged at her core, as he reached for her ponytail and pulled the hair in front of her shoulder. Grayson widened his stance, and there it was again. That twisting, jabbing, numbing sensation in her spine. What *was* that?

She waited for Grayson to put his hand back in his pocket or down to his side, but he never did. A single finger brushed the underside of her chin, lifting her face toward him.

Then up a little farther.

She couldn't avoid him any longer and fixed her stare on his. His eyes were as stormy as her thoughts. They wandered lower…lower…down her neck to where her necklace lay. Had the oxygen left the room? No one had ever looked at her with such familiarity—not even Kyle.

There was something else hidden in the sculpture of his face—an expression she didn't recognize. Longing? How could it have been longing? Grayson didn't know anything about her. But, when his gaze tracked back and forth across the base of her neck, it was as if he were reading her life story in that thin, gold strand.

He cocked his head to the side, and Cassidy's throat closed.

Was he about to kiss her?

She was misreading him again, just like she had that morning, when she'd eaten his breakfast. Just like when she had assumed the worst about his intentions with the historic district. But the heat climbing up her arms was undeniable. She was frozen in time.

His lips parted as if he were about to speak. Perhaps he did, and she couldn't recollect.

He bent forward, and her heart stalled. "You have some paint on your neck."

She wished her entire body was covered in paint, so he couldn't see her crimson flush. He had barely looked at her when he came into the room so upset about the wall color. Now, all she wanted was for him to look away, but he couldn't seem to take his eyes off her.

There was a genuine smile on his face. It wasn't a smirk or his usual incredulous glower. He wasn't grunting and moaning. Was this the real Grayson? A mix of polished perfection and teasing afternoon glances?

He stepped back before Cassidy could blink.

She coughed to clear her throat. "Uh, so you aren't upset with me?"

Grayson's hands went back into his pockets. "I'm not pleased, but you will repaint this before tomorrow."

Cassidy blinked a few times. Had that incident been

a figment of her imagination? Did Grayson time travel to a parallel universe, brush the hair away from her face, and breathe the same air that she breathed, or had that been an illusion?

"I am meeting Lance, my partner, for dinner tonight. Feel free to stay as long as you like. Otherwise, I'll see you first thing in the morning. Colton said I have you all day, per the amended Clause III under Expectations." He walked toward the door, the air suddenly condensing enough for her to breathe.

What was she supposed to say?

Grayson looked over his shoulder with his signature smirk. "And don't keep me waiting next time."

CHAPTER THIRTEEN

HE SHOULDN'T HAVE DONE THAT. TOUCH HER, STAND close to her.

There had been hesitation in her voice the moment he walked in the front door. Was she nervous he wouldn't like the color? Because he didn't; it was *yellow*. It was nothing even remotely close to the pastel, fern green he had selected.

Now he was about to have dinner with Lance, and all he'd be able to think about was how she was going to scrub the paint off her skin. With a loofa? Maybe she'd just soak in a bubble bath until the flakes peeled off.

His body tensed at the thought of Cassidy in a bath.

Cassidy had been vulnerable in the kitchen, her timidity triggered by his disappointment. He wasn't entirely sure if her reaction was because she had to please him, or if she wanted to.

The mere idea that Cassidy could possibly want to please him was enough to send him into overdrive.

Every atom in his body reacted to her. Even from feet away…miles away…she expedited his every move.

Lance strolled in through the front door of Richard's and immediately made eye contact with Grayson. Removing his coat and giving an appreciative glance at the waitresses, he sat. "I need to talk to you about the quarterly reviews I had with my interns."

Grayson leaned back into the bench cushion. "We have a meeting about it on Monday. It's not Monday."

"I'd rather talk to you about this in person than in front of our senior associates from the other floors. First of all, did you see the way that waitress avoided you like the plague a minute ago?"

"Please, tell me there is an ending to your story."

"Grayson, my interns are terrified of you. During the reviews, they kept asking 'will Mr. Grayson be here?' and I'd say, 'no,' and they'd immediately relax."

"You wanted to work with the younger staff and train them. I can't help that you've decided to hire incompetent college graduates to do data analysis for you."

Lance laughed sardonically. "I only hire from Ivy League schools, per our mutual agreement. And sometimes they make mistakes, but that's how they learn."

"Well, they're making plenty of mistakes my team has to clean up. So, what exactly is the problem?" Grayson intertwined his fingers on the table cloth.

Smile fading, Lance briefly gazed at the ceiling. "The women at the office are a little scared of you. They just don't understand your…intensity."

There was an easy solution for this. "Teach them to understand me."

This wasn't the first time Lance had lectured him on this, but that's why Grayson had hired Lance in the first place—to talk to people. Grayson did the work. Lance blabbed his mouth, and his interns messed up their spreadsheets in an attempt to learn, then Grayson's team picked up the pieces and closed the deal. It just worked. When would Lance accept that Grayson preferred to stay behind his microscope? People didn't change. Grayson knew that.

Or, perhaps people just didn't know how to reveal all their layers, like Cassidy. She was impulsive, stubborn, and obnoxious, yet she had the power to awaken emotions Grayson had long buried.

After their meal, Lance tapped his fingers on the tablecloth. He wanted to say something, because he was doing that nervous flinching thing with his hands. *Tap, tap, tap.*

Grayson stared at Lance's wild drumming fingers. "Is there anything else you wanted to talk about?"

Lance stilled. "I spoke to a lawyer today about your little stunt on Ike."

Now, Grayson stilled.

"You need to stop this thing with Cassidy, Grayson. I know you better than anyone. I'm glad you've been avoiding her. For once, your personality flaws are working toward something good. We can work around the house thing until it's done, but you need to keep your distance." Lowering his voice to a whisper, Lance leaned forward. "If word gets out about you stealing a soldier's letters, and then hiring his fiancée for your own pleasure, because your dead sister *told* you to, all the work we've done will be for nothing. We'd likely have no say in what happens to the second High Tower, even though our research will be conducted there. The children's home certainly will be demolished, since no one will want to listen to a thief—I'm referring to you here—and you'll likely go to prison again."

Grayson folded his napkin and placed it on the table, staring down at it. "I get it. You want me to back off." It would probably be a bad time to tell Lance that he almost kissed Cassidy hours ago. And technically, she worked for Colton, so Lance's statement wasn't as bad in reality. Grayson thought he and Lance were in agreement about Cassidy. But, that was before a lawyer got involved.

Grayson lifted his eyes to Lance's.

Lance sighed. "Just try. That's all I'm asking. Just continue to be yourself and don't talk to her. But lighten up on my interns, will ya? Some of these kids are going to be great associates for us, someday. They just need a little patience." After the waitress picked up their plates, Lance smiled. "Cassidy is pretty, though. I didn't know what to expect, but she's a stunner."

Grayson rose from his chair, and Lance followed. "You met her?"

Lance flipped through his wallet. Grayson did the same, so they could both leave a tip. "Yeah, didn't she tell you?"

When Grayson stood in front of Cassidy earlier, how could they have spoken in anything but a whisper, with his face inches from hers? "Like you said, we don't talk much."

After Grayson's dinner with Lance on Thursday, the two of them pulled an all-nighter playing catch up. There was an endless amount of paperwork that didn't seem to ever go away.

Over the weekend and the next Monday, Grayson didn't return to the house to check on Cassidy. He was far too busy at the lab, but he also wanted to show Lance he was making an effort to keep his distance. When possible, he spent the nights working in his office. Every other time, he went to the house when he knew Cassidy wasn't there. Even though he didn't see her, the distance didn't keep him from thinking of her.

—

From: Cassidy Thatcher
To: Grayson Daniels
Subject: Punctuality

Dear Grayson,

I'd like to point out that I have not violated Clause III of Expectations. In fact, I am taking a sledge hammer to your kitchen floor right now.

—

She had attached a picture of herself with a sledge hammer and the stovetop clock to her right indicating the time. He couldn't tell if she had repainted the kitchen walls or not since the image was zoomed in.

—

From: Grayson Daniels
To: Cassidy Thatcher
Subject: RE: Punctuality

Dear Cassidy,

Please change back the time on my stovetop. You and I both know you tampered with it.

G

—

A light knock sounded at his office door, interrupting his thoughts. "Mr. Daniels, here is my analysis report." Bianca stood as far from him as possible, but close enough to hand him her stack of papers.

She was one of the new interns. She could have easily given this report to Lance...unless Lance was testing him. "Why, thank you, Bianca. I am impressed and very grateful that you got this done on time."

She nervously eyed the room. "Really?"

No, it had been due Monday afternoon. It was Tuesday morning, but he wasn't about to say that.

Bianca flipped her long black hair and stood taller, a wide smile on her face.

Grayson examined her. She was a polished, young, professional girl. Early twenties, fresh out of college.

Lance paid a lot of attention to Bianca. Grayson didn't think anything romantic was going on between the two, especially since Lance had signed an agreement not to screw staff members, but agreement or not, Lance still managed to hire the most beautiful—unqualified—women.

This was just one deadline; it didn't mean Bianca was incompetent. She could very well be one of his associates within a few years, if she could learn how to read a clock.

"Thank you for this." He waved the report and expected her to leave, but she just awkwardly stood in front of his desk, crossing her legs.

She crossed her arms uncomfortably.

Grayson eyed her curiously. "Is there something I can help you with?"

She remained twisted like a pretzel. "Yes. Sir, I was wondering if I could take this Friday off. My little brother is getting—"

"No." Grayson didn't need to think about it. Right now, everyone in the office needed to be dedicated to their projects. There would be no time off unless given proper notice, per their office policies.

Lance's words from dinner last week flooded his mind. Grayson could try to compromise here. He stood behind his desk. "Okay. You may take Friday off."

Bianca beamed and strutted out of the office.

He sat, satisfied. And Lance thought Grayson couldn't communicate well with women. He scoffed. Grayson pulled up his email on his computer and wrote a message to Cassidy.

—

From: Grayson Daniels
To: Cassidy Thatcher
Subject: House Meeting

I'd like to meet with you and Colton this evening to discuss the living room. Lance, Colton, and I are leaving town within the next two weeks, and I want to make sure we are on the same page before our trip. Let me know what needs to get done.

G

—

From: Cassidy Thatcher
To: Grayson Daniels
Subject: RE: House Meeting

Colton is working late tonight, and I have dinner with Mya. Can we do tomorrow morning instead?

—

From: Grayson Daniels
To: Cassidy Thatcher

Subject: RE: RE: House Meeting

I'd prefer tonight. You and Mya can have dinner at the house with me. I need Colton working on the lab. What time should I expect you?

—

Cassidy's responses usually came fast. Grayson sighed and stared at his phone, waiting for her name to pop up in his inbox. What, was she writing a novel? Tomorrow wasn't going to work because he and Lance had interviews for the secretarial position all day.

His desk phone rang. "Yes, Lance?"

"So, I was thinking we could go to Richard's tonight and come up with a game plan for our upcoming trip. I need to prep."

"I have plans with Cassidy tonight." Well, if she ever emailed him back. The line sounded as if it had been disconnected.

Lance sauntered down the hallway from his office and swung open his door. "I thought we agreed you were going to back off? Now you're scheduling a late-night rendezvous with her?"

Grayson lifted his eyebrows and crossed his hands on his desk. "I am meeting with her to discuss business. That is all." Really, he even invited Colton. This was entirely innocent.

With an incredulous grunt, Lance sat on Grayson's black couch. "You're going to be the death of me. You know that, right?" Lance snorted and rested his head on the back cushion.

"I told you, I'd try to keep a reasonable distance. I won't let anything happen to the lab."

Sitting upright, Lance ran a hand through the scruff on his face. "Screw the lab, Grayson. I just don't want you to get arrested over this. Yes, the lab is important, and I know what I said on Thursday, but I'm worried about *you*. You're family to me." Standing, Lance sighed, shrugged, and headed back to the door. Before exiting, he turned to face Grayson. "Please, just be careful. Think about the long term. And I'm begging you, don't fall in love with her. I'm heading out for the day, so we'll talk later."

Grayson nearly laughed as Lance walked back to his office. Love? Long term? Grayson's phone beeped, and Cassidy's name appeared on the screen. His heart beat turbulently as he swiped to read her newest email.

—

From: Cassidy Thatcher
To: Grayson Daniels
Subject: RE: RE: RE: House Meeting

We will be at the house at 7:00 p.m.

—

Relieved she agreed to tonight, he checked his watch. He had two hours to get home and either make dinner or order something. What would the girls like to eat? When he had first arrived in town at the beginning of summer, they'd prepared ribs—ribs that were inedible, nearly scorched to ashes, and neatly foiled and placed in his refrigerator. So, meat wasn't entirely out of the question.

He'd pick something up on the way to the house.

Stopping at a restaurant he thought the girls would like, Grayson bought an array of finger foods. Balancing the paper bags in his arms, he walked into the kitchen. As soon as he reached the island, he dropped his head and laughed.

Cassidy hadn't repainted the kitchen wall like he had asked. Instead, it was that same horrendous Easter yellow.

Groaning, he lifted his eyes and smiled. She was a feisty one. She'd likely keep it that color until the end of the project or until Grayson decided to repaint it himself.

Taking a few dishes out of the cupboard, he stacked them on the dusty island counter. Something looked different in the space, but he couldn't quite tell what that was. The time he spent at home was minimal, but he was starting to enjoy the distance from the lab.

The low hum of an engine pulled into the driveway next door. The girls were a little early. He walked to the front door, and smiling, he swung it open.

Cassidy walked through the entrance with two cans

of paint in her hands. Her face was flushed, and she had a sports bra on under her overalls. The sun's glow on her hair and bare shoulders made him hold his breath.

Grayson held the door open wide for her, and she passed under his arm.

She lifted her eyes to his and smiled. "You'll like these colors. For the wall." Nodding, she walked toward the kitchen, and her hips had complete control over his gaze as he followed her.

He wanted to say something snarky like, "you were supposed to repaint this wall days ago," or "you're disappointing me," but when she turned, crouched, and exposed more of her bare ribcage through the slit in her overalls, he couldn't find the words. She banged loudly on the floor a few times with a hammer, causing him to jump.

That's what was different. Cassidy had sanded the boards on the floor. He had thought she wanted to switch to tile...maybe she'd changed her mind. Either way, he couldn't help but trust her. But he'd be sure to be more specific, if she ever asked for his opinion on paint colors again. Next time, he'd go with her.

Cassidy stood and shuffled toward Grayson. She had been talking this entire time, but Grayson's mind had been elsewhere. "...Mya will be here soon. But I need to tell you something before you find out somewhere else." She looked away and bit her bottom lip.

"The anticipation is killing me."

She smiled sheepishly. "Mya got into an Insta-war with someone last week."

"A what?"

"Ugh. She went to college with Mya, and they've been competing ever since. Who's richer. Who's skinnier. I've only met her a few times." Her face flushed that beautiful shade of pink again. "Long story short, Mya said she lives here. Or, in the mansion next door."

Grayson could watch her ramble all day. She squeezed his arm as if trying to get his attention. Couldn't she see that she had all of his attention?

Nodding, Grayson bowed his head down to her. "I understand."

Cassidy shook her head and took a step back, and the imprint of her fingers faded from his skin even through his suit jacket. "I don't think you heard me."

Mya told someone she lived in the mansion next door. He had heard Cassidy just fine.

The front door knob jiggled, and footsteps drew close. Detangling her hair from an updo, Mya shook her head and let her thick locks cascade over her shoulders. "Why the silence?"

Cassidy turned and fiddled with the food on the counter.

"Don't tell me all at once." Mya placed her purse next to the sink. "What's going on?"

Grayson leaned his lower back against the kitchen sink and crossed his arms. "I hear you live next door."

Mya's jaw dropped, and she gawked at Cassidy. "You told him?"

He stepped in front of her. "No, it's okay. I get it."

Flushed and slouching, Mya shook her head. "I'm sorry, Grayson. I just don't have a job yet, and everyone thinks I'm a loser. It was the first thing that came to mind. I just blurted it out. Have you ever lied to protect yourself?"

Shrugging, Grayson smiled. "Your food is going to get cold."

Mya eyed the arrangement on the kitchen island. "Yaaas, you got egg rolls." Picking one up, Mya groaned in satisfaction. "I haven't eaten all day. Can we sit somewhere? I can't bear to stand in this pantsuit any longer. I need to take all of my clothes off right this second."

Cassidy gaped at Mya, although Grayson wasn't sure why. It wasn't as if Mya offered to strip or anything. She was just stating how uncomfortable she was.

Cassidy's lips firmed into a thin line. "You aren't at the *pole studio*."

Again, Grayson didn't have a clue what they were talking about. He collected some of the takeout boxes and led the girls into the partially furnished living area. The leather couch Cassidy had fallen asleep on was shoved in the corner, a lamp sat adjacent to it, and a square mahogany table lay in front of the fireplace. He set the food down on the table and walked to the kitchen to grab the rest and some plates.

When he returned, Mya was sitting on the couch and Cassidy on the floor that had been swept clean. She picked at a chicken kabob with her legs crossed and her hair re-tied into a fresh knot atop her head.

Mya removed her jacket. "Grayson, could you give me some advice?"

He didn't know what Mya could possibly want advice on. He nodded. "I can try."

"How do I get rich?"

Whipping her head around so fast the air around her face nearly whistled, Cassidy coughed.

Mya eyed Cassidy. "What?" She shrugged and gave Cassidy a *stop looking at me like that* face, her blue eyes playful. "Cassidy and I are practically broke. I've had three interviews within the last five days, all of which have been unsuccessful, and Cassidy's boyfriend won't write to her. Oh, on top of that, my husband is leaving me."

Cassidy turned her face away, as she nibbled on an egg roll. "These are good, Grayson. This is quite a diverse spread. Thank you." She avoided his gaze and scratched the underside of her forearm.

Mya's eyes were undoubtedly on him, as he stared at Cassidy, but he didn't care. There was hurt in Cassidy's expression. Her lips were in a slight frown. Her shoulders slumped at an angle foreign to her body. Tempted to reach out and rub her back, he clenched his fists in protest.

Laying his legs flat in front of him, he leaned on one arm while moving his shoulder closer to Cassidy's.

Shifting away from him, she shoved the egg roll into her mouth.

Mya crossed her legs on the couch. "Did I say something I shouldn't have? I do that a lot."

Cassidy smiled and filled a plate of stuffed mushrooms, egg rolls, sweet and sour meatballs, and miniature pizza pinwheels. She handed the plate to Mya behind her.

Watching Cassidy reach for a second plate, Grayson

took it from her and filled it with the same items she had given to Mya, then handed it to her.

Lifting her head, Cassidy smiled weakly. "Thank you."

Grayson grabbed the last plate and filled it with everything the girls didn't want. "If you were mine..." He stopped himself.

Cassidy gazed at him with intensity. What else was in her green gaze? Appreciation? He wasn't sure. She had never looked at him that way before. Her voice was barely audible. "If I were yours...what?"

What to say? There was no way he could tell her that he would write her every day so she'd never doubt that she had complete hold of his heart.

He cleared his throat. "If you were mine, I'd write to you every day, that's all."

"Oh." Snapping her face away again, she put an entire pizza roll into her mouth.

Mya munched on another egg roll. "I think Cassidy just has a hard time understanding people. Especially me. I don't mean any harm. She's too sensitive."

Too sensitive. *That's* why people didn't understand him. "No, I get what you're saying. Apparently, people have a hard time understanding me, too."

Mya uncrossed her legs, sat up, and examined Grayson. "I don't get it. I understand you just fine."

Grayson smiled. "Thank you, Mya." He looked over at Cassidy, who was nibbling on an egg roll again. "And you?"

She gazed at him from the corner of her eye. "What was that?"

"Do you understand me?"

A smile formed on Cassidy's lips, and she laughed lightly. "Hardly. I don't know when you're upset, if you're being literal or not, or if you're just being...*you*."

Grayson rubbed the back of his neck. "You sound like Lance." If Lance were here, he'd likely give Cassidy a high five. The two seemed to think the same things about Grayson's character.

He laughed at the thought of comparing Cassidy to Lance. While their lectures sounded the same, they couldn't be any more different. Cassidy devoted her heart and time to a lowlife who didn't deserve her, writing him letters and worrying about his wellbeing, while Lance couldn't keep his eyes focused on one woman for more than a few seconds.

Cassidy guffawed. "Yeah, that man and I couldn't be any more different. He came by before the weekend. He left blueprints...and some other stuff."

Nodding, Grayson eyed Mya, whose eyes were closed as she slowly chewed on a stuffed mushroom.

Mya groaned. "These are so good." She stood to come to the table to get more before sitting down. "Since you two have such a hard time communicating, why don't we work on this? I learned a few things from my marriage counselor. How different could this be?"

Cassidy shook her head. "Mya, I really don't think you're the best person to give relationship advice."

Grayson nodded. "Okay. How can Cassidy and I better our relationship, Dr. Rivers?"

Mya set her plate aside and stood in front of them. She was barefoot, although Grayson couldn't remember when she had taken off her shoes. She paced in front of the fireplace and Cassidy eyed Grayson as if he had poked the bear.

"Cassidy, Grayson, do you trust each other?"

Cassidy shrugged, and Grayson nodded.

"Good. Cassidy, have you ever considered having an affair?"

Cassidy pinched her eyebrows. "What? No. I would never be unfaithful to Grayson. Uh—I mean, Kyle."

Mya halted and quirked her lips to the side. "That was a weird question. Sorry, I'm just repeating the questions that our therapist gave us. Um...okay, I have a good one. Why do you want to work on your relationship?" Nodding in satisfaction, Mya continued to pace.

Grayson cleared his throat. "I guess, I want to see where this goes. I'm not good with people or so I'm told, and if you believe I need to improve, then I will fix myself for you."

Mya clapped. "Grayson, that was really good. Great job articulating your needs. Okay, Cassidy, your turn."

Cassidy rolled her shoulders. "I can't be in a relationship where there's no communication." She fixated on the far corner of the room. "I am the kind of person who needs reassurance that I'm doing things that make you happy, and when you don't talk to me, it makes me feel...I dunno."

Grayson smiled. "This sounds like a breakup."

Cassidy erupted in laughter.

Mya picked up her plate. "That was great, guys. Now we're past the awkwardness. Cassidy, you need reassurance, and Grayson, you want to improve...what, exactly, did you want to improve on?"

Cassidy was still smiling. God, she was beautiful when she laughed.

Grayson waited for her to make eye contact with him. "What do you want me to fix?"

Sitting, Mya picked at the rest of her food. She was in a world of her own, staring at the ceiling and being completely content with herself. Grayson was in another universe where only Cassidy existed.

Looking up at him, Cassidy whispered, "Can you smile more? I like it when you smile." The gleam in her eyes was back. The glow behind her irises was unmistakable.

Grayson leaned away from her and looked down at his plate, the heat of her eyes still on his face. "You're asking a lot." When she didn't say anything, he lifted his gaze to hers. He lowered his voice. "But I think I can do that for you."

CHAPTER FOURTEEN

DISHES CLANKED IN THE BACKGROUND AS MYA STROLLED into the living area. "I don't know why you said he's a tyrant. I really like Grayson."

Cassidy held her breath and stretched her legs out in front of her on the floor. She liked Grayson, too. Although, she would never say it out loud.

Mya reached behind her shoulder to scratch an itch. "In the kitchen, he was telling me about Lance and how they met in science class in middle school. How cute is that?"

That numb, twisting sensation jabbed at Cassidy's stomach again. Mya getting along so well with Grayson didn't sit well with her. Or maybe Cassidy had just eaten too many of those pizza pinwheels. "Super cute." She found it difficult to place charisma behind her words.

Instead, there was jealousy. Mya was so approachable and infectious.

Mya flopped on the couch and sighed. "Yeah, like,

when I say dumb things, he doesn't look at me like I'm stupid, you know? He just smiles at me, and it's really sweet."

"Why would he? You have an impressive degree in photography."

A chuckle escaped Mya's lips. "I know…but I know what people see when they look at me." She gazed at the ceiling. "They see a blonde-haired dummy who needs to drop thirty pounds."

Grayson came in to pick up the rest of the leftover food. "That's not what I see when I look at you, Mya."

Snapping her head to gaze at Grayson, Mya lifted her eyebrows. "Thank you, Grayson. If only there were more good men like you in the world."

Cassidy made an explosive sound from her chest. It was a mix of a laugh, a cringe, and a growl. And here she was thinking Mya and Grayson wouldn't get along at all, that Mya would cower under Grayson's crass tongue, but instead, they were two peas in a pod.

Grayson smiled at Cassidy. She didn't know where to look other than to the leftovers in his hands, as he turned and headed toward the kitchen.

That tingling in her stomach traveled to her throat, and she coughed and coughed to get rid of it.

At the same time, Mya cleared her throat.

Grayson called over his shoulder. "I'll get you some water, Cassidy."

After nodding incessantly through her coughing fit, Cassidy examined Mya on the couch. Her legs were flung over one arm, and her head lay on the other, her eyes closed, a small smile on her lips.

"Mya?"

Mya opened her eyes and turned to face Cassidy.

"Am I a bad judge of character?"

"Yes."

Cassidy's heart fell. "Wow, take your time to think about it."

Sitting up, Mya leaned forward and whispered, "Take Grayson, for example. I don't know why you said he was a brute. He's such a gentleman."

Grayson was also sort of handsome, a little witty, mildly sophisticated. Cassidy fiddled with her hands and rubbed her bare ring finger.

Mya giggled. "And he totally has the hots for you."

Cassidy shot Mya a confused look and was met with the biggest smile. The sparkle in Mya's eyes was intense, as if Cassidy were staring at a pile of diamonds. "I don't know what you mean."

"I'm just saying, Grayson and I connected on another level tonight. Maybe it's a full moon or something. I can read him like a book."

If only Cassidy could do the same. "And what does the *Book of Grayson* say? That he's attracted to tall supermodels? That's not me."

With an incredulous expression on her face, Mya rested her head back down. "Let's just say he didn't offer to bring *me* a glass of water."

Mya was being ridiculous, but her words seemed to lift weight off Cassidy's lungs. The oxygen that had been stripped from the room miraculously came back and her stomach stopped performing an uncomfortable circus act.

Grayson Daniels didn't have feelings for Cassidy. Or did he? She couldn't recognize the difference between a smirk and a grin or determine his mood from his body language.

Shaking the idea from her head, Cassidy brushed some flyaway strands from her forehead and stared into the worn-out fireplace. "Even if he did, I have Kyle. And until that's over, nothing can happen between me and Grayson."

Surprised by her words, she turned to see if Mya had been listening. Cassidy blew a stream of air when she saw her cousin dead asleep.

Grayson walked in carrying a glass of water. He still had his dress shoes on, his shirt was partially unbuttoned at the top, and his hair was deliciously disheveled—in an unattractive way, of course.

Afraid to make eye contact with him, afraid to see if Mya was right, Cassidy stared at his black leather shoes as he approached.

Grayson's feet stopped a few feet away from where she sat. "She's a deep sleeper, huh?"

Cassidy looked up at him. "You have no idea."

His eyes were downcast toward an empty spot on the floor.

Mya groaned and stirred on the couch.

Grayson hadn't been looking at Cassidy a second ago, but now his eyes bore into her. Oh God, he needed to look away. He was making her nervous. He held out his hand to her, and she stared at it.

After a long pause, she put her hand in his as he led her out of the living area and simultaneously handed her the glass of water, which she took with both hands to escape the sear of his touch. Wrapping her fingers around the glass, her fingertips brushed his, and she could have sworn she heard his breathing hitch.

He turned to face her when he reached the kitchen counter. "How is Mya with secretarial work?"

Cassidy laughed. "Terrible. She had an interview last Thursday to be a bookkeeper, and they were severely disappointed."

He tilted his head to the side. "Is she a fast learner?"

Nodding, Cassidy quirked her lips to the side. "Yes, she's a hard worker. She just needs guidance."

"Can she answer a phone?"

"Of course."

"Would she be interested in coming to my office tomorrow morning? Lance and I are holding interviews all day for a secretarial position. Pay starts at $23 an hour."

He had to be joking, but his sweet eyes told her otherwise. "Yes! She'll be there." Cassidy nearly jumped to hug him, but she refrained.

He smiled and cast his gaze downward and away from her. It was a tender expression. One of happiness.

He lifted his eyes. "Should we go to the loft to talk about the house?"

Grayson guided Cassidy up the stairs to one side of his bedroom that had a small desk. The entire walk to the loft, his hand was on the small of her back, scorching her skin through the thick denim.

He guided her up and let her sit on the chair behind

the small oak desk. She ran her hands along the top of it in admiration, and he leaned against the corner.

Pulling out his phone from his pocket, he placed it next to him on the desk. "Like I told you, I'll be leaving town soon with Colt. I just want to make sure we're on the same page, so you and Colton can coordinate. I'd like to avoid any kind of miscommunication."

Cassidy nodded. "I'll be sure to let you know what I'm doing. I'll send you pictures of furniture, and I can probably have the fireplace done in about a week. I'll have to verify with Colton, but I don't see why we can't work out details while you all are gone. There won't be any communication issues. I'll make sure of it."

Grayson laid out his hand flat on the desk inches from hers—she didn't move. "I'll email you every day."

She had no doubt he would email her every day. Part of her knew that Grayson Daniels was a man of his word.

Fixated on the proximity of their hands, she nodded again. "I guess I'll wait, then."

What were these feelings? Confusion? Good God, lust?

Betrayal?

Cassidy avoided eye contact as long as possible, until Grayson's finger found the bottom of her chin. She still only managed to stare at the base of his throat. This was the second time he had touched her there. The first time, she had completely misread his intentions.

Paying close attention to how his shoulders slouched casually, she trailed her eyes down the loose ripples of his dress shirt. She only partially had to imagine what was underneath.

Why was she even thinking about his muscles?

This was a work meeting. They already got through their communication issues earlier, thanks to Mya, but why did this feel entirely foreign to her?

Because this was not a work meeting.

This was Grayson's hand under her chin and her avoiding his alluring blue eyes at all cost, in fear of admitting her attraction to him. She could not—would not—let herself say it out loud.

Had he been speaking this entire time? Everything around her whittled away into silence. And was she standing or sitting? She couldn't feel her legs. Grayson had sat her down in his chair the last she remembered.

Did he spike her water with some weird Kool-Aid concoction he created in his lab? But she hadn't even taken a sip yet.

Grayson shifted his weight to the other foot. She would know, she was staring at them.

He breathed softly. "Cassidy?"

She whipped her head to look him in the eyes. She shouldn't have done that. She melted. "Yes, I agree to that. Sounds like a great plan."

The acute attention behind his gaze sent a feral burn into Cassidy's core.

He looked pained, almost hungry, in the way he stared at her. "Okay, then."

She couldn't do anything but nod and nod and nod.

Pulling away, he straightened his shoulders and held out his hand toward the door, telling Cassidy to lead the way. She stood and left the home office with Grayson in her wake.

When she reached the kitchen, Mya was there washing something in the sink. She reached for the glass of water in Cassidy's hand. "Let. Go. Cassidy." She pried Cassidy's fingers away one by one until her clutch released.

Cassidy struggled to speak. "We should go. Our meeting is done." The words came out breathy and constricted.

"Ok-a-ay," Mya sing-songed, dried her hands, and turned to Grayson. "I guess, I'll see you when I see you, GrayGray. Thanks for the talk tonight. It was fun."

Cassidy grabbed her purse, while Mya searched for her clothes that seemed to be everywhere. She left toward the living area in search of her jacket.

It was just the two of them once more, and Grayson stepped closer. He always seemed to do that, step closer.

Clearing her throat, Cassidy pointed behind her to the two cans of paint she arrived with that evening. "I'll repaint the kitchen tomorrow."

He shook his head.

"But I thought you hate the color."

He laughed. "Yes. It's terrible."

"So…you *don't* want me to repaint it?"

Grayson smirked, but it wasn't his usual glowering tug of the lips. This was almost…flirtatious. "Since you have a hard time understanding me," he stepped forward again, "I do not want you to repaint this wall."

"But—"

He hushed her with his index finger on her mouth.

His skin on her lips was more intoxicating than under her chin. She needed to get out of this house. Guilt and betrayal stabbed at her heart.

"Don't repaint it," he repeated, and the warmth of his touch was gone.

Mya walked out with articles of clothing in her hands. "I found my jacket."

Cassidy smiled at her cousin. Even completely disarrayed and half-dressed, she still looked stunning.

Walking up to Grayson, Mya kissed him lightly on the cheek. "See you tomorrow."

What was Mya doing?

Cassidy's jaw dropped. She had never seen Mya act this way with a man. She wasn't being her usual frisky self. She didn't stick out her breasts in an attempt to rub against Grayson's arm. She didn't even brush his chest seductively when she kissed him on the cheek.

Mya widened her eyes at Cassidy. "What? Why are you looking at me like that?"

Shaking her head, Cassidy smiled at Grayson and walked out the front door.

Grayson may have thought he was making himself clear, but Cassidy was even more confused than ever. If not about him hating—then not hating—the pastel yellow walls of the kitchen, it was that she couldn't understand her heart.

CHAPTER FIFTEEN

Mya was the worst secretary Grayson had ever had.

Lance scoffed. "I say, she lasts three weeks."

From Grayson's office, the two of them watched Mya decorate and re-decorate her desk. She was obnoxiously bright in a slim-fitting pink dress, and whenever the phone rang at the front desk, it looked as if she just put every client on an eternal hold.

Based on her current performance, Mya wouldn't last until Friday.

It had been two days since Grayson convinced Lance that Mya would be the best thing that ever happened to the High Tower Lab. Oh, how his lies were getting good.

Lance turned to face Grayson, shook his head, then left.

Come lunchtime, Grayson walked over to Mya and leaned over the counter. "Mya?"

She looked up at him with an innocent stare.

He leaned further over her counter to examine her computer screen. "Are you browsing job openings right now?"

She closed all open windows and leaned back, her hands folded neatly next to her keyboard. "Maybe?"

"You're terrible at this."

Mya let out the breath she was holding. "That's exactly what I told you in our interview, and you still hired me."

"You need to get better."

"How? No one has shown me anything. I didn't come out of the womb this fabulous. This took time, Grayson."

"Mya, it's Mr. Daniels here."

She put her hand up as if cutting him off. "Oh, hell nah. Don't even start with me GrayGray."

Jesus Christ. What had he done? This scenario was all sorts of backward.

Lance came out from behind the partition wall. "How have your first few days been, Mya?"

Grayson stepped forward. "They're great. She's amazing, just like I thought."

Mya cleared her throat. "But you just said..."

Setting a stack of papers at the edge of her desk, Lance folded his hands in prayer in front of his chest. "Do you think you can help me bind some documents together? They're due at 2:00 p.m. It's critical that they get mailed out today."

She had a blank look on her face, and Grayson

nodded his head in hopes Mya would somehow mirror him.

Sure enough, she nodded her head slowly. "Sure?"

Lance clapped his hands and walked off. "Thank you, Mya."

Grayson couldn't help but notice the flush on her face. He lowered his gaze and stepped out of the way, as if he were interrupting some intimate brain wave she was trying to emit.

Mya snapped her head to Grayson with another blank look on her face.

"Use your words, Mya. Why are you looking at me like that?"

She blushed. "I don't know how to bind documents."

Grayson tilted his head to the side and inhaled. "It's lunchtime. I'll show you. Follow me."

He was wrong about Mya. She wasn't just bad at answering phones, she was awful at just about everything. Grayson had to reprint two of Lance's reports because Mya inserted them into the machine incorrectly.

When she finally seemed to have a handle on things, Grayson handed her small stacks, and she would punch and bind them. They seemed to be gaining efficiency when Mya yelped, and the machine stalled. The jarring screech of machinery jamming echoed through the print room.

She beat on it with a closed fist. "I hate you, little machine. Ow." She looked at her finger and put it in her mouth. Eyeing Grayson, she whispered, "Paper cut."

Grayson turned the machine off, unjammed it, and angled his body toward Mya.

For some reason, she couldn't meet his gaze. Her hands lay limp at her sides. "I'm never going to get a job I'm actually good at, am I? I'm going to be the laughing stock of New York. My friends, if I can even call them that, can't even look at me. I know what they say behind my back. I am defined by my failing relationship with Brian."

She chewed on her upper lip and swayed in her six-inch heels.

He didn't know what to do. Per company policy, Grayson would usually defer personal issues like this to HR on the twentieth floor. But this was Mya, Cassidy's cousin, and he wanted to be the one to help her.

Grayson stepped forward and brushed her hair off her shoulders. "No one defines Mya Rivers." He placed his hands on either of her shoulders, until she lifted her empty gaze to his.

A small smile tugged at her lips.

"Come here. I'll show you how to do this and still keep your fingers." He held out his hand, and she passed him stacks of paper that he ran through the binding machine.

She spoke freely and without hesitation. "You know, when I first started working here, I thought you and Lance were rich."

Grayson chuckled. "Yeah, Lance likes to spin that story. We're really not that interesting."

She snorted. "No kidding. I also thought you owned this entire building. What the heck? You only manage the first two floors." She scrunched her face, her statement masked with a hint of disgust.

"Are you disappointed?"

She shook her head, then nodded. She eventually decided on a shrug. "A little, I guess. You're just different than I thought."

He grabbed all of Lance's papers, some bound better than others, and handed them to Mya. "Sometimes we can't help what other people think about us. We can only change how we view ourselves. Now, take these to the fifth floor, they'll send them out for you."

Nodding, she walked out of the copy room gracefully. He wasn't sure how she didn't fall through the grates that lined the floors in her needle-pointed heels. That was wildly impressive.

Grayson waited for Mya to return to her desk. When she did, her phone rang. She looked up at Grayson in horror.

"Answer it," he instructed.

She reached for the phone and put it to her ear. "The High Tower...Lab?" She pulled the receiver away from her ear and whispered, "It's for you. What do I do?"

"Forward it to me."

She shook her head. "But you're right here. Can't you just talk to him?" She tried to hand him the receiver, but he held out his hand and pushed it back to her.

"Tell him, 'Mr. Daniels is in his office, would you like me to forward you to him?'"

She repeated his phrase and nodded her head at him.

"Say, 'Please hold.'"

She did.

Grayson reached over the countertop ledge and forwarded the call to his office. Before retreating, he gave her a small smile and rushed to his office to pick up the call.

Cassidy walked the familiar hallway and spotted Mya's rear poking out from behind a wall. "I see you." She couldn't help but laugh as she walked through the glass doors that were propped open.

Mya dragged a box on the floor and stood. "It's too heavy for me. I'll have Grayson do it." She tip-toed to the back of her desk and sat down with a smile across her lips. "Welcome to the High Tower Lab, how may I help you today?" She crossed her legs and batted her eyelashes.

"You'll have Grayson do it? Well, I see who's in charge now." Cassidy laughed. "We were going to get groceries today. Did you forget?"

Lance appeared from behind a wall and smiled at Mya. "Mya, God, thank you for sending those documents out today. You're a life saver." He hustled to the end of her desk and acknowledged Cassidy with a nod. "Hi, Cassidy." His green eyes were softer today. His posture wasn't so tense.

Cassidy smiled weakly and looked down at her

brown cutoff boots. Today, she tried to not look like a hobo, in case she ran into Grayson. It seemed like every time he saw her, she was in overalls and covered in dirt. She wore a loose, white blouse that she managed to save after the apartment flood and her favorite pair of jeans.

Lance's voice was smooth when he talked to Mya. He wasn't tight-lipped with her as he had been with Cassidy the week before. She scanned their interaction. Mya used her hands to speak, and Lance watched patiently. He placed his hands in his pockets casually, as Mya's continued to float in the air.

He tilted his head to the side. "We should get lunch sometime. Purely professional."

Mya lifted one shoulder. "I'm actually super busy, but maybe next month?"

Lance's eyes widened, and a sheepish expression blanketed his face as he elegantly turned on his heel toward the back of the laboratory.

Mya cleared her throat and faced Cassidy. "Just a second. I have to get something. Wait here." She scuttled into a room in the back, and Cassidy watched her disappear.

She couldn't remember the last time Mya had so much energy. Perhaps the nuclear radiation was charging her up like a bunny.

As she stood there, Cassidy couldn't help but let her eyes search for Grayson. Low whispers filled the space as a few polished men and women trickled out of the office, one at a time.

Grayson crouched over one of the microscopes in the back where a young girl in a short lab coat practically tugged on his sleeve. She held a clipboard, and by the desperate pleading in her eyes, she needed his attention.

He tried to wave her off, but she continued to nudge his elbow. His shoulders raised and his back curved as he inhaled. Standing tall, he turned his face toward the girl and also caught a glimpse of Cassidy. He did a doubletake of her standing by Mya's desk.

Cassidy had never seen Grayson fully decked out in his geek-wear before. Only in *Science with Grayson*, which was nothing like seeing him in the flesh. Her breathing stalled.

The girl in front of him still tried to get his attention, but his eyes were preoccupied. A trail of heat traveled from Cassidy's forehead to her toes and back up again, following the path of his eyes.

Once he made eye contact with her, she mouthed "smile" while drawing an arc over her own lips with her index finger. She pointed to the girl standing in front of him.

He turned his face away from Cassidy and gave the girl before him the most awkward grin. Cassidy's heart warmed at his failed attempt to act normal.

A soft ring echoed from Mya's desk, and Mya shuffled, cursed, and hurried out to answer it. "This is the High Tower Lab, how may I direct your call?...Mr. Daniels is in his office, would you like me to forward you to him?...Please hold."

Seconds later, the phone in Grayson's office rang. From the other side of the office, he pointed in the girls' direction and winked. God, Cassidy liquefied. The girl with the clipboard threw her head back in frustration and followed Grayson into his office with a pen in her outstretched hand.

Mya cleared her throat. "Sorry, today's been a little crazy. What were we talking about?"

Leaning on Mya's countertop, Cassidy smiled. "Groceries? Today?"

Mya's expression sobered. "I'm sorry, Cassidy. I completely forgot. Grayson needs me to bind some documents for him by tomorrow morning, and he's going to teach me how to read lab results so when clients call, I can answer the basic questions about the atomic structure of their samples. And, I need to plan a trip for the boys next week to Seattle. They're going to be talking about the new lab downstairs, and it's kind of a big deal for Grayson. Phew. Super important stuff for the guys. Is that okay? Can we maybe go tomorrow?"

Cassidy smiled. "It's fine, Mya. Really. I can go by myself."

Cassidy didn't know what to make of this encounter. She'd only been at the High Tower Lab for mere minutes, but it seemed as if an entire season passed before her eyes.

Mya's phone rang again, and she lifted her shoulders. "Hi, Grayson. Okay, I'll tell her. By the way, you have a call on line two."

Cassidy crossed her arms and playfully tapped her foot against the linoleum flooring.

Mya hung up and smiled at Cassidy. "Grayson says, you don't have his permission to leave yet."

Permission? She snorted. No man had control over

her. Taking a few steps back, she retreated to the hallway. Before turning for the elevator, she tossed a glance toward Grayson's office. His back was to her, and he had his phone nestled in the crook of his shoulder as he finally signed whatever that girl was holding out for him.

With a relieved look on her face, she sauntered out and approached Mya, handing her the clipboard.

Mya's movements were graceful and smooth. She stuck out like a sore thumb in terms of clothing, but she had the biggest smile on her face. And that familiar interaction between her and Grayson? It seemed effortless and easy.

Cassidy's stare followed the path of the tables back to Grayson who held his phone to his ear with one hand and was looking straight at her.

This time, she didn't look away. He didn't drop his gaze, either. His face was a blank canvas until he mouthed, "smile." Then he smiled.

And, God, it was the most breathtaking thing she'd ever seen.

CHAPTER SIXTEEN

GRAYSON STEPPED OFF THE HIGH TOWER'S PRIVATE JET, and a wall of humidity closed around him. Droplets formed on his eyelashes, and he blinked them away, his eyes stinging from the raging wind.

Lance followed him down the stairs, trying to hold an umbrella steady over them both. "Do you think we could convince the High Tower CEO to get the lab our own private jet?"

Grayson shook his head. "I doubt it. The only reason he let us take the jet is because he's in love with Mya."

Lance patted his chest, looking for something. "She's only been with us for two weeks; can you imagine the things she'll do in a few months? She's amazing. Okay, so we have a meeting with investors this afternoon at three, then we have a break. Oh wait, I still need to confirm that. I'll have to call the others tomorrow, too—"

"I already took care of it, Lance. You really do worry too much." Grayson patted his own pockets to double check he hadn't left his phone on the plane.

Lance's tone was filled with irritation. "I told you, I'd take care of it."

Grayson huffed in amusement. "It would have taken you five hours. Even asking you to come to my office is a ten-step process for you."

"I get it from you, you know."

Throwing his head back, Grayson laughed. "I organize in advance to prevent issues down the road." He tossed a glance over his shoulder, as they reached the last step to the tarmac. "You stress about petty things and try to micromanage them. There is a big difference."

Grayson didn't need to see Lance's face to know he was rolling his lips in contempt.

Lance spoke through clenched teeth. "Yeah, sure."

Lance could dish the insults and call Grayson the introvert of the century, but he sure didn't like when the tables turned. It had been the same in college. Grayson excelled easily in their science and business classes. Lance was a top-tier student as well, but it wasn't as effortless for him.

Being competitive, Lance pointed out Grayson's personality flaws more and more, as their undergraduate academic career came to an end. It was as if that made Lance feel better for not being as good in everything.

When Grayson had to repeat the last semester of his senior year, Lance hadn't poked fun then. There was this mutual understanding that they were even. Different, but even.

Now that they were older, more mature, Lance's jabs were attempts to "help Grayson see his flaws."

Lance interrupted Grayson's thoughts with grumbles and groans about the rain. They rushed into Jackson Jet Center, their pilot close behind.

The middle-aged man smiled at Grayson. "I didn't close our flight plan in the air, so I'm going to do that now." He pointed to a computer in the back of the lobby. "Your luggage will be brought to you shortly."

Grayson shook hands with their pilot. "Thanks, Alexander."

"Thanks, Alex. We'll see you in about two weeks." Lance wandered off to the side door and waited for his bag. "This rain sucks, man. I don't know if I could live in the Pacific Northwest."

Cassidy was from the Pacific Northwest. Granted, it was more inland and not as rainy in Montana.

Grayson turned to face Lance, who stared out the window at the cloudy, dark sky. "I don't know. I can't imagine it being too bad living on this side of the country."

Lance laughed and brushed water droplets off his jacket. "I can't imagine you anywhere but New York. The best time of year around here is fall. Every other time it's either sunny or raining, and you never know what you're going to get."

Grayson didn't know what that meant. Lance was having one of his moods again where he seemed to know everything about everyone. "Well, I can imagine myself here."

"*Well*, I can't." Lance locked eyes with Grayson and shrugged. "Luggage is down. Let's get out of here."

After picking up their rental car, Lance drove them to The Four Seasons Hotel near downtown Seattle. "Wow, Mya really set us up. Girl knows how to treat us like kings."

That comment made Grayson smile. Mya had quickly become the best secretary he had ever had. She brought a much-needed energy to the lab.

In Seattle, Grayson and Lance were going to give a presentation on the High Tower Lab remodel and their research goals moving forward. Lance would do most of the talking, as usual. Jason, who owned all the buildings between McNolan and Oak Park, would arrive the next morning and discuss his involvement on New York's Landmarks Preservation Commission and talk about the construction of the second High Tower.

The High Tower's CEO would come later in the week with Colton, likely on Friday so Colton could focus on putting out fires for the majority of the week.

Unbuckling their seat belts, Grayson and Lance exited the car and walked to the front desk of the hotel.

Lance dealt with the reservations, flirting a little with the female staff, and Grayson turned his back to wait for Lance to finish.

Eventually retreating from the front desk, Lance walked to Grayson's side. "Okay, I'll meet you this afternoon to go over my spiel. Typical drill: You do the introductions, I'll fill in the gaps, and you close and answer questions about the new lab."

"Room key?" Grayson laid out his palm, and Lance handed him a plastic card. "I'll see you at 2:00 p.m."

They parted ways and Grayson settled into his room. He hardly glanced outside to look at the water and mountain view before stripping out of his rain coat, placing his suit jacket and tie on the bed, laying down on the white bedspread, and pulling out his phone to check his email.

———

From: Grayson Daniels
To: Cassidy Thatcher
Subject: Seattle

Dear Cassidy,

This is the first of many emails to you. I trust you are behaving in my absence.

On a side note, I've decided to paint the bedroom blue.

———

He sat up and searched the luggage he had placed next to his bed for his laptop. He had a few hours to run through some lab results from his associates before meeting with Lance again.

His phone dinged.

—

From: Veronica Amelia Gomez
To: Grayson Daniels
Subject: Catching Up

Darling Grayson,

I heard you're in Seattle. I'll be in town this weekend, if you'd like to get a drink.

With all my heart,

Veronica

—

He groaned, locked his phone, tossed it beside him on the bed, and exhaled. That woman just didn't know when to stop. Seeing her at The Jamaican a few weeks ago stirred rage in the pit of his chest. Now, she was a vulture just waiting for her time to feast.

She wouldn't have the opportunity. After their fallout ten years ago, she piggy backed on her father's success and started her own company that eventually went bankrupt. And now that Grayson was contributing to the success of the research at the High Tower, she had appeared out of nowhere. It wasn't a coincidence, and he wouldn't fall for it.

Veronica was looking for a second chance at something. He just wasn't sure what her angle was yet.

His phone vibrated, but he ignored it. He pulled out his laptop to check Lance's proposals and his own team's submissions for new and upcoming projects. Falling into the rhythm of work, the frustrations of the day dispersed and the fog in his mind cleared. Eventually, time didn't feel stagnant and minutes turned to hours until a reminder for Lance's 2:00 p.m. meeting popped up on his screen.

He reached for his tie and saw a notification from Cassidy on his cell. He opened his email app.

—

From: Cassidy Thatcher
To: Grayson Daniels
Subject: RE: Seattle

Blue? Have you lost your mind? You need to have the bedroom painted white. It'll look way better with your bed frame. Your bed, by the way, is enormous.

Sincerely,

Cassidy

—

Grayson laughed and opened a text message to her.

Grayson: So...you've been spending time in my bedroom?

He could visualize her flustered face—her perfect blush—while reading his text, and it made him smile. He sent his message, then set his phone aside to get some more work done.

Later that evening, after meeting with donors and listening to Lance share their ideas about not demolishing the children's center, Cassidy was still on his mind.

He hadn't heard from her all day. Had he crossed a line with her? He drove himself mad with wonder. Meanwhile, he and Lance shook hands with new acquaintances, old friends, and random people who were brought along for their meetings. He drank wine and tried his best to socialize without sounding crude or annoyed. But when an investor suggested tearing down the children's center to build a gym for building tenants, Grayson guffawed and said that was the stupidest idea he'd ever heard.

Breath.

Another breath.

Lance jumped in, suggesting some alternative options for "relaxation." Perhaps a tennis court or a climbing gym on the far end of the new tower. He deflected the conversation away from Grayson's obvious agitation.

After their meeting, Lance turned to Grayson as they entered one of the restaurants on the first level of the hotel. "So, you don't care about fitness?"

A choked grunt escaped from Grayson's throat.

Lance bowed his head so low his chin skimmed his chest. A low chuckle erupted from him. "Remember when we'd go with rich-man Parker to his meetings? You got your closing skills from him. What do you think he would have said to that guy?"

A sly grin appeared on Grayson's lips. "Parker would have said exactly what I did. I made him proud today."

Lance laughed. "Yeah, calling an investor stupid is on the top of your list of accomplishments." He looked at Grayson. "No, he would have said something like, 'Have you ever been homeless? Broke? Abandoned? My boy, Grayson, has. You should try it. It builds character.'"

It was Grayson's turn to laugh.

After dinner, they had drinks with a previous client who was in town. He talked about his family and his newborn baby, and how he believed the baby wasn't his. Grayson wasn't at all interested in this man's family drama, but he nodded and drank his whiskey, while Lance talked about his own parents who were visiting extended family in Italy.

All Grayson wanted to do was text Cassidy and ask how her day was. His hand was fixed over his pocket so he'd be ready to respond quickly if she messaged him.

She sent nothing.

Occasionally, Lance eyed him. It was a look that said Lance knew what Grayson was thinking, but that couldn't be possible. Lance could scowl all he wanted, Grayson had other things on his mind.

He'd tried to keep his distance from Cassidy at first. He had kept his word to Lance. But spending time with her and Mya, and seeing the distant look in Cassidy's eyes when Kyle was brought up, Grayson's resolve evaporated. The need to fill that emptiness inside her was overpowering.

After giving their presentation on the new High Tower Lab for the umpteenth time the following Monday, Grayson and Lance were ready to retreat to their rooms. Jason and Colton had left for New York just about as fast as they came. Grayson and Lance hardly had any time to talk to them as they conducted their business in different areas of the hotel. Still not having heard from Cassidy, Grayson was getting anxious and eager to return home as well.

Lance walked into the elevator next to Grayson. "I know what you're thinking, Grayson."

"I highly doubt it." He pushed the button for the twelfth floor.

"How is Cassidy?"

It was none of Lance's business. Grayson emailed her every morning and evening, just like he said he would.

"I know you're thinking it's none of my business," Lance whispered.

Grayson stared straight ahead as the elevator doors shut.

"Do you have feelings for her now? You can tell me, you know."

When *hadn't* he had feelings for Cassidy? Protectiveness, trust, surprise, happiness, lust. She brought the full color spectrum into his otherwise grayscale life.

Grayson sighed. "What if I do?"

Lance rocked on his feet.

Grayson lowered his voice. "I can't help it, Lance. It's like I'm tethered to her." He wasn't sure if Lance could hear the declaration.

The elevator dinged one floor at a time, stopping at intervals to pick up one or two hotel guests with towels, searching for the balcony pool area.

A pause was placed on their conversation when others were in the elevator, but when alone again, Grayson turned to face Lance. "You can try to pull me away from her, but I'll go straight back."

Lance nodded. "Okay."

Okay? That was it? For months, Lance had badgered Grayson about Cassidy. Lance begged Grayson to back off when they were on Ike, and Lance continued his sermons long after they arrived on solid ground. Now, all of a sudden, it was okay?

Shaking his head in exasperation, Grayson waited for the elevator doors to open on their floor. When they finally did, he stormed out, but Lance grabbed him by the bicep. Grayson didn't want to get into this with him, again.

Lance's eyebrows pinched together in concern. "I'm not saying I like it. If her fiancé finds out, this could cause problems for you. Our lawyer said so himself. As your business partner, I'm asking you to back away. As your friend...I haven't decided yet. I want you to be happy. Although, I don't know how you could possibly be happy after letting her paint your kitchen yellow. That's just wrong."

Grayson relaxed and smiled. That wall was a hideous color, but every time he looked at it, it radiated

Cassidy's charisma and stubbornness. It was everything he adored about her. He wouldn't change that for anything.

Lance tilted his head as if examining him. "I support you. Just like I always have. I even support you wanting to protect the children's center, even though the rest of the city wants to tear it down for the second High Tower. This is more than a way of getting over Katrina's death."

His fascination with Cassidy had started out that way, a desperate attempt to be forgiven by a ghost. He didn't mean to fall for Cassidy in this way, but he had.

Lance ran his free hand through his mahogany hair. "I even think I saw you smile this morning. In fact, you should bring her on that camping trip you promised Jason you'd attend."

Grayson groaned. Why had he said he would go to that? Oh, that's right, because Jason had the impressive ability to spam text at the worst possible moment.

Wiggling his eyebrows, Lance let go of Grayson's arm and took a few steps back. "I'm just saying." He shrugged, smiled, and turned toward his room down the hallway.

Grayson filled his lungs with a steady stream of air. He didn't want to disappoint Lance, and even though Lance still had his concerns, that simple "okay" was enough. Grayson hadn't been able to breathe this freely for weeks.

He would pursue Cassidy if she'd have him. And he wouldn't feel criminal about it.

That Monday passed, and the rest of the week flew by even faster. Lance attacked each meeting with finesse, and Grayson sealed the deals. The investors interested in funding the High Tower expansion were enthusiastic about their plans and generous with their money. Most people were curious about the new laboratory, and Grayson enjoyed talking about what they'd do with that new facility.

"We will need to send all these people invitations to the lab's banquet at the end of summer," Grayson reminded Lance as they walked to their rental car. Grayson kept checking his phone. Cassidy still hadn't replied to any of his emails or texts, and he was starting to get worried. "I think it'll be the best one yet, considering construction is almost done. I'm surprised more people here were interested in our lab construction than the High Tower expansion."

Nodding, Lance pulled out his tablet and jotted down some notes. "We should also invite the city's veterans. What do you think about that? The banquet is for us to give back to our interns and associates, but I feel that would be a nice ending to our chapter on Ike. Maybe we could actually fill a venue this year." He laughed.

Grayson smiled. "Yeah, I like that a lot. Don't forget to invite the kids at the children's home, too. I want them there."

Raising his eyebrow, Lance coughed lightly. "You sure?"

"Just keep them…confined. If I hear anyone cry, or see any kids running around causing trouble—"

"Okay, I'll take care of it. Don't worry." Lance laughed, as Grayson sauntered to the passenger side of the vehicle.

Lance fastened his seat belt and started the engine. "Want to grab an early lunch?"

Grayson pulled out his phone to write an email to Cassidy.

—

From: Grayson Daniels
To: Cassidy Thatcher
Subject: AWOL

Cassidy,

It's Friday. I haven't heard from you since last Wednesday. Are you receiving my emails? Are you okay?

G

—

Grayson put his phone away and turned to Lance. "I'm sorry, can you repeat that?"

Putting the car in reverse, Lance look over his shoulder. "Do you want to grab lunch?"

Nodding, Grayson put his phone into his breast

pocket. "I'm worried about Cassidy. I haven't heard from her since last week."

Lance paused. "Colton's probably slave driving her."

Yeah, that's the last thing he wanted to think about. Colton never seemed to be able to keep his eyes off Cassidy when she was around. No one could.

Grayson shrugged. "Colton was only out of town for a day and a half, I can't imagine him doing that to her." Something poked at the base of Grayson's skull. He reached behind his head to massage there. "She's incredibly responsive. I just know something's wrong."

He had probably pushed the boundaries of professionalism by texting her and asking if she was in his bedroom.

Grayson fidgeted with the smooth material of his pant leg, then fumbled around in his suitcase, searching for something, but by the time he unzipped it, he couldn't recall what the item was. He watched the trees pass by outside in a blur. Closing his eyes, he took a deep breath.

Lance's voice was in the background, but Grayson didn't pay attention. He was sure there were words like, "don't worry," and "I bet she's okay." Or perhaps he was asking Grayson if he was alright.

He opened his eyes and grasped his phone in search of Mya's desk number.

"Good morning, Grayson. What's up?" Mya's cheerful voice calmed the squall line traveling through his chest.

He was just overreacting. "I just wanted to check in on you. How are you doing?"

"I'm great! You should promote me."

Grayson couldn't help but laugh.

Mya sighed. "I'm just trying to comfort Cassidy, you know? She's barely at our apartment. She just kind of hangs around your house and pulls out floor boards all day."

"What do you mean you're comforting Cassidy?" A slight chill passed down his spine.

"Oh, she didn't tell you?" Hesitation flooded Mya's voice. "I don't want to—"

"Tell me what happened," he demanded.

"It's Kyle. Her douchebag of a boyfriend—sorry, *fiancé*—broke up with her last week. She's a total wreck, but she won't let me near her."

It was no wonder she'd been so silent.

Grayson lowered his head. "I see."

He should have been relieved that things were over between them. Hadn't he shielded and tried to protect her from Kyle while sailing the Atlantic?

The thought of Cassidy hurting ignited an unsettling sensation in his gut. But, the fact that she didn't want to tell him what was going on in her life bit at his heart, especially after trying so hard to build somewhat of a trust between them.

Apparently, he wasn't trying hard enough.

Mya's Lambo was parked behind his Jeep. Grayson didn't know if that meant he should be more worried or relieved. Grayson fumbled with his wallet, paid the cab driver, and slowly walked away from the vehicle toward his hedge.

When he reached the front door, it was unlocked.

He swung the door open. "Cassidy? Are you here?"

Pausing, he listened to the sounds of the house for footsteps, an echo, the sound of her hammer beating on something. There was only the hammering inside his chest. Grayson had continued to email Cassidy through her silence, in hopes that she would eventually open up to him, but she never did. He even extended his stay in Seattle a few extra days to give Cassidy some space. Since she seemed to find comfort in his home, he didn't want her to feel like she had to leave. Yet at the same time, all he wanted to do was see her.

Grayson entered the living room. "Cassidy, answer me."

She lay on the couch, her face turned away from him. She stirred in the dim-lit room.

Worry consumed his heart, and he walked toward her. "Cassidy, sweetheart?"

Sitting upright, she wiped her eyes and turned to face him. Sniffling, she kept her gaze at his shoes. "I'm sorry, Grayson. I was so tired. What time is it?"

He wasn't sure what the time was. It was mid-afternoon. The living room looked about the same as when he left it—his stone fireplace still as beat up as before. He rushed to her side and sat next to her. "Will you talk to me?" He brushed her hair away from her face and saw tear streaks down her face.

She looked more empty than sad.

Cassidy covered her face with both of her hands,

and a letter fell onto her lap. Grayson picked it up.

Cassidy,

I really love you a lot, but I don't see this working long term with me here, and you in Montana. We're too different, you know? Everything is going so well here. I'm advancing like crazy and getting promoted. I just don't think I have time for a relationship right now. When I come home, I'll reach out to you, and we'll see if I still have feelings for you, okay?...

Out of all the honorable men in the military, Cassidy had to give her heart to the loser of the lot. Grayson didn't need to read the entire letter. The thing was five pages long and seemed to only talk about Kyle's needs and wants.

After having met the guy, Grayson assumed Kyle completely lost interest in Cassidy. Or perhaps he was afraid that Cassidy would leave him, and he wanted to be the first to cut ties. Either way, it cast disappointment over Cassidy's beautiful face.

Looking back down at the letter, it was dated near the end of spring while Grayson had still been on Ike. It was practically the end of summer now. He rubbed Cassidy's back, and she easily leaned into him. He wrapped his arms around her and cradled her head into his chest.

Kissing the top of her head, he whispered into her hair. "When did you get this?"

She sobbed silently into him, and he only held her tighter. "It's been sitting in my pile of mail for God knows how long." She sniffled. "It was there the whole time on the passenger seat of Mya's car." She nuzzled into him and wrapped her arms around his waist.

He rocked with her, as she told the story from the beginning. How she found the letter, how she was so elated. And now, all she wanted to do was rip her own heart out, so it wouldn't ache anymore.

"Grayson, it hurts. My heart hurts." She squeezed him tight, and he ran his hands through her hair.

"I'm here. Everything is okay."

She pulled back quickly, her eyes puffy and swollen. She swallowed a cry and sat up straight. "I'm sorry. This is so unprofessional of me." Laughing at herself, she turned and stared at the hardwood floor at her feet.

Grayson reached for her hand and placed it in his own. He brushed his thumb against her soft skin. "What can I do to make this better?" His heart swelled for her. He wanted to hold her to him once again and transfer her suffering to himself.

She gazed at their hands and hiccupped. "Can we talk about something else? Maybe about you instead of me?"

Grayson nodded.

She sat expectantly. Did she want him to share something, or was she going to ask him a question? He wanted to hold her and make her pain go away.

She sniffled again. "Have you traveled anywhere nice lately? Tell me about it."

If talking to her about himself was going to ease her pain, he would do it. "I don't take vacation." That probably wasn't the comfort she was seeking. He cleared his thoughts. "This last spring, I was doing some training on an aircraft carrier—"

She snapped her head up. "Oh my God, were you on Ike? Did you know Kyle?" There was hope in her eyes. "Did he ever talk about me?"

What to say? Grayson had been on Ike, and Kyle *had* talked about Cassidy, though never in a good way.

Cassidy blushed, and an alligator tear welled in her eye. "Augh, I'm sorry. I shouldn't—" *hiccup* "—drag you into this."

With his free hand, Grayson reached to brush away her tear, as it trailed down her flushed cheek. To protect her, he did what he thought was best. He leaned close to her and whispered, "I don't know Kyle."

She was sitting too far away. He tugged on her hand, and she scooted closer to him, her eyes wide with sadness. He wanted to touch her, soothe her, but didn't know how much was *too* much. He didn't know the right things to say.

Grayson released her hand and lifted his arm for her to rest under. "I know I can't make the pain go away, but I'm here for you."

She smiled weakly and leaned into him, her head on his chest, droplets of water falling from her eyes and staining his suit jacket. "I sacrificed everything for Kyle. My dream job was in New York, but I settled for an okay life in my hometown. I love my hometown, don't get me wrong, but ever since my parents died, it just feels empty there."

"How old were you?"

"Sixteen."

He continued to brush her hair with his fingertips. "I lost someone when I was sixteen, too."

There was a force field around them, an aggravated magnetism. It was unsettling, yet at that moment, Cassidy sank into him, and they became one. They lay there, Cassidy pushing into Grayson's side, as she breathed short, shallow breaths.

She rested her cheek against his chest. "My parents died because of me. *Me*, Grayson. I ran away from home, and they came to try and find me. They died that same night. And, the last thing I said to them was 'I hate you.'" She sniffled and wiped her tears off with both hands. "That was the last time I ever got really angry at someone to the point of yelling. Then you, of course. And Mya makes me angry sometimes. But you seem to frustrate me more than anyone else. Everyone I care about leaves me."

I won't leave you, he wanted to say. Part of him felt responsible for this. Stealing her letters was a catalyst for Kyle breaking her heart. Grayson would never tell her. Yet there she was, her cheek resting on his heart, where a small lavender envelope permanently resided in his breast pocket.

He tried to be as still as possible and inhaled through his diaphragm so Cassidy's head wouldn't abruptly rise with his chest. "With all the things that happen in space and time, there's no way that one instant could have possibly been your doing."

A hollow laugh left a trail of warmth down Grayson's chest. Cassidy's shallow, choppy breaths deepened, until her eyes finally closed.

Grayson squeezed her shoulder comfortingly and smoothed out her baggy sweatshirt. She had placed her shoes to the side of the couch, and her toes curled and flexed, as she fell into a deeper sleep. Cassidy willingly snuggling up to him was unlike any other sensation. They had managed to lean over slightly, her body cuddled into his as he half-lay on the leather couch in his living room. Sadness still registered on her face, but her tears dried and the muscles in her cheeks relaxed.

A week had passed since Grayson fell asleep on the couch with Cassidy in his arms.

Mya opened the front door holding a stack of papers. "How is she? She's barely at the apartment, and she won't talk to me." She passed the pile to Grayson and shivered. "Jeez, it's getting chilly outside. This summer has gone by way too fast."

Cassidy had barely spoken to him after he woke up alone on the couch. He wasn't sure if he should tell Mya that detail. "She hasn't really spoken to me this week. She'll start to strike a conversation, but her mind is elsewhere. She's been painting the loft all week. I don't know how many layers she thinks she needs, but she's in there every day." He pointed upward. "It's Saturday, and I bet you she'll be up there painting all day."

Mya's head dropped, and she sighed. After a long groan, Mya lifted her gaze. "Is she crying?"

"Not anymore. That stopped on Wednesday."

She couldn't hide the bitterness in her tone. "Good. Maybe she finally saw Kyle's true colors. He was a jerk."

"Yeah. Had a smug face, too." Grayson placed the paperwork on the kitchen counter and realized what he had just said.

"So, you've seen a picture of him? He kind of looks like a bull dog to me." Mya rolled her eyes and twirled a blonde lock around her index finger.

He needed to be more careful. He leaned against the counter top. "Is there anything I can do to help?"

"We need to do nice things for her, and get her out of the house."

Grayson smiled. "I have an idea."

Fifteen minutes later, Grayson began making an early lunch. Mya offered to help, but when she managed to burn a teaspoon of butter, he demanded she go away.

She sat at the newly finished island, a stunning glass counter with a matte design etched into it. "So, what's the plan?"

Wasn't it obvious? "I'm going to make her lunch." He rubbed his palms against his jeans and adjusted his sweater.

Mya's jaw dropped. "That's your grand idea? Cooking for her? Do you not know women at all?" She threw her hands up in the air.

Grayson thought this was a great idea. He turned off the stove, frustrated. "Do you have anything better in mind?"

"Take us *out*. Let's go do something. Take her to the museum. She loves that dinosaur stuff. Give her a tour of your lab—"

Laughing, Grayson crossed his arms over his chest. "You think giving Cassidy a tour of my research lab is a better idea than cooking for her?"

She nodded.

Women were impossible.

But he did have another plan. He took his phone out to text his buddy from the Cooper Hewitt to see if they could make it happen.

Cassidy came around the corner with her hands covered in white paint, and she nodded toward the sink, indicating she needed Grayson to get out of her way.

He obeyed. "Are you hungry, Cassidy?"

She shook her head. "No, not really. Hi, Mya. I've missed you. Sorry I've been gone so much." This was a start. At least, she was talking.

Grayson looked to Mya, and she flicked her hand out, as if urging him on.

He eyed Cassidy. "You're coming with me today."

Mya palmed her face and shook her head.

Cassidy didn't take her eyes off her white fingertips as she scrubbed her hands.

Grayson cleared his throat. "Would you…like to go somewhere today?"

Cassidy's head spun around to meet him. There was a hint of a smile across her lips mixed with interest. The urge to lean forward and kiss her was irrefutable.

She turned off the sink, dried her hands, and straightened her T-shirt. She paused for a long moment. "I guess, I should get out of the house. Should I change?"

Smiling, he cupped either side of her face. "Just get in my car, and let's go."

She stared at him, and when he realized his hands were on her face a beat too long, he quickly dropped them to his sides.

Cassidy turned to Mya. "You coming?"

Putting her hands up, Mya shook her head. "Nope. I have no desire whatsoever to go anywhere. I'm going to hit the pole this afternoon."

Whatever Mya meant by "hit the pole," he wasn't going to ask.

Cassidy looked up at Grayson in that innocent way that gripped his heart. "Okay then, I'm ready."

He could sense her excitement the entire drive. She had no idea what was coming. He couldn't believe she could be any more beautiful, yet here she was in his car, that stunning, show-stopping sparkle in her eyes. The sadness in her expression seemed to be replaced with curiosity.

She turned to face him. "I'm kind of nervous. Where are you taking me?"

He continued to drive, and when he reached the High Tower, he parked in the garage adjacent to the building.

She unbuckled her seat belt and laughed. Her tone was filled with humor. "You brought me to work with you?" She couldn't stop giggling, and it was damn near the cutest thing.

His eyes bounced between her wide smile and her playful stare. "I didn't know you found my work so amusing."

"No, I actually find what you do fascinating. I've watched all of your videos." Her face sobered, and she looked away.

So, Cassidy Thatcher *had* done her research on him. "You've watched all of them?"

She scratched the side of her neck, something Grayson recognized as one of her nervous mannerisms. Nodding, she kept her face turned away. He wanted to see that perfect blush.

His knuckles turned white over the steering wheel, and he cut the engine. Guiding her through the sanitation chamber and to the elevator, he pointed to the fern planter to his left. "This, here, is my fern. I found my lab coat here. Thank you for hiding it so well."

There was that pink shade he had been waiting to see. She shook her head in amusement, but he knew she didn't regret shoving his coat into the dirt.

When they were inside the elevator, he pressed the button for the second floor. "My mentor, Parker, loved the view from the sixty-eighth floor of this building. His favorite restaurant used to be there, until it closed down. Someday, my main research lab will be on that level."

Cassidy looked up at him. She placed her hand on his forearm, and even though he had on a cashmere sweater, her touch singed his skin in the most delicious way.

Before she could pull away, he laid his hand on top of hers.

The elevator dinged.

He wanted to tell her what she did to him, but it felt too soon. Grayson pulled away and dropped his hands to his sides. "We're here." But they weren't. The doors hadn't even opened yet.

Pushing her to his office, he draped his lab coat over her shoulders and smiled. "The circumstances are different this time, but I think a lab coat suits you."

Cassidy laughed. "I promise, I won't throw it into a planter." She lowered her gaze. "I'll hide it better next time," she mumbled.

She was almost herself, although her eyes were still as hollow as they were that night when she wrapped her arms around his waist and pressed her cheek into his chest. He would find a way to fill that hollow gaze.

He gave her a little tour as he waited for his friend to arrive. There were moments when Cassidy stared into space. She disconnected from the world, and in those instances, Grayson stood close to her in hopes that she would come back.

But, she didn't cry.

When he talked about Poppy, he had her full attention. In fact, Cassidy didn't look at the microscope at all. She watched his hands as he spoke and stared at his lips, which made him nervous. He couldn't help but stumble on his words with her penetrating eyes glued to him.

As they walked into his office, Cassidy removed Grayson's lab coat. "Do you usually stutter when you give tours of your lab?"

"Aren't you funny." He wasn't about to tell her that it wasn't the talking that made him stutter.

"I'm just kidding." She giggled.

He hadn't heard her laugh like that ever. It was so… Cassidy. Goofy and free.

"I know." He was about to reach for her when movement came from the front of the office. "Cassidy, I have someone I want you to meet. Put the coat back on."

Cassidy did as she was told and followed him out of his office.

"You're looking good for a retired man, Doc." Grayson smiled at Dr. Pinkerton and took the box of samples out of his hands.

Dr. Pinkerton's eyes crinkled, and his smile widened when he saw Cassidy. "Cassidy? How great to see you. Grayson didn't tell me I was meeting with *you*. I haven't heard from you since last year."

A small gasp escaped Cassidy, her eyes widening in surprise when she saw Dr. Pinkerton. They shook hands briefly, which turned into a welcoming hug.

She pulled away and shook her head in disbelief. "When I first got to New York, I tried to call you, but they said you were retired. It's so wonderful to see you."

Grayson was the one who was thoroughly confused. "Well, it looks like we can skip introductions." He turned to Cassidy. "I asked Dr. Pinkerton to bring some artifacts from his last dig. I thought maybe you could use my lab equipment and get some hours toward your degree. He's agreed to approve of your hours."

Those eyes of hers bore straight through him. She didn't blink. She swallowed hard once before nodding. Grayson laid his palm out, indicating for Cassidy to go ahead, and he stepped back.

Dr. Pinkerton laid out the artifacts and waved Cassidy closer. From a distance, Grayson observed their familiarity and the easiness in the way they communicated that illustrated the depth of their relationship. He had no idea Cassidy had contacts at the Smithsonian Institute. Perhaps that was the opportunity she left behind to be with Kyle. He tried to assemble the pieces of her life.

For the first hour, he sat in his office, writing emails. After 3:00 p.m., Grayson's stomach roared, and he picked up a late lunch for everyone, only for them to analyze samples of chicken under the scope.

When Dr. Pinkerton left, Grayson took out his Bunsen burners and showed Cassidy what a pipette was.

She looked up at Grayson. "How did you know I needed more lab hours for my degree?"

He pulled away from the work station and smiled down at her. "Colton may have said something to me when I tried to fire him."

She tossed her head back and laughed. "You tried to fire Colton? But don't you need him for the lab downstairs?"

"There are other architects."

"But he's your friend, yeah?" She walked around him and into his office a few paces away.

His eyes followed her every move. "Yes."

She sighed in feigned exhaustion. "Grayson Daniels, you are a piece of work." She dropped down on his black leather couch, pressed up against the window, and rested her head against the back cushion. "What made you change your mind? Did he blackmail you?"

Not really, but close.

Grayson took slow steps and stood in front of her. "Not *exactly*."

Her head snapped up, and she grinned. "Colton totally blackmailed you. Go on, tell me what it was."

Grayson crossed his arms. "You're amused by this, aren't you?"

She nodded. "I want to know what power Colton has over you."

It had nothing to do with his friend, and everything to do with the power Cassidy had over Grayson.

He crossed his arms. "Colton had my back when I needed him. Now, he takes every opportunity to remind me."

She tilted her head to the side and raised her eyebrows. "And now he owns your soul?"

Grayson smirked and nodded.

She shook her head. "No, the Grayson I know— favor or not—would have done whatever he wanted anyway."

He stood with his feet shoulder-width apart and smiled down at her rosy cheeks and flirtatious eyes. She was killing him.

Cassidy crossed her legs and folded her hands in her lap. "You're being difficult. Will you tell me why you didn't fire him?" She hadn't smiled like this for weeks.

On the surface, Grayson was fulfilling his word to Colton—in exchange for Colton's loyalty, Grayson was to jumpstart an ambitious architect's career. But under the glass facade, there was an undercurrent that swelled for Cassidy. Somewhere along the way, the need to protect her from Kyle in order to gain forgiveness from a ghost transformed into a wild fascination. Grayson didn't just want to protect her anymore. She stirred an array of emotions within him. Frustration, lust. He needed more.

He stepped closer until his knees were inches away from her. "You."

He must have sounded like an idiot, because Cassidy didn't say anything in response.

Eventually, she let her hands fall down to her sides on the couch. "Well," she lowered her voice, "thank you. For everything. And for today. I really needed this." She hugged his lab coat tighter around her torso.

Grayson examined her as she uncrossed her legs and stood. Confusion passed over her face. Her green eyes scanned the room as if in thought.

She finally looked at him. "And Dr. Pinkerton… Grayson, that was an incredible gift, putting me back in contact with him. I don't even know what to say."

Grayson strode behind Cassidy and helped her out of his lab coat. "Your smile is enough. How come I've never heard you talk about archaeology?"

She lifted her shoulders. "I can't talk to Mya about it. She supports my decisions, but she is also very good at making me feel like an idiot. She judges me a lot. And Kyle? I definitely couldn't talk to Kyle about it, because he just didn't understand my career goals." She brushed some dust off her hands, and Grayson watched as the flecks of dust floated to the ground. "When I was younger, all I ever wanted was to work at the Cooper Hewitt." She looked down at her hands and picked at a remaining strip of paint on her thumb. "I chose Kyle over everything else in my life."

Grayson strode to the rack next to his door and hung up his lab coat.

Cassidy's eyes scanned every part of the room but never fell on him. Was she scared Grayson was going to judge her, too?

Her sweet voice continued to infiltrate the space. "You know, I thought things were changing with Kyle." She finally looked up and nodded as if the movement would help her get the words out. "He contacted *New York's Eye*, and they offered me a commissioned article because of it."

A lump formed at the base of Grayson's throat, and he swallowed to try and clear it. "Oh yeah?"

"I was thrilled. But then I moved here...and what's funny is that after working with Colton, I don't know if I want to be an archaeologist anymore. I really like what I'm doing now. Not that I want to jump ship or not get my degree or anything, but I don't see why I can't love both, you know?" She laughed lightly. "I've been so lost these last few months. Everything I thought I wanted has changed." A hint of desire flared in her eyes.

Grayson wasn't sure if it was excitement, or if she felt the same electricity between them.

She huffed. "I haven't even started writing the article. Knowing Kyle was behind it just makes me sick, and it's due at the end of September."

He stood in front of her. "Are you sure he was the one behind it?"

She nodded adamantly. "Oh yeah. I wrote to him

about it. Only him and Mya know. And now you."

Grayson's chest constricted. There were so many things he wanted to tell her. "If you love both archaeology and architecture, you should pursue both."

Cassidy examined him with intensity and quirked her lips to the side. "I can't have *both*, Grayson." She practically snorted the statement, as if Grayson's words were ludicrous.

"Why not?" He stepped closer to her so they were toe to toe, and she had to tilt her chin higher to maintain eye contact with him. "Choosing doesn't always mean sacrificing. You *can* have both." He paused. "Just stay away from the paint aisle, alright?"

She playfully slapped his shoulder with the back of her hand and rolled her eyes. "Ha. Oh really? *You're* one to criticize. Why are you so terrible with people? I mean, it's really bad. You're so awkward."

He laughed from deep within his chest. "I just want to be left alone, that's all."

"But you work so much..." She looked around his office and lifted her palms. "We're even at your lab on a Saturday—for fun." Her lips quivered with amusement. "You need to let people in."

Grayson reached to tuck a strand of hair behind her ear. "Work is the only thing that doesn't disappoint me. I see immediate results, and I can fix things quickly. Relationships aren't necessarily like that, so I avoid them. Anything else you'd like to pry about?"

She bit her bottom lip and shook her head.

He reached for her hand. "Let's go."

Staring at his outstretched palm, she intertwined her

fingers with his, and he led her back to his Jeep. He opened the door for her, waited for her to get in, and sauntered to the driver's side.

After giving Cassidy a private tour of the High Tower and a personalized lab day with Dr. Pinkerton, every day that passed seemed to get better for her. Mya walked around the house and the office with an *I told you so* look on her face. On Friday evenings, the three of them watched movies in the living room and squished onto the same couch—Cassidy in the middle and Mya and Grayson on either side. Grayson's favorite part of Friday evenings was when Cassidy said goodbye before the weekend.

The fourth weekend after her breakup, she was reserved and shy.

The fifth weekend, Mya flung herself on him, and Cassidy leaned in for an awkward side hug.

The following weekend, Cassidy was the first to hug Grayson, and it lasted longer than any of their other hugs combined.

This Friday, the second week of September, Mya kissed Grayson on the cheek. Cassidy surprised him by doing the same.

His heart called out for her. He spent the entire evening thinking about her lips, so close to his. Mya's intentions were so clear, so easy to decipher. Cassidy, on the other hand, was his favorite kind of complex formula. He could tell she was close to opening her heart and accepting that she was approaching a theoretical limit—a final destination.

He prayed that final destination was him.

CHAPTER SEVENTEEN

GRAYSON HAD BEEN A WONDERFUL DISTRACTION, BUT after the seventh weekend without Kyle, Cassidy had a terrible dream, recollecting all the memories of their relationship.

She moaned. Why couldn't the douche canoe float out of her mind?

There was unfinished business with Kyle. She wanted to ask him "why," and "when did he know?"

Would she take him back?

Would he even want her?

She sat cross legged in her living room, her new laptop balancing between her knees, trying to think of something to write about Mesoamerican culture. The more she thought, the more she resented writing the article. A foul taste erupted in her mouth, and she closed her computer, set it aside, and turned away.

"Stop thinking." She beat her head lightly, stood, and shuffled to the kitchen to make some coffee.

This happened every time she tried to write. And Karen Joseph had essentially given her a prompt to write off of. This was her archaeology career on a silver platter. She moaned.

Her phone rattled on the counter, and she saw a text message from Grayson.

Grayson: Can I bring you anything?

That man. He was not helping her feelings at all. The fire in her core went ablaze at the thought of him.

He looked at her differently.

Touched her differently, longer.

Every one of his movements was for her, and she relished the fact that he made an effort for her. She was falling for Grayson Daniels, and that was dangerous. Or was he just an emotional rebound?

Cassidy recalled her most recent interactions with him and how he never pulled away from her. He was attentive, kind. He hadn't yelled at her for quite a while, which was a huge step for him. He still only shared small pieces of his life, but he was a different man compared to the cold, crass scientist she first met.

He probably yelled at all his associates in the lab and fulfilled his angry word quota before interacting with her.

She smiled.

Then Kyle crept into her mind. It was always when she was happy. Guilt exploded in her heart for being happy.

Her phone buzzed in her hand.

Grayson: Stop neglecting me. Do you need a distraction?

She couldn't help but laugh. It came out as a croak, or a cry. It was as if he knew what she was going through. And not just on the surface. Grayson understood her grief as if he was the mere reflection of her. Not even Mya understood Cassidy's whirlwind of emotions.

She typed a message in reply.

Cassidy: Yes.
Grayson: I'm coming to pick you up.

It was Tuesday morning, and Grayson was playing hooky to come to the rescue. *Don't smile. Don't smile.* But she couldn't help it. He did that to her.

She showered, dressed casually for the unknown, and forty minutes later, there was a knock at her door. As Cassidy opened it wide for Grayson, he eyed the small apartment space. He was wearing dark-wash jeans and a heather-gray sweater that hugged all of his muscles.

She held the door open for him. "No suit?"

Walking inside, he ran his hand through his hair, and then down the side of his unshaven face. "For you? Never." He stepped inside. "I see what you both mean now when you say the 'pole studio.'" He stifled a laugh.

Cassidy closed the apartment door. "It's Mya's favorite hobby now. None of her old fruitcake friends would ever consider taking a pole fitness class, so she knows she's safe from those trolls." She held her arms out wide and spun for him. "Welcome to our humble dwellings."

Grayson placed his hands on her shoulders and turned her to face him. "Pack a bag for three nights. You're coming with me."

It was Cassidy's turn to laugh. "What? I can't. I have work."

"Technically, you work for me. And I say, we're going camping."

Taken aback, Cassidy squinted her eyes and searched Grayson for truth. Cassidy loved camping, but this was so sudden. Grayson hadn't mentioned anything about a trip, and he meticulously planned everything.

Waiting for her response, Grayson eyed her curiously as if that would get her to speak.

She shook her head. An image of Kyle flashed before her eyes, then she nodded, only to shake her head again. This was too fast. Grayson was probably just being nice, but then again, his eyes were so warm today. They were opening up and swallowing her whole.

She wanted a distraction, and camping was it. "Okay. I'll pack a bag."

Grayson's face was etched with surprise. He stood there motionless. Finding his expression amusing, she ran into her room and packed her bags. *Camping with Grayson might be fun.*

She texted Mya and Colton and left a note on the kitchen counter.

After getting Colton's authorization to take a few days off, she collected more random items and tossed them into a tote.

She turned to Grayson. "Tent? I don't have anything here."

He blushed. Grayson Daniels blushed. "I have one tent, but I was planning on sleeping in the hammock. The tent is all yours. It's supposed to rain in Vermont the next few days, so if that's the case, would I have permission to stay with you?" He rocked on his feet. "I can also sleep in the car. Whatever you feel comfortable with."

He was so handsome when he rambled. His deep, melodic voice sang to her. She must have been drooling because Grayson glanced at her as if she had something on her face. She wiped her chin for good measure.

Clearing her throat, she stood tall. "Um. Let's decide when the time comes. Let's go. You know, I've only been to Vermont once. This is so spontaneous of you. I'm kind of excited."

Grayson waited for her as she locked the apartment door, then led her down the staircase and through the pole studio. "To be honest, I've known about this trip for a while."

Knew it.

"I have been meaning to ask you if you'd join me, but...you know. Stuff happens. I didn't want to push while you were still vulnerable."

Where was the demanding man she used to despise? Had Grayson always been this caring from the start, but she just didn't see it?

The car ride was awkward. Grayson didn't listen to any music while driving, stating it "messed with his concentration." Tempted to fiddle with his radio, Cassidy stopped herself.

Grayson was in such a good mood that it was rubbing off on her. If the man didn't want music, she could accommodate that.

She started humming to herself.

"My God, Cassidy. You can't keep a tune. I have never heard someone so off-key in my entire life." Grayson threw his head back when they approached a stoplight, and a burst of air escaped his throat in an exaggerated laugh. "Who taught you to sing? Darth Vader?"

Cassidy glowered. "Mya taught me to sing when I was eight years old, thank you very much."

That shine in his eyes warmed her heart. His contagious smile lit up his entire face. She wanted to reach for him.

She wanted to know everything about him.

Weeks ago, when they spent time together at his lab, she had the opportunity to ask him anything. He was there for the taking. But she couldn't find it in herself to ask him about being an orphan, or the children's home and if he was, or wasn't, trying to protect it. They were finally on good terms—great terms, actually—and she didn't want to encourage an argument.

After he selflessly helped her gain more laboratory hours toward her degree, she'd rather assume the best of him. Her Grayson could never do any harm to anyone. Eventually, he would share facts about himself, and she would be ready.

One hour passed.

Then two.

The car seemed to slow down, and Cassidy allowed herself to close her eyes, but when she opened them, the car was in the exact same spot. "Are we moving at all? How long have we been stationary like this?"

"Five hours. There's a pretty big accident ahead. Everyone's heading to the festival by the river." It sounded as if Grayson was trying to apologize for the traffic.

She had never heard him apologize for anything.

She had accepted that this was what made Grayson so mysterious. She wondered what happened to him to make him that way. Maybe he was just used to getting what he wanted, and the traffic gods were sick of it.

Grayson's sweater bunched at the shoulders. His knuckles turned white as he gripped the steering wheel, his annoyance obvious by his labored breathing. Whether he was annoyed with the road or himself, Cassidy wasn't sure.

She reached out to touch his arm. "It's okay. I don't mind at all. I enjoy spending time with you."

Immediately, he seemed to relax, and his hands fell from their death grip, one of them interlocking with hers.

He looked down at their intertwined fingers, then up at her. "I just want this to be a good trip for you."

She remembered each and every instant he touched her, but nothing had been as electric as this.

The pulse in his wrist throbbed wildly. It matched the cadence of hers. His skin was soft, but not too soft, and although the strength of his hands was visible in the way his muscles corded around his wrist, the pressure he placed on her skin was exquisitely tender.

There was no misunderstanding him this time. Grayson wanted her.

She continued to stare, as did Grayson. She couldn't recall who initiated this, but it felt right.

Looking back to the road, Grayson placed his free hand on the wheel again, and they sat motionless. "We're almost out of the state."

Cassidy was just fine where she was.

As she examined Grayson's profile, something new sparked within her. It was as if an emotion had lay dormant in her chest all her life only to reveal itself in this single moment.

Selfless, check.

Honest, check.

Grayson, the most unapproachable person, fit the bill, and she only realized this in a stupid traffic jam on the way to Vermont. She was happy and didn't feel guilty about it. She almost laughed to herself.

As the car moved, she released Grayson's hand so he could focus on driving, but he still managed to touch her one way or another, whether it was his elbow grazing against hers while leaning on the center console or patting her knee every fifteen minutes.

She watched as the sun tracked across the sky until a loud *pop* sounded from outside, jerking her forward. "What was that?" She looked over her shoulder to see if they ran over a coyote or something.

The car limped to the shoulder, and Grayson told Cassidy to stay in the car while he checked it out. He walked around to the passenger side, Cassidy following his every movement with her eyes. A few minutes later, he was back at the driver's side of the car stripping his clothes off. Good God, the man knew how to take off a sweater.

He had a white T-shirt underneath, and he opened his door to place his sweater on his seat. "Flat tire." He closed the door and went to Cassidy's side to open it for her.

She looked up at him. "I thought you told me to stay inside." Grayson was a literal man, so she took his comment factually.

He leaned inside. "Ever fix a flat before? Let me show you." He was so close, she could smell his clean scent.

Cassidy had only gotten one flat tire in her life, and that was when she met Kyle. But Kyle did everything for her; he never showed her how to do it herself. She stared blankly back at Grayson.

He laughed. "I want you to be able to take care of yourself if you're ever stranded. Get out."

She groaned. "I just *love* a demanding man."

Grayson guided her to the back passenger side and demonstrated how to fix a flat. She grunted and groaned, but it was a ruse. This was even better than *Science with Grayson*. More intimate. She found it hard to pay attention to what he was doing, because she was so focused on the way his muscles bulged through his clothes. Shaking her head to wake up from her daydream, she fell backward on her butt.

Squealing, she clutched Grayson's arm and pulled

herself back up. "That's poison oak a few feet away. Be careful."

Grayson didn't lean away from her touch. He helped her up and let her put all the tools away. She purposefully placed the wrench where the screwdriver needed to go, just so Grayson's hand would reach across her and put it in its rightful place.

She found every excuse to be close to him. "Thank you for showing me how to do that, Grayson. I'm pretty worthless when it comes to cars. Mine actually broke down right before I moved here. I sold it and used that money to buy a one-way plane ticket here."

He was doing that thing again, that charming smirk paired with compassionate eyes. It was as if he reached into her soul and found her future there, and now he was showing it to her.

Grayson guided her to her seat and waited for her to buckle up. When he was back inside as well, she looked over to him, and he smiled at her. He started the car and put it into drive.

Turning on the radio, Grayson mumbled, "You've been patient with me, so you can listen to music."

Cassidy laughed. "Are you rewarding me, Mr. Daniels?"

He smirked again, but this time, it was devious. With the sun beginning to set, his features became more playful. Maybe in the darkness he wouldn't be able to see her obvious stare.

After three more hours and barely moving a mile, Grayson turned the music down. "I think we should stop for the night. This traffic isn't going to let up. Tomorrow morning, we can decide if we want to continue to Vermont or go back home."

Yawning, Cassidy agreed. "What is this camping trip for, anyway?"

"This guy, Jason. He owns all the buildings between McNolan and Oak Park, where the second High Tower is going to be built. I'm trying to stay on his good side, but this camping trip was poorly timed, so here we are."

Cassidy smiled weakly. She had so many questions about the second High Tower. She wanted Grayson to finally open up to her about his life. In time, she reminded herself. They could finally go days without arguing or misunderstanding each other. She wanted this to last.

They pulled into the first hotel.

A few months ago, Cassidy would have never imagined Grayson spending the night in anything less than a five-star resort, yet here they were, walking into the Motel 6 lobby together.

She waited and watched their bags as Grayson took care of the rooms. She hadn't heard from Mya yet, so she checked her phone.

Mya: Hey, hooker. Got your message. Have fun with GrayGray. Can you ask him if he thinks I've lost a few pounds? But don't be really obvious about it, K? I've been counting calories like a mathematician. I wonder if anyone's noticed. See you in a few days.

This life was easy. Mya was happy, Cassidy was on the way it seemed, and Grayson wasn't as sour as he had been in June. For once, everything was going as planned. It was just a different plan than she had originally laid out.

Grayson kept his head low as he walked toward her. "You know how I asked you if we could share a tent if we really needed to?"

Cassidy nodded.

"Would you mind if we shared a room? There was only one left…and it has one bed. I'll sleep on the floor and keep my hands to myself. Scout's honor."

Laughing, Cassidy grabbed the room keys from him. "Were you even a Scout?" She doubted it. "I could use a serious nap right now." She ventured through the hallway, until they approached their room. Flinging the door open, Cassidy launched herself on the bed and stretched. "I love you, bed."

Grayson walked into the restroom and turned on the shower. "I'm going to take a quick shower. Get some rest."

The room was dark other than the restroom light that was now a sliver spanning between the base of the door jambs.

Cassidy hummed to herself. *I'm not a bad singer.*

She yawned again and closed her eyes.

Something clawed at Cassidy's back, and she woke up screaming.

Grayson jumped up from his sleeping bag he had laid down on the floor. "What is it? Are you okay?"

Cassidy looked behind her. "Something bit me."

Turning on the bedside lamp, Grayson crawled to her on his knees and twirled his finger at her. She spun around.

He lifted the back of her T-shirt and huffed. "Take your clothes off."

"What?" She yelped and backed away from him, pulling her T-shirt down. "Is this you trying to be funny? You said you wouldn't touch me. What happened to Scout's honor?"

Grayson raised an eyebrow. "I was never a Scout, and you have a rash all over your back. It looks like poison oak. Take off your clothes."

Cassidy crawled further away from him. She was not going to take off anything. "I don't think I touched it. How did I get it?"

He held out his hand for her. "It doesn't take much for someone allergic to it to break out. Sweetheart, your back is completely blistered. Let me help you."

"I don't want you to get it, though." She held tightly onto her T-shirt.

"I'm not allergic to poison oak."

She rolled her eyes. "Yeah, and you are a Scout, too." She laughed, but Grayson didn't seem to find any of this funny.

His face was cold, and his chiseled jaw clenched. "Before I went on Ike, I needed to get a series of medical exams done. It was in order to get this little badge that lights up around radiation exposure. My doctor here in New York suggested I get an allergy test, which I thought was pointless, since I'm not allergic to anything. If you won't take your clothes off, come here, so I can. You don't want to spread the oil all over you."

Okay, so Grayson couldn't have lied about that. But she wasn't about to get naked in front of him. "I'll go take a hot bubble bath, and you can come in when I'm inside the tub and covered, okay?"

"Don't take a hot bath. Take a cold bath. Lukewarm at the most. No bubbles."

Cassidy's jaw dropped. "Are you serious?"

Grayson's hand was still extended. "Let me help you. Trust me."

"There's more poison oak where I come from than here in New York. Or Vermont. Wherever we are. I am the expert here."

"Actually, a few years ago I conducted a research—"

"*Don't*. You win. You're the expert. I'll go take a totally unenjoyable bath." She took his hand, and he led her to the bathroom where he turned on the bath for her.

"Sit in here, and I'll be right back. Face that way," he pointed toward the back tiled wall, "and expose your back to me."

He left the bathroom, and she stood there awkwardly for a few moments.

She hesitated. "I can take care of it myself," she yelled into the empty space.

Her back itched like she was being burned alive. She grabbed hold of her T-shirt and twisted it side to side along the length of her back to relieve the pain. It only intensified. She lifted her shirt and examined the rash through the mirror.

Her back was bruised, and it looked as if puss was ready to spill from the swollen blisters. Okay, so maybe she did need Grayson's help.

She stripped bare, careful to slip out of her clothes as easily as possible. She sat in the lukewarm water, her hands covering every visible part of her. Then she waited for Grayson to return.

She could sense him before she saw him, and she tightened her arms to cover her chest. The air around her bare shoulders shifted. He turned off the faucet and dumped something inside the tub. It looked like flakes of oatmeal. She swooshed one hand around, stirring the oatmeal in the water to make it milky and mask more of her body. She looked over her shoulder and watched, as he scooped oatmeal from a cylindrical box and dropped it inside a sock.

Cassidy turned her face. "Where did you get the oatmeal?"

"I wasn't sure what would be at the campsite, and I didn't know if you liked oatmeal or not." He leaned closer to her.

He lightly rubbed the sock on her back.

She sighed in relief as the burning sensation neutralized. "Where did you learn to do this?"

Massaging her back with the oatmeal-filled sock, he hesitated for a beat. "My little sister, Katrina. She was allergic. She'd roll around in the wildflowers with Lance, and both of them would be covered in blisters the next day. Lance was on his own," he laughed, "but I took care of Katrina before our parents could find out. They didn't like her playing by the water because of the poison oak there. The oatmeal works best if it's cooked first, but this will do for now. I have some chemicals in my bag we'll use next."

She flinched. "You have *what* in your bag?"

"Chemicals. I'm a scientist. I carry this stuff around."

Because that miraculously explained his resourcefulness.

"I'll mix a clay, and we'll put that on your back. It'll suck all the oils out. We'll rinse you with cold water and do that for a few hours until the itching subsides." He continued to scrub her back.

Grayson's free hand found her shoulder while the other moved in repetitive cyclic motions around her back.

She didn't know what to say. Thank you? Sorry?

She took a deep breath. "I didn't know you had a sister."

Where his fingers lay gently on her shoulder, she turned and rested her cheek on them. The oscillating touches on her back ceased, and she lifted her cheek only for Grayson to turn her face toward him.

He breathed softly next to her ear. "I was sixteen when she died."

She remembered him saying he lost someone when he was sixteen. No words could ever make that pain go away. He ran the back of his index finger across her cheekbone and down to her chin, along the side of her neck, and atop the slope of her shoulder. She held her breath as he seemed to memorize her features. Naked in front of this man, albeit sitting in a tub full of murky water, she wasn't exposed. He didn't look at her as if he saw weakness and vulnerability.

There was leashed desire and restrained passion. Grayson Daniels needed to be freed, and Cassidy wanted to be the person to do it.

As if sensing her thoughts, Grayson grinned slightly, only one side of his lips quirking upward. He dipped the sock into the water and continued to lather her back. After she shivered from the cooling water, Grayson stood and reached for a towel. He placed it on the ledge of the bathtub and leaned close to Cassidy's face.

She turned her lips up to him.

She closed her eyes, and he placed his mouth on the curve of her shoulder.

He missed. She was right there for the taking, and he *missed*. She ached for him, and her desire grew as he left the bathroom and closed the door.

She sat for a few minutes in the cool oatmeal water. After another shiver coursed through her body, she stood and unfolded the towel Grayson left for her.

He knocked lightly on the door. "Pat yourself dry." He was too controlling. But now everything he said was irresistibly cute in a torturous kind of way.

She laughed to herself. "Can you give me some clothes from my bag?"

The door creaked as it opened enough for him to hold one of his T-shirts and a pair of boxers out for her. "These will be more comfortable for you. Don't worry, they're clean. Let me know when you're dressed."

"How about you let me know when you're going to kiss me," she mumbled.

"What was that?" he called out.

"Oh nothing. Just muttering to myself." It only took her a few minutes to dry her hair and put on his clothes. They swallowed her. "Okay, I'm dressed. Where to, Master?" She thought that was funny, but Grayson didn't seem to get the joke.

The bed had been stripped of its sheets. A blanket and his sleeping bag lay atop it. "Lay here so I can put this stuff on your back."

"This stuff" was a coffee cup filled with green goop that resembled clay.

He pointed to the sleeping bag, and she crawled inside.

He kneeled in front of her. "Can you lift the shirt?"

She laid on her stomach with Grayson's sleeping bag zipped halfway up, covering her lower body. She lifted his shirt above her shoulders. His hand was on her again, rubbing the paste along her spine. The cool sensation of the clay drying…Grayson's warm hand…it was ambrosial. She allowed herself to close her eyes, as Grayson shared this new part of his character with her.

Grayson laid next to her on the blanket, and she turned to face him.

Her sleepy eyes could barely stay open. "How long were you rubbing clay on my back and washing it off? I feel amazing."

It was dark, but she could see the outline of his smile. "A few hours. It's about two in the morning. Get some sleep. You've had a long day." He pulled his sleeping bag over her shoulders.

After realizing Grayson was going to sleep next to her, she couldn't seem to get her eyes closed. They were pried open as if she were getting Lasik surgery. She stared at him, following his silhouette and trying to read his body language. But he just lay there with his face turned to her.

Cassidy was still lying on her stomach, and she folded her hands under her chin. "Why did you ask me to come with you?"

"I wanted to spend time with you. Why did you say yes?"

"Well, you're tall, smart, you don't have a lot of scars on your hands, you drive a nice car…"

Grayson laughed. "Is that your checklist?"

Yes. "No. Of course not. I'm just trying to be…I dunno. Charming?"

Was she not charming?

He laughed again. "Okay, give me your list. Let's see how I score."

Oh God. She couldn't do this. She wasn't about to do this. Cassidy reading her perfect boyfriend checklist to Grayson Daniels would be like a kindergartener who liked to draw stars trying to describe space to an astronaut. He would just laugh at her ridiculousness or worse, make her add more categories or even footnotes.

She started with the basics. "Do you have all of your own teeth?"

"You've got to be kidding."

"Teeth are important."

He sighed in exasperation and turned to face her. "Yes, I have my own teeth."

Cassidy cleared her throat, suddenly more nervous. "How many women have you slept with?"

Did he just groan in agony?

"Okay, that answers my question," she mumbled nervously. "Have you ever been to prison?"

Grayson shifted a few inches away from her.

"Of course you haven't, you're Grayson Daniels. I can't imagine you breaking the law." She laughed. "This is dumb, I told you—"

"Five. I've been with five women." He paused. "And yes, I've been to prison."

CHAPTER EIGHTEEN

How was he going to explain this to her?

Guilty for already having been dishonest when it came to Kyle—to protect her, he reminded himself—this was an opportunity to show her he deserved her trust.

She didn't say anything. It didn't even seem like she was breathing. She lay there waiting. Or panicking.

A few beats passed, and she wiggled inches away from him, turning to her side and covering her chest with crossed arms. She was already covered, but the shadow of her arms grabbing and tugging at every loose end of his T-shirt indicated that she was uncomfortably exposed.

He teetered on the edge of a breath. "Oh, for God's sake, Cassidy." With humor behind his tone, he smiled, but the room was pitch black. Hopefully she'd be able to hear the lightness in his words.

"What did you do?" Her voice was almost inaudible.

Not sure where to start, he said the first thing that came to his mind. "It was my senior year of college."

She laughed, and even in the darkness, he could sense her relax. "Let me guess. A wild drunken party? A night in a cell is hardly a sentence, Grayson."

It wasn't a drunken party. And it wasn't for one night. He rolled on to his back and gazed up at the ceiling, his chest compressing wildly. "My girlfriend had just gotten in a fight with her parents. They didn't like her spending time with me, because I wasn't their class. I picked her up one evening at dusk, about 7:00 p.m., and she cried and cried, as I drove. I didn't even know where I was going, but we just drove around. Lance kept calling, because we had a project due the next morning."

Cassidy had adjusted her position, and she held her head with her hand propped up on her elbow.

"I turned onto Oak Park, so I could pull over and talk to her, but out of nowhere, this little girl came zooming out on a little pink bike."

Cassidy gasped. "You hit her?"

"Yes." Even in the dark, Grayson could see Cassidy had her palm over her mouth. "I killed her."

Cassidy dropped her hand. "That was an accident, Grayson. It's not like you intentionally hurt her." She reached for him, and he didn't stop her hand from laying on his chest.

"That's not what the court saw. Veronica wanted us to run. I told her that would be a felony, and she broke out into hysterics again. She said she would fix this with her father being a hot-shot lawyer and all. I didn't know what her father would do for me, considering he already didn't want me and her in a relationship, but I had to have faith that she would take care of it.

"In court, Veronica was completely protected. Me, on the other hand, I didn't have the cleanest past. When I was sixteen, I was kicked out of the house, I broke and entered into the cottage I live in today. It was a pool house then. It belonged to Parker. I told you about him. Before that, I was in foster care, until I was about nine."

Cassidy's fingers tensed on Grayson's chest. "She stood up for you, though, right?"

Grayson shook his head. "No. She claimed it was distracted driving, because Lance had been calling me. Who were they going to believe?"

"How long were you there?"

"Six months. When I got out of prison, Lance called his friend to keep it out of the public. The guy says he's a lawyer, but that's not what he really does. All that remains is the fact that I had to repeat the last semester of my senior year of college and that I was involved in a car accident. Colton and Lance had my back. I owe everything to them."

Leaning forward, Cassidy rested her forehead on his chest. "I'm so sorry, Grayson. What was her name?"

Running a hand through her long, silky hair, Grayson kissed the top of her head. "Paige."

Understanding transmitted through Cassidy's breath. "What happened to Paige's family?"

"She didn't have a family. She lived at the children's home on Oak Park."

The next morning, they decided to drive back to New York City instead of continuing to Vermont. Cassidy's back was considerably better. Grayson laid cold towels on her, while she slept to ease the swelling. But even after all their efforts the night before, Grayson caught glimpses of her rubbing her back against the car seat like a black bear against a tree.

She sat quietly, reading.

He broke the silence. "What is that?"

Cassidy didn't look up from the book. She had hardly made eye contact with him all morning, but they moved around the hotel room, like they'd done this a hundred times before. It was swift and effortless.

She laughed. "It's a book Mya suggested to me. It talks about the Universe and how we can use science to help us understand relationships and whatnot. It's by Jessica Minasian."

Grayson had never heard of it.

They drove in amiable silence, the radio turned off, and Cassidy reading her book. Traffic was still terrible, but they were able to get to Cassidy's apartment just after noon.

He walked her to the door.

Mya flung it open before they reached the top landing of the stairs. "I heard your voices, why are you back so soon?"

Cassidy mumbled something under her breath. "I touched poison oak."

Mya backed away. "Well, I would offer to cook you

something, but I don't know, does chicken soup help with that? I have to head back to the office here in a sec."

Grayson and Cassidy laughed in unison while Mya turned and went into the bedroom.

Cassidy turned to face him. "Thank you for taking me camping." Her smile bore into him, opening his heart and filling it with her light. "I had fun, sort of."

Grayson closed his eyes and cringed, as a soft hand caressed his face. He opened his eyes, and she pulled him down to her, kissing his cheek. They were communicating, finally on a level of understanding.

She didn't say goodbye, or if she'd be at the house later.

Before she could back away, Grayson gripped her hand in both of his. "Kyle." He averted his eyes and gazed at their interlocked hands.

She stepped closer. "What about him?"

"I know it hasn't been long, but do you think you're ready to move on?" He cleared his throat. "Maybe with me?" He lifted his eyes to her.

Her smile was warm and exuberant. "Yes."

Yes with him, or yes to moving on? Jesus, he wasn't good at this. He wanted clarification. But, part of him worried she only meant that she was ready to leave Kyle behind, and there was no future for them. After cleaning her wounds, taking care of her all night, and connecting with her on a deeper level than anything he'd ever known, he'd rather live with the illusion that she wanted him than hear her speak the truth.

He pulled away from her and stepped back into the

hallway. "I'll check on you tomorrow. Maybe I'll see you later today, if you decide to come to the house?"

She nodded.

Before leaving, he called out to Mya. "Hey Mya, do you need a ride to the office? I'm going to change, head to the office to pick up some things, and work from home today."

"No, thanks! I'll see you there!" Her voice was muffled and faint.

Grayson walked into the High Tower that afternoon, and Lance left his conversation with Bianca to greet him. "I thought you'd be gone all week. I'm glad you're here."

Hadn't Lance been the one urging him to go on that stupid trip? "You seem thrilled I'm here. Did your precious interns screw up my spreadsheets again?"

Lance smirked. "Ha ha, very funny. Yes, but I fixed it."

Grayson dragged in a lazy, amused breath and sauntered toward his office.

Lance followed. "Grayson..."

Oh no. Grayson knew that tone.

"...I need you to watch my niece this afternoon."

Shaking his head, Grayson put his hands up. "I only came to pick up some paperwork. I am not going to babysit your—"

"Uncle Grayson?" Pitter patter sounds came from around the corner. A head of platinum blonde hair flowed in her wake as she ran up and hugged Lance's leg.

Grayson eyed Lance and glared at him. "I can't."

He looked to Jessica's little, round face. Her bright blue eyes. Her Mary Janes.

Why did she have to wear Mary Janes?

Lance put his hands in front of his chest in prayer. "I'm begging you. My sister came home early from Italy, and she had to leave town again this morning. I told her she could drop Jessica off, hoping one of the associates could watch over her, but they can't. I have training all day today, so I can't keep her with me. Please, she's looking forward to spending time with you."

Jessica smiled, and Grayson grimaced. "Uncle Lance says you can tell me a story about princesses and cooties."

Lance patted her head. "Coyotes, Pup. Not cooties."

Jessica rolled her eyes. "Hello-o-o, that's what I said." She crossed her arms in front of her chest.

Grayson ached all over. His muscles felt as though they had rot. He wanted to fall to his knees. After staring at Jessica for at least a minute, he eventually raised his eyes to Lance. A scowl scrunched his face. "No."

Grayson walked to his office.

"Wait, Grayson," Lance pleaded and followed him. "Jess, go play with…something. There are lots of things in my office. I'll be there in a few minutes."

Grayson tried to close his office door on Lance, but Lance stuck out his hand to stop him. Grayson turned to face Lance and clutched a lapel of his lab coat. "How could you ask me to watch her?" He shoved Lance away. "She's the spitting image of…"

Lance ran his hands through his hair. "She misses

you, Grayson. It's been two years since she's seen you. Skype can only do so much. She loves you."

Growling, Grayson lowered his head and dropped his chin to his chest. After a few breaths, he lifted his eyes. "Skype was hardly bearable, Lance." He held out his hand toward Lance's office where Jessica sat on the floor playing with a paper weight. "Do you *see* her shoes? You're trying to kill me," he laughed in disbelief, "you're honestly trying to kill me."

Putting his hands up, Lance sighed. "Okay. I'll ask someone else. I'm sorry I even asked. I mean, you're only my best friend."

Lance turned and left Grayson's office.

Well, for Christ's sake.

It was just one day. Lance had Grayson's back time and time again.

Before Lance got halfway to his office, Grayson called out, "I'll do it."

Lance clapped, turned, and beamed. "Thank you." He walked to his office door. "Jessica, come on. Come play with Uncle Grayson. Be good. He's grumpy today."

Looking to the ceiling, Grayson regretted this decision already. But Jessica was smiling, and Lance was smiling, so at least he was doing something right.

Grayson walked to his office, Jessica trailing behind him. He sat behind his desk, and she came up to the front of it, her eyes barely visible from behind the wood laminate.

Shifting in his seat, Grayson wasn't sure what to say to her. "Go...sit."

She walked to his side of the desk and climbed onto his lap. "Will you tell me a story?"

Grayson leaned back in his chair and folded his hands over his stomach, Jessica sitting expectantly on his knee. "There once was a businessman. He was an investment banker who made a terrible negotiation..."

She yawned. "What about a princess? Tell me the story of the Princess of the Coyotes."

No. That's what he should have said. He wasn't ready for this. Jessica's tiny fingers fiddled with the tie he had put on after dropping Cassidy off, and she stuck her hands in all of his pockets, probably looking for candy. She pulled out Cassidy's letter from his breast pocket.

An unimaginable force closed around him. He closed his eyes tightly. The image of Jessica holding Cassidy's letter shifted something in him. It was as if Katrina were there, on his knee, with Cassidy's words in her hands.

He filled his lungs with air, counted to ten in his mind, and slowly exhaled. Opening his eyes, he took Cassidy's letter back from Jessica and placed it in his pocket. "There once was a girl. She was six, so, your age. She had long, blonde hair, like an angel."

Jessica's eyes widened. "I have blonde hair!"

Grayson ran his hand over her head. "Yes, you do. The princess loved to run through wildflowers with her two...guards. They hid behind trees, but she could always find them."

Jessica rested her head on Grayson's chest, her little arms draping around his waist.

"One day, the Princess of the Coyotes had to make a

big decision. Heaven opened up and told her, she could stay on earth, or live amongst the gods forever."

Popping her head up, Jessica's eyes widened.

"The princess chose to live amongst the gods, so she could forever watch over those she loved."

Jessica rolled her eyes and pushed herself up. "That's a dumb story. If I were her, I would have chosen to play in the wildflowers."

Grayson picked Jessica up off his lap and set her on the floor. "I think that would have made a better story, too." Standing, he reached for Jessica's hand. "Want to get some ice cream and hang out at my place?"

Nodding fervently, Jessica grabbed Grayson's hand.

He reached for some papers, bugged Lance about a car seat, and they left the High Tower together.

On the drive to Laramie Hill, Grayson let Jessica choose the radio station, and she sang obnoxiously to every song, while eating her ice cream cone. She wiggled in the back seat and looked at him through his rearview mirror with a wide smile on her face, as she sang to him.

It was off-key. It was loud. But just like Cassidy's singing, to his ears, it was perfect.

Mya's car was parked by the hedge, meaning Cassidy had dropped Mya off at the office and came to do some work on the house. Or maybe she just wanted to see him. He smiled to himself.

Grayson exited the car and walked to where Jessica sat to help her unbuckle her seat belt. She lunged out of the car and ran toward the house with her arms outstretched, as if she were a bird.

Before he reached the front steps of the house, Cassidy opened the front door.

Is this what life with her would be like? Coming home to her like this?

Jessica stood still in front of Cassidy. Jessica started talking gibberish, and Grayson watched them interact. Cassidy crouched down, and Jessica gave her a little hug before going inside.

Leaning against the door jamb, Cassidy grinned, and Grayson stepped closer.

She sighed. "Oh Grayson, I thought you didn't like kids…"

He had said that, hadn't he? Grayson reached for her. "Can I hug you?"

She nodded, and he wrapped his hands around her waist, pulling her to him.

"I want to talk to you about last night," he began, but Cassidy lifted her finger up to stop him.

"I do, too. But *after* you see the new floors in the living room." Smiling, she pulled him inside, and Grayson's jaw practically dropped. "Do you like it?"

The original scuffed floorboards had been entirely replaced with dark wood.

Cassidy released her hold on him. "I need to polish it, but do you like it?"

He nodded. "I love it." He reached for her again, but Jessica came around the corner, and he backed away. Jessica was gone just as fast as she had come, and Grayson attempted to reach for Cassidy again. This time, he was successful. "Maybe you could teach me how to polish the floors? We could do it together."

She threw her head back, exposing her neck. If he lowered his head just a little, he'd be able to kiss her there if she didn't move. "And I filled the pool. No reason to have one if you're not going to use it, right?"

He lowered his head and nuzzled the crook of her neck. He had hoped to fill the pool up with dirt and never use it, but he wasn't about to dampen Cassidy's mood right now.

"I also made dinner, if you're hungry. I know it's only four, but we had a long night."

Jessica ran to them squealing. "Cassidy made cookies, Grayson. Can I have one? Ple-e-ease?"

He just couldn't get a moment alone with Cassidy. He laughed and squeezed her gently to avoid irritating her back, as he pulled away from her.

They ate spaghetti in the kitchen. Cassidy and Grayson sat next to each other at the barstools, and Jessica sat everywhere else. She couldn't seem to stay still.

After eating, Jessica turned to Grayson. "Can I go outside to play?"

He nodded, grateful for the privacy with Cassidy he'd been thirsty for all afternoon. "Stay on the grass." He eyed the swimming pool that was clean and filled to the top. "And stay away from the pool—I mean it."

"Okay, okay," she sing-songed, as she skipped through the back door of the kitchen.

Grayson looked at Cassidy. "Should I go out there with her to make sure she doesn't get hurt?"

Cassidy laughed. "She'll be *fine*, Grayson."

He relaxed and gazed at her, soaking in every delicate detail of her face. "Last night was…nice."

She nodded.

Nice? Last night was a camping trip from hell, yet all he could think to say was, "nice."

He wanted her to speak, but she didn't. She just smiled, and he couldn't help but do the same.

After gazing at the lines of her face, he rubbed his palms against his slacks. "So, next week is the High Tower Lab's banquet. It's usually a small, intimate thing, but this year has been pretty big for us with the construction on the first floor. Lance and I are going to try to fill out a venue this year. Will you be my date?"

She nodded again.

This whole talking to people thing was far easier than he thought it would be. But, he didn't want to talk anymore. He reached for her hand and pulled her up.

She walked to stand between his opened knees. Her hands lay at her sides, and Grayson placed them around his neck, as he massaged her waist. A raging wildfire of desire coursed through his body.

"I think," he began, before sitting taller to bring his lips closer to hers.

"Hm." Her groan was soft and laced with passion.

He reached further.

Behind Cassidy, there was a splash and a scream. His heart went into overdrive. Pulling away from her, he stumbled off the barstool and knocked it over, as he threw himself toward the noise. The slapping of water, the high-pitched shriek. His heart beat fast and irregularly.

Jessica flailed in the swimming pool. He bent over and reached for her. "Grab my hand, Jessica. Come on."

"I can swim, Uncle Grayson." She laughed and splashed around. "Watch me swim!"

He leaned further, grabbing at her, but she spun away from him. The quarters of his suit jacket skimmed the top of the swimming pool, and she went under.

Jessica sank to the bottom of the pool and pushed up, her head bobbing out of the water as she took a breath and went back under.

He reached into the water, deeper, deeper, and grabbed the first thing he could, which was a fistful of hair.

As he pulled her head out of the water, Jessica opened her mouth wide, a pained expression passing over her face. A second later, she cried. She held onto Grayson's wrist with both of her hands, scratching at him and the sleeve of his jacket.

After dragging her to the edge of the pool, he gripped her arm and yanked her out of the water in one swoop. "I told you to stay in the grass!"

Jessica's eyes welled with tears. "It was an accident." She held onto her head where Grayson's hand had just been.

"I told you to stay in the Goddamn grass, Katrina! If you'd only listened to me, this would have never happened! You'd still be alive, do you hear me?" She was eye to eye with Grayson on his knees. He held her shoulders and shook her.

"Uncle Grayson." Her face contorted in fear. "I'm Jessica."

He shook her harder, and tears streamed down her face, as she wailed. How much time had passed? Three seconds? Four?

Cassidy ran up behind Jessica and pried Grayson's fingers off her.

She pulled Jessica behind her and crouched down to touch Grayson's face. "Grayson?"

Swatting her away, he glared at her. "This is your fault," he seethed.

Cassidy stood as well and put her hands on her hips. "What do you mean this is my fault?"

He pointed at the swimming pool. "'She'll be okay, Grayson.' I should never have listened to you. And, you should have asked my permission before filling up the pool."

"Permission? Grayson..." she reached for him again, and he recoiled.

Looking at Jessica, he held out his hand for her. "Let's go. I'm taking you back to the office."

Jessica hid behind Cassidy, and when he took a step forward, she screamed again, hid her face in the back of Cassidy's thigh, and wrapped her arms around Cassidy's knees.

Cassidy put her hand on Grayson's chest with firm pressure, pushing him backward. "Stay away from her. I'll take her." She picked Jessica up and stormed into the house. "And don't you *ever* look at me like that again."

How had he looked at her?

The way Jessica hid when he reached for her was indication enough.

He sat by the swimming pool, images of Jessica

flailing her arms ripping open old wounds. He wasn't sure how much time had passed, but the sky began to darken, the ripples in the pool settling, and then ceasing, as if untouched.

The front door opened and slammed shut. Grayson stood and walked into the kitchen. "Cassidy—"

"You scared her to death, you bastard!" His face was met with a hard slap. "What is wrong with you? She was just playing. It was an *accident*. Why did you yell at her like that? You yelled at *me*. After seeing you like that—" she shook her head and backed away "—I can't do this with you."

Grayson reached for her shoulders, but she smacked his hands away.

"You are incapable of having normal relationships, Grayson."

He wanted to make this right, but hearing that phrase for the umpteenth time set him over the edge. He spoke through clenched teeth. "I *have* relationships."

Cassidy beat her palm to her forehead for emphasis. "I don't think you understand what I'm trying to say."

He tossed his hands up. "You sound like Lance. I've heard this 1,000 times."

"Well, let me tell it to you in a way that you might understand. Since we apparently still have communication issues, I'm going to break your relationships down to a particle level."

This was going to be lovely.

She put her hands on her hips. "Quarks."

He raised a brow. "Are you really giving me a science lecture right now?"

Her face reddened. "God, how did that book put it?" she muttered. She pinched the bridge of her nose and lowered her hand. "In order for a quark to be stable and create an unbreakable bond with another quark, it must become lighter or go through particle decay."

"I know what a quark is, Cassidy." This was pointless, but the agonized look on Cassidy's face made him take pause. He had put that expression there. He held out his hand for her. "I'm listening."

"Grayson," she exasperatedly placed her hand in his, "you are carrying so much mass that you are incapable of bonding with another person. You need to let go of whatever is holding you down. Consider it a personal particle decay, so you can bond with someone else...with me."

In the hundreds—thousands—of times Lance had tried to explain this to him, nothing was as clear as when it passed through Cassidy's lips. He sat down on the bar stool and gazed at the wall separating the kitchen and the living room.

Ever since Katrina's death, he'd been holding on to his grief. Every time he looked into a body of water, there he was, a sixteen-year-old boy, holding his dead baby sister outside their house.

"My parents had tried for years to conceive. They couldn't, so they adopted me. Shortly after, they became pregnant. They even called me a miracle." Grayson gazed past Cassidy's shoulder. He scoffed. "Some miracle."

"Katrina was only six. I found this silver bracelet by the canal in our backyard, and Katrina wanted it. She begged for it desperately. 'Grayson, I want it, please!' God, I can hear her pleading for it now. You know, she was the cutest thing. When the sunlight hit her hair, it was golden. It was like a little halo around her perfect face." Grayson laughed to himself as the vivid memory of her flooded his mind. "I told her she couldn't have the bracelet, that it was for Mom. I asked her to stay by the grass, and I left to put the bracelet in our mother's jewelry box.

"One minute later, I ran outside to play hide and seek with Katrina, and I couldn't find her. I thought it was some sick joke. She always did that with Lance and hid in the weeds from me. I searched and searched for her. I ran back to the house, but she wasn't there.

"Then I saw a little yellow head bobbing up and down in the canal."

He closed his eyes tightly.

Cassidy placed a hand on his shoulder and stood closer to him. His hands naturally found her waist, and he opened his legs for her to step inside.

"I chased after her, but the current was strong that day. Her arms flailed around just like Jessica's." He shook his head, and Cassidy wrapped her fingers in his hair. "I did what any stupid teenager would have done and jumped in after her."

Her blue eyes begged for help. As he got closer, their fingertips touched, but he couldn't grab ahold of her. Her fingers were slippery, and so small. He could tell she was fading, panic etched on her face, her mouth stretched wide with fear. She choked on water, and the brightness in her eyes transformed into fear, as she tried again to reach for him with her tiny hands. He swam fervently, angrily, but she went under.

A tree had fallen into the canal, and Grayson prayed they would be caught in its branches. He reached in front of him, blind, and grabbed onto something, anything, praying it was her. His hands grabbed a fistful of her hair and pulled her out of the water, as his pant leg caught on the fallen tree.

He cried out for her. "Katrina! I'm here. Stay with me." Cradling her body in his arms and working his way to the edge, he pulled himself one-handed out of the water.

He laid Katrina down in the dirt and tried desperately to save her. Chest compressions...breath...chest compressions...nothing. The halo around her head was drenched, her skin cold and wet.

After two hours of CPR and crying out for help with no one coming, Grayson knew she was gone. He carried her lifeless body the half mile back to their house.

Grayson swallowed hard and leaned his forehead against Cassidy's chest. "My parents stopped talking to me then. Their only child was gone. Their only *real* child. And they blamed me for it," he whispered into the fabric of Cassidy's T-shirt. Breathing in her scent, he nuzzled his face into her.

Before Katrina's funeral, Grayson had snuck into his mother's room to grab the bracelet his sister had wanted so badly. He slipped it on her nimble wrist before she was put in the ground, so he could honestly say he gave her everything she ever asked of him.

Cassidy was silent, her shallow breaths the only thing holding the space together around him. He knew she understood his grief. She continued to run her fingers slowly through his hair.

He raised his eyes to look at her. "I know my past doesn't excuse how I treated Jessica, or you, but so many people have come and gone in my life. I don't want one of those people to be you."

She cupped his face and kissed his forehead. "Someone once told me that 'with all the things that happen in space and time, there's no way that one instant could have possibly been your doing.'"

"Cassidy—"

"You don't need to explain anything. You should go upstairs and get some rest." She tugged on Grayson's biceps, and he stood up. She guided him toward the stairs.

Halfway up the stairs, he turned to face her. "Are you staying?"

She nodded. "Yes. First, I'm going to drain the swimming pool."

He watched as she went back into the kitchen. How could one woman be so incredible? How could one person change his perspective, so completely?

If this is what life would be like with Cassidy—bonded on an unseen level—he would take it.

CHAPTER NINETEEN

THE WEEK AFTER GRAYSON OPENED HIS HEART TO HER had been unimaginably perfect. Every morning, he would come to her apartment, make breakfast for her and Mya, then take Mya to work with him while Cassidy went to Laramie Hill.

He opened doors for her and pulled out her chair. He loved her cousin and cared for her like she was his family, too.

"Mya, I've never felt like this." Cassidy put her toothbrush away and adjusted her tank top.

With tired eyes, Mya nodded and leaned into the door jamb of the bathroom. "I know. And I can't begin to tell you how happy I am for you."

Lifting her shirt up, Cassidy turned around to bare her naked back to Mya. "How does my back look?"

Mya ran her fingers across it. "I can't even tell that you were crusty and blistered just last week. Can Grayson mix me up some DIY wrinkle cream?"

Cassidy lowered her tank and smiled. "He probably could." She walked to their bedroom and scrunched her face at the array of gowns on the bed. "What's this?"

Mya walked in behind her and lifted one of the hangers. She held a velvet dress close to her body and spun around. "Grayson took me shopping today after work. It was pretty much a makeover for me, although he would never call it that. He said I'm too fabulous and needed more laboratory-worthy shoes. He seems to think my heels are going to get stuck in the grates or something. Anyway, he had to leave for a meeting with Lance, and of course, I kept shopping. I bought these dresses for you." She set the hanger down and beamed the brightest smile.

Cassidy lowered her gaze back to the three dresses laying on the bed. "What about you?"

"Why would I buy anything for myself?" Smiling, Mya lifted another dress off the bed and held it up to Cassidy's body. "You'd look amaze-balls in this one."

Cassidy watched Mya run her hands over the silk, the velvet, the chiffon. Mya seemed genuinely happy. Cassidy remembered just months ago, Mya thought she'd never be able to live without a five-bathroom penthouse. Cassidy's heart soared.

Grayson had something to do with the change in Mya. When Mya doubted herself, Cassidy often overheard Grayson tell Mya she was beautiful. Then, he'd walk over to Cassidy, cup her face, press his hand to her lower back, and whisper to her that she was his quark.

God, that man.

Cassidy gravitated toward the sleeveless, plum velvet dress. When standing next to Grayson, it would bring out the ocean hues of his eyes that she loved so much.

She looked to Mya. "I thought you were going to come with me."

Shaking her head, Mya laughed. "Oh no, this is practically your first legit date with Grayson, and you are going to enjoy it and then tell me all about it. Pick one, then let's return the other two, because I saw this charming table I'm dying to get for our living room."

Cassidy's phone rattled on the bedside table, and she reached for it, smiling when she saw Grayson's name.

Grayson: I have someone coming over to bring you some dresses. Don't worry, I didn't pick any of them out.

Laughing, she replied to him.

Cassidy: As much as I love you spoiling me, I already have a dress. Leave me alone, I'm pampering myself.
Grayson: Send me a picture of your dress.
Cassidy: Why…?
Grayson: So when I introduce you as my date tomorrow night, people won't think I'm color blind because I don't match you.

And so she sent him a picture.

There seemed to be no graceful way to get into this dress.

"Mya? I'm bloated, and I need your help zipping this up."

Cassidy squirmed, twisted, and sighed in exhaustion. The thing had fit like a glove last night. Maybe binge drinking wine and watching reruns of *Science with Grayson* in the bathtub late last night was a bad idea.

"Mya!" She groaned. "I can't zip this up. I'm fat as a cow."

Mya danced into the bathroom. "Did someone call for a fat cow? I am here to save you, bean pole."

Letting her arms fall limp, Cassidy sighed and let her head fall back.

Investigating, Mya lifted up the dress at all angles. "It looks fine to me," she murmured from underneath the fabric. "Oh, the price tag is stuck in the zipper."

Cassidy watched Mya's reflection in the mirror as she bit the plastic string holding the price tag, latched on to the zipper, and slid it up Cassidy's back.

Mya shuffled out of the restroom and into the hallway. "He's here! I'll get the door."

Cassidy wasn't ready yet.

Mya's voice pierced through the walls. "Hi, lover. Looking snazzy."

Grayson's low reply absorbed into the walls, and Cassidy couldn't make out what he said.

"Wait here, she'll be done in a second."

"More like a million seconds," Cassidy mumbled. "Mya, can you *please* come here?" She tried to sound calm, but her heart raced. It was a big step for her and Grayson, and it was an important event for him. She wanted this night to go well.

Mya waltzed in. "He's going to die when he sees you in this dress. I'd be protruding out of the seams by now with my holy tits." She giggled. "What is the big fuss about? You sound like you're having a panic attack."

Cassidy looked down to her feet. "I'm going to trip over this thing. I feel like it fit just fine last night, what happened?" The thin, velvety material bunched at her feet. She was even wearing three-inch heels.

Mya quirked her lip to the side. "Well, we did drink a lot of wine before bed. I have just the thing." She retreated into the hallway and toward the bedroom.

While waiting for Mya to come back, Cassidy touched up her makeup. Her hair was in a loose bun, tendrils falling around her face. Her eye makeup was minimal, with a light dusting of bronze flecks. Her lips were a sheer plum that Mya suggested she wear—the color was gorgeous.

A minute later, Mya walked in with an unrecognizable pair of shoes.

Cassidy raised her eyebrows. "What are *those*?" They resembled heels, but they were much, much higher.

"They're my hooker heels."

Cassidy tossed her an incredulous look.

"Hey, if you want me there in spirit, you need a touch of slut. Put these on. They'll fix the material you're swimming in."

The shoes were terribly uncomfortable, and Cassidy walked as if her head were in the clouds. "I feel like I grew a foot." Cassidy took a deep breath and stood in front of Mya. "How do I look?"

Mya sighed and leaned her head to the side. "You

look stunning, Cassidy. Now go out there and have the best night ever."

Cassidy entered the hallway, and Grayson waited with his hands in his pockets, observing the bare walls. He turned to face her, and his eyes filled with hunger.

He watched her. She watched him. Nothing else existed in that moment. She took an uneasy step forward. These heels were going to be the death of her.

His posture was primal, as he met her halfway. "You look beautiful."

For once, she didn't have to crane her neck to look at his freshly shaven face, even though he still had a good seven inches on her. "I like your tie." She traced the textured design from the base of his throat down to where the fabric disappeared behind the lapels of his black suit. He smelled of Old Spice and sandalwood.

He grabbed her hand and led her outside to where a black Jaguar was parked. A man in a black suit opened the door for them both, and Grayson guided her in first.

She held back a smile. "This is fancy, Grayson."

They sat in amiable silence. It was dark, but even in the darkness, she couldn't take her eyes off him. As they entered the freeway, light shone on his face, followed by a blanket of black, as they drove under the streetlights that cast an iridescent glow.

His gaze was fixed on her as well. It seemed as though every time they passed under a lamppost, Grayson's knee was a few inches closer to hers than before.

When they arrived at the venue, photographers lined either side of the staircase leading to the main entrance.

Grayson exited the car first and held out his hand for her. They walked hand-in-hand up the marble stairs, and when they reached the final landing, the cameras directed their blinding flashes to the next couple arriving.

He held the door open for her as she entered, and a swoosh of warm air engulfed her. Women were in floor-length gowns, men were in suits and ties. She spotted Lance in the corner, talking it up with a few women. He leaned in close to them as if he were whispering a secret —or something completely inappropriate, since two of the girls blushed feverishly.

There were men and women in Marine uniforms. Air Force. She turned to face Grayson. "You invited veterans?"

Glasses clinked, and the chatter was low. Music crescendoed in the background, although she hadn't a clue where it came from.

Grayson grasped her waist and walked her to the table closest to the podium. "Did I actually do something right for once?"

She laughed and nodded. "My father was in the Navy. He would have loved this. I think this event is just perfect. This banquet is for the lab, right? There are so many people here."

"Yes, we invited more people than usual this year. We have another banquet in the spring for the entire High Tower. That's usually an enormous event that Lance and I have little involvement in. You and Mya will really like it."

Talk of the future made her giddy.

He pulled out a chair for her to sit down, and a voice called out behind him. "Grayson Daniels, so nice of you to finally show your face. You bailed on the camping trip."

Cassidy and Grayson spun around.

Grayson released her waist and shook hands with the barrel-bellied man. "Jason, I'd like you to meet my… person, Cassidy."

Bowing her head and smiling, Cassidy reached for Grayson's elbow and laced her arm in his. "So, *you're* Jason?" He was shorter than she expected. From what Grayson had told her about Jason owning all of the buildings on the block the second High Tower was being built on, she expected a giant of a man with bold features and a firm handshake. Jason was as cute as a bear with his Teddy Roosevelt glasses. "Grayson was actually super adamant about going to Vermont."

Jason's eyes widened. "Really? He's rejected all my offers every year, since I've met him."

She nodded. "If I hadn't leaned back into poison oak, Grayson would have made it. So really, I'm the one to blame."

Holding his stomach, he rolled out a laugh. "You're telling me Grayson made you sit in poison oak, just so he didn't have to go? Oh, Cassidy. I like you."

Wow, this guy knew Grayson pretty well. She shrugged. "I guess in a way, yes, he's the exact reason I rubbed poison oak all over me." She smiled weakly and turned to Grayson in hopes he would say something, but he just gawked at her.

Jason burst into laughter as Grayson moved his hand

back around Cassidy's waist and squeezed her in a way that said, "you're going to pay for that."

Jason patted his chest and turned to look behind him. "I left my phone somewhere. I'd better go find it before my wife does. She's been threatening to destroy it, because I'm on my email so much." He was about to spin around, when he leaned toward Cassidy and whispered, "What she doesn't know is that I have two spares in my desk drawer at the office." He winked and left.

Grayson turned to her. "So, my beautiful date…"

Oh, she loved those words coming out of his mouth.

"…I didn't know anyone could make me look worse than I already do. So, now we're telling people I made you rub poison oak all over yourself?"

Cassidy cringed and raised her shoulders. "It seemed like the best thing to say?" She rolled her gaze to the floor, embarrassment plastered on her face. "I don't really fit in with these people, Grayson. I feel like I'm going to say something dumb." She laughed nervously, and her ankles wobbled.

Grayson placed his hand under her chin and lifted her face to meet his. "Do what I do. Ignore everyone."

She tossed her head back and laughed, almost losing her balance while doing so.

Grayson's hands were now around her waist, and he eyed her up and down. "I can't take my eyes off of you."

Cassidy wanted to memorize the passion in his eyes, the feel of his touch on her skin. She lifted her chin as if in invitation.

How had they gotten to this place? How did this

man find her and breathe his fire into her? He brought out her rage, her passion. The trust and faith that had died inside of her, Grayson revived.

She read his lips when he mouthed, "May I kiss you?" She nodded slightly, expecting him to lean forward.

All he did was turn his head to look behind him.

Lance came up to both of them, concern lacing his features. "Grayson, did you invite Rony?" He was breathless and aggravated. "By your muteness, I take that as a no."

Cassidy turned toward Grayson. "Who's Rony? Is he someone I know?"

Grayson shook his head.

Best to let the boys deal with their worries. Cassidy grasped Grayson's arm. "I'm going to hit the ladies' room."

On shaking ankles, she made it down the hallway and to the restroom. There was only one other girl in there, fixing her lipstick. She looked like a movie star, her jet-black hair shining like she just stepped out of an Herbal Essence photo shoot.

Cassidy stepped up next to her. "That color looks great on you. Red lipstick like that washes me out."

The girl pouted and eyed Cassidy through the mirror. "Yeah, I bet it does."

Brushing some loose strands of hair back into place, Cassidy couldn't help but feel a little insecure around this perfectly polished woman. Cassidy took out her own lipstick and reapplied.

The woman laid her fingers out as if she wanted Cassidy to kiss her knuckles. "I'm Veronica."

Veronica? As in Grayson's ex-girlfriend? Cassidy kept a calm face, but inside, she wanted to claw at Veronica's face.

Cassidy could see why Grayson was attracted to Veronica. He hadn't mentioned how stunning she was, but why would he? She looked nothing like Cassidy. She was immaculately tall, sculpted like a goddess, sophisticated. Cassidy was petite and pretty ordinary, in terms of looks.

Standing almost eye to eye, Cassidy didn't accept Veronica's limp fingers. Instead, she presented her own. "I'm Cassidy."

Veronica cringed as she looked at Cassidy's hands. "I see you came here with Grayson. Are you together?"

Technically, they weren't together yet. Or were they? They hadn't had that conversation, but she knew it's what both of them wanted. "Yes, Grayson and I are together."

"Uh-huh."

What was that? Cassidy squared her shoulders. "Yes, we've been together for a while now."

Veronica made that sound again. It was between a grunt and a sigh. Doubt mixed with humor. "See, the thing with Grayson is he has a hard time letting things go. Take our relationship, for example. I had dinner with him in early spring. What is it now, almost fall? And you came along…when?"

Cassidy straightened her dress. "I don't know what you're talking about. I'm sorry, but I have a date to get back to. It was so nice to meet you." She turned and headed for the door.

"Oh, Cassidy?" Veronica sang. "You forgot your lipstick here by the sink."

God. Cassidy paraded to the sink, retrieved her lipstick, and smiled at Veronica. "Thanks, Veronica."

"Please, call me Rony."

Wasn't that the guy Lance just talked about? Cassidy swiftly left the restroom, and Grayson was waiting around the corner for her.

He had his hands in his pockets. "You were gone for a while. I was nervous you walked out on me." His face was laced with worry and lust.

"Why would I walk out on you?" She giggled and stepped closer to him. "On a side note, I met Rony just a second ago. She's a real piece of work."

He outstretched his palms to her, and she accepted them.

"Why didn't you correct me earlier when I assumed she was a guy?"

He licked his lips, and his eyes gained intensity. "It didn't seem important."

The more she thought of it, the more he was right. It wasn't important.

He released her hands and cupped her face. He stroked her cheeks lightly with his fingertips. "If I'm not making myself clear, just ask me. I'll tell you anything, baby."

He leaned forward, and their lips met. They breathed together in a sweet embrace. His fingers stroked the underside of her chin as he pressed into her.

Visions of him consumed her. Him and his electric glances, his heated touch.

Everything was him, him, him.

Closing her eyes, she let him take from her what he needed, but he only gave. He was tender, gentle, and poured himself into her. Their chests were inches apart, the hypnotic pull of his chest bringing her heart closer to his until they were completely and wholeheartedly one.

Minutes passed. Hours passed. She didn't know how long Grayson had been leaning over her and caressing her face.

He pulled away, but she kept her eyes closed.

Leaning his forehead against hers, she smiled, her eyelids fluttering open, and her hands found his biceps.

He leaned into her. "After two quarks bond, when they're separated, they always find their way back to each other. Did you know that? And if there's enough force to completely tear them apart, they instantaneously duplicate so they aren't alone." His hands brushed her shoulders, her arms, all the way down to her waist. "Near or far, know that I will always be with you."

They mingled, they danced, and Lance and Colton gave a series of speeches in the background about the new laboratory. The kids from the children's home even came out for a half hour to entertain the adults. They wore suits and silk dresses. They smiled unlike any child Cassidy had ever seen.

Grayson, even though he couldn't admit it, had a heart of gold. He had a desire to give back, whether it be to right the wrongs of his past or keep Paige's memory alive. Cassidy had no doubts about him anymore. He had never specifically stated whether or not he supported the children's home being demolished, but it didn't matter because she knew that his intensions were pure.

She watched, as he tossed a young boy in the air, and couldn't help the passing thought that that he would make a good father. After a short intermission, they retreated back to the area that was set up for them, and Grayson led Cassidy to their table. He pulled out her chair.

When she sat down, she noticed that many of the seats around them were empty. She leaned into Grayson, and he placed his hand on the small of her back. "Are there guests missing?"

He nodded. "The VA asked if some of their wounded veterans could come later," he lowered his head to look at his watch, "they should be here shortly." He rubbed her back. "Apparently, some of them just got out of surgery, but they wanted to be here. We didn't want them to feel like they had to stand around the whole time or anything like that."

She continued to gaze at him. He had thought of everything.

Lance sat beside Cassidy and smiled at her. "Cassidy, you look lovely today."

His mood had significantly shifted toward her after she brought Jessica back to the High Tower. They had spoken about Grayson, why Jessica was crying, and why Cassidy had been the one bringing the young, wailing girl back to the office.

STOLEN WORDS

Lance glared at Grayson. "Grayson." He jerked his head in greeting and bitterness smothered his tone.

Grayson nodded and cast his eyes downward.

Putting her hand on Lance's knee, Cassidy leaned toward him. "He's really sorry."

A sound escaped from Lance that sounded like a snort that had been dragged through hot coals. "Grayson, apologize? I'll get a first-row ticket to that event."

"Is Jessica doing alright?" Cassidy pulled away from him and folded her hands in her lap.

Lance lifted his shoulders and unbuttoned his jacket. "When my sister got back to town in the evening, all three of us watched a movie and binged on ice cream. Jessica woke the next morning not remembering a thing. She literally asked when she could see Grayson again." He rolled his eyes in disbelief.

Footsteps approached from behind Cassidy, and a female voice exclaimed with excitement. "Kyle?"

That's what it sounded like anyway. *Kyle.* Or "hi." Grayson, Cassidy, and Lance turned around to face a woman in Navy blues, her hair pulled back into a low bun. She glowed and radiated happiness.

Standing up, Grayson reached his arms out to her. "Mary? God, I was hoping I'd see you again." His hands shook nervously as he reached out for her. "Lance, you remember Mary from the ship, right?"

Grayson and the woman hugged lightly, but one of Mary's arms was limp, and she returned Grayson's embrace singlehandedly.

He pulled away from her. "Mary, what happened to your arm?"

She quirked her lips to the side. "I'm glad it wasn't the first thing you noticed about me. I had to get elbow surgery, and my joint got infected. It was terrible, eating away at my flesh and bones. They had to remove it."

Cassidy put her hands over her mouth. "Oh my God, that's horrible."

Mary smiled widely. "I took a bullet for my best friend. She's alive, and that's all that matters to me."

Grayson gestured to the seat beside him.

Eyeing Cassidy with raised awareness, Mary grabbed Grayson's hand. "Is this the girl who wrote you all those letters?" She looked to Cassidy. "You must really love this guy."

Cassidy shook her head. "You must have me confused with someone else. I'm Cassidy Thatcher."

Mary nodded with a Cheshire cat grin on her face. "Oh, yes. You're the one."

What an odd statement. Cassidy turned to Grayson. "Grayson, did you have a girlfriend before meeting me? I don't know, maybe you had dinner with other girls?"

He cocked his head to the side. "Don't be silly."

This must have been an inside joke or something that Cassidy wasn't latching on to.

For a few minutes, more soldiers trickled into the venue and filled the empty seats. Grayson talked to Mary for a while, holding her hand, and she gave him quick nudges with her good shoulder.

Cassidy saw a mirage of Kyle in a wheelchair and turned her face away. Even though she had decided he was in her past, she couldn't help the disappointment that resurfaced when she thought about him. That unfinished business.

She turned her head again, and the illusion of Kyle was gone.

"Cassidy?" a male voice asked.

As she turned her head, all the blood seemed to escape her body. Lightheaded, she shook her head to rid herself of this hallucination, but it wouldn't go away. "Kyle?"

He was in his uniform, his hair neatly trimmed, one of his legs in a cast. He sat in a wheelchair with a smile on his face.

Was he happy to have broken her heart or what?

He reached for her, and she pulled away. "Cassidy, I've missed you. What are you doing here?" Her movement must have caught Grayson's attention, because Grayson placed one of his hands on Cassidy's shoulder, as they remained seated. "Grayson?" Confusion passed over Kyle's face, then recognition.

Cassidy whipped her head back to look Grayson in the eyes. "Do you know each other?"

Kyle wheeled closer and held out his hand to Grayson. "Grayson...I mean, Dr. Daniels, trained the Reactor Division on Ike. We had a lot of conversations. He taught my class."

Cassidy turned in her seat to face Grayson, and his hands grasped her knees. "Grayson, your hands are shaking." She placed hers over his.

There was a pause before Grayson's eyes met hers. She saw the truth there.

Shaking her head, Cassidy pushed his hands away. "You told me you didn't know Kyle."

He leaned toward her, but she stood.

Grayson followed. "You were in pain, sweetheart. I didn't want to hurt you."

Kyle meandered around in his wheelchair. "Sweetheart?" He eyed Cassidy with surprise. "Are you dating this guy?"

Pain loomed over Grayson as if he were anxious for her answer. Cassidy could see the dark clouds above his head.

Her confusion and annoyance dissipated, and she looked down at Kyle. "It doesn't matter because you *dumped* me, remember?"

Grayson's eyes softened; he was speaking to her with his gaze alone. What was he saying?

Kyle tossed his head back and cackled. "That was only because you never wrote to me, Cassidy. You know, I wouldn't do something like that unless I knew you'd moved on. I still love you."

He reached for her hand in that graceful way he always did, and she pulled away.

Mary stood up, her face scrunched up in confusion. "Kyle?"

Both Grayson and Kyle turned to face her.

What is going on?

People were looking their way now.

Cassidy grabbed Grayson's hand and pulled him into the nearest hallway. "Why does Mary keep calling you Kyle? Why did she ask if I sent you letters on Ike? I'm so confused, Grayson. Please explain this to me."

His face was blank.

"Say something, anything," she pleaded. "My past and my future are both standing in front of me, and I need to know what's happening. I need closure."

He reached for her hands and placed them on his chest. "I do know Kyle," he sighed, "I lied to you about that, because I didn't want you hurting." He cupped her face, his soft hands calming the storm inside of her. "He was in the air wing. He wanted to take my class to be a nuke, but he struggled, so I failed him. It was only partially personal."

Partially. "What do you mean *partially?*" She grasped his suit lightly and dug her fingers into his chest. "Don't tell me it's because you thought it wasn't important."

He ran his fingertips down to the tops of her shoulders and paused. With one hand, he reached into his breast pocket and pulled out a lavender envelope. It was weathered and worn. It looked like the stationery she always used, but she couldn't be sure. Cracked and folded, it looked as if it had been read a thousand times and then a thousand times more.

Grayson stared at the envelope. "After being on Ike for four weeks, this letter was accidentally given to me." He handed it to her. "It became my most prized possession."

Opening it, she gasped when she saw her handwriting. "This is mine."

He nodded.

She didn't give it back to him and held it to her chest. "So, you got one of my letters to Kyle. I still don't understand, Grayson. It seems like fate brought us together." She smiled, but he didn't smile back. Why wasn't he smiling?

"I didn't just steal this one letter, Cassidy. I have all of them."

Cocking her head to the side, she examined the letter in her hands once again. "I don't understand."

Grayson placed his hands on her face, cupping it softly. "It was supposed to be one letter, one time. But then I met Kyle—" he looked away briefly "—and I just couldn't give it to him. I couldn't give any of them to him. Mary saved them for me. She didn't know my name. I knew you were short on cash, so I called *New York's Eye*..."

"*You* called them?" All this time she had thought it was Kyle who orchestrated the Mesoamerican article. "And what did you have to do to make that happen?" Her voice wavered.

He avoided her gaze.

She couldn't help the yell that escaped from deep within her heart. "Tell me!"

"I told them that if they gave you the feature article, Lance and I would let them write an exposé on the new lab. They're always writing exaggerated articles, and I wanted them to have the truth for once."

"So, the feature article was given to me as an exchange deal?" The fact that it had nothing to do with her skill or talent and everything to do with manipulation shredded her. She couldn't look at him. She took a step back, and Grayson grimaced. "You ruined my engagement. You read my private letters to my fiancé. Did you manipulate my job with Colton, too?" With every word, her rage grew. "Don't answer that. I don't believe you right now."

What hurt the most was that he did this all out of pity.

She had taken risks.

Mya had taken risks.

He was sawing her heart open.

She turned her back to him, and his hands caressed her bare shoulders again. She rolled her shoulders and stepped away from him. "Don't touch me. Can't you see I don't want to be anywhere near you right now? Answer me. Did you have dinner with Veronica after meeting me?"

He cringed.

Throwing the letter and envelope at him, she removed her heels and stormed off toward the exit.

"Cassidy." He chased after her, and she told herself not to turn around. "When you took my workers, I didn't know it was you at the time. I had no idea. We would have met anyway." Desperation was thick behind his words.

She spun around but couldn't find the words to say.

"Cassidy, say something."

Embarrassment. Shame. Betrayal. She couldn't fit her list of emotions on any piece of paper. "I don't believe in fate or the Universe, or any of that nonsense. I can forgive you for being a pig and for not knowing what to say. But you lied to me, Grayson. Multiple times. You made me feel like I was worth it. But it was all fake. I can't forgive you for that."

Cassidy's face portrayed an array of grief, heartache, and distrust. He wanted to reach out for her, to tell her it was okay, but it wasn't okay.

Lance had warned him that this would happen. Had he listened? Partially.

Everything was partial. Partial truths, partial actions.

The one person he gave the entirety of his devotion to was walking away from him.

He wouldn't leave her. It was his silent promise to her on Ike, his declaration of feelings for her now.

She turned and exited the venue from the back door. A car was parked next to the handicap accessible ramp, and even from a distance, Grayson could tell it was Kyle getting inside the vehicle.

Kyle leaned his head out of the SUV. "Cassidy? Come with me," he shouted and waved at her.

The closer she got to him, the more panic rose in Grayson's chest.

"Cassidy, don't go." He lunged for her and grasped her hand. "You can't get down there without crossing the bridge, and it's closed. Please, don't do this. Let's talk. I'll tell you anything, baby."

A deep pond and water fountain lay between them and Kyle. Cassidy whipped her hand away and kept walking.

Grayson begged. He pleaded. He didn't know what to say that could make this evening disappear. He wanted to see her face one more time, her beautiful smile, her head tossed back in happiness. The woman in front of him was broken. She threw her shoes to the side. She put one leg in the shallow pond and then the other.

"Where are you going?" He knelt on the pond's ledge and held out his hand for her. Holding his breath, flashes of Katrina, and now Cassidy, bombarded his mind. "Don't do this, Cassidy." He didn't recognize his voice.

Not turning around, she slid deeper into the water. It was her only way out, and it broke his heart knowing she wanted to get away from him that badly. He tried to grab the fabric of her dress to pull her back toward him.

She whipped herself free and fell deeper in the water, her chest nearly covered.

Grayson flinched as she waded halfway to the middle of the pond.

Did second chances exist? Before Ike, before Cassidy, he would have said no. But now, seeing the woman who he'd latched his heart onto float away from him, he was not about to let the past repeat itself.

He put one foot into the water, then the other. He didn't even bother stripping off his jacket as he charged for her.

Reaching her in a matter of seconds, she squirmed in his arms. "Don't fight me, Cassidy. I'm not letting you go."

Her face was tear-stricken as he turned her to face him. "Don't touch me." She sobbed and rocked her shoulders from side to side to try and free herself.

"Cassidy, I love you."

She closed her eyes tightly.

"Did you hear me? I love you. Please don't go. Stay with me. Be with me." He held her close to him and breathed in her sweet scent.

She kicked and continued to swim away from him, taking his heart with her in the process. She pulled away while he continued to tug on her dress, her arms, her waist.

Together, they made their way to the closest ledge, and he grasped both of her shoulders, trying to keep her from getting out. The water was only knee deep, and Cassidy tried to stand. Her body seemed to succumb to exhaustion, and she looked at him, barely able to get to her knees. Even in the darkness, her gaze was emotionless, hollow. Her rage from earlier seeped from her body in uncontrollable pants.

He grabbed her hands. "Don't leave me."

"There are so many questions I need answered. And right now, I don't trust you. If you love me, you'll let me go, Grayson." She tried to tug herself away from him.

He looked down at her limp hands and his shaking ones. Lifting his gaze, he was met with mixed emotions.

She tore herself away so fiercely, it didn't give Grayson a chance to respond. Kyle's driver had just made it up the hill to the pond and helped Cassidy down the steep embankment.

Kyle's hand outstretched, and she took it and climbed into the vehicle.

CHAPTER TWENTY

"HEY, BABY GIRL, CAN YOU GET ME SOME WATER?"

Cassidy stood from the couch and went to the kitchen to get Kyle a glass of water. "Can you not call me that?"

"And can you bring me my meds, too?"

She went into his bedroom to get his medication. When she sat back down, he gave her a pat on the leg.

"You're awesome. How does it feel to be back in Montana?"

She didn't know how to answer that. The words of endearment didn't sit well with her, either. For the last two weeks, all she had thought about was Grayson. Her mind was everywhere but the present. It was as if she hadn't come back to Montana with Kyle, after all.

Grayson's face haunted her. She waited for a demanding email, but none came. She broke her business contract with Colton. She ran from New York. Again.

"Cassidy?" Kyle yawned and sank further into his leather couch. "Let's go on a date this afternoon. It's been so long since we've seen each other, and I want to do something nice for you."

Cassidy believed that leaving with Kyle was the right thing to do. He needed her right now. God, she was so angry that Grayson lied to her about not knowing Kyle. Lied to her about hoarding her letters. Lied about everything.

Now, Cassidy was helping Kyle get situated in his new apartment. He told her to stay with him, but she insisted that she stay in a nearby hotel instead.

She adjusted her seat. "I'd like that, Kyle. Can we go now? I'm starving. I haven't eaten since yesterday morning."

He shrugged. "Oh, I didn't mean now. Can we wait a few more hours? I'm really not hungry."

His response took her by surprise. "Oh. Should I order take out or something instead?"

Turning to face her, he smiled. "You're amazing."

This was far from the date she had pictured. Even just to catch up. Kyle walked around with some help, and he was sleeping all the time. His leg was broken, but it wasn't like he was immobile.

She held her palm out to him. "Do you have a card I should use?"

"You aren't paying for it?" He reached into his pocket and dug out a handful of cash.

After she called for Chinese delivery, she walked over to where Kyle had his leg propped up and his arm slung over his eyes. "You never told me how you hurt your leg. Were you wounded in action?"

He rolled his eyes. "Oh, baby girl, you don't want to hear about my heroic acts during times of war. It's too soon. I don't think I'm ready to share the story with you."

She nodded and smiled weakly. "Sure. Yeah. Do you mind if I call Mya? I haven't spoken to her for two weeks. I'm sure she's mad at me."

Kyle was asleep.

The Chinese takeout came, and Cassidy ate alone while contemplating a text to Mya. Cassidy took out her phone and opened her messages.

Cassidy: Mya, I don't know how to explain this. I just needed clarity.

It took fourteen minutes for Mya to respond.

Mya: Did you find said clarity?

Relief opened Cassidy's airways, and she could breathe once again.

Cassidy: Not really. How's Grayson?
Mya: Oh, he's great. How are you?
Cassidy: Great.

Cassidy hadn't been to her parents' graves since their

funeral. Her heart couldn't cope with the fact that their deaths had been her fault. She fought the urge to see them—to face the fact that they were really gone.

Living a false reality that they were "out of town" comforted her.

Seeing their marble headstones brought a rush of adrenaline through her body, as if she'd passed through a stone wall.

"I need your advice, Mom," Cassidy whispered, as she lay in between her mother and father's graves. "I'm sorry I haven't come to visit." The sky was gray and fog formed in the foothills. She curled up next to her mother and ran her fingers along the headstone. "I miss you."

The banquet seemed like a distant memory—a nightmare that she had awoken from and couldn't retell any of the details. But she tried. She spoke every word slowly, relaying every detail to her parents as the sky grew dark.

"...and now I'm here, wishing you were here to tell me what to do."

A breeze swooped by, and a raindrop fell on her face. It was just a little trickle, like heaven was crying with her.

"Mya and I live over a pole dancing studio, now." She laughed, and a hiccup escaped from deep in her throat. "Can you believe our Mya has changed that much?" Guilt started to corrode her insides. "I've lived an adventure-filled life, Mama. I wish you could see me now."

Luckily, Cassidy's phone had died, and she couldn't check her messages. She was tempted, though. She kept pressing the power button in hopes that it would turn on just long enough to see if she had any missed texts.

The torture of the unknown was her new addiction.

Limbo seemed her only option at this point.

The sky seemed to fall in heavy drops of rain. Cassidy turned to her parents, kissed the ground above each of them, and whispered, "I'm sorry."

When she returned to her rental car, she wiped her tears and plugged her phone into the charger. She hadn't found the advice she desperately needed, but the door leading to her past seemed to close.

Cassidy's phone buzzed as soon as she stepped into Kyle's apartment. "Smithsonian Institute, Cooper Hewitt" flashed on the screen. Kyle was still asleep on the couch, so she crept into his bedroom, closed the door, and whispered, "Hello?"

"Cassidy, it's Dr. Pinkerton."

Her heart raced.

"I heard you earned the feature article in *New York's Eye*. I'm looking forward to reading your piece."

She nodded, then realized she needed to use her words. She spoke as softly as she could. "Yes, I was commissioned the article, but...I don't think I'll actually finish it in time."

"Are you alright? I can barely hear you." He sounded concerned.

"I'm...great. I just can't raise my voice."

"Ah, I see. Well, Cassidy I've recommended you for a full-time position at the Cooper Hewitt. I hope you'll consider it."

Her jaw dropped. "But...I'm..." What could she

say? "A *full-time* position? Like, I'll be paid? I don't have enough internship hours yet, Dr. Pinkerton. I don't have any type of degree."

He chuckled. "Grayson has offered his new laboratory on the first floor to help with that. You and I can analyze dig samples at the High Tower Lab to help you finish your archaeology degree, and you can work at the Cooper Hewitt as well."

Her eyes ached.

She beat on her chest hard to bring it back to life. She wished her parents were alive, so she could ask for their advice. They'd know what to do. Wasn't this the offer of a lifetime? Working at one of the best museums and finally earning her archaeology degree? But what then?

His laugh bellowed through the ear piece. "That man can't stop saying all these amazing things about you."

She wanted to ask him what Grayson had said about her. She wanted to ask how Grayson was and if it looked like he was getting enough sleep. Because she wasn't. Was this Grayson's attempt to get back with her?

The thought of Grayson bribing her with another pity position made her nauseous.

"To be honest, Dr. Pinkerton, I've been thinking about pursuing architecture. I know the Cooper Hewitt is huge on that, perhaps that's why I fell in love with the museum in the first place. In hindsight, I think I knew architecture was my path all along but didn't know enough to pursue it. I know this is crazy, but my time in New York really changed my perspective on things." A light knock sounded at the door behind her. "Can you give me some time to think about this? Thank you so much for your call, I just have some personal things to deal with."

"Yes, yes, Cassidy. Take all the time you need. Let me know when and if you're ready to talk."

She hung up and opened the bedroom door.

Kyle stood there on his crutches. "Jesus, Cassidy. Could you keep it down? I'm trying to sleep. Did you order some food for us?"

It's right on the table if you'd just look. She nodded in the general direction of his small kitchen.

He hobbled and opened a few of the boxes. "It's cold, but thanks anyway."

"Hey, Kyle?"

He looked up at her with disinterest.

"What do you think about moving to New York? I mean, they have a wonderful VA there. You wouldn't have to travel so much when you're deployed...would you be open to discussing that with me?"

He shook his head and grabbed a fork from one of the drawers to his right. "We decided on Montana, because it's where we're from. And it's cheaper here. You know you can't afford New York."

She stood taller. "I'd like to finish my degree in archaeology and start pursuing architecture."

Kyle rolled his eyes. "I thought we were done talking about New York. And why do you want to go into architecture now? You can't keep jumping around from thing to thing. You're getting too old for this."

"I'm not *jumping* around, and I'm twenty-seven. I

realized, I'm passionate about more than one thing. Why can't you be more supportive?"

"Why can't you start a blog or something you can do from home?"

"I don't want to stay at home all the time, Kyle. I want a career. Something I love doing. And while you were overseas thinking of ways to break up with me, Grayson opened up all these doors for me to explore what I love to do."

Slamming the fork down on the table, he growled. "Can we *not* talk about him?"

Cassidy recoiled.

"What's gotten into you? I know, he was a nice little rebound, but he ruined our relationship. You didn't ask my permission to do any of that stuff. I've forgiven you."

"Excuse me?" She crossed her arms over her chest. "Permission? Forgiven me? I haven't done anything wrong. I feel like I've finally found a place I can thrive, and I don't understand why you can't support that."

"Yes, *permission*. That's how it's always been, Cassidy. Have you forgotten? I thought we were finally working on things, and everything was good, until today." Kyle reached behind his back to dig his fingers into his shoulder and massage there. "You've never been this argumentative. What's gotten into you?"

That's because he had never challenged her the way Grayson did. She could forget Grayson, but she didn't want to. "What if I told you I got a second chance at my dream job?"

He lowered his hand and clutched the kitchen

counter. "I'd say, you need a new hobby. I'm tired of hearing about this."

Fire burned in her stomach. "Archaeology isn't just a hobby, Kyle. It's something I went to school for. I wish you'd stop saying that."

"You have to make sacrifices, Cassidy." He spoke as if she didn't understand English. "New York changed you. You never used to be," he waved his hand up and down at her like she was a wild animal, "like *this*. I don't like this side of you. Besides, why would you want to go back to New York—are you listening?—with all those people there that lied and screwed you over?"

She shivered.

God, what would Mya do in this situation? Or Grayson?

Even though Grayson lied to her, he didn't make her feel like she was sacrificing anything. He opened up his heart, and she knew he tried to help her in the ways he knew how.

Cassidy looked away and took a few calming breaths. "After the banquet, you talked about pressing charges on Grayson. Are you going to do that?"

Laughing, he nearly shoved the takeout boxes away. "There you go talking about him, again. And I have already pressed charges. Do you know how much money I am going to get out of this? I won't ever have to work again."

She would have understood if he wanted to press charges because Grayson stole his fiancée. She would have understood if he wanted to press charges because he was heartbroken and lonely on Ike.

Money? Was that really the first thing he thought about?

Cassidy was just a stepping stone in Kyle's plan for life. "Did you have internet access on Ike?"

Kyle rolled his eyes and shrugged. "Yeah, I guess. I was on Facebook a few times."

And he never once thought to message her.

He continued to shovel food into his mouth and spoke through mouthfuls of fried rice. She couldn't stand him.

She walked up next to him and moved his one crutch to the side. She seethed. "You didn't even think about writing me a letter? I mean, I met Mary. She seemed like she could have helped you. You didn't have any problem breaking up with me."

Kyle sighed. "I told you, you never wrote to me, so I didn't know what to do. I'm sorry, Cassidy. Really, I am. Please calm down." His face softened, but she wouldn't fall for it.

How was it that getting no apology from Grayson felt better than this lousy apology from Kyle?

"Besides," he continued, "did you see Mary? She has one arm. I can't imagine her being useful at all." He laughed to himself. "Can you imagine her in battle? What is she going to do, slap someone with her empty sleeve?"

"That's *enough.*" She grabbed her purse from the kitchen table and walked to the front door. "I never want to see you again."

He stopped chewing.

"First of all, I don't need your permission to do

anything. I moved to New York to start a new life, and I did. Without you. I don't need you, Kyle. I don't even want you. You've been treating me like crap since the first day I met you, and for some reason, I let you. I don't know what you thought would happen with me coming here, but it was a mistake. I don't love you anymore."

"Where are you going?" Limping toward her in his cast, he put his hands out in question.

Breathe.

She smiled.

He had given her exactly what she needed: closure.

She reached for the door handle, took a breath, and squeezed it. "Home."

CHAPTER TWENTY-ONE

G RAYSON'S DIET CONSISTED OF STALE CRACKERS AND whiskey.

His stomach ached. Or, was that the side effect of a broken heart?

The bathroom in his house needed painting, but he couldn't get himself to do it. He couldn't pick any color without being reminded of Cassidy.

There was paperwork that needed to be taken care of, but he stacked it among the other piles of things in his kitchen, on the floor of his house—anywhere there was an empty space.

Grayson couldn't stand being at the High Tower Lab. Knowing that he'd taken Cassidy into every room, walked her down every hall, and brushed against her in his office, he avoided the lab whenever he could.

The only place he hadn't taken her was the men's restroom, so when he did go to work, he found himself taking far too many bathroom breaks. Every room was a dungeon.

He couldn't even stand being at his house, knowing she worked so hard to fix it up for him.

Everywhere he looked, Cassidy was there with a chain around his heart. He texted her every day, only to delete the message before sending. He even called her every morning and every night only to hang up quickly before it rang.

The first few days, he was in shock. Grayson walked around in denial, believing Cassidy would stroll through the front door, singing a terrible off-key tune. But that never happened.

The pitch of Cassidy's voice faded from his memory, but he remembered every word she had said.

Her smile, those awful clothes he first met her in, the stunning woman underneath. His phone buzzed, and he didn't even bother looking at it. He knew it wasn't Cassidy, so why care? It was likely Lance bothering him yet again.

Grayson was on his first vacation in sixteen years. A vacation from life. He slept all day and stared at the ceiling all night. "God." He groaned and rubbed his eyes. The pain was supposed to go away. He rubbed at the empty spot in his chest. He didn't know the cure for losing her.

He reached for his phone that was sitting on the living room table and brought it to his face. It was, indeed, Lance.

Lance: You coming in to work? People are starting to worry...text me.

Another text followed almost immediately.

Lance: Don't worry about that Kyle guy. I heard he broke his leg during lunch hour trying to do a backflip off the starboard side of the ship. What kind of sailor breaks his leg jumping into the water?

Grayson tossed his phone on the ground, grabbed his glass of whiskey, and stood to walk to the fireplace, where he stared into its fireless depths. Thoughts of Cassidy continued to flood his brain.

He took a few steps back, until his heels bumped into the couch behind him. He needed to feel closer to her. With one lazy hand, he dragged the couch around the wall and into the next room. He faced it toward the kitchen sink and grimaced as the legs scratched the floors Cassidy worked so hard to finish. She never did teach him how to polish the floors. His heart cried out for her.

Images of Cassidy danced around his mind, as he slouched into the couch and gazed at the ceiling for what seemed like endless minutes. Succumbing to the memory of her, his eyes followed Cassidy, as she walked barefoot across the hardwood floor. It was like she was there, bending over to choose paint colors. She looked up at him, and those tendrils of hair fell into her eyes like they always did, begging him to brush them away.

He stared at the yellow space in front of him. He

raised his glass up in a toast to the ugly wall he loathed. The color was still the ugliest thing he had ever seen, yet he couldn't turn his face away. No, it was absolutely perfect...because it was hers.

His fantasies were interrupted by a knock at the door. He groaned. His muscles tingled after his efforts of dragging the couch to the kitchen—that alone was too much movement to handle.

The knocking continued, and Grayson ignored it. From his peripheral vision, Lance's silhouette appeared through the back door, and he knocked.

"It's unlocked," Grayson mouthed with his arm slung over his eyes.

Grayson could hear Lance remove his sport coat and put it on the barstool. The couch underneath Grayson sank further. Grayson continued to lay there.

Lance placed his hand on Grayson's shoulder. "You should get up."

"You *just* texted me. You know that, right?" Grayson spoke into his arm which was still covering his face.

"Yeah, and you didn't respond. I'm worried about you."

Grayson sat up slowly in obedience. Lance looked concerned...and tired. He had dark circles under his eyes, much like the circles under Grayson's.

Grayson leaned back down. "You look like hell."

"You look worse."

A sound came from the hallway, and Mya appeared in the kitchen with a basket full of laundry. "Oh, honey." She sat next to Grayson and put her hand on his shoulder. "I know you're hurting, but this isn't the way to live. You need to go after her."

Lance sat there dumbfounded. "What are you doing here?"

Mya cocked her head. "Please. Collecting dirty clothes."

The three of them sat on the small couch, Mya leaning on the arm rest, Grayson in the middle, and Lance at his other side.

Grayson turned to face Mya. "Have you heard from her?"

She nodded.

He sat up quickly. "Did she ask about me?"

Mya pushed on his shoulder, until his back was against the cushion. "Lay down. I'm going to cook you dinner."

"No." Grayson stood and held his hands out to her. "As much as I love your company, you are the reason I am eating crackers."

She shifted her weight to one hip. "You are impossible." Turning, Mya walked to the fridge and took out one of her protein shakes. She placed it to her lips and took a drink.

Lance swallowed hard. "I've never seen Mya in normal clothes. I didn't know cotton could stretch like that."

Grayson glared at Lance. "It's a polyester blend. And Mya is absolutely off limits, Lance."

Lance pulled out his phone and spoke in a hushed tone. "We need to talk to our lawyer, Grayson. I can also get Brian Wittington involved. He's getting back from Dubai this week. I can set up a meeting with him."

Grayson didn't know why Lance was practically whispering. It wasn't like Mya didn't know what was going on.

The following weekend, Grayson dragged himself out of bed to meet Brian. They met at a small café, and Brian dressed casually in jeans and a T-shirt.

Grayson's phone vibrated. It was Mya. He lifted a finger to Brian. "I'm sorry. This is important." He turned away slightly. "Mya, are you okay?"

"Grayson, how do I turn on the dryer, again? Do I put this white powder stuff in it and just press 'start'?"

He smiled at her inability to do normal, everyday tasks. "I'll take care of it when I get home. You have your cooking class tonight, right?"

"Yup. Right after my pole dancing class. I put all the dirty clothes where you instructed, but you're going to have to take care of it when you get home. My clothes are piled in there, too. Thanks in advance. K, bye." She hung up.

Turning to face Brian, Grayson shrugged. "Mya Rivers, she's kind of my roommate right now. She's not involved in this." He felt the need to explain.

There was a distant look in Brian's gaze. "Yeah, I know Cassidy and Mya. Mya's living with you now?"

Grayson tilted his head from side to side. "Not really. She has an apartment, but she's been spending a lot of time at my place ever since this whole…thing."

Brian licked his lips. "And how is Mya doing? Is she happy?"

Grayson nodded. "Yeah. Lively, flirty, crazy. If you know Mya, you know how she is. She's my secretary now, too."

"Secretary?"

Both of them laughed, and Grayson ran his hand through his hair. "Her first week was rough, but I haven't had anyone better work for me."

Before Grayson could ask how Brian knew the girls, Brian lowered his head, took a deep breath, and said, "Well, thanks for taking care of her. Let's talk about your situation."

Grayson explained everything to Brian, from what happened on Ike to Cassidy and him meeting by chance, only to meet in person again under different circumstances. He talked about Mary and how he didn't want her getting into any trouble. He wanted to settle this all outside of court. What he did was wrong, and he'd do what he had to make it right again.

Brian didn't take notes. He didn't record anything. He listened patiently, attentively, and when Grayson finished, he shook Grayson's hand. "I can only fix so much, Grayson. But I'll see what I can do."

Grayson dragged his feet, as he walked into the High Tower after having been on "vacation" for four weeks.

He saw the glances, rather, he could *feel* them, because he didn't have the energy to make eye contact with anyone. Hell, he didn't have the passion to shave, let alone raise his eyes to greet someone.

He finally got to the second floor. Maybe no one would see him.

Pens tapping on desks, the murmur of voices, everything seemed so loud. He couldn't possibly still be hungover. He hadn't had a drink since before meeting with Brian. His ears rang, his eyes rolled, and Grayson just wanted to get to his office.

Lance must have seen him, because he shot out of his chair and rushed down the hallway. Good thing Lance held the door open for Grayson, because he would have just walked straight through it. It would have moved eventually.

His face laced with concern, Lance breathed heavily. "I wasn't expecting you in today. You're wearing sweat clothes—"

"I'm ready."

Shaking his head in confusion, Lance's brow furrowed. "Ready for what? Certainly not work."

"Help." Grayson leaned the back of his thighs on his desk and looked down at his feet. He had worn two different socks. "I need you to help me fix myself. I'm ready for your sermons. Help me change."

Lance approached slowly, until his feet were in front of Grayson's.

"I need her back." Grayson's voice was cracked. "Everywhere I look, she's there. I don't know what to do, how to reach out to her. I clutch my phone to my chest every day, waiting for her to give me a sign, but she doesn't. My nightmares of Katrina have been replaced with those of Cassidy swimming away from me." He eventually managed to raise his eyes to Lance.

They stood in the center of the office, eyeing each other with varying levels of worry in their expressions, their breaths.

Lance pointed to the black leather couch, and Grayson eventually moved there to sit. "Take notes, Grayson, because I don't ever want to repeat myself again after this. First, for once in your life, you're going to apologize. Then, we'll work on the other parts of your flawed character."

CHAPTER TWENTY-TWO

CASSIDY DIDN'T ACCEPT THE FULL-TIME POSITION AT THE museum, but she did accept Dr. Pinkerton's help to finish her archaeology degree, so she could move on to pursue architecture. Her time spent with Colton opened her eyes to an entirely new profession, and she didn't see why she couldn't pursue both her passions. Once she left Kyle's place and arrived at her Motel 6, she called Dr. Pinkerton, and they came up with a game plan for the following Monday.

But there was another phone call she dreaded to make.

She waited anxiously as it rang.

"*New York's Eye*, you're speaking to Karen Joseph."

Cassidy inhaled. "Karen. Hi. It's Cassidy. I'm calling about my commissioned article—"

"Oh, it's fantastic, Cassidy! I thought the team emailed you. A very different twist, very emotional, I wasn't sure if the editors would go for it, but they love it. I don't know how you did it."

What? Cassidy called to apologize to Karen for not meeting her deadline. "Um…"

"I'm happy you called because we're running this edition a little early. We gave your assistant one of the first prints. Congratulations, Cassidy. The editors are thrilled with the content."

This conversation was so confusing. Fear pooled in her throat. Cassidy hadn't even started to write an article on Mesoamerican culture, let alone submit it. She didn't have an assistant. Karen continued to speak about upcoming magazine editions and how she'd love to keep Cassidy's name on file.

Thoroughly confused, Cassidy kept the phone pressed to her ear in a daze. She continued to say, "Uh-huh," and "Yes," as Karen spoke.

The temptation to call Mya was overwhelming. Cassidy stopped herself. She had walked away from New York without a word, isolating herself to deal with the conflict that stirred within her. She'd been in Montana for nearly five weeks, and Mya had barely spoken to her since she left. She only sent a sporadic text every other day to ask if Cassidy was doing okay, and Cassidy would respond with the same word—great.

Cassidy's phone buzzed, and a text from Mya flashed on the screen.

Mya: Open the door.

Cassidy stood up from her bed and walked the few paces to the front door.

Mya stood there with a wide grin on her face. "Tell me you missed me."

Cassidy's jaw dropped. "How did you know I was staying at this hotel? And Mya—"

"Wait. Before you tell me you miss me, hear me out." Mya stepped inside, removed her red pumps and knee-length jacket, and placed them next to the small window at the side of the room overlooking nothing but bricks. The hotel had been squished between two existing buildings. Windows hardly seemed necessary. "I forgive you." She sighed. "I know what it feels like to have someone you love betray you." Mya sat on the edge of the bed. "I even forgive you for leaving me alone, scaring me to death when I couldn't find you, and making me do laundry." She shook her head. "I had to cook for myself and feed myself. That's no way for a woman to live. But you know who was there for me the entire time?"

Cassidy shrugged.

"Grayson. He enrolled me in a cooking class, can you believe it? He said that if I didn't learn how to boil an egg, then I'd never be successful. So, naturally, I listened to him. He opened his tiny, itty bitty, hermit house to me. He supported me, even though I could tell he was hurting. He cares about me, your cousin, someone he has absolutely no romantic feelings for." Mya licked her lips. "He's broken without you."

Lowering her head, Cassidy moved to sit on the bed

next to Mya. "So much has happened these past few weeks. I didn't mean to abandon you."

Mya cocked her head to the side. "I'm listening. You were going to tell me how amazing I am."

Cassidy couldn't help but laugh. "You, my cousin, are amazing." Cassidy sat on the bed next to Mya. "I called *New York's Eye* today, and they said I had already submitted an article. And something about an assistant. Did you submit an article to them on my behalf?"

Mya shook her head. "No. I just assumed you weren't going to submit one. You seemed to be happily distracted working with Colton. I wasn't sure what you were going to do after you left us."

Left us. Why did Mya have to say it like that? Cassidy only managed a whisper. "I guess, I'll find out soon enough, because she said they're running this edition early."

Reaching into her purse, Mya pulled out a white envelope and handed it to Cassidy. "This is from him."

Him. Cassidy couldn't even bear to think his name.

It was thick and had multiple sheets of paper inside. She pressed the contents in between her fingers praying it wasn't a Dear John letter from Grayson. She was too late. Shaking her head, she gave it back to Mya. "I can't open it. Please, can we just talk about everything that's gone on? I don't want to be on bad terms with you—"

"Open. The. Letter." Shoving it into Cassidy's hands, Mya turned her face as if that was going to give Cassidy privacy.

Slowly, she broke the seal and pulled out the lavender envelope Grayson had showed to her at the banquet. The edges were even more worn. The face of the paper was severely weathered as if Grayson had continued to read it again and again.

She held it to her chest and reached into the white envelope to see if there was anything else for her—a sign maybe? She'd even take a demanding Post-It note. She would take anything as long as it was from him.

An ivory sheet of paper was neatly folded inside, and she pulled it out. Running her fingers across the deckled bottom edge, her heart raced as she finally managed to look at the words inscribed on the page.

Cassidy,

I fell in love with you twice. First, when I received this letter and again in New York.

What I did was wrong, and I am so sorry. I never meant to hurt you.

At the banquet, you said that if I loved you, I would let you go. As much as it pains me, inside this envelope you'll find my heart. I don't seem to be in need of it anymore.

Love,

Grayson

She couldn't lift her eyes off his words. His elegant, blocked script embodied his personality, his signature as passionate as his gaze.

Mya turned to face her and shrugged ever so slightly. "And?"

Cassidy sniffed. "I'll tell you everything on the plane back to New York." She was going to let Grayson explain everything from the beginning.

Mya filled Cassidy in on what she had been doing the last few weeks. "Grayson lost about ten pounds, because he refused to eat my food. If only I were so lucky to drop that much weight. I really didn't think you could screw up spaghetti, but I did. So that's when he helped me find a cooking class." She beamed. "I can cook Italian…"

Cassidy tried to listen, but all she could think about was how slow this plane was moving. She held Grayson's letter to her heart as if that would let him know she was coming back for him.

"…and you'll never believe who's in my cooking class." Mya's eyebrows raised for emphasis. "Isabella and her BF forever and ever, *Veronica*." She rolled her eyes. "I've never met Veronica before, but she held her hand out to me like I was a peasant. Like, was I supposed to kiss those boney fingers?"

Looking over to Mya, Cassidy smiled, grateful that they could fall back into their relationship so easily. Cassidy laughed. "Trust me, I know that handshake of hers. Please tell me you made a better meal than her."

Mya nodded. "Way better. All she could talk about was Grayson this and Grayson that."

Cassidy's ribcage ached with longing.

"She totally burned her meal, because she wouldn't shut up. She's trouble. During the class, she just couldn't get over the fact that she apparently screwed Grayson over, and he hasn't forgiven her yet. I mean, that's not how forgiveness works. And get this, her full name is Veronica Amelia Gomez." She laughed out loud like it was the funniest thing she'd ever heard.

Cassidy didn't get what the joke was.

Looking at Cassidy incredulously, Mya snickered. "Her initials, Cassidy."

That didn't explain anything.

Exasperated, Mya leaned her shoulder against Cassidy. "V.A.G. No wonder Isabella is such a demonic bi-atch, her best friend's name is Vagina!"

CHAPTER TWENTY-THREE

COLTON BEAMED. "I HAD TO PRETEND I WAS CASSIDY'S assistant, but it's done. The lady was super skeptical at first, but after she saw both articles were written by you, she was putty in my hands, man."

Lance stared at Grayson with worried eyes. "Are you sure you want to do this? There's no turning back once that magazine publishes this tomorrow morning."

The three of them sat in Grayson's office, Lance on his black leather couch, Colton in Grayson's desk chair, and Grayson in one of the small arm chairs.

Grayson sighed. "Yes, Lance. For the hundredth time, yes."

Shifting in his seat uncomfortably, Lance tapped his foot nervously. "Brian won't be able to cover this up."

Sometimes, Lance just needed to calm down. "I know."

Colton spun around lightly in Grayson's chair. "You

realize that once this gets out, we're all off the second High Tower expansion? You might even lose your job."

Grayson nodded. "I've made sure that you two are safe. Really, Colton, you didn't even know about this until a few weeks ago. I don't think I'll be able to keep my promise to you, though."

Raising his eyebrows, Colton nodded. "There will be other jobs. I got to work on the lab downstairs which turned out to be a huge success. Don't worry about me, Grayson. I say, you've kept your word just fine."

Lance sighed. "If you get arrested, can I keep Mya?"

Grayson smirked. "Yes. God knows you need all the help you can get."

"Good, because I'm going to need her help to hire another batch of interns in a few weeks. You're going to give me permission for that, too."

It had been a few days since Mya left New York to find Cassidy. His heart ached for Cassidy, but knowing Mya was with her comforted him. All he wanted was her happiness, and if him not being in her life gave her that, then he would try to accept that.

Although, his track record for "trying" was crap.

Lance and Grayson's lawyer couldn't fend Kyle off for much longer. Brian kept his word and tried to make the drama go away, but it didn't stop the calls from reporters. Soon, the police would get involved.

New York's Eye did their interview as promised. Lance and Grayson spoke of the laboratory, and Lance even clearly stated that they didn't own the entire building—they just managed the first two floors. That was a big step for him. Image was important to Lance, almost as important as it was to Mya, but even she had changed drastically in the timeframe Grayson knew her.

While teaching Mya how to do her own laundry at the house, she had mentioned that she didn't think Cassidy would submit an article after finding out about Grayson's involvement behind it. So, he wrote a personal essay to submit instead.

He wrote about Katrina's death and how finding Cassidy's letter on Ike was his second chance at forgiveness. He described his distaste of Kyle and how his innocent need to protect Cassidy quickly transformed into something deeper. The hardest part was recalling Cassidy walking away and the way he jumped into the pond after her, just like he had jumped in after Katrina.

Grayson knew his days were numbered, and he'd likely go back to prison. He just didn't know when. He didn't want there to be any confusion on what happened. No false articles in *The New York Times* or someone dragging Lance or Colton into this mess.

He wanted to take full responsibility and without a doubt, set the story straight. If anything about his personal life was to be plastered on the internet, it was at least going to be the truth.

Colton leaned back and stared at Lance, then at Grayson. "We have your back. If they come for you tomorrow, is there anything you want us to do while you're away?"

Grayson nodded. "Rich-man Parker's place. I want you to find a way to buy it."

Lance stood. "*That's* your farewell request?"

Turning to face Lance, Grayson rubbed his eyes with the pads of his palms. Exhaustion pulled at his every limb. He didn't want the morning to come. "When word of this gets out, like Colton said, we'll be off the second High Tower build. I'm certain the children's home will be demolished, even after all our efforts. I want to transform Parker's home to be suitable enough for all those children. I need you to promise me, you'll make that happen."

Turning to Colton, Lance nodded.

Colton bowed his head in acceptance.

Grayson rubbed his hands together. "And, I want to name it after Paige."

Lance tried to lighten the mood. "Jesus, Grayson, it's not like you're going to be locked up forever. Lighten up."

The three of them sat in Grayson's office until the sun rose. They drank whiskey and talked about everything going on in their lives. It wasn't friends catching up. It was goodbye.

Grayson drove back to Laramie Hill, climbed through his hedge, and took a long, hot shower. After putting on Cassidy's favorite outfit of his, a worn-out T-shirt and jeans, he sat on the couch that still rested in front of Cassidy's wall. After long minutes, he walked outside and dangled his feet off the edge of his empty swimming pool.

Footsteps crunched on the gravel, and a hard knock tapped on the front door. He could hear it from the other side of the house. This was it. He had been in such a deep trance, he couldn't hear any sirens. There weren't any red and blue lights that bounced off the stone and brick of the walls. With sluggish limbs, Grayson stood and strolled to the front of the cottage.

He stopped breathing. The world stopped spinning, and everything floated around him in slow motion.

Cassidy stepped off the gravel pathway toward him.

She held the most recent publication of *New York's Eye* in her left hand and small puddles of tears welled in her eyes.

Her voice wavered. "I went to the High Tower, thinking you'd be there. Then I saw this on the stand out front."

He lunged for her and in two steps pulled her into him, lifting her chin and kissing her impatiently. He didn't know if she had come back for him or if she was a hallucination, but he would have one last taste of Cassidy Thatcher.

He wrapped his arms around her waist and pulled her tight against him. She was warm, and her hands clutched his sleeves. He couldn't stop murmuring, "I'm sorry, I'm sorry," against her lips.

Slowly, she pulled away from him, and he continued to grasp at her.

Her chin quivered. "Tell me you still love me."

How could she not see his desperation for her? It was in the way he looked at her, the way his hands clasped her waist.

She didn't need to ask him twice. He leaned his forehead against hers. "I love you."

The whistle of sirens filled the air, and Cassidy dug

her face into Grayson's chest. "Why did you have to write this? I was coming back for you. Why?"

He combed her hair with his fingertips. "I'm ready to let people in. This was going to get out, eventually. I'd rather it come from me."

Her arms tightened around him. "Say it, again."

"I love you." He whispered sweet nothings in her ear until the sound of police cars were right outside the hedge walls. In these last moments, he savored her scent and refreshed his memory of the inflections in her voice. He let her touch engrave his body, so she'd be with him always. "And, you don't have to say it back, Cassidy. Say it when you're ready. And believe me, I'll be yearning for the day when I hear you say the words."

Grayson didn't need to turn around to know someone was behind him. "Grayson Daniels, you're under arrest for mail theft."

Cassidy didn't release her grasp around his waist as his arms were pulled away and cuffed.

"You have the right to remain silent. Anything you say can and will be used against you in a court of law."

Cassidy shook her head in Grayson's chest, as the officer pulled him backward. She stayed tethered to him.

"You have the right to have an attorney..."

Grayson tried to lean forward. "Cassidy?"

"...If you cannot afford one, one will be appointed to you by the court."

"Cassidy." He spoke louder.

She looked up at him.

He gazed into her eyes. "Wait for me."

Another officer helped the first pull Grayson through

the hedge. Cassidy was forced to release her grip, but she still managed to follow.

"Yes. I'll wait for you." Her smile was weak, but her expression was filled with hope. "I will visit you whenever I can. I'll write to you every day."

She leaned her forehead on his chest and sobbed as he placed his chin atop her head one last time. He couldn't help but smile into her hair. She leaned back to lift her eyes to his as the officers guided Grayson into the back of the cop car.

The window was open, and she reached for his face in disbelief.

He leaned forward and kissed her cheek, the other, and then her lips once more. "I love you," he whispered against her skin.

Words brewed on the tips of her lips as if she was lost for words. "Why are you smiling?"

"Because, finally, your letters will be addressed to me."

EPILOGUE

PRISON IS THE SAME AS I REMEMBER. INMATES BEAT ON their cells all day long and yell profanities at each other.

Duke is still here in 118. He hasn't changed one bit. The middle-aged man continues to buy toothbrushes, file them down, and believe he's the reincarnation of the Count of Monte Cristo, and he's going to dig himself out. Except I don't think he realizes we're on the third floor.

My cell is small and quaint. There's a toilet in the back corner, and I have a mirror that the other inmates say is glass. I believe it's stainless steel, but I'd have to see its atomic structure to be sure. I tried convincing a guard to let me take a sample home after my six months are up, but he said that was forbidden. Jesus Christ, it's just for research.

At least, I don't have a cellmate. I'm grateful for that. I was worried I'd get paired up with some loon. I don't think I need to worry about the guys here, because for some reason, everyone in this place thinks I've committed a crime worse than mail theft. "Mail theft" must be code for something. I have no idea. But today, I was inducted into the brotherhood gang, and my new brothers keep trying to tattoo shamrocks on my face.

Lance would be pleased to know that I fit in just fine here.

If you'd be willing to spend your life with an ex-convict, when I get out of here, maybe my shamrock brothers can be my groomsmen. What do you think about that?

I love you.

Grayson

THE END

YOUR WORDS

Now, to the most important thing—you! Your words mean more to me than my own. Thank you for taking the time to read *Stolen Words*, and thank you for sharing your opinions on your blogs, Amazon, and all other platforms. It only feels right that we finish together. There's no me without you.

> "I am new to this wonderful author so I wasn't sure what to expect. But one thing is for sure...SHE NAILED IT! I couldn't put it down! I went into this book blind. I would give this book 5 out of 5 STARS! The ending BLEW me away!"
>
> — KAIT-CUDDLEMEBOOKS

> "India Caedmon knows how to start a conflagration that has the reader rooting for her lovers! Her

appealing and quirky characters are irresistible and draw the reader effortlessly into her story. Anyone would think these two thrown together would be a disaster! How could they possibly learn and grow from each other, let alone ignite into love?"

— NANCY REYNOLDS

"Both Grayson and Cassidy deal with tragic guilt, living behind borders not allowing them their true happiness. Grayson and Cassidy learn, that all the things that happen in space and time, there's no way that one instant could have possibly been their own doing. Until that one serendipitous moment when the wrong letter was put into the right hand."

— AUTHOR OF THE SECRET SERIES, GINA A. JONES

"Grayson Daniels is complexity personified. His Prince Charming night with his nearly won Princess (Cassidy Thatcher) takes on nuclear level explosions. How can so many good intentions shatter and hurt so hard? Every well-sculpted character grew through this bittersweet comedy of errors."

— RUSTY HOUGH BADER

"I need to say that the story is catching since the first glimpse. You start reading it and you get a feeling that tells you you need to keep reading to know what will happen next. Both stories, Grayson's and Cassidy's are really sad, but they are realistic and make you understand their personalities, their flaws, their insecurities and also their dreams."

— IRENE GRANADO

NUMBER INFINITY

Are you ready for Lance's story?

High Tower, #2
A Standalone Contemporary Romance
COMING SOON

THE BANDIT'S JOURNAL

Firearms, #1
A Historical Romance Series
COMING SOON

ACKNOWLEDGMENTS

To my parents, thank you for supporting me in every aspect of my life. My list of goals on goals seems to get longer every day, and you support me through all of it. It'll always be the three of us—forever. I love you with all my heart and everything that I am.

Ariana, you've been with me from the very beginning of this journey, and I'm so grateful for everything you do. You inspire me. You make me better. You're there when I break down, and you're there to help me rise. You took this to the finish line with me, and I know I say this every day, but you're amazing.

CJ, you are such an incredible artist, and I am honored to work with you. Thank you for having my back from day one. You are my inspiration. You're my girl for life!

Sebastian, to say thank you is not enough. You're my diamond in the rough, man. Every time I see "Cooper Hewitt," I'm going to laugh (or cringe). Thank you for watching out for me. I couldn't have done this without you.

Marnye, you once told me that we can control what we write, but we can't control how others interpret our words. At the time, that seemed so trivial, but looking back, your advice has sculpted the way I write and view the world. Thank you.

Tim, I don't know what I would do without you and Silverton Agency. Thank you for your hard work, your dedication to me as an author, and the life you bring to our industry.

Rupa, your creativity is unbound. I'm so thankful for our friendship. You truly are the best graphic designer I've ever met.

My alpha readers Sophie Hainsworth, Jade D. Knightly, Celia Mai, Rupa Lahiri, and Michelle Hanton, we've come a long way, girls! Thank you.

My beta readers Jasmine Warren, Kaley Cardinal, Hannah Dewey, Maddy D., Jessica Wolford, and Kayla Cruz, your blunt opinions took my final draft to the next level. I am so thrilled to have found my Caedmon Clan. I am beyond grateful for your brilliance.

Most importantly, thank you readers. I write for you. To those of you who have been with me since the creation of NDP Book Review, I flove you crazies. To those of you who found me much later, you fuel me. Thank you, thank you, and thank you.

Bisou bisou 💋 💋

Indy

India Caedmon is a twenty-something hopeless romantic who believes in old-fashioned romance and the power of handwritten letters. When she's not engulfed in make believe, she is a structural engineer. She enjoys flying planes in the Idaho backcountry, swimming, yoga, and paddle boarding with her border collie, Apollo.

India particularly loves conjuring up a variety of ways for Mr. Right to woo her...until that *actually* happens, she'll just have to write about it.

Join the Caedmon Clan!
www.IndiaCaedmon.com

www.ingramcontent.com/pod-product-compliance
Lightning Source LLC
Chambersburg PA
CBHW051545250626
47157CB00001B/185